The
Trickster's
Sister

R. Chris Reeder

Black Rose Writing | Texas

First printing

ISBN: 978-1-68433-677-7
PUBLISHED BY BLACK ROSE WRITING
www.blackrosewriting.com

Printed in the United States of America
Suggested Retail Price (SRP) $22.95

The Trickster's Sister is printed in Chaparral Pro

*As a planet-friendly publisher, Black Rose Writing does its best to eliminate unnecessary waste to reduce paper usage and energy costs, while never compromising the reading experience. As a result, the final word count vs. page count may not meet common expectations.

For my son, August, who gave me the courage to write it.

You'd better hope and pray

That you make it safe

Back to your own world

You'd better hope and pray

That you'll wake one day in your own world

'Cause when you sleep at night

They don't hear your cries in your own world

Only time will tell if you can break the spell

Back in your own world

—Shakespears Sister, Stay

The
Trickster's
Sister

Prologue

Blink. Blink blink. Blink. The tiny red orb, flickering in the dark, flew across the room and landed in a pile of dirty socks before shooting back into the air. It sputtered briefly and then flared back to life, darting one way and then the other, searching for anything to distract itself from the ennui that threatened to engulf it. Out of the stillness, a voice keened softly to the orb as it meandered along the walls and ceiling of what most people would swear was a perfectly normal bedroom in a perfectly normal house in a perfectly normal suburb.

"Hello, red dot, my old friend,
I've come to stare at you again,
Because you're not the homework I should be doing,
The history paper that I am...eschewing,
And I hope that word...means what I think it means,
...I like baked beans,
'Cause that's the sound...of laser pointer...by which I mean this magic laser pointer that was given to me by an old woman in an abandoned appliance store but now it doesn't seem to be magic anymore since all it does is make a regular red dot on my ceiling while I should be doing my homework and now this is the end of my song."

The singing was replaced by soft clapping and the whispered roar of a crowd.

"Applause. Applause. Wild applause. No, no. No money, I couldn't, no, I could never accept money for my art. Well, if you insist."

Brynn sighed.

Everything had been so weird lately, ever since she got back from the Land of Annwfyn. Annwfyn, the mysterious Otherworld. Annwfyn, home to goblins and demigods and clockwork chickens. Annwfyn, the Land of Not Enough Vowels. Why couldn't everything just go back to normal, she wondered for at least the millionth time. After she defeated the villain, sent the boss goblin packing, and saved her baby sister, she figured she could slip back into the regular life of a moody and socially incompetent fourteen-year-old girl in Jeffersonville, Indiana.

Except, of course, for the tiny little point that she wasn't exactly a girl. She was a goblin, a shape-changer from another dimension, capable of disappearing and turning into a white raven and granting wishes and bringing bad luck and a whole host of various other abnormalities that she didn't care to think about. And also, she wasn't fourteen anymore. She was fifteen now, as was clearly displayed on the gigantic, homemade banner from her recent birthday party, a party attended by every single one of her friends, by which she meant her best and only friend, Makayla. The Jeffersonville part, though, that was normal. As normal as could be. She sighed again, flopped back onto her bed, and sighed once more with extra drama, just for good measure.

She listened to the silence all around her. Everyone else in the family had been asleep for hours. At least she was pretty sure that her parents were, and she thought her brother probably was, although he rarely came out of his room these days. When he did, he was so quiet and sullen that it was hard to tell when he was in and when he was out. Her parents blamed it on the events of the previous year. Having your house assaulted by a demigod, having your sister go missing, finding out that you're a goblin, it had been rough on him, her parents insisted. But, honestly, Brynn couldn't really tell the difference. He'd been quiet and moody before it all went down and he was quiet and moody now. After everything that had happened—the near destruction of their house, the discovery of their magical origins, the advent of supernatural powers— he was still the same old Conn, more interested in the week's new comics or in re-reading the Oz books for the umpteenth time than in engaging with the world around him.

She squinted at the ceiling. She needed to make a decision: work on her homework (sensible), try to sleep (useful), or procrastinate some more (probable). She was just reaching for the laser pointer again, for some more procrastinatey goodness, when she heard a noise. It came from outside, or at least she was pretty sure it did. It was close, that much she knew.

She crawled out of bed, sidled over to the window, and pulled the curtains aside. There was a shadow on the street. This, of course, wasn't unusual to Brynn, but the fact that it was moving slowly down the sidewalk, seemingly of its own volition—that definitely caught her attention.

There was a streetlight in front of the house, but there wasn't anything nearby that would potentially cast a shadow of that shape (vaguely humanoid, distinctly creepy), or really any shape at all. There was nothing between the streetlight and the shadow and yet there the shadow was, huddling in the darkness just on the other side of the fence that separated her yard from the sidewalk. Brynn craned her neck around to see if there was something she could be missing, some forgotten tree or misplaced shopping cart (after all, shadows didn't just exist without anything to cast them), but she couldn't get a good vantage from the little window of her corner room.

She was just about to crawl out onto the roof and investigate (despite the fact that she knew this was a terrible idea) when her phone rang. Keeping her eyes locked on the shadow, she reached out her hand to find it. On the second ring, the shadow's head snapped around. The next instant, the shadow dissolved away with the wind.

"Who the hell," she muttered, "would be hanging out in front of our house at this time of night?"

Brynn picked up her phone and slid her thumb across the screen to answer it.

"Hey."

"Jeffersonville Weird Crap Information Hotline," the voice on the other end intoned scratchily. "How can I assist you?"

There was a brief pause. Brynn squinted suspiciously at the phone.

"You called *me*, Makayla."

"I know. It's still so weird being able to call you."

"It's just a phone. Lots of people have phones."

"Yes, but *you* have a phone now," Makayla said. "Your parents won't even let you watch TV. You have a phone!"

"Indeed."

"Welcome to the future!"

"You don't have to say that every time we talk on the phone."

Makayla chuckled under her breath and gave up the well-practiced pretense.

"Why did your parents finally let you get a phone, anyway?" she mused through a mouthful of something crunchy. Popcorn, Brynn guessed. It was her favorite midnight snack.

"They might have felt bad after I was nearly killed by an interdimensional demigod."

Brynn's eyes were still searching for the missing shadow. Her fingers were still on the handle of the window and her feet were still restlessly tapping the floor, urging her to follow whoever or whatever had been lurking outside the house.

"Why did you call?" Brynn asked absently. "I'm busy."

"Seriously?"

"Yeah." Brynn hesitated. "I'm, uh, doing my homework," she added falteringly.

"Really?"

"Yeah."

"Were you playing with the laser pointer again?" Makayla accused playfully.

"Maybe."

"Did it do anything other than being a dot?"

"No."

"It's just a laser pointer," Makayla insisted.

"Um, no, it's a laser pointer I got from a magic lady who runs a magic appliance store and who also gave me a magic apple."

"And a grenade."

"Yes. And a grenade."

"But it's still just a laser pointer. I mean, that's all it is, right?"

"I don't know," Brynn said. "I've been using it every day for the last year and the batteries still haven't run out."

"That's weird."

"Yeah. I actually tried to check it out a couple times but every time I get the battery panel open, I get this weird tingly feeling all across my face and then I pass out. When I wake up, the battery panel is back on and the laser pointer is hidden in one of my shoes. And for some reason my fingers smell like garlic and then I burp a bunch."

"That's also weird. Maybe you should leave it alone."

"Maybe."

"You don't sound convinced."

"I'm not," Brynn sighed. "But seriously, why did you call?"

"I heard something outside again tonight. My Ma was busy with the boys so I snuck out to see if I could find it."

"You really shouldn't do that. It could be something like me, which means it has powers. Or...and perhaps more likely...it could just be an actual dangerous person because those exist and sometimes they are out at night on streets."

"I was okay," Makayla assured her. "I brought the baseball bat with me. The one I destroyed a demon with."

"It wasn't a demon. It was a fetch."

"Whatever. I brought the bat. I don't have goblin powers—"

"Coblyn."

"Whatever. But I brought the bat."

"Okay."

"I saw a shadow moving down the street so I followed it."

"Did you find anything?"

"Nah," Makayla said, followed by more crunching. "Probably just a raccoon. I think a family of them've moved in. Our garbage is always messed up lately."

"Yeah. Ours too."

Brynn paused.

"I saw a shadow tonight too," she said.

"What the hell. Why are weird people—"

"Not necessarily people," Brynn interrupted.

"Resuming. Why are weird people or weird not-people wandering around outside our houses?"

"I don't know. If it is anything...unnatural...I promised my parents I wouldn't go chasing after things like that. You know, after what happened last time."

"Yeah. I remember. I was there."

There was a flicker of movement outside Brynn's house on the sidewalk.

"There it is again," Brynn said softly, her feet itching to move. "I have to go."

"What is it?"

"Um..."

"Brynn. What is it? Because if it's something weird, you told me not thirty seconds ago that you promised your parents you wouldn't go chasing after things like that!"

"I don't know...what it is...exactly."

"Brynn. What are you going to do?"

"I think maybe I might go chasing after things like that."

"Sigh. Be safe, B."

"Always. I can disappear, you know."

Brynn hung the phone up and almost before she knew what she was doing, she was sliding the window open and clambering out onto the roof. She felt within herself, drew out the hollow nothingness and disappeared into the night. Her transparent body dropped from the edge of the roof onto the lawn and her transparent feet padded across the grass toward the sidewalk.

A flicker of movement drew her eye. A shadow twitched on the sidewalk and vanished around the corner, behind the house. Brynn followed it. The shadow flickered in and out of visibility. It leapt from circle of light to circle of light, just on the edges of the darkness, just on the edges of Brynn's perception.

Brynn tried to pick out details as she slunk after it. When she could get a good look at it, which wasn't often, it did seem to be humanoid, it did seem to possess head, trunk, limbs, all the traits one would expect to see in a human or human-like being, but not the other attributes, namely solidity, color, mass. It was just a shadow, flitting along through the night, pursued by an invisible goblin girl, and Brynn could hardly believe that this was actually what her life was like now.

She shook her head and as she did so, she noticed a flash of color among the vaguely defined limbs of the shadow. The shadowy legs moved it along, but the shadowy arms were clutching something, Brynn was sure of it. What it was clutching, though, she couldn't make out. She urged her feet to move faster, trying to follow it, trying to catch up.

Then she rounded a corner and there on a brick wall, the image thrown by a particularly powerful streetlight, she could see the shadow, clearly visible. She hugged the corner, the edge of the bricks pressing into her skin, and peered around, hoping her invisibility could protect her from whatever she was chasing. Because she could see it now. She could see pointy ears. She could see long, sinewy limbs and curling toes and spindly fingers. She could see a tail thrashing impatiently behind it. It was still a shadow, but now it was a shadow with a shape. It raised its arms and Brynn finally saw what it was carrying. A baby. The shadow had a baby in its arms—

swaddled and asleep, but definitely a baby. A human baby and not a shadow at all.

Brynn gasped. She pulled herself back behind the corner. She knew she had to move and she knew she had to move quickly. She let her body coalesce back into visibility. She searched within herself, found the ancient, gnarled knot and drew it forth, feeling the power and swiftness that came whenever she adopted her goblin form. She counted to three and then ran, swifter than the wind, around the corner, back to where the shadow stood, but no sooner had she begun to move than she knew it was too late. The shadow was gone and so was the baby. Whoever it was, whatever it was, had simply vanished, taking the baby with it.

Looking around, she realized that she was standing in the middle of the streetlight's glow in her goblin form, fully visible and liable to give a heart attack to any oblivious humans who might wander by. Embarrassed and frustrated, she flickered out of visibility and plodded toward home, before stopping in her tracks.

"Wait a second," she muttered to herself. "Pointy ears. Tail. Stealing a baby. It can't be. He wouldn't. He promised."

An image of her father in his goblin form rose unsettlingly in her mind. She tried to compare it to the shadow she had just seen, but she couldn't be sure if they were the same figure or if it was only her doubts and fears eating at her. But who else in Jeffersonville had pointy ears, a tail, and a history of baby-stealing?

After everything that happened last year, it was nearly beyond comprehension that he would do it again, that he would steal another baby. After their whole family was nearly killed. After all those other families were nearly destroyed.

"He couldn't," she whispered. "He wouldn't go back on his word like that, I'm sure of it."

Brynn seethed with rage, her tail twitched, and she ran toward home to find out.

"I guess I'm not that sure," she grunted, her legs flying over the pavement.

When she arrived home, she jumped nimbly to the roof, then shifted back to her human form and climbed through her bedroom window. Still invisible, she snuck down the hall to her parents' room, eased the door open and peeked inside.

Her mother was in bed. Alone.

"Damn it," Brynn whispered under her breath. "I knew it."

Fuming, she turned around, ready to chase down her missing father, but had taken only two steps when she bumped into him. He was carrying Brynn's baby sister, Hero, now just a year old. Brynn jumped back, her surprise snapping her back into visibility.

"Brynn," her father whispered, clearly startled but trying not to wake the baby. "What are you doing?"

"Nothing," she said, trying to convey both innocence (for herself) and suspicion (of him), which wasn't terribly successful. "What are *you* doing?"

He yawned and grinned wearily.

"Hanging out with Hero."

Brynn grinned in spite of herself. This was a familiar refrain in her family these days.

"Surprise, surprise," they said together.

"Your mother's been up so much with her the last few weeks," her father continued. "I wanted to give her a break. So I've been walking with the baby. Not like she needs it. This kid could sleep through a tornado. Everything okay?"

"Yeah, I was just worried..." Brynn hesitated.

"About what?" her father asked.

Brynn studied his face but could see no trace of guilt, no sign that he'd sprinted home and somehow managed to make it back before her, completely unwinded. She didn't want to accuse her father without proof. Maybe she'd just imagined it. She shook her head, her jaw clenched.

"It's nothing."

ACT 1: SHADOWS

Chapter One

Having a goblin for a best friend wasn't always easy. But it wasn't like there were a lot of other contenders crowding around hoping to audition for the role. Makayla kicked at an imaginary pebble as she shuffled along the street, her hands thrust deep in the pockets of her hoodie, her backpack full of homework she knew she probably wouldn't have time to do until everyone else in the family was asleep.

Ever since they'd got back from that other world, whatever it was called (Makayla still couldn't quite figure out how to pronounce all the weird words that Brynn was always talking about), Brynn and Makayla were stuck together even tighter, bonded by the extraordinary terror of the danger they'd been through and the overwhelming relief at having somehow survived it.

And even when Brynn was pensive, moody, distracted, as she often was these days, even when she disappeared into nothingness, even when her waifish exterior evaporated only to be replaced by the now-familiar pointy ears and tail, Makayla still stuck by her. What else could she do? For that matter, why would she want to do anything else? Brynn was all she wanted. Everyone else in this loser town could go to hell, for all she cared.

Makayla looked back over her shoulder. Was someone whispering back there? Her breathing quickened. Her chest tightened. The back of her neck felt hot, which quickly spread to her cheeks, forehead, ears. She put her hands on the straps of her backpack, gripped them tightly, felt the solid fabric against her hands, tried to breathe as deeply as she could.

"Nah. Just the wind. Keep it together, me. Just normal wind noises like wind always normally makes." She whispered under her breath, trying to keep herself calm. She said it again out loud, not caring if anyone overheard. "Keep it together. It's just the wind."

After everything that had happened last year, she was no fan of strange noises, surprises, shocks, anything out of the ordinary, anything that deviated from her usual routine. Even a pop quiz could send her into a tailspin, her mood plummeting into a funk she had a hard time rousing herself from.

She rounded the corner by her house and bounded up onto the porch. She swung the door open and it collided with a magnificent tower of Legos and saucepans that clattered to the ground in dramatic fashion. Makayla sighed and rolled her eyes.

"Ma," she called. "I'm home. In case you didn't hear the ear-shattering din from the toys the boys left everywhere. Once again."

As if on cue, with capes and scarves flying behind them, three boys of various heights ran by, nearly knocking her over.

"Siblings!" Makayla shouted, her breath still ragged. "Stop your insanity right now!"

There was no response other than an even louder crash from the kitchen.

"Did you just break something?" Makayla called.

There was a long silence. Finally, one voice called out uncertainly.

"No."

"Should I come look?"

The response was quicker this time, all three in unison.

"No!"

Makayla sighed.

"Where's Ma?"

"She went out to pick up dinner. She'll be back soon."

"Okay."

Makayla peeked out through the living room curtains. The street seemed strangely deserted. Out of the corner of her eye, she caught sight of a shadow twitching, disappearing, and reappearing under the next streetlight. Its formlessness coalesced into form, a tall, impossibly tall form. The shadow shimmered in the wind, an overcoat or possibly a cloak fluttering behind it.

Makayla looked at their yard. The air outside the house was quiet and the trees were still. Makayla looked back at the streetlight. The shadow remained, still blown by a wind that seemed to exist nowhere else. She saw the head of the impossibly tall figure snap around as if a sound, somewhere out of sight, had caught its attention. Then the shadow strode off and was instantly lost from her view.

Makayla gulped, the flushed heat returning to her shoulders, her neck. Her cheeks felt numb and she tried to calm her breath, which threatened to catch in her throat.

"Well, who the hell was that?" she whispered, although she knew there was no one around who could possibly answer this question.

"Siblings..." she called out, willing her voice to convey a calm that existed nowhere inside her. "I need you to...just come in here, will you? I'll read you a book. Or something. Here in the living room."

Three heads slunk warily into view and peered out from behind the edge of a doorway.

"You'll read to us?" the youngest asked suspiciously.

"Yeah." Makayla offered her most self-assured smile. "Sure."

"You never want to read to us," the second brother insisted.

"Well, today I do. Come in here. Sit on the floor and I'll read to you."

The three boys ran to grab books and the necessary accoutrements for the chosen stories, which consisted of laser pistols, race cars, and one sticky, uneaten licorice whip.

As they assembled their treasures, Makayla settled herself on the couch. "Yes, I'll read to you," she whispered to herself, "as long as we're nowhere near that window."

Chapter 2

In the morning, the events of the previous day were already blurry, her memory of them hazy and imprecise, and by the time Makayla met Brynn after school for their walk home, she had already mostly convinced herself that she must have imagined the impossibly tall shadow with the cloak flapping in the otherworldly wind.

They walked their usual route, past the vacant lot, past the Asian grocery, past the seafood restaurant. The man in the foam rubber fish costume was in his usual position, waving his usual sign, although he studiously avoided their gaze these days, sometimes going so far as to hide behind the corner of the building when he saw them coming. Brynn insisted she'd had some kind of interaction with him, but Makayla found it hard to believe that whoever was in there had any interest in the world around him, since all he did was stand there in his stupid fish suit every day.

"Look up there," Brynn said, grabbing Makayla's arm and pointing down the block.

"Where?"

"Up by the appliance store. What is that?"

There was something flitting around in the shadows in the alley behind the store, but Makayla's eyes couldn't make any sense of it. There was a noise too, a muffled metallic screeching, like someone trying to use a prybar inside a sleeping bag.

They approached the appliance store cautiously. Everything was silent and dark within, as it had been every day since they'd returned from Annwfyn. Brynn was still claiming she'd been inside and talked to the old woman who ran the place, but Makayla didn't know what to think about that part of Brynn's story. Then again, in Makayla's part of the story, she'd been frozen in a pillar of light on the bottom of a lake that didn't exist anymore, so who was she to cast aspersions?

They heard the screech again and ran around to the back, but there was nothing there that could have possibly made the noise they heard.

"What a second," Brynn said. "Where'd the dumpster go? Isn't there always a dumpster up against this wall?"

"Yeah. There is. Looks like someone pushed it down to the end of the alley. And what the hell is that?"

Makayla walked up to the patch of wall where the dumpster usually resided. The brick here was unnaturally bright, red as the sunset, as if the dumpster had been fitted tight against the wall ever since the building was built and the bricks behind had never been exposed to the grime and fetid air that inhabited the alley. Makayla knelt down. In the midst of the patch of unfaded bricks, there was a door. A door no taller than Makayla's knee. A door made of the purest, brightest wood that either of them had ever seen, with a glass knob the size of a quarter and a glass knocker twisted to look like climbing vines.

"Who could even use a door like this?" Makayla whispered.

"I don't know," Brynn answered with a shrug. "Not me. Not you. And the old woman I met was way bigger than this door."

Makayla leaned in closer, peering at the unnaturally vivid wood.

"Look at those...those scratches. On the edge."

"They look fresh. Do you...I mean, whatever those sounds were, do you think they might have been coming from here?"

"You think someone was trying to break in?"

"Maybe."

"Who the hell would want to break into an empty appliance store?" Makayla asked as she stood up and brushed off her knees.

"It's not really—"

"Yeah, I know. And what were they using? A pocket comb? Nail clippers?"

Brynn cocked her head, her eyes searching for something far beyond the grimy alley.

"Why would shadows we can't see try to break into a door we can't use?"

"Okay," Makayla responded slowly. "More creepy than I was thinking, but yeah, why?"

"I don't know. Let's get out of here."

They walked away, leaving the appliance store and the mysterious door behind, trying to make sense of what they had seen.

"So...whoever it was," Makayla finally asked after ten minutes of silent trudging, "they were big enough to move the ridiculously heavy dumpster but small enough to break into a door the size of my cat?"

"It doesn't make sense—"

"Is a summation of our lives for the last year, yes. *Nothing* makes sense. What the hell is going on?"

"I don't know. After we got back from Annwfyn, everything seemed so good for a while. My dad stood up to the strange little man and Finian was gone and nothing was suspicious and no children were missing and everything just seemed so good."

Makayla stopped and looked at Brynn.

"It's different, though, now, right?"

"Yeah," Brynn acknowledged sadly.

"What happened?"

"I don't know."

"When did it happen?"

"I don't know!" Brynn harrumphed, thrusting her hands even deeper into her pockets. "It's like someone said, 'turn gloominess up one percent,' enjoyed the feel of it, and then just kept doing it. 'Turn it up.' 'Turn it up.' 'Turn it up.' 'Should I stop?' 'Nah, keep going!'"

They trudged on.

"Um…" Brynn puffed out her cheeks. "While we're on the subject of unusual goings-on…"

"Out with it."

Brynn hemmed and hawed but it finally came spilling out of her.

"Conn got into a fight today."

"Wait," Makayla scowled. "Conn. Your brother?"

"Yeah."

"The dude who just sits in his room reading comic books and never talks to anybody?"

"Yep."

"The dude who is so difficult to notice that he was marked absent five times last year on days he was actually in class?"

"That's him," Brynn said.

"The dude who's so quiet that one of his teachers thought he was an exchange student who doesn't speak English?"

"Your opinion of him is noted."

"How...wait, did someone, like, trip him and he scraped his knee or something?"

"Nope. An actual bare-knuckled, punching, had to be pulled apart by sensible adults, sweaty, bloody, probably going to be suspended, fight."

"Okay," Makayla said with a grimace. "That's...yep, that's weird. So someone just walked up and started pummeling him?"

"Also no. In true Bizarro-world fashion, Conn started shoving some eighth-grader. The other guy threw a punch, so Conn tackled him to the ground, got on top and started pounding his face."

Makayla nodded solemnly.

"So, yeah, well...supporting our theory here...things are now getting so weird and grim in Jeffersonville that the quietest guy we know took a swing at someone twice his size."

"Yeah."

Makayla grabbed Brynn by the shoulders and looked her square in the eyes.

"Dude. If I wake up in another dimension again, I am so going to kick your ass."

Brynn smiled.

"Duly noted. Maybe we'll wake up there together."

"Nah. That's no good. Who'd rescue us then? Blond chick with the sword?"

"Doubt it. She pretty much split."

Makayla checked her phone.

"Oh, crap. I'm going to be late."

Brynn squinted at her suspiciously.

"Late for what?"

Makayla shook her head.

"It's nothing. I just...I got to go."

She trotted off briskly, leaving a best friend staring suspiciously in her wake. She hated to keep secrets from Brynn, but she wasn't sure what else she could do right now. Makayla stuffed her hands into her pockets and tried to squash the guilt back down into her gut. When she finally glanced back over her shoulder, Brynn had disappeared.

Chapter 3

In a booth carved from stone, in the far corner of what would likely be called a bar, sat an unusual duo. One was small and rumpled, with a tweed vest and bow tie, a wizened face and piercing eyes. He was drinking an aromatic wine from a wooden cup. The other was large and blocky and seemed to consist primarily of bands of knotted muscle hewn from stone. Veins of glittering ore striated his bulk and his eyes glowed of their own accord. His limbs were powerful, his trunk bulky, but he moved gently as he lifted a tankard (which seemed to be carved from the same stone as his flesh) to his mouth and drank deeply from the steaming contents within.

There were no windows in the room. Beings of all shapes and sizes were flitting about, or sitting, or hovering in midair, or clinging to the wall, hunched over drinks. A multi-armed bartender tended to them all, his limbs stretching this way and that, delivering drinks, collecting empty vessels, delivering nuts, hot coals, spicy insect fritters, bowls full of pink sludge—whatever his clientele desired, he made available.

Once the large, rocky being had drained his tankard and called for another, he spoke to his much smaller companion.

"So remind me: what exactly did the little coblyn call you?" he said with a smirk.

"Strange. Little. Man," the other noted dully, clearly insulted at the appellation.

"To be fair, 'little' is an apt description for you at the moment."

"Only compared to some."

"And I would imagine your appearance would seem 'strange' in their world. 'Man' is a relative term, of course, but it would suffice for the coblyn's purposes. Why do you take offense at this?"

"Stop trying to justify it, Lwmpyn!" the smaller of the two grunted, before draining his own cup. Another appeared in his hands almost instantly.

"But why is this troubling you?" the creature carved from rock replied, throwing up his gargantuan hands. "An insignificant coblyn child referred to you by these words last year and since then, you have prattled about it incessantly every time I have been in your presence."

"I'm having a hard enough time trying to concentrate lately. Every time I sit down and make a go of tending to my paperwork, some urgent matter or another comes up. I'm months behind on tracking the changelings."

"But instead of seeing to this task, you complain to me, yet again, of this imagined slight."

"I glower at you."

"Oh come now, Ysbaddaden. Have another. Sulk some more. This paperwork can't be all that important, can it?"

"In the grand scheme of things, that could perhaps be viewed as correct," the bow-tied being acknowledged. "The changelings will flow whether or not the logs are up to date. But if I don't do it, eventually someone will be sent to check on me, and I'll offer excuses, and there will be yelling, and teeth will be gnashed, and someone will be left in an uncomfortable position, and it will most likely be me. So I just need to sit down in my office with the requisitions and the invoices and the tracking sheets and the book and I need to record the thefts of the human children and the changelings who've replaced them. Where the stolen children came from. Where they're going. Who they've been delivered to. Who they've been replaced with. Beli knows how I ended up with the maintenance of the Logbook, but I did, and there've been dozens, maybe hundreds, of relocations that aren't recorded now."

At that moment, a thunderous bell echoed through the bar, through the halls, and through the caverns beyond.

"Ah," Lwmpyn sighed, draining another tankard, "the bellows call. Must get back to my labors. Although, speaking of being behind on work, I need to reserve some energy so I can make progress on my dissertation tonight. I've been lost in it for months."

"What're you studying? I always forget."

"I'm not sure you forget. I think you always nod off when I try to discuss my research with you."

Ysbaddaden shrugged in agreement. Lwmpyn sighed and looked him straight in the eyes, speaking as clearly as possible.

"The Internecine Period of the Inter-Regulus Struggle. You know, back when we had a King. Well, Kings. And a Queen. All trying to kill each other."

"Fun times."

"Indeed."

Lwmpyn rose and stretched, cracking his wrists, neck, and various other portions of his anatomy, then laid a handful of coins on the table. Ysbaddaden followed Lwmpyn toward the door. He looked up at his towering companion, who filled the vast majority of the narrow aisle between booths and bar.

"You know, I've never asked. How do you even get in here? You're twice as large as that door."

"Bodies are only what you imagine them to be."

Lwmpyn pressed his enormous bulk against the doorway and his rocky flesh oozed and morphed its way through before reconstructing itself on the other side, a mound of muscle and flint once more, a mound who waved a casual farewell as he made his way back to the kitchens.

"Well, that's a useful skill," Ysbaddaden muttered under his breath. "But I suppose I must get to it."

He gave a deep sigh, straightened his rumpled vest, then navigated his way through the warren of hallways, antechambers, courtyards, mounds of earthenware, lounging rooms for the pwca and dressing rooms for the bwbachod (who insisted on at least three full changes of hair, clothing and regalia everyday) until, at last, he arrived at a scuffed wooden door.

After murmuring a few words of opening, he prodded the door open with his boot and it swung noiselessly inward, revealing a comfortable den with shelves lining every wall—shelves full of books, quills, parchment, and the remnants of many, many unfinished meals. In the center of the room was an imposing desk, much too large for a figure his size, but he had inherited it from the previous occupant of the office and within a week, he'd grown so accustomed to the outsized furniture that he'd never bothered to have it changed.

He heaved himself up onto the chair, heaved together a towering mound of paperwork that stood to one side, and finally, heaved open the Changeling Logbook, the enormous tome that took up the vast majority of the vast surface area of the desk.

"Let's see," he muttered to himself, "exactly how far behind am I?"

He flipped through the papers: the requisitions, the dispatch orders, the changeling tracking sheets, all the mundanity that went along with the simple task of stealing a human child, sending it off to whichever demigod or resident of the upper echelons desired it for their amusement, and replacing said child with one of their own, with one of the Tylwyth Teg.

"Last month," he said, separating a swath of papers and setting them aside. "The three months before that," he added, setting an even larger swath aside. "August, 1543," he wheezed, pinching a single sheet of parchment and staring at it. "You're rather late to the party, aren't you? And woefully misplaced. I wonder whatever became of you." He looked nervously around before snapping his fingers guiltily. The sheet of yellowed parchment burst into flame and disappeared. He shrugged. "I suspect it worked itself out. I have no doubt I would have heard about it sometime in the last four hundred years if it hadn't." He flipped through another two feet of parchment. "And another six months. How in the blue blazes did I let this slide?"

He scowled, tapping his fingers furiously on the massive pile of overdue paperwork.

"Okay, Ysbaddaden. Time to buckle down. If you set to work now, keep your head down, and plow through this, you could have it done in what? A month? Perhaps two? If you don't stop for food, water, recreation, social visits or interruptions from underlings and vague acquaintances."

He flipped the pages of the book to the most recent entries that had been completed before he had—through no fault of his own, he assured himself—left off his bureaucratic duties. He stared at the figures in front of him. He cross-referenced the figures with a small parchment binder he retrieved from beneath a mostly empty mug. He flipped a few pages back and checked the figures there, then flipped ahead again. He shook his head. Something wasn't right here, but he couldn't quite put his finger on it. He took a deep breath and concentrated. All of a sudden, the letters and numbers went out of focus, swam around the page, and rearranged themselves in a completely different order. He shook his head and rubbed his eyes. The figures stayed in the same place.

"Well, what infernal chicanery was that?"

He was reaching into a nearby bin for a scrying lens when the office door burst open and a small, iridescent being with olive skin and wings the color of honey flew in and circled the room near the ceiling, screaming at the top of her minuscule lungs.

Ysbaddaden sighed.

"And there it is. The interruption I knew was coming."

He waited patiently while the undersized woman continued her oversized screams.

"Boss," she screamed. "Boss! Baaaaawwwwwwss! Boss! Boss! Boss? Boss! Boss!"

Ysbaddaden tried to catch her attention, but her body was a blur as she frantically flew and screamed.

"Slow down, Myfanwy," he called, waving his hands above his head. "Slow down! I'm worried you're going to—"

The winged being did indeed, as he'd feared, careen directly into a tureen he had (for some reason) stored on the very top shelf. It and she tumbled to the ground. The tureen landed bottom-side-up and immediately began quivering. Within a few seconds, it was glowing, and then sparking, and then exploding.

"That was my best tureen," he said.

The winged creature sat, covered in the remnants of the mostly evaporated soup and tureen. Her eyes finally focused and she directed her words at Ysbaddaden instead of to the room in general. Her volume, however, had not decreased.

"Boss! You got to come!"

"Fan. Whatever it is, can't you handle it yourself? For once?"

She shuddered with nearly incoherent rage.

"I handle all the things for you all the time," she screamed. "All the time! So many things! Which is my job. My station. And I try not to complain."

"Maybe you could try harder?"

Beams like gleaming daggers flowed from her eyeballs.

"Not the time?" Ysbaddaden whispered.

"Hardly! As I was trying to say: You are needed. Promptly. Indubitably. Unforeseenly."

"I am?"

"You are."

"For?"

"The furnace at the salamanders' estate has gone out of commission," Myfanwy said, wagging her microscopic finger. "She says her stomach's gone funny."

"The salamander's stomach?"

"No! The furnace's stomach! Pay attention."

"Yes, well—"

"As I was saying," Myfanwy continued, glaring at her superior, "her stomach's gone funny and the temperature is dropping. Dropping quickly. If the temperature in the estate falls too low, things would get very squirrelly indeed! I mean, the salamanders could...they could..."

"They could die."

"Or possibly...or possibly..."

"Explode. Yes, I know."

"But probably...oh my. Probably..."

"Both," they said together.

Ysbaddaden sighed.

"You're right, Fan. You're always right. Let's go," he said, grabbing his vest and buttoning it up as they left. He gave a brief and guilty glance back at the enormous ledger, the Changeling Logbook, already forgetting the strange and disconcerting behavior of the figures within.

Chapter 4

The final school bell rang. Makayla found her way to her locker and loaded up her backpack. She tried to set her feet toward the meeting spot, the stop sign where she always met Brynn after school, but her feet hesitated. Her feet had been hesitating all day. *She'd* been hesitating all day, she admitted to herself. She was supposed to meet Brynn to walk home like they did every day. Except she wasn't going home today. And she wasn't sure she wanted to tell Brynn why.

It was a good reason. It was an important reason. But the reason had to do with Brynn. Plus (and she hated to admit it), the reason made her feel like crap about herself. She couldn't handle talking about it. Or talking to anyone. Or talking.

She walked toward the meeting spot. She walked away. She walked toward. And away.

"Damn it," she whispered, her face flushing.

She walked away from the meeting spot and she kept walking away and this appeared to be her feet's final decision.

She pulled out her phone. Her thumb flashed over the screen.

forgot 2 tell u, she texted to Brynn. *can't walk home 2day I have a thing*

A thing? Brynn texted back, and Makayla could almost feel the exasperation pouring out of the six letters. *Another thing? U will tell me what this "thing" is at some point won't u?*

Makayla stared skyward. There was nothing she hated more than keeping secrets from her best friend. But she didn't know what else to do. Brynn would freak out if she told her where she was actually going.

she shrugs, Makayla texted after a long moment of thought.

did u just narrate ur shrug to me?

she nods

jesus M fine have ur secret

There was a long pause before the next message flashed up on Makayla's screen.

Brynn sighs

cya, B, Makayla texted, but there was no further response.

Makayla pulled her hood up and stuffed her hands into her pockets. She would tell Brynn soon, she promised herself. Sometime soon. Just not today.

She walked on, but a funny feeling crept up her neck almost as soon as she began moving. She looked around but didn't notice anything unusual. She put her head down, hoping to hide her face under her hood, and kept walking. She was across the street from the seafood restaurant when she noticed that the man in the foam rubber fish costume wasn't moping and dragging his sign along the ground like he usually did. He was waving, waving at *her*, waving frantically. This creeped Makayla out more than anything else. She walked faster.

A noise started to intrude on her as she walked, like a bee was buzzing around her. No, not around her, she realized. Inside her, just behind her eyes. And then it wasn't just one bee, but a cluster of bees, buzzing through her thoughts, almost as if a radio was following her, tuned to a station that didn't exist. Her neck went hot and her breath went ragged. She looked over her shoulder, trying to find the source of the sounds, but there was nothing. No. Wait. Not nothing. A shadow.

There was a shadow behind her, lurking around the corner of a coffeehouse, an impossibly tall shadow with a cloak flapping in the wind. It twitched and flickered. It emerged from behind the corner of the building, and it was now clear that the shadow was moving on its own, not cast by anything that Makayla could see, at least nothing in this world—a shadow without a source, a figure without light or mass—and it was then that Makayla began to run.

She heard footfalls behind her, but they were raspy, unclear, staticky, as if the feet were pushing their way through white noise. She ran faster, but the noise drew closer, the raspy footfalls, the buzzing static in her head. She ran faster, but so did the noise, and then the noise was around her, surrounding her, inside her.

She closed her eyes in terror. The static was upon her and it was all she could hear. Her body convulsed and there were knives behind her eyelids and there were knives in her ears, pricking at her, cutting her, slicing her psyche, delving into her, removing her secrets. Then there was fire, lines drawn in fire, tracing intricate shapes all through her being, through the air around her, on the sidewalk she stood upon, on the air she was breathing. She could see the lines of fire, even though her eyes weren't open.

Then without warning, it was as if the air—all the air on the street, perhaps the whole city—was sucked away and there was nothing, nothing at all, for just the briefest of moments. When the air rushed back in, when she gasped for breath and the air filled her burning lungs, her eyes opened wide and she knew that whatever had been following her, whatever had been with her, inside her, pricking her and pulling her and burning her, it was gone. As quickly as they had arrived, the sound and the shadow were gone. There was no one around. No people, no shadows, no sounds. The world was silent.

Makayla blinked back tears. Whether it had actually happened or whether her brain had imagined the shadow and the noise, there was nothing she could do about it now. She had somewhere to be and her feet were going to take her there.

Chapter 5

Ysbaddaden set his jaw in a determined clench. He felt ruffled, fatigued, unwell. His eyebrows felt moist and his tongue felt dry. His knees ached and his stomach grumbled. The last two weeks of his life had not gone well and that was likely a drastic understatement.

On their way home from solving the crisis at the salamanders' estate, he and Fan had somehow found themselves smack dab in the middle of an amphibious amphora heist (crisis number two), and as soon as they'd broken that up, an envoy arrived to announce that a swarm of Loquacious Locusts were demanding an immediate audience with the directorate (crisis number three). Once he'd diverted the swarm with empty promises and vague assurances of alchemical appropriations, he'd had to intervene between Fan and the instigators of crisis number two who had come back for retribution after Fan's over-enthusiastic arbitration had led to the collapse of their secondary martial boulangerie. That brouhaha was crisis number four. No sooner was that tamped down than he'd been interrupted by a family of gwyllion whose cavern had been vandalized by a band of pwca colts and while he was trying to make peace between these two factions (crisis number five), the salamanders exploded, which meant he hadn't solved crisis number one nearly as thoroughly as he thought he had. Crisis number six was a massive fire which took nearly three days to extinguish, and (long story short) it had been nearly a fortnight and he still had made no progress on the Changeling Logbook.

But he had decided that, once and for all, today was the day. All crises had been extinguished. He'd canceled all meetings, instructed all underlings to keep away, and notified all relevant emissaries, legates and harbingers that he was not to be disturbed. The wheels of bureaucracy must turn. The rivers of red tape must flow. The long-neglected pile of papers must needs be sorted, organized, recorded, and today was the day.

He settled himself in on his chair. He arranged his binders. He neatened the pile of parchment. He double-checked that his supplies for the day (primarily soup and mulled wine) were still in place. He loosened his bow tie. It was time to work.

He heaved open the cover of the Changeling Logbook, retrieved the top piece of parchment from the towering stack, and prepared to make his first entry. He took his quill in hand, checked the parchment, checked the book, but his quill did not yet move. He pored over the records in the Logbook. He'd seen these entries countless times, had entered most of them himself, had double-checked them, revised them, cross-referenced them, but today, as he looked at them, something wasn't right.

He stared at the figures on the page. They were smudgy and ill-formed. Ysbaddaden harrumphed. He prided himself on his attention to detail as well as his exquisite handwriting. He stared at the figures again, leaning in close. He took his thumb and wiped it over the offending section. The figures came away in a clump. He shook his hand to free them. The black mass that had been masquerading as figures in the Logbook landed on the floor with a splat.

"What in Beli's name is going on?" he whispered, peering even closer. "There's something under there."

But before he could continue his examination, the door to his office opened, ever so slightly, and a tiny head fluttered into view. Ysbaddaden sighed.

"Yes, Fan?"

"Oh. Hi, boss."

The tiny figure fluttered there in midair, her head still poking through the doorway.

"Do you need something?"

"I do. I really do. But you told us not to bother you today."

"I did. I really did. I would really like to not be bothered today."

Ysbaddaden stared at Myfanwy. Myfanwy stared back. The tiny figure gave a high-pitched whine from deep inside her tiny body, as if the words within were threatening to burst forth whether she willed them to or no. The whine increased in intensity and volume, and Ysbaddaden wondered what would happen if he let it continue. Her eyes grew wide, her cheeks grew red, and finally, Ysbaddaden decided that his curiosity likely wasn't worth her passing out, or exploding, or whatever it was that happened to those of her race in these situations.

"Fine, Fan. Out with it."

The breath exploded out of her, a keening scream which immediately turned into a torrent of words.

"Okay, okay, okay, boss, I am so so sorry to bother you but I really didn't know what to do, there's just so much...so much...so many...things...and I didn't know what to do, and I tried to get Clychau to help me, but he said he was under strict instructions to leave you alone and I said yes that's what *I'm* trying to do, I'm trying to leave you alone, I'm trying to solve the problem by myself but he didn't understand. So I kicked him and then I had to escape because he tried to kick me back and he is, as you know, much much larger than me and I really didn't want to get kicked. So I escaped and I tried to find someone else to help me, anyone at all really, but no one was around or they were busy or sleeping or drunk so I went by myself but I got there and I realized I actually don't know how to turn things into other things...or back from things into the original things which is what I really needed to do. But like I said, I don't know how to do that so I thought maybe I could learn! So I asked someone at the library about that and they said yes, it's something you can learn to do, but it would probably take ten to twenty years of constant study and I really didn't think I had that kind of time. Although I thought about it for a while because you said you really really didn't want to be disturbed, but I didn't know if that meant for ten or twenty years or maybe less. So I tried to start studying and I checked out a book and everything but I think maybe there's a prerequisite before you can learn about turning things into other things because I didn't understand that book at all! So I returned the book and it was heavy, so I was kind of tired, so I had a snack, but then I remembered the problem was still happening and I hadn't found a solution and neither had anyone else as far as I could tell. So I had a good little scream and a cry about it but that didn't solve the problem—of course—but it did make me hungry again so I had another snack and then I couldn't think of what else I could do so I came here and I opened your door and stuck my head in and waited and then you told me to talk so I told you this story."

Myfanwy paused for breath. Then she smiled and was silent.

"Fan?"

"Yes, boss."

"You still haven't actually told me what the problem is," he said, with as much patience as he could muster.

"Oooooooh. Yeah. I guess I haven't."

Ysbaddaden waited but no other words seemed to be forthcoming.

"Fan."

"Yes."

"Please tell me what the problem is before I dump you in another tureen."

"Oh, right!" she said, her eyes going wide. "The problem. It's a big one! Okay, so you know those monkfish they've got in that pond down in the courtyard?"

"Yes."

"They...the monkfish, I mean...well, they turned into monks."

"Monks?"

"Yeah, monks."

"So...just to clarify," Ysbaddaden said, "the monkfish— the supremely ugly, creepy fish I like to keep down in that pond to deter others from enjoying my favorite courtyard and also I keep them there for making my favorite dish, monkfish chowder—those monkfish..."

"Yes, those."

"Have turned into..."

"Monks."

"By which you mean…"

"You know, monks," Myfanwy said, throwing up her tiny hands. "Guys in long robes. Tonsures. Mostly humorless. These ones are preeetty scowly."

"What…what are they doing?"

"I don't know. Chanting and not eating meat and accusing each other of apostasy, I guess. You know. Monk stuff."

"Does this require my attention?"

She said nothing, just nodded so vigorously that it rocked her tiny body back and forth in the air, her eyes as wide as he'd ever seen them.

"How many monks?" he asked.

"I would say…approximately…two or three…thousand. Give or take."

"In the courtyard?"

"They've spilled out a little bit."

"Yes, I would imagine they have."

She nodded just as vigorously.

"Out of my favorite courtyard," he continued.

"Yeah."

"Most likely trampling my beloved Irrational Petunias?"

"Indeed."

He put on his vest.

"Very well. Lead the way. We should probably let the metamorphosists know. We'll most likely need their assistance."

"I'm on it, boss."

She flittered away as he closed and locked the door, giving one more look at the suspicious Logbook, which seemed determined not to let him finish his work. As soon as the door closed, the black mass that Ysbaddaden had wiped from the book began to move, inching across the floor, up the table leg and across the desk, before sliding up the binding, across the parchment, and settling itself back into place on the page with a tremulous hiss. And then, with a blast of cold air, the book slammed shut.

Chapter 6

The next day, Makayla met Brynn at the usual place, by the usual stop sign, for their usual walk home. Brynn didn't mention the fact that Makayla missed the walk yesterday which Makayla was grateful for. They walked, mostly silent, lost in their thoughts, kicking at the fall leaves that covered the sidewalks. Brynn seemed to be building up the nerve to ask a question, which she finally did, but it was so quiet that Makayla could barely hear her.

"Hey...can you come over?"

Makayla stopped short.

"Why do you seem so nervous about asking me that? I come over all the time."

Brynn groaned.

"There's something...there's something kind of weird I want to show you."

"I don't know, man," Makayla responded, arching her eyebrows, "the last time you said you wanted to show me something weird, I ended up in another dimension."

"Yeah, I know. Sorry about that."

"Is that going to happen this time?"

"Us ending up in another dimension?"

"Yeah. If I come over and see your weird thing, are we going to end up in another dimension again?"

Brynn shrugged and grimaced hopefully.

"Sure," Makayla answered quietly, her chest tightening. "Let's see this mysterious weird thing of yours."

They walked the rest of the way in silence. When they arrived at Brynn's house, it was empty. They dropped their backpacks off in the kitchen. Makayla gave an inquiring look until Brynn nodded solemnly, cocked her head toward the stairs and said, "come on."

Makayla followed Brynn down the stairs to the den in the basement, which had been the setting for a horrific battle the year before. A creep named Efnysien (who was apparently some kind of interdimensional demigod) had taken over their school pretending to be a kid named Finian. He'd kidnapped Makayla and taken her to his court in Annwfyn, home of the goblins. After Brynn rescued Makayla, Efnysien followed them back to Earth and took Brynn's family captive before he was slain in the battle in the basement. But it had taken a heavy toll. Brynn had been heavily burned. Her baby sister had almost died. And Brynn said her father told her not to put too much stake in Efnysien's death—it had apparently happened to him before.

The room was desolate and empty. The furniture, which had been scorched or crushed or slashed or all of the above during the battle, had been sold or destroyed. One wall was entirely covered in a set of built-in bookshelves, but all the shelves were empty. The archaic hardwood paneling was singed. The ceiling was blackened. A seemingly random pattern of lines was burned into the wooden floor. Makayla could make no sense of them. They ran edge to edge, a mass of intricate charred chicken scratches, inscrutable scorched hashtags. The only other things that Makayla could see in the room were the bloodstains—on the floor mainly, but also a few on the walls.

"No one comes down here anymore," Brynn said quietly. "We keep meaning to clean it up. My parents want to have it renovated or have professional cleaners in or something. But I think what we all kind of want to do is pretend this room doesn't exist anymore."

Makayla nodded but didn't say anything. It was the first time she'd been down here since the attack. The room was devastated. The air felt menacing. 'Otherworldly foreboding' was the phrase that sprang to mind and it was a phrase she didn't care for at all.

"When Finian came here and did the things he did," Brynn continued, "his blood burned these...these shapes into the floor."

Makayla knelt down to look more closely at the hardwood floor, criss-crossed by hundreds of scorched lines, lines that connected, intersected, blossomed like malignant mildew stains, intent on reaching every corner they could.

"Those railroad-track-looking things?" Makayla asked, morbidly entranced. "That are scratched all over the floor? His freaking blood did that?"

"Yeah," Brynn answered softly. She wrapped her arms around herself, clearly caught up in the memory.

"What the hell are they?" Makayla's voice was shaky.

"I think they're runes."

"What?"

"Runes," Brynn repeated. "Some kind of old alphabet, I guess. They don't look like any of the ones I could find online, but I think that's what they are. We tried scrubbing at them a little, but we couldn't get them to go away. They've just been sort of...sitting here ever since, but..."

Brynn took a deep breath, shaking her head.

"But what?" Makayla prompted her.

"I came down here the other day. I touched one. And it was hot."

"Hot?"

"It burned me."

She held up a bandaged finger.

"Crap, Brynn. Are you okay?" The other girl nodded. "That doesn't make any damn sense," Makayla said, staring at the floor.

"I know. But it burned me."

Makayla reached out toward one of the spidery lines etched into the floor. Before her fingers could touch the wood, she hesitated.

"I can feel it from here. It's like there's a fire inside the lines. Why isn't the floor on fire?" Her voice grew louder, her eyes wider. "Why isn't the whole damn house burning down?"

"Good question, Makayla," Brynn responded, no hint of emotion in her voice.

"Wait a second," Makayla said, her brow furrowing. "Are all of them hot?"

The girls investigated, careful to keep their hands and feet clear of the lines that burned, shuffling around the edges of the room, hunkered down, following the heat from one set of scorch marks to another.

"No," Makayla said finally. "Only some of them. These ones over here next to each other are, but then these aren't...and then...these ones are."

"There's a section of them here," Brynn said. "Look. The heat travels straight across, from here to that bloodstain."

"And here...the hot ones go from here...over to the wall, crossing the ones you found."

"There's a pattern."

"Yeah."

"In a line." Brynn shook her head. "No. Lines. The burning runes here make a line, and then those ones do, too."

"Damn it," Makayla hissed. "Are the runes making more runes?"

"What would that even—"

Before Brynn could finish the thought, there was a noise upstairs. A noise that sounded like a blanket was trying to knock on the front door. If the blanket was wet. And full of bones. The girls snapped their heads around and gulped, nearly in unison.

"Front door?" Makayla whispered.

"Yeah."

"You expecting anyone?"

"Nope."

They padded as quietly as they could up the stairs and down the hallway. Brynn peeked out the window of leaded glass at the top of the heavy wooden front door, then scurried back to Makayla.

"Nothing there," she whispered.

"Weird."

"Yeah."

"Nothing at all?"

Brynn shrugged uncertainly.

"I don't think so," she said. "Just a shadow."

"A shadow?"

Brynn nodded.

"There's a shadow," Makayla repeated, "knocking at your front door?"

Brynn nodded again, her hands fidgeting with nothing.

"That's creepy," Makayla said.

"Yeah."

Makayla squinted at Brynn.

"It's not the first time it's happened, is it?"

"No," Brynn responded, unable to meet Makayla's eyes. "It's not."

Chapter 7

Makayla didn't linger at Brynn's house. She needed to get home to make herself dinner and the discovery of the runes scorched on the basement floor didn't increase her desire to stay much longer anyway. As she plodded along, hands deep in the pockets of her hoodie, eyes firmly on the sidewalk in front of her, she caught a sliver of movement out of the corner of her eye—a shadow twitching along a concrete stairway.

She turned to look and it was gone, but when she started moving again, there was another flicker, a tremor of darkness across the street, and then it was by the streetlight, a spasm of gloom. She quickly realized that it wasn't the same shadow flitting from corner to corner. There were shadows all around her, like the one from the other day, but more now, lingering all along the edge of her vision. They were getting braver, getting closer, encroaching on her. She quickened her pace.

A panic threatened to overtake her. She avoided one shadow, then another and another, turning down streets she didn't know, crossing from one side of the street to another and back again, anything to avoid the shadows which crowded her from every direction. She kept trying to make her way toward home, but lost her direction, then found it, then lost it again, and without realizing where her feet had taken her, she ended up in a playground, one she didn't recognize.

The playground had clearly been built decades earlier. The metalwork was solid and thick, with chunky welds holding each piece of the tarnished jungle gyms and swing sets in place. There was even a merry-go-round, one of the old-school metal ones, a relic from another era. This was the type of playground just waiting for some city council or neighborhood association to tear it down and replace it with brightly colored plastic and mass-produced animal images, all cushioned with a few inches of shredded rubber tire.

There was a little boy on the other side of the playground, no older than four. He had something in his hands, and it took Makayla a few moments to recognize what it was, because it wasn't something she expected to see in the hands of a young child. The boy had a hacksaw and he was cutting through one of the metal bars which formed the steps of the largest, sturdiest jungle gym. He finished his cut, pulled out the bar, and added it to the sizable pile of metal bars on the ground next to him. And without even pausing to admire his handiwork, he set the saw to the next step and got back to work.

Makayla looked around. There was no sign of the shadows. There was also no sign of this kid's parents. Although his back was to her and his head was lowered, she could see that he was well-dressed, with a vest, a bow tie, and khaki slacks. The hacksaw was rusty, with peeling yellow paint and a worn silver handle. His movements were methodical and almost skilled, as if hacksaw use had been a part of his life since he'd been able to walk. Makayla knew she should keep moving, should hurry home, but she also knew that four-year-olds shouldn't be alone at playgrounds, especially four-year-olds with rusty hacksaws. She cleared her throat. The boy did not respond. She waved. The boy did not respond.

"Why are you doing that?" she said, forcefully but calmly.

The boy answered quickly, but did not slow the pace of his work, nor did he look up at Makayla.

"I need some metal bars. Well, they're bars for now. I'll sharpen them later. Then they'll be stakes. Sharp, pointy stakes."

"I don't...I'm not sure that's a real good idea," She knelt down next to him. She still couldn't see the boy's face. "You know, I have younger brothers and I think you might be a little too young for a...for a rusty hacksaw."

"I'll be fine, Makayla, don't worry."

He kept working, still without looking up at her. She cocked her head.

"How did you know my name?"

The boy shrugged. He kept sawing. Makayla clenched her jaw and also her fists. She had younger brothers, three of them. She could deal with misbehavior. She knew how to deal with kids who didn't listen.

"I'm going to take that hacksaw now."

The boy shrugged again. Makayla tentatively reached out for the hacksaw. The boy did not object but also did not slow his work. Makayla plucked the saw carefully from his hand and then reached for the pile of metal bars he had already cut free.

"Yeah, I'm just going to take these too."

The boy finally paused once Makayla had taken the saw from him, his body going slack. But now he flexed both hands, grabbed the bar he had been cutting, and began to pull, trying to break the thick welds through brute force alone.

"Hey...um...are your parents around?" she said gently.

The boy did not respond. He pulled, straining against the metal, grunting with effort, his tiny hands white as he struggled to move the metal bar. Nothing else happened for some moments, just a small boy trying to accomplish a clearly impossible feat, but then a chill went up Makayla's spine as the bar moved, just a bit. He pulled again, a muffled scream of fury escaping from his diminutive frame. The bar moved again. Only a fraction of an inch, but a clearly noticeable fraction. The boy snarled. He let go of the bar and rubbed his hands together. He took three deep breaths, then leapt off the ground and kicked the bar with both feet. The bar clattered to the ground and the boy landed nimbly on his hands, then pushed himself back to his feet in a graceful spring. He picked up the bar with a muted sense of satisfaction.

Makayla's concern for the well-being of this preternaturally strong preschooler was quickly evaporating. She backed away, her arms encumbered with the hacksaw and the dismembered remnants of the jungle gym. Once she reached the edge of the playground, she turned toward home. She gave one quick glance over her shoulder and saw that the boy was now sitting motionless on a swing, watching her depart. He was holding the recently freed metal bar, tossing it absently, spinning it in the air, catching it again. It was the first time Makayla had seen his face. It was the normal face of a four-year-old boy. Except for the eyes. She couldn't say why, but something about his eyes was wrong. She picked up her pace. When she looked back again, the boy had disappeared.

There were no shadows now, no creepy kids. Just her and her footsteps and her racing heart. Now that she was alone, wandering streets she didn't know, the panic overtook her. Her chest tightened. Her head went so fuzzy it was hard to see through the haze. The back of her neck burned and the flush spread to her cheeks, her forehead, her shoulders, her chest. And there was nothing she could do about it. She tried to slow her breathing down but she couldn't. She kept her eyes down. She put one foot in front of the other. That's all there was to do. If she just moved one foot, and then the other, eventually the feeling would pass.

"Not now," she whispered. "Not now."

But that's what she always said when it happened. Even if she could package these feelings up and unbox them at a more convenient time, would that really help? No, of course not. Better to keep them bottled up deep inside. If they escaped a little bit, like now, when she was alone on the streets, so be it.

When she was able to control her breathing enough to form coherent words, she pulled out her phone and pressed the pointy-eared icon on her screen, the one she'd assigned to Brynn.

"Hey," Brynn answered, "what's up? You just left. Did you forget something?"

"No," Makayla said, willing her voice not to shake, not to belie the scream struggling to force itself from her lungs. "I, uh, I forgot. My parents took the boys over to my Grandma's house for the night. I told them I wanted to stay home."

"Okay?"

"Yeah, I decided I don't want to stay home. Can I crash at your place tonight?"

"Sure. But remember, my place has creepy burning lines in the basement."

"Yeah, I'm good with that. My perspective on the perilousness of the creepy burning lines has changed suddenly."

Makayla hung up. It wasn't a lie. The rest of her family really was going away for the night. She'd been looking forward to curling up by herself on the couch, watching some TV that her parents would never let her watch when they were home. But not now. Now all she wanted was to be anywhere but there. Anywhere but a place with no other people. Anywhere but alone.

Chapter 8

Thirty minutes later, Makayla was already beginning to believe that she must have imagined the crowd of shadows, the super-strong pre-schooler, all of it. If it weren't for the hacksaw and pile of metal bars that she'd stashed under Brynn's porch, she would have been sure it had just been her imagination run amok. For now, she let the memory of it drift away like clouds on the wind. She was curled up on the couch, socks off, hair up, eating popcorn with her best friend and pretending to do her homework. Well, *she* was pretending. Brynn actually seemed to be engaged with her textbook, her brow furrowed in concentration. Makayla gave a deep sigh and poked Brynn in the side with her foot.

Brynn widened her eyes in mock fury. "If I don't finish this by tomorrow," she hissed, "I'm toast."

Makayla relented, picked up her book again, and decided to give the War of 1812 a shot. Two paragraphs in, her eyes grew heavy and she was just starting to ponder the benefits of a little nap on the couch when the front door flew open, startling her back to awareness.

Brynn's little brother, Conn, slammed the door shut behind him, threw his backpack across the room, glowered at the girls and stormed through the living room. They heard the door at the bottom of the basement stairs open and slam shut. Brynn and Makayla stared at each other in amazement.

"Did he...did he have a black eye?" Brynn whispered.

"Yeah, dude. He did. Your brother has a big old shiner. And a couple of cuts on his face too."

"That's crazy."

"Do you think he got in another fight?"

"Well, he must have," Brynn said, wrinkling her nose. "Right? Where else would he get a black eye?"

"At this rate, he's either going to get his ass kicked or get expelled," Makayla said. "What is going on with him?"

"I don't know." Brynn sighed moodily. "I wonder if there's a goblin version of juvie."

"Or military school."

"Or scared straight."

They were just about to giggle at this when a piercing scream of frustration rose from the basement, immediately followed by a blinding flash in the window and a peal of thunder that shook the house.

"What was that?" Makayla whispered. Her hair felt like it was standing on end.

"I think...I think it was lightning," Brynn answered, her eyes wide.

"Where did it hit?"

"Close. Very, very close."

They went outside. The air was silent and still. Makayla pointed. There was a scorch mark on the wooden fence in front of Brynn's house. A piece of the fence was smoldering, small flames licking the wood. Brynn ran over, kicked at it, and doused the flames with her foot. She stared at the burnt fence, then looked to the sky and back again.

"I...where did it come from?" Brynn asked, bewildered.

"What do you mean?"

"Where did the lightning come from? It's not raining. There are no clouds. It's been clear all day. Look. There's the stars. Stars everywhere."

"No clouds," Makayla muttered.

"None."

"Then where the hell did the lightning come from?"

They stared upward. Makayla, almost without knowing it, reached out her hand. Brynn took it and they stood there together under the cold, clear sky, while just beyond the edge of their vision, shadows moved in the night.

Chapter 9

When they came downstairs the next morning, Conn was at the breakfast table, still with his black eye, staring into a bowl of cereal. They decided not to sit down. They grabbed their backpacks, said goodbye to Brynn's parents, and headed out the door for the walk to school.

A shadow darted across their path. Then a couple more. They put their heads down and hurried on. So intent were they on ignoring the flickering shadows which flitted all around them that, when they turned the corner, they barely noticed what was in front of them, or rather, what wasn't. Makayla's feet ground to a halt.

"What the hell," she blurted out in surprise.

"Huh?"

"Look, Brynn. Look where we are."

Brynn finally pulled herself back to the moment, away from the shadows, and looked at the street in front of them.

"What the hell," she blurted out in surprise.

"Yeah, that's what I said."

They were standing on a sidewalk, near an alley, and between them and the alley was a slab of concrete, clean as if it had just been poured. There was no dirt, no debris, no grass growing between the cracks, nothing to indicate that anything else had ever been here. But something had. They had seen it just the day before. And every day before that as well.

"Where did...the appliance store," Brynn stammered, "where did it go?"

"I have no freaking idea."

"I mean, it was here yesterday. Right?"

"I'm pretty sure it was."

"This is where the appliance store goes. This is where it's supposed to be."

"Yeah."

"It's an appliance store! Appliance stores do not disappear!"

"As a general rule, I believe that is correct."

They stared at the clean, smooth concrete where the appliance store had once stood. The store where Makayla had seen Brynn disappear for the first time. The store where Brynn had met the old woman and prepared for her trip to Annwfyn. The store where they had found the tiny door with the glass handle. But now it was gone. There was nothing left, just smooth concrete in front of an alley. Makayla shuddered. They ran the rest of the way to school.

Chapter 10

That day after school, there were no shadows on the walk home, which Makayla was grateful for. She was less thankful for the fact that the disturbingly strong kid from the playground was across the street from her house, watching her. She waved at him. He didn't wave back but his eyes remained locked on hers. He was holding the metal bar that he had ripped from the jungle gym, only now it had been sharpened into a vicious point. He stared at Makayla dispassionately while he stabbed the sharpened rod into a telephone pole over and over again, never taking his eyes off her.

She shuddered, turned away from the boy, and was about to run onto her porch and bound through the front door to get away from him when she noticed that her house looked hazy, as if she were looking at it through a raincloud. Then she spotted a shadow at the corner of her house, an impossibly tall shadow with no figure to cast it and no sun to throw it. She saw another shadow by the porch and several more huddled near the front window and then she realized there were dozens of them. Now she knew why there were no shadows on the walk home. They were here. They were all around her house. Their nebulous arms were linked, clutching at each other, holding tight. But what were they doing there? Trying to keep her out? Or the rest of her family in? The boy across the street continued to stab the telephone pole. She was caught between a phalanx of shadows and an incredibly creepy, perhaps sociopathic, preschooler. She did the only thing she could think of: she called Brynn.

"I just got home," Makayla panted. "There's shadows all around my house."

"Mine too." Brynn's voice sounded hollow.

Makayla looked at the drifting darkness of the shadows as they clasped each other. Some of the arms were beckoning her toward the house or perhaps taunting her, she couldn't tell.

"I don't...I don't want to go through them," she said to Brynn.

"You don't go through them, right?" Brynn's voice tightened, as if she were trying to convince herself as well as Makayla. "I mean, they're shadows. We can step over them. Or around them. It's just a shadow on a sidewalk. You're not going to break anyone's back by stepping on a crack."

Neither of them laughed at her attempted joke. There was a heavy moment of silence before Makayla hung up. She walked to the edge of the shadows. Brynn was right. It was just a shadow on a sidewalk. And on the other side of the sidewalk was her home, full of comfort and parents and siblings and love.

She closed her eyes and stepped over the shadow. Instantly, she knew that Brynn was wrong. Very, very wrong. Everything went out of joint. A blast of cold air hit her from every direction at once. A thousand needles pricked her skin and every bit of moisture was sucked from the air. Her throat was too dry to swallow, her eyes were too dry to blink, the skin on her hands was cracking and peeling, her fingernails were shriveling at the edges, and all around there was nothing but hazy darkness—no house, no sidewalk, no sky, just hazy darkness and a coldness that was draining every bit of warmth and moisture from her body.

Her body shook. She shivered convulsively, desperate to escape the chill. She lost her footing but didn't fall, her body held somehow aloft in the nothingness. There was no up, there was no down, just darkness, all-consuming darkness— then suddenly there was a flash and she saw through the emptiness, saw through the cold, into a shadowy glade under a sunless sky—and then there was another flash. This time, she saw a pair of eyes, the darkest eyes imaginable. They were staring at her, piercing her soul, sucking everything from her that was her and there was nothing to fill the void. All the things that made her who she was were being drained away and the hollowness that remained was being filled with the nothingness that surrounded her. Makayla screamed but there was no sound. Makayla screamed but there was barely any Makayla left.

But as suddenly as it had begun, it ended, and she was on her front porch, on the other side of the shadows, a few steps away from her front door. She gasped for breath, found there was air all around her, which filled her up, filled the gaping nothingness inside her. She swallowed. She blinked. She checked her hands, which were still there, not bleeding. Her fingernails had not peeled away. She was there, she was whole, but her house was still surrounded by shadows.

She leaned against the wooden siding on the porch and called Brynn. Brynn answered but didn't say anything.

"I don't think they're just shadows," Makayla said, her voice dry and cracked, a voice that had almost been taken from her by the darkness. "They're more than that. I went through them. I saw a land with a sunless sky. I saw a pair of black eyes that I know I've seen before. I went through the shadows, Brynn. I almost got ripped apart."

There was no response. Not for several minutes. Even longer, maybe. But finally, the voice on the other end, as dry and hoarse as Makayla's own, said two words:

"Me too."

Chapter 11

Ysbaddaden sat at his desk, glowering at the Logbook. He was mentally daring the book to do anything, anything at all, to prevent him from doing his paperwork. The book did nothing but Ysbaddaden glowered at it all the same. He threw open the cover, daring the book to respond. The book did nothing. He opened the book to the relevant page. The book did nothing. Feigning nonchalance, Ysbaddaden turned his back, pretending to reach for something on the very top shelf. Then he snapped back around and jumped into his seat, eyes darting, searching for anything the book might have done while his back was turned. The book had done nothing.

"Hmm," he said. "Playing coy today, are you?"

He picked up a quill, dipped it in the ink, and moved the nib toward the page. The book did nothing. He moved the quill closer. The book continued to do nothing. A tiny drop of ink fell from the quill and landed on the page beneath. The book remained still and motionless and absorbed the ink, as books usually do when one spills ink on them. Ysbaddaden pursed his lips determinedly.

"Fine, then," he said sharply, "it seems we've come to an understanding. I have work to do, and you—" He pointed stridently at the book. "You are going to let me do my work." The book remained silent, which he took for acquiescence. He dipped his pen in the ink, set the nib to the page, and began to inscribe the first letter, whereupon the office door immediately flew open with an earsplitting crash. Ysbaddaden's quill slid across the parchment, leaving a messy ink splotch behind.

Something between a growl and a whine came from deep within his throat. He laid his quill carefully to the side. Myfanwy fluttered into view and poked her head in.

"Boss," she said quietly.

Ysbaddaden did not respond.

"Boss."

Ysbaddaden did not respond.

"Okay, boss, I hate to bother you with this—"

"I also hate for you to bother me with it, and I don't even know what it is."

"Well, it's just that the gwragedd down the hall are quarreling with the bwbachod next door over the temperature of the pond. See, the bwbachod say they need the pond cooler, but the gwragedd say they need it warmer, but the bwbachod say the steam is disrupting their wardrobe routine, but the...but the...boss, are you smiling?"

"Why, yes," he said, realizing that it was true. "Yes, Fan, I believe I am."

Fan looked confused.

"But...but..."

"So, the situation you described," he cut in, alleviating her bewilderment. "That's the whole crisis?"

She cocked her head at him. Her confusion rendered her silent, a condition she was rarely to be seen in.

"That's the entirety of the problem?" he reiterated. "That's all?"

Fan nodded. He sighed with relief.

"This is…this is a minor disaster at best. Send Bubbles to deal with it."

Fan smiled and drew herself as straight as she could while hovering in mid-air.

"Got it." She gave an earsplitting shriek. "Bubbles! Come here, Bubbles!"

"Fan. Fan. Fan." He tried to gain her attention while she continued to scream Bubbles' name. "Fan!"

"Yes, boss."

"Not so loud. He's just across the hall."

"Got it, boss."

A man, or a mostly man-shaped being, shuffled into the room. He wore long brown robes of a rough-hewn material and plain leather sandals. The hair on the crown of his head was shaved, leaving a ring of brown wisps along the edges. His robes were soaking wet up to his knees. His face was nearly expressionless. He gurgled.

"Have you been standing in the fountain again, Bubbles?"

The robed man nodded and gurgled.

"I don't know why we were able to turn all the other monks back into monkfish," Ysbaddaden said. "Except for Bubbles here."

Bubbles stared vacantly into space, his jaw slack.

"Yeah. Me neither. He's kind of growing on me, though," the tiny winged woman said, looking at the monk with vague affection.

"If only he were more understandable."

There was a moment of silence, which was broken by another gurgle from Bubbles.

"Gurgle," Bubbles said. "Salvē! Te adiuvāre possum?"

"Hello, Bubbles," Ysbaddaden said. "Yes, we need your help."

"Gurgle," said Bubbles appreciatively, which he followed with, "Meum nōmen Bubbles est."

"Yes, Bubbles, I know." Ysbaddaden spoke more slowly. "We need your help."

"Gurgle," said Bubbles. "Hōc bonum est!"

Ysbaddaden nodded and smiled, then used a series of broad gestures while he spoke, doing his best to make sure Bubbles understood him.

"Down the hall."

Bubbles thought for a moment, then pointed and gurgled.

"Yes, that's right. Down the hall, there's a pond. It's used by the gwragedd and the bwbachod who work here."

"Mihī placet lingua latīna!" replied Bubbles. He paused. "Gurgle!"

"Focus, Bubbles," Ysbaddaden said, bearing down on him. "I need you to go to the pond and just…just sit in it for a while. I suspect that will dissuade everyone from arguing over it for at least a few hours. Long enough for me to get some work done. Can you do that?"

Bubbles stared vacantly at the wall and gurgled for a surprisingly long amount of time. Finally, Ysbaddaden snapped his fingers, which brought Bubbles' attention back.

"Bubbles! Can you do that for me?"

Bubbles stared at Ysbaddaden. Ysbaddaden stared back.

"Nōn intellegō!" Bubbles shouted.

Ysbaddaden sighed.

"Go to the pond," he said loudly, each syllable sharp and distinct. "Sit in the pond. Stay there as long as you want."

He stared at Bubbles with all his might, attempting to cram the instructions into the monk-y fish-man's head with all the force of his will. Bubbles' eyes were vacant. They were vacant. They were vacant. And then suddenly, they lit up. His arms flew up over his head. He gurgled loudly and merrily.

"Cōnfestim reveniō!" he shouted and ran out of the room.

"Close enough," Ysbaddaden muttered.

He sat down again, preparing to work, but mere moments after Bubbles had departed, an unbelievably loud noise filled the room, a noise of squelching and popping, as if a plastic tube of raw meat had burst open, only the tube of raw meat was a mile long and had popped open because it collided with a jet plane. Ysbaddaden's eyebrows flew up. So did Myfanwy's. His jaw clenched. So did hers.

"Fan," he said.

"Yes, boss," she said quietly.

"Will you please go and see what that noise was?"

"Yes, boss."

The tiny woman flitted out of the room into the vestibule which led to the hall and immediately returned with a sour look on her face.

"Oh, boss," she said, and she appeared to be both grimacing and crying, "it's...it's Bubbles, he...he...he..."

"Out with it, Fan, spit it out."

"Bubbles, he...well, he turned back into a fish at what was probably the worst possible moment."

"A fish?"

"Yeah, a fish. Only instead of shrinking back down to fish size when he turned back, he...oh my, he grew. He grew a lot."

"He grew?"

"Yeah, I think so, but maybe he grew too much, because I'm not sure how big fishes are supposed to get, but it looks like he got preeetty big and then...um..."

"And then?"

"And then after he grew...I think he sort of...exploded."

"Exploded?" Ysbaddaden asked.

"Yeah."

"He didn't."

"He did."

"While he was growing?"

"Appears that way, yeah."

"So...the hall? Outside my office?" Ysbaddaden asked, dreading the answer.

"Is kind of...full...of fish...flesh. And fish skin. And...yep, quite a bit of fish guts, too."

"How full?"

Fan shrugged and pinched her mouth closed, clearly not wanting to answer.

"A puddle?" he insisted. "A thin layer? Spread end to end ankle deep?"

"More...more than ankles, boss."

"How much more?"

She gauged it with her hand.

"Almost to the ceiling."

Just at that moment, muffled screams were heard from somewhere down the hall.

"I think it might be pouring out of the hall and into some of the rooms now too."

The first set of muffled screams were joined by more.

"Yeah, I think some of the bwbachod next door might be sort of...trapped."

The muffled screams were growing less distinct and more panicked by the moment. Myfanwy cocked her head and listened intently for a brief instant, a confused furrow upon her brow.

"I think...I think they might be drowning."

"In fish?"

"Yeah. It kind of sounds like that. Doesn't it?" She frowned. "Drowning in dead fish. Exploded dead fish."

"Which means our minor disaster is now..."

"Less minor. More apocalyptic. Little bit of utterly revolting on the side."

A thin trickle of exploded fish flesh began to trickle under the office door.

"That's...that's most unpleasant." Ysbaddaden shivered.

"Well, if you think that's unpleasant, you're really not going to enjoy what's happening in the hall right now."

Ysbaddaden stared at the Logbook.

"What is wrong with you?" he asked it.

Another squishy explosion echoed through the room. Another set of muffled screams joined the chorus.

"Boss! Quickly! The disaster is getting significantly more disastery by the second!"

Ysbaddaden continued to stare at the Logbook.

"You are beginning to be my least favorite book."

"Boss! Hurry!"

"I'm coming."

Ysbaddaden pulled on a pair of galoshes. He grabbed a shovel, a machete, and a headlamp, and marched solemnly into the hall. The office was still for a moment. Then the Logbook fluttered in a nonexistent wind and, once again, slammed shut.

Chapter 12

There was an awkward silence around the dinner table at Brynn's house. The two adults and two teenagers nodded and smiled nervously. Makayla tried to break the silence and perhaps move things along.

"Mr. McAwber. Mrs. McAwber," she said politely, looking each of them in the eye.

"Hi, Makayla," Brynn's father said.

"No need to be so formal," her mother added.

"Yes, absolutely," her father continued, "you've been such a good friend to Brynn, especially with all the…"

"Unfortunate events," Brynn's mother provided.

"Yes, especially after the unfortunate events of last year, and we really appreciated your…"

"Discretion."

"Yes, your discretion. After all, if the entire city of Jeffersonville found out that we were…well, you know…"

"You're goblins," Makayla said matter-of-factly. "I have no problem with this. It's actually kind of cool."

"Yes," he continued, "but asking you to keep a secret from your family…it's a terrible thing to ask someone to do."

"It's cool," Makayla shrugged, taking another bite. "Families got to have their own things sometimes."

"Sure," he said, his eyes squinting and peering upward as if he were trying to convince himself of this, "maybe sometimes they do." He then looked sternly at Brynn before shaking his head and mouthing, "no, they don't."

Brynn sighed and rolled her eyes.

"Well, like I said," he continued, "we really appreciate you keeping our little secret. I can't even imagine what would have happened if the entire city found out." He blew out his cheeks. "Well, I suspect it would have been bad." He pondered this for a moment. "Really bad. I mean, what would the general populace of a city this size—here in the Midwest region of the United States—what would they do if they found out that goblins not only exist, but that their children were attending school with two of them—"

"Gaf," his wife whispered, tapping his arm.

"Yes, dear."

"Gaf, we should maybe get back on task."

"Right. We actually wanted to have this chat for a reason, didn't we?"

"We did."

He gestured for her to continue.

"We appreciate you coming over and chatting with us," Brynn's mother said with a genuine smile. "After what Brynn told us, we thought the simplest thing to do would be just to sit down with you two girls and have a...have a little talk. Right, Gaf?"

"Right, yes. Sit. Just like we're doing now." There was another awkward silence. Brynn's father stood up abruptly. "Um...coffee?" he asked Makayla and then pointed in various directions. "Do you drink coffee? What about water? Juice? Juice box?"

Makayla's lips curled into a slight frown.

"I haven't had a juice box in quite a number of years, actually."

"We're fifteen now, Papa," Brynn said.

"Right, right. No juice boxes, then."

Makayla smiled.

"I'm good with water."

After Brynn's parents found out about the encounter with the shadows (Brynn had been the one to let it slip), they insisted Makayla be invited over for a movie night sleepover. Said sleepover, however, turned out to be merely a pretext for the two adults to sit the girls down and insist that supernatural goings-on in town should probably be reported to the supernatural adults in town. By which they meant themselves, and definitely not (and this part was directed squarely at Brynn) the Salmon of Knowledge, the Old Woman in the Appliance Store, or the Mysterious Librarian. And once that groundwork had been laid, the two adults got down to the real business of prying information from Brynn and Makayla while also politely offering them refreshments.

"So," said Brynn's father.

"So," said Makayla, doing her best to contribute.

Brynn's mother cocked her head at her husband, gesturing with raised eyebrows toward the girls.

"Right," he said, plowing ahead, "yeah, I...well, that is, we...we just have a few things we want to ask you about..."

"About the irregularities," Brynn's mother added.

"Abnormalities..."

"Popping up around town..."

"That you girls have been seeing..."

"Experiencing."

"Can you tell us what you saw?" Brynn's father asked.

Makayla and Brynn were both silent, unsure what to say.

"I know," Brynn's mother said. "It's hard."

"They were…" her father gently prodded, "that is, what you said you saw…they were shadows, correct?"

"Yeah," Makayla answered hesitantly, "but the thing is, Mr. McAwber—"

"Gaf. Please."

"Okay. Gaf. Right, we're not being formal here." Makayla grimaced uncomfortably. "They weren't just…shadows. They were more than that. They were shadows when there was no sun. They were shadows that were moving on their own. They were shadows that followed me, that buzzed and filled my head with nothingness. They weren't…" she finished weakly, "they couldn't be just…shadows…not in any way that I've ever thought of that word."

"And is that the same thing you saw, Brynn?" her mother asked.

Brynn nodded.

"What did they look like?"

Brynn and Makayla looked at each other.

"Tall, right?" Brynn said to Makayla.

"Yeah," she answered, the memory making her shudder, "incredibly tall."

"With like…something floating in the wind behind them—"

"Even when there wasn't wind—"

"Like a…coat…or a cloak or something."

"So," Brynn's father summed up, although he added details that Brynn and Makayla hadn't said out loud, "very tall, very thin, grasping hands, and a cloak blowing in the wind even when there's no wind around?"

"Yeah, that sounds about right," Makayla said.

Brynn's father nodded gravely, a frown upon his face, his brow furrowed. There was a long silence.

"So what does it mean?" Brynn finally asked.

"Nothing good," he said. "Nothing good at all."

"What can we do about it?"

"That...that is a very good question. And the answer is...probably nothing."

"Nothing?

"Nothing. What's happening is beyond anything I've experienced. It doesn't make a damn bit of sense."

"But Mr....Gaf..." Makayla asked, "have you been seeing them too?"

He nodded. And gulped.

"I have."

"Me too," Brynn's mother added softly.

"And that...that right there, is what is so troubling," he said, reaching for his wife's hand. "If there was just one of these...these shadows floating around, we could blame it on an overactive imagination, or a stomach bug, or an errant bit of mystical mischief that maybe got trapped here last year."

"But if we've all seen them..."

"And in these numbers..."

"Then...yes, something is definitely happening."

"But the exact nature of the something is what we don't know."

"And the not knowing...considering what we've seen..."

"And felt..."

"The not knowing is what truly has me disturbed."

Makayla took another drink of water, trying not to notice how much her hand was shaking. If anyone in the whole universe would know what was going on with the shadows, she expected it to be Brynn's parents. The fact that they were just as much in the dark as she was left her cold to the tips of her toes.

"So...you guys are magic beings with superpowers," she asked.

Brynn's parents both shrugged.

"And the two of you are quote unquote 'disturbed' about what's going on?" Makayla asked hesitantly.

They nodded.

"Well, that's goddamn terrifying, Mr. and Mrs. McAwber, and I apologize for both the swearing and the formality."

"It's okay, Makayla," Brynn's mother said warmly. "Considering the circumstances, I think both are warranted."

Chapter 13

The week after that was full of shadows. Shadows around their houses, shadows lurking behind the school, shadows on the sidewalk, shadows clinging to the sides of buses, shadows tiptoeing along the power lines, shadows floating along the rooftops, shadows in the sky.

The creepy boy with the bow tie seemed to be following Makayla around. He never approached her and he never spoke to her. He did, however, now have a friend: a girl about his age, wearing a yellow sundress and carrying a scalpel. They were joined by two more, and then two more, until the pack of preschoolers numbered an even dozen. They didn't speak, just stood on the side of the road, watching Makayla as she walked to school. They were all neatly dressed. One of them had a chisel. Another had a bulging canvas grocery bag slung over her shoulder, stained with a dark liquid, and Makayla didn't even want to think about what might be inside.

But worse than all of that, worse than the encroaching shadows, worse than the hollow-eyed children who were following her around, worse than the general sense of gloom and foreboding infecting their town, was what Brynn said to her on their walk home.

"We're moving," she said, and Makayla felt the bottom drop out of her world.

"What the hell, Brynn," she answered sharply. "Who decided this?"

"Well, not me, obviously," Brynn snapped back.

"Yeah, I know, but I mean...did your dad get a new job or something? Are you moving somewhere to be closer to family and I'm realizing as I'm asking that last one I don't even know what that would mean for a family of goblins—"

"Coblyns."

"Whatever."

"It's not my fault, Makayla," Brynn said, her jaw clenched, clearly trying not to cry.

Makayla closed her eyes and took a breath.

"I know," she said. "I'm sorry, I'm just...I feel like I got punched upside the head, you know?"

"I know. I wanted to find the best way to tell you, but I didn't think there was one. I feel like crap too. There was a...a big fight last night."

"What do you mean? With who?"

"Me," Brynn said with a shrug. "My mom. My dad. And he...he actually raised his voice. I've never heard him do that before. It was...unsettling."

"Yeah, your dad is one calm dude."

"Yeah."

"What about Conn? What does he think?"

"No idea. He was gone. Stormed in after the fight was over and went straight to the basement."

"Your brother has some crap going on," Makayla said, shaking her head.

"To put it lightly."

"So...what happened?"

"My dad's been trying to figure out what's happening in town. Consulting someone...something...I don't know, I didn't really understand all of what he was saying."

"That sounds more like your dad."

"Yeah. But he can't find anything out. He thinks whatever's going on is weird and probably dangerous, but he has no clue what it is. And then he said we needed to leave."

Makayla was silent. Brynn looked to the sky, her eyes wet.

"I asked them why—why would we run from a problem? I said we have to figure out what's going on, right? They said no, whatever's happening in Jeffersonville is levels beyond anything they've ever seen before. They said they'd talk to your family, try to give them some help. But they said we need to protect ourselves. And that maybe…maybe when we leave town, the problems will leave too. My dad said that goblins bring bad luck with them sometimes, that maybe we brought bad luck to Jeffersonville, that maybe…maybe Jeffersonville will be better off without us."

"I won't be better off without you," Makayla said quietly, but she wasn't sure that Brynn heard her.

"They said there's no reason not to move," Brynn continued. "I mean, I guess we came here in the first place because the strange little man told us we had to. Now that he's gone…there's no reason not to leave."

"So what does that mean? You're going to go chill out somewhere for a while, see if everything dies down here?"

"No, Makayla. We're leaving. We're leaving for good. We're going back to California."

"When?"

"Soon. I guess we never actually sold our house out there. Or it never completely existed in this dimension. Or both? I'm not sure. Something in between real estate and metaphysics means that our old house is still out there in California waiting for us, and we're going back to it."

The rock in the pit of Makayla's stomach was growing with each passing moment.

"There's...there's already a truck parked in front of our house," Brynn said. "It showed up this morning. My parents are already boxing stuff up."

"Damn it."

"Indeed."

"No, I mean, damn it, Brynn! You're going to leave me in this town full of noises and shadows and burning runes and weird kids and you're just going to go off to safety and me and my family are what? Condemned to creepiness and lurking shadows for the rest of our lives?"

"I mean...who knows...maybe the weirdness *will* follow us out to California. Haven't you always said this was the most normal town on the planet until I showed up?"

"Well, yeah," Makayla mumbled. "But I always kind of meant it in a good way. Not in a the-weirdness-is-threatening-my-very-existence kind of way."

"I don't know what to do," Brynn said weakly, her emotions now spent.

"What *can* you do? We're fifteen. There are some decisions that are...out of our hands. You made your case. Your appeal was denied."

Brynn nodded.

"So what now?" she said softly.

Makayla gazed down at the sidewalk.

"How long?" she asked after some thought.

"I don't know. A week. Maybe less."

"Well, we should probably try to make the most of that time."

"Yeah? How?"

"Spend it together, I guess," Makayla shrugged.

Brynn smiled.

"So just like normal then," she said.

Makayla smiled too.

"Yeah. Just like normal."

Chapter 14

Ysbaddaden sat staring at the Logbook, his fingers drumming on his desk. He was developing a twitch in his left eye. His stomach churned.

"Why is it every time I try to sit down and finish up this blasted paperwork, something blows up?"

The door flew open and Myfanwy screamed in.

"Something blew up!"

Ysbaddaden stared at her, slowly rising to his feet. He was about to scream, throw something, gnash his teeth, tear his hair. But as he stared at the quivering woman hovering in front of him, screaming about yet another disaster seemingly sprung from nothingness solely to divert him from his duties, a wellspring of stubbornness bubbled forth from deep within him. He decided he would stay here, on this chair, come hell or high water, until the paperwork was done. He clenched his jaw, folded his hands, and looked straight into Myfanwy's eyes.

"You deal with it, Fan," he said resolutely. "I give you the authority."

"You...you what?"

"I give you the authority. Here...take this...ladle," he said, retrieving one from the army of earthenware that cluttered his shelves. "This is my Ladle of Authority. It's a badge of office. It means if you run into anyone who questions you, all you have to do is say, 'look, this is my Ladle. It means I'm in

charge. I'm the one holding the Ladle, so, as everyone knows, that means I'm in charge.' Yeah? And then you deal with the problem."

"*I* deal with the problem."

"Yes."

"Because I have the ladle."

"Exactly."

"Yeah…boss…I'm not exactly sure about this…" Her voice trailed off. Ysbaddaden stared at her blankly until she continued. "But I guess I'm just going to take this…ladle…"

"Ladle, capital L, Ladle of Authority."

"Okay, I'm going to take this Ladle…and I'm going to go deal with this problem."

He nodded.

"Because I'm in charge."

He nodded again.

"And everyone has to do what I say."

Her eyes glinted. His squinted.

"*Everything* I say?" she said, her wings fluttering anxiously.

"Well…"

"You *said so!*"

"Fix the problem, Fan. Don't let this get out of hand. Let's not have a repeat of the Great Pudding Disaster of 1287."

"That wasn't my fault!"

"It was pretty much your fault."

Myfanwy sulked.

"*I love pudding!*" she screamed, more ferociously than he had ever heard her scream anything before, and he had heard her scream a great many things, both profound and mundane, over the course of more centuries than he cared to think about. She also scowled ferociously.

"I know," he said after her scream had faded. "Fix this problem and you shall have pudding."

"Promise?"

"I do."

"Puddings of various flavors and consistencies?"

"Yes."

The tiny woman pulled out a heretofore unseen cap, put it on, and fitted it down low over her brow. She adjusted the cap authoritatively and then saluted.

"I'm on it, boss."

She flitted out of the room.

"Where in blazes did she get the cap from?" Ysbaddaden muttered, but waved the thought away and got back to work.

He sat down, picked up his quill, and made to open the enormous book before something caught his eye. He pulled out his scrying glass and gave a closer look to the cover. His fingers grasped a tattered bit of thread, barely perceptible. He gave a gentle pull. A few inches of the thread came free from the binding but remained attached. He pulled again. A few more inches were revealed. He kept pulling and pulling until yards and yards of thread were in his hand, and the binding of the cover kept unravelling and unravelling until suddenly, with a poof of dust, the cover disappeared entirely, leaving a distinctly different cover in its wake, a cover which was wrapping a distinctly different book.

The revealed book was much brighter and much smaller than the previous book had been, a slim volume with six words on the cover: *A Succinct History Of The Rheum*.

"Wait a second," Ysbaddaden growled. "What in Beli's name happened? Where did my book go? Who would want to meddle with the Changeling Logbook? Who would even know how?"

He stared at the book perplexedly, then spoke three sharp, guttural words under his breath. Immediately, there was a sound as if a sheet of paper made of a hundred cats was folded into an origami swan and then set on fire. A blast of cold sucked the air from the room and for a few moments, all was silent.

The book on Ysbaddaden's desk quivered, twitched, lay still, then quivered and twitched again. The book jumped slightly into the air, gave a sound like a muffled firecracker, and then letters, numbers, punctuation marks, ink splotches, tables, sums—all the contents of the book—exploded outward, filling the air with their substance so that he could hardly see. Behind the haze, something landed on the desk with a distinctly unbooklike clank. Ysbaddaden cocked his head curiously, his eyes going wide. He waved a hand in front of his face. The letters and numbers were still floating thickly in the air like motes of dust, concealing the something on his desk, the something that was glinting in a distinctly unbooklike way. Ysbaddaden gave a gasp, which he immediately regretted as he inhaled a cluster of diphthongs.

"That does not look like a book," he said, coughing out a subordinate clause.

He waved his hands furiously and the fog of characters began to clear away. There on his desk lay a small silver cauldron about the size of his foot. It had two handles of brass and three feet of iron. He picked it up and examined it rim to rim and top to bottom. He sniffed it and his nose wrinkled in distaste. He squinted at it, holding it close to his eyes. Above one of the handles, he found a small stain. He flaked a bit of the stain off with his fingernail and examined it, then laid it on his tongue. He spat it out but nodded knowingly.

He retrieved a flat knife from the shelf and scraped the rest of the stain into a vial, which he stoppered. He located a satchel among the detritus in the room and gathered some materials he thought might be useful: his scrying glass, a small sack of smooth round stones, several flasks, and some cutlery for good measure. He went into the hall and locked the door behind him.

He unstoppered the vial and took another good whiff. Closing up the vial, he sniffed around in the hallway. A faint odor lingering on the stale, underground air led him down the hall. The odor led him to another hallway and through a door. It led him up one stairway and down another. It led him across a courtyard and through a garden. It led him near a pond and around a quarry. It led him to a tower he had never entered. It led him to the basement of that tower.

The smell led him to an underground path which twisted and turned, as underground paths are wont to do, until it led him to a simple wooden door. A door he did not expect. He stared at the door for a full five minutes.

"Well, I did not expect that," he finally said.

But despite his lack of expectation, he turned the handle and entered just the same.

Chapter 15

Makayla was at the dinner table at Brynn's house again. The mood was even more somber than it had been the last time she was here. The room was bare. Everything was in the moving truck outside except for four sleeping bags and the dinner table. Brynn said her parents wanted to have one last nice meal in the house before they left in the morning, although Makayla wondered how delivery pizza eaten on paper plates could be considered 'nice.'

"Thanks for coming to dinner, Makayla," Brynn's mother said, her voice wistful.

Makayla only nodded.

"It's...this has been a hard decision to make," Brynn's father added. "I know it's the right one, but we also know it will be hard on our kids. You and Brynn have been so close since we arrived, you've been such a good friend for her, we thought it was only right that..."

"That you join us for our last meal here," Brynn's mother finished his thought.

There was a long silence. The pizza was growing cold on the counter. Brynn's father made as if to speak, but stopped himself, the words evaporating in his throat. He stared gloomily at the table. His wife took his hands, tears welling in her eyes.

"It's weird," Brynn said finally. "I hated moving here. I hated this house when we got here. I hated it. And then I loved it. All of a sudden, it was my favorite place. And the really weird thing is I don't know when that happened, when I started loving it more than any place I ever had. But then...I also don't know when I started hating it again." She paused, her nose wrinkling in thought. "Well, no, that's wrong. I don't hate it. It just doesn't feel like ours anymore."

"I know, sweetie," her mother said. "I think...I think I felt the same way. It hasn't felt like ours for a while."

"Since the attack, it's been hard to feel comfortable here," Brynn said, her words clotted with frustration and sorrow. "I mean, I know we're safe, but I don't *feel* safe."

"And once you stop feeling safe, it stops feeling like home," her mother agreed.

"Yeah."

"And once it stops feeling like home, it stops feeling like a place that's ours."

"Although," Brynn's father added, "technically, it is still ours."

"Wait, I thought you said you sold it," Makayla said.

"Hasn't happened yet," Brynn answered. "We're leaving the keys and the paperwork—"

"So much paperwork," her father cut in.

"With Linda," Brynn continued.

"She's a real estate agent who lives down the block," her father said. "She said she'd take care of it for us. And in the end, it doesn't really matter. We can't come back here. We made a good go of making a home here for ourselves, in this part of the country—"

"A couple times now," Brynn's mother added.

"But it didn't work," her father continued, nodding, "either time. We don't belong. It's time for us to go and leave this town to the people who belong here."

He was trying to comfort Makayla, make her feel better about their imminent departure, but was clearly failing miserably. There was another long, morbid silence, finally broken by Brynn's mother.

"We should eat," she said.

"Yeah," Brynn's father said, trying to pull himself up from the morass of his own thoughts.

"Before the food gets cold."

"Colder," Brynn said with a smile.

"Should I get Conn?" Brynn's mother asked.

"Yes, please," her father said. "We should all be together."

"I just think he's been taking this so hard," Brynn's mother said. "All of this. The discovery about who he actually is, the attack, the strange things happening around town. I think they've really hit him, maybe even harder than they've hit any of us."

"He's at a...difficult age," her father responded.

"I think all of Conn's ages have been difficult," Brynn whispered to Makayla.

Makayla smirked. Brynn's mother gave Brynn a sharp look. Brynn rolled her eyes.

"Where is he?" Brynn's mother asked.

"I think he's down in the basement again," Brynn said.

Her mother nodded and walked down the stairway which led from the kitchen. They heard her knock on the door at the bottom of the stairs and call softly.

"Conn?"

"I'll be out in a minute," a voice grunted sharply, muffled by the door.

"Conn, it's time for dinner, you should come on upstairs."

There was no response from the sullen voice behind the door.

"Why are you in there anyway?" Brynn's mother continued. "It's still all burnt and it smells terrible."

"I like it in here," the sullen voice responded sullenly. "I feel less alone in here."

"You've been down there a lot lately."

"Yes, like I said, I like it in here."

"Conn, terrible things happened in that room. It's one of the reasons we're leaving."

There was no response. A frigid silence spilled forth from behind the door.

"Conn?" Brynn's mother called. "Conn?"

There was still no response. They heard her pulling at the door.

"Gaf, I can't get it open. I think it's locked."

Brynn's father looked confused.

"That...that door doesn't have a lock."

Brynn's father tramped down the stairs to join his wife. Brynn and Makayla heard him knocking gently on the door, then less gently.

"Conn?" he called. "Conn?"

Brynn and Makayla exchanged glances, then padded softly down the stairs to see Brynn's father pulling harder and harder on the door, to no avail.

"I don't know what's going on," he said. "Conn, come out of there now!"

There was no response from the room behind the door. Brynn's father gave a quick, guilty glance over his shoulder at the girls standing on the stairs.

"Sorry about this, Makayla," he muttered, as his body shimmered and changed before her eyes into something much different, something much less human-looking. His skin was now pale green, his ears were elongated and arched, and a long beard trailed from his pointy chin. His eyes were golden, his fingers and toes long and spindly. A tail twitched behind him, and a jewel flashed in the hollow of his throat.

"This body is just so much stronger than the other," he said, before his leg flew out, kicking the door with such force that Makayla could feel it in her gut. He kicked again and again, each blow more powerful than the last, but the door did not budge. He looked despairingly to his wife, who said, "let me try," as her body shimmered and changed.

Her skin was now so black it seemed to absorb the light around it, a darkness broken only by the stars and galaxies which whirled inside it. Her hair, on the other hand, was now so bright that it hurt to look at and glowed with a light of its own.

Brynn's mother put one of her hands on the basement door and whispered softly to it, as if she were consoling it or offering a secret. The door whispered back and then disappeared, replaced by a sheet of water standing in the middle of the door frame, clear and still. Brynn's mother walked through the water and into the scorched den. She glanced quickly around, but even before she entered, it was clear that the room was empty.

"He's gone," she said.

"How could he get out of there?" Brynn's father asked.

"He couldn't," Brynn's mother answered, despair rising from her voice as the stars within her skin grew fiery and sharp. "There's no other door. No windows." She shook her head, and her glimmering hair rained tears of starlight upon the floor below. "He's just gone."

ACT 2: MISSING

Chapter 16

The first thing Brynn's family did was head out into the neighborhood to see if Conn was still nearby. They tried to keep it quiet but a few of the neighbors heard, and then some families from school found out, and then there was a full-fledged search party roaming the streets, the parks, the schools, the libraries, anywhere they plausibly thought Conn could have reached in those first few gut-wrenching hours. As more and more of the city got involved, the search expanded into the woods, malls, rivers, lakes, highways, truck stops. No one found anything. Not a single trace. Not a single clue.

An eleven-year-old boy was missing, had seemingly vanished into thin air, and it was all anyone in Jeffersonville could talk about. It was splashed across the front page of every newspaper, the lead story of every local news report, for weeks.

Makayla came home exhausted every night, after helping with the search or providing comfort for the family in distress or helping them unpack the moving van. She couldn't stand to see Brynn hurting like this, and she knew there was nothing else she could do, but it was still killing her.

Eventually, after too many weeks, with every search turning up fruitless, with every lead turning up dry, with the citizenry exhausted and the media moving on to other things, Brynn's parents called it all off. The search was a failure. Conn was gone. There was nothing else to be done. Nothing but wait. And hope.

Chapter 17

Well, nothing else that humans could do, anyway. Those of the goblin persuasion took it upon themselves to move on to less traditional methods of seeking answers. Brynn had been spending every available moment in her basement, the room she had last seen her brother in, studying the runes that were burned into the floor. She took pictures with her phone. She printed the images, cut them out, glued them together. She scrawled shaky images on ream after ream of dollar store printer paper.

"I figured something out," Brynn said to Makayla, not looking up from her current sketch. It had been a week since the search was called off. "Something about the runes."

"Yeah, there's runes everywhere. We know that."

"No, not those runes," Brynn grunted, gesturing vaguely. "The other runes. Those...those lines we found, the heat signals that are making lines on the floor. I figured out what they're doing. Look."

She pulled the cap off a thick magic marker, checked her notes, drew a long black line across the floor and then added another.

"Whoa, dude!" Makayla shouted, trying to grab Brynn's arm. "What are you doing? That is...that is going to ruin the resale value of your house."

Brynn sniffed in frustration and resumed her work, drawing line after thick line on the basement floor, her wispy hair wild about her head.

"Yeah, I don't think selling the house is the first thing on my parents' minds right now. Not until we find Conn. And even if we do, I suspect the burned-up basement full of creepy runes isn't going to be the number-one selling point."

She waved Makayla off until she was done. She made a line, checked her notes and made another line, again and again, until a series of distinct shapes were traced on the floor. The shapes were like nothing Makayla had ever seen before, and even though she didn't know what the characters meant, didn't know if they meant anything at all, they made her skin prickle and her breath stutter.

Brynn stood up, her work complete. She put her hands on her hips, surveying the basement. Then she ran over and grabbed her papers.

"So, look," she said to Makayla, showing her one of the drawings. "The runes we found, the hot ones, the heat signals...these are the shapes they're making."

Makayla examined the figures in the drawing, which matched the figures Brynn had now traced out on the basement floor.

"They're different from the little runes burned into the wood," Brynn insisted, jabbing her finger at the paper to make her point.

"What do you mean?"

"I checked out all the smaller runes. There's hundreds of them, but there's actually only twenty individual characters. They just repeat in different patterns. I went over the whole floor three times."

"Only three?" Makayla muttered.

Brynn squinted at her, then shrugged, her compulsion to continue her point overcoming her frustration.

"Only twenty. *These* twenty." She waved one sheet in front of Makayla's eyes, then replaced it with another. "But then the other runes, the burn-y runes, they look like this. See...totally different shapes!"

"Okay. So...so there's a bunch of little weird shapes—"

"Twenty!"

"Right...and those little weird shapes are making some bigger shapes—"

"Thirteen. There's thirteen of them. Only thirteen. And I think...I really think there's some connection between them. I just haven't found it yet. I'm missing something. Something really basic, I know I am..."

Brynn took out her phone and started taking pictures of the figures she'd drawn on the basement floor.

"I don't...Brynn...they're just shapes. They don't mean anything. I know what happened down here was really hard, but I think...I think that dude just trashed your den. He's gone now, and your family is fine, but your brother is missing and your den is trashed."

"No, Makayla, look. Look at this one here, how it curves upward into this loopy spike, but all the small ones burned into the floor have only straight lines..."

As Brynn continued to talk, Makayla saw that her eyes were sunken. Her clothes were dirty. She looked as if she hadn't showered or brushed her hair in at least a few days. Makayla took a discreet whiff. "Oof," she whispered. Maybe more than a few days. Brynn was still talking.

"Brynn," she said gently.

Brynn was still talking.

"Brynn!"

Brynn finally heard her and looked up from her drawings.

"You need a break," Makayla said with as much firm insistence as she could muster. "Look at yourself. You don't look good. And you do not smell good."

Brynn pursed her lips and was about to object. Then she gave a hesitant sniff to her pits, grimaced and hacked.

"Let's go...go at least put on a clean shirt, huh?" Makayla said, leading Brynn gently toward the door. "And then maybe we could take a walk? Or something?"

"I'm going to bring these, though," Brynn said, holding up her unkempt wad of drawings and photos. "Maybe some fresh air will show me what I'm missing."

"Maybe. Come on."

Brynn nodded silently and a few minutes later they were out the door. Makayla led them aimlessly around the neighborhood. They paid no attention to where their feet took them, just walking in silence, but eventually (Makayla wasn't quite sure how), they ended up at the library.

Before Makayla could stop her, Brynn pushed her way through the doors, a look of wild determination on her face. Makayla followed her, hoping to pull her back outside, but Brynn strode quickly ahead, too fast for Makayla to catch her. As they wandered in and out of stacks, up and down staircases, Makayla wondered why the building seemed so empty and was just about to ask Brynn about the lack of people when they came face to face with a librarian, an older man, clean-shaven, with silver hair and an argyle sweater vest.

"It's you again," Brynn said.

Makayla cocked her head curiously. She had never met this librarian before but Brynn had talked about him.

"Indeed," the older man said.

"Are there any, you know, any other librarians that work here?"

"Certainly." He paused while the girls remained silent. "I'm sure there are." There was another silence. "Probably." The girls still did not respond. "That's not important. Now what do you need to know?"

"I need to know about these," Brynn said as she pulled out her sheaf of scribbled diagrams and the pictures she'd taken of the intricate runes. "Can you help?"

"Where...where did you find these?" the librarian asked.

Brynn pulled out her phone and flipped through the pictures of her basement floor, showing him each one for less than a second.

"Did you take these pictures yourself?"

"I just want to know what they are, what they mean," Brynn said, pocketing her phone.

"Do you want to know what they are or what they mean?" the librarian said slowly, his eyes twinkling sharply. "Those are two very different things, especially when we're dealing with those pictures you showed me."

"What do you mean?"

"Well, they're a type of...alphabet."

"Runes, though, right? They're runes?"

"Perhaps," the librarian said, his eyebrows arching high above the frames of his glasses.

"Perhaps? Well, I think they're freaking runes," Brynn said, her passion and exhaustion overwhelming her, "and if they're runes, that means they're a language, and if they're a language, they mean something."

The librarian said nothing.

"Right?"

The librarian continued to say nothing.

"Right?"

Brynn and the librarian stared at each other, a soundless showdown, neither wanting to flinch or back down. There was an intensity in Brynn's eyes Makayla had never seen there before. And whatever that intensity was, the librarian eventually gave in to it.

"Well, of course they mean something," he said. "Everything means *something*."

Brynn glowered at him.

"You were way more helpful last time," she hissed.

He pursed his lips and tapped his foot, looking to the ceiling. Brynn did nothing but stare at him again. Makayla followed her lead this time, still unsure exactly what was going on but hoping to contribute to the bizarre matchup of wills if she could.

"Fine," the librarian said after several minutes of this silent standoff. "Come with me."

He led them up a winding staircase into a part of the stacks that Makayla had never seen before. The older man searched the stacks and quickly found a huge, dusty, leather-bound volume. He flipped through page after page of runes, alphabets, characters and figures that meant nothing to Makayla, until he found what he was looking for. He stopped, unconsciously bringing his hand to his mouth.

"Oh my," he said quietly.

There was silence as the girls waited for him to say anything further. He did not.

"What...what does that mean, 'oh my?'" Brynn said finally.

"May I see the pictures again?" he asked politely. Brynn pulled out her phone and handed it to him. "Well, the runes here," he said, flipping through the photo gallery until he found the image he sought, "the ones which seem to be inscribed on some kind of...hardwood flooring?" The librarian looked at Brynn. Brynn shrugged as if she had no idea what he was talking about. The librarian rolled his eyes and continued. "Well, the runes seem to be Ogham...but the patterns you found, the ones you've drawn..." He pulled out several sheets of Brynn's drawings from the crumpled wad. "Here and...here...well, these shapes, these figures...these..."

"Runes?" Makayla provided.

He nodded.

"They *are* runes. But ones much older than Ogham. Much, much older."

He laid the drawings side by side with the book, transfixed. Brynn tried to get his attention, but he waved her away with a hiss. Finally, she put her hands over the pictures. He looked up at her, frustrated.

"Hey," she said. "Old dude. What does that mean?"

"It means...it means I'm going to need some time with these," he said, gently prying the rest of the sheaf of drawings out from under Brynn's arm. "I'll let you know when I know something."

"How will you do that?" she said.

"Trust me," he said vaguely. "I'll find you."

He handed her phone back, picked up the book and the entire bundle of drawings and was somehow gone before either of them were able to object.

Makayla and Brynn were left alone in a seemingly empty library, deep in the stacks. The girls waited quietly, but nothing happened until, several minutes after the librarian had vanished, a bank of lights flipped off at the far end of the building. Then another bank of lights went dark, and another, until the whole building was being plunged into darkness.

"Is...is the library closing?" Makayla asked. "It's like two in the afternoon."

Another set of lights went out, closer to them this time, with what seemed to Makayla to be a distinctly judgy clank.

"We should probably go," she said.

"Yeah."

Once they were outside, Brynn gave a smile of quiet triumph.

"I told you they weren't just shapes."

Makayla gave her friend a wide-eyed stare, punched her, and then they walked away together under the autumn sky.

"Ow," said Brynn.

Chapter 18

There was no answer when Makayla knocked on Brynn's door a few days later. This was unusual, as Brynn and her family were always home these days, waiting by the phone, worrying, sitting silently with each other, trying to pass the time while hoping for the unhopeable. Makayla turned the knob, opened the door slightly, and called in.

"Brynn? Mr. and Mrs. McAwber? My parents sent over a casserole. I told them you've been ordering a lot of pizza. They thought you might like a home-cooked meal."

There was still no response. She opened the door farther and stepped inside.

"Hello?"

"It's okay, Makayla, come on in," Brynn called faintly from the upper floor of the house.

Makayla set the casserole on the kitchen counter and headed upstairs. Most of the house was dim, but there was a light coming from Brynn's parents' room. Makayla pushed the door open and saw Brynn's mother lying face down on the bed, looking distinctly non-human. The skin of her back was so dark it seemed to swallow the light of the room, except for the glowing pinpricks of stars, galaxies and comets that swirled and moved over its surface. Her hair glowed with a light of its own, a halo of starlight above the darkness of her skin. Her head was resting on the pillow, her eyes were closed, and she wasn't wearing a shirt.

Makayla's eyes went wide and she yelped involuntarily.

"I am so sorry, Mrs. McAwber!" She jumped back into the hallway, slammed the door shut, and shouted uncomfortably. "I thought I heard Brynn's voice coming from up here somewhere."

"It's okay, Makayla," Brynn's mother called softly. "Come on in."

Makayla pushed the door open again. She now saw that Brynn and her father were in the room as well. Brynn was sitting on the bed and her father was examining his wife's skin, following the various shooting stars and galaxies which moved within it.

"What...what is going on?" Makayla asked hesitantly.

"We're checking," Brynn's father said vaguely, clearly distracted.

"Checking for what?"

"Checking for Conn. It's unlikely we'd find him here...but we still check."

"What do you mean, you're checking for him?" Makayla asked. "Do you mean he'd be inside there or something?"

Brynn's father chuckled.

"No, no," he said, "nothing like that. But the markings, they might...in certain circumstances...show us where Conn is. We check every night."

"Is it...is it a map?"

"Of sorts. Only..."

"Only not of Earth," Brynn said dryly.

"So, it only shows other planets?" Makayla asked with a confused frown.

"No," Brynn's mother said with a smile, opening her eyes for the first time, "nothing in this dimension at all, actually.

But other lands are here if you know how to look, and also other times. And thoughts and feelings and truths. And family. It's a map of all those things. For those who know how to read it."

"And if someone could put that in terms I could even remotely understand, I'd be awful grateful," Makayla said.

"Well, the relevant point here," Brynn said, "is that if Conn wasn't on Earth anymore, if he had skipped off to Annwfyn or something, he would show up on this map. I mean, I don't think he could get to Annwfyn, anyway. It took me weeks to figure out where the nearest entrance was and I was only able to get there 'cause I can turn into a bird. I don't think Conn's rabbit abilities would cut it."

"No. I can't imagine he went to the burial mounds," her father said. "So he's somewhere. Somewhere close."

"Relatively speaking," Brynn replied.

"Yes, relatively speaking. He is somewhere in this dimension, and given his age and current abilities, I find it unlikely he's been able to get too far."

Suddenly, Brynn's mother's eyes went white. A flash erupted deep within her skin and a wave of light moved outward from her back, spreading like a circle in the water, up her neck, down her arms, to her forehead, to her fingertips. She gasped. And just as suddenly as it had appeared, the wave of light fell into darkness.

"What was that?" Makayla asked, her voice hoarse.

Brynn's mother's eyes went back to normal and immediately filled with tears.

"It was Conn," she whispered. "He was there." She gathered a sheet around herself and sat up wide-eyed on the bed. Brynn's father put an arm around her.

"Where did it go?" Makayla asked quietly. "The light, the flash, what happened to it?"

"I don't know," Brynn's mother said.

"Has that ever happened before?"

"No. Nothing close."

"But if he showed up there...even for a second..." Brynn turned to her father, pleading.

"Then we've been searching in all the wrong places," he sighed wearily.

"Which means...what does it mean?" Brynn asked him. "What do we do now?"

"It means...it means we're going to need some help," Brynn's father said.

He looked to his wife. She nodded. He got up, pulled a small duffel bag from the closet and started throwing clothes into it.

"Papa?" Brynn asked. "Where are you going?"

"I'm not entirely sure yet. But there are some...people...I should talk to. If Conn has ventured out of this realm, the police aren't going to be able to help us anymore. But there are a few...people...I might could ask about it."

"I couldn't help noticing your eyes flicker over to me every time you said the word 'people,'" Makayla said. Brynn's father grimaced guiltily. "They aren't people, are they?"

"Not so much, no."

His bag now packed, he leaned over his wife, whispering good-byes.

"Take care of them," he said, nodding to the girls.

"I will."

"And kiss the baby for me."

"I will, Gaf," she said, smiling through her tears.

He wrapped his arms around Brynn. When he let go, she held on.

"But what do *I* do?" she said.

"Nothing. You stay here. Help take care of the baby."

"But..."

"No buts. I don't want you sneaking off into another world again."

"But...I'm not going to do that. I just want to help."

"I have to find some answers," he said. "I'll be back as soon as I can."

And once again, Brynn's father packed his bag and left for destinations unknown. Makayla watched as Brynn slipped out of her own skin, her body shifting, her skin changing hue, her fingers lengthening, her tail whipping around her. Makayla watched as the young goblin put her arms around her mother and rested her head on her shoulder. Then there was nothing, nothing but silence, for a long while as moonlight streamed in through the open window. If it weren't for the baby waking, crying, needing food, love, a clean diaper, they might have stayed there longer, silent despair etched on their faces. But there was a baby and the baby was crying. So they wiped each other's tears and did what they could do: take care of someone who needed them.

Chapter 19

"Where are we going?" Makayla asked, struggling to keep up with Brynn, who seemed to be on a mission.

"My dad is going to look for answers, right?"

"Yeah."

Brynn shrugged.

"Well, so am I," she said.

"Didn't he tell you not to?"

"No. He told me not to leave this dimension. I'm not going to leave this dimension. I'm not even going to leave Jeffersonville. I'm just going to talk to someone."

"And I'm coming with you to talk to this person?"

Brynn nodded, then stopped and turned to Makayla. Her mouth opened, she started to speak, but then frowned.

"Not a person, though," Makayla said, supplying the obvious answer.

Brynn nodded, then turned again and strode off, Makayla following as best she could. They rounded the corner and Makayla suddenly realized where they were. Brynn slowed to a halt and waved at the man in the foam rubber fish costume, who stood, as always, in front of the seafood restaurant. When he saw them, he jumped slightly and scurried into the alley on the far side of the building.

"Wait a second," Makayla said skeptically. "That dude?"

Brynn nodded.

"Trust me," she said.

They followed the man in the fish suit into the alley. He was standing near a dumpster, pretending not to look at them. Makayla realized she didn't know where his real eyes were, but his big, plastic, fish eyes were pointedly pointing anywhere but at the two girls. Brynn walked up to him and planted her feet.

"I need answers," she said, as if a sad man in a fish suit could somehow provide them. "I desperately need answers. I know you're not supposed to give me any, but...please. The appliance store is gone. The old woman is gone. My dad is gone. The librarian...I can't find him. I don't know what's going on with that guy, but he hasn't been any help."

The man in the fish suit stared at the wall. His sign wobbled nervously in his hands.

"And I guess you probably know all of this already. That's your job, right, to know things? You're the Salmon of Knowledge. But...my brother is missing. He's gone. And not just gone from Jeffersonville, he's gone from Earth, from the whole freaking dimension. I ran into some...some nasty things when that happened to me last year, and I barely made it out, and he's younger than me, and he's the kind of kid who just wants to stay in his room and read comic books, you know?" She gulped and wiped her nose with the back of her hand. "I'm his big sister! I'm supposed to be the one protecting him and I've been doing a really, really crappy job of it lately. If something...if anything happens to him, I don't know what I'm going to do."

The man in the foam rubber fish costume turned and looked at her. He set his sign down. He pulled out a yellowed pad of paper and a stub of pencil from somewhere deep inside his fish suit. He wrote out a note and handed it to Brynn. Makayla read it over her shoulder.

Even if I were to break
The oldest rules that bind my existence,
There is no knowledge that I can provide.
I cannot divulge a location that I do not know.
I cannot tell you of a journey
That has passed out of my sight.

"Okay, I thought you were kidding about this guy," Makayla whispered to Brynn. Brynn shook her head.

"If you can't tell us where he is," Brynn said to the fish, "could you...could you just point us in the right direction? Tell us somewhere he's been recently?"

The man in the fish suit passed her another note.

The sight of the Salmon of Knowledge,
As vast as it may be,
Is limited in scope by the cycles of life,
By the powers that move above,
By the winds that whistle through time.
Were I to have my kin with me,
My brother, my sisters three,
Even our combined power could not ferret out this answer.

"Please," Brynn pleaded, her voice sharpening. "Please. Give me anything. Who he was with. Who he's talked to. What he's been eating. Anything."

He scribbled and handed over another slip of paper.

All I can tell you is this:
The question you ask me is wrapped in darkness.
The forces that have engulfed your brother

Are beyond understanding for those in this plane,

Unfathomable, impenetrable, obscure,

Inscrutable even by the cleverest of coblyns.

He passed another note.

And the mind of your human companion

Could not even comprehend the topic

In a very broad and general sense.

"Dude," Makayla said. "You're a fish. There's no need to be insulting. I'm just trying to help."

The man in the fish costume gave the barest hint of a shrug.

"So that's a no," Brynn said.

I cannot provide the help you seek.

"And you're sure you're telling the truth?"

Telling the truth is what I do, Branwen the coblyn.

It is all that I do and it is all that I am.

"Okay then."

The man in the fish suit continued to stare at the wall. His sign was blowing listlessly in the wind. Makayla and Brynn looked at each other, and then back to the fish, but it was clear that the conversation was over. As they walked away, the wind brushed a piece of paper up against Makayla's leg. She picked it up and read.

Be careful.

Shadows have descended on Jeffersonville.

Do not trust your eyes.

Do not trust your ears.

Listen only to your heart.

Makayla glanced back over her shoulder, but the man in the foam rubber fish costume was gone.

"Could that dude be more cryptic and alarming?" she said.

"I know, right?"

Brynn smiled, but Makayla could see there was no smile in her eyes. There was nothing there but fear.

Chapter 20

The outer door was unlocked, as Ysbaddaden knew it would be. The door in front of him, however—the inner door, a larger, much more ponderous door—was most definitely locked, as he knew it would be. He fidgeted in the large, stone antechamber for nearly a full minute before he made up his mind, drew a smooth stone from his satchel, laid it near the lock and whispered a short, guttural phrase. The lock clicked and he eased the door open.

"Hello, anyone here?" he called softly. "I've got a delivery...very important, um..."

He rooted around in his satchel for a moment.

"Apparatus. Very important, vaguely defined apparatus for delivery."

There was no answer. He peeked into the large office behind the large door, which seemed to be empty. He sighed in relief and slipped inside, closing and locking the door behind him. He'd never been inside this office before, although he'd certainly had plenty of meetings in the antechamber outside. Plenty of loud, screamy meetings, in which the screaminess had almost always been pointed in his direction. This was possibly his least favorite place in the entire compound.

"Well, the directorate certainly wouldn't be happy if they found me in here," he muttered. "Have to make this as quick as can be."

He gave a couple thorough sniffs of the pungent air.

"The book...the book is definitely here. Why would the book be here, of all places..."

He let his nose lead him through the office, past the desk which seemed to be made for someone two or three times his height, past the desiccated remains of several Effluvial Junipers, past the bookshelf littered with volumes written in a language he was certain had died out millennia before. He followed his nose until it led him to the far wall, which was perfectly, pristinely blank. He pursed his lips and felt around the smooth stonework. It took him only moments to find the hidden latch that opened the secret door hidden in the masonry.

A room opened up behind the door, a room filled with strange equipment of burnished brass and oiled leather, with antiseptic odors and a dusky glow permeating everywhere but emanating from nowhere. Ysbaddaden widened his eyes, taking the room in, then shook his head and squinted.

"I don't even want to speculate what these are used for," he muttered.

On the far wall, set apart from the equipment of indeterminate use, were three wooden chests. Ysbaddaden followed his nose and opened the first chest. It was full of smaller versions of the brass and leather appliances which lined the walls. He grunted and slammed it shut. The second chest was empty save for a sigh that escaped along with a feeling of furtive yearning, a feeling that passed through him, making him shiver and release a sigh of his own. Once the feeling had passed, he turned to the third chest.

He put his hands to the lid, hoping that his search might be over, hoping that he could get out of this office before anyone found him here, hoping that this fraught mystery could finally be concluded. He flipped the lid open and there, simply lying on the bottom of the chest, was the Changeling Logbook. He couldn't believe it had been so easy. All he had to do was haul it out of here, get it back to his office, and this whole ridiculous fiasco would be over. He breathed a sigh of relief and bent over to heft the massive book out of the chest, but when he picked it up, he immediately knew something was wrong. The book weighed no more than the delicious mascarpone tart he'd managed to pinch from the kitchens the night before.

The surprise threw him off balance and he stumbled, fumbling the book. It fell on the floor and landed with the lightest of whiffs, despite its massive size. His eyes widened and he gritted his teeth. He stared angrily at the impostor lying innocently on the ground, then knelt down beside it and flipped open the book, anxious to uncover this mystery and depart before he could be found.

The instant his fingers touched the cover, however, the entire book dissolved. The pages, cover, bindings, everything within it crumbled into dust and a whispered breath of cold air. The dust and chill floated in the air for a moment, then coalesced on the ground into three serpents made of shadow that slithered away, burning the floor in their wake. One of the serpents brushed against Ysbaddaden's hand as it went, scorching it raw. He smelled burnt flesh and felt his skin bubble. He yelped and clasped the limb against his chest, but clamped his mouth shut when he heard a noise in the hall outside the office.

He flipped the chests closed as quietly as he could, slipped out of the secret room, eased the door closed, and whispered a small glamour. He chose a form that no one would recognize and that no one, in fact, would quite be able to identify or remember afterward.

No sooner had he done so than the office door burst open, and an imposing pwca charged in, his long ears twitching, his bristly tail twitching behind him. He was wearing an official breastplate marking him as one of the constablery and his helmet featured a crest of bright red wiry hair. He whinnied loudly and pointed angrily at the tiny figure before him.

"Caught! I caught you!" he shouted authoritatively in a voice that seemed accustomed to shouting in an authoritative manner. "There you are! You are not supposed to be here! You made so much noise and set off so many alarms!"

"I'm so sorry, sir," Ysbaddaden squeaked in the meekest voice he could muster. "Am I...did I come into the wrong office?"

The pwca shoved a thick finger covered in wiry hair into Ysbaddaden's chest.

"I should say so! Breaking into the Underminster's office! This is a serious transgression! You have transgressed!"

"The Underminster, ah, yes, good, I got so lost on the way here, I was worried that I might have ended up in the wrong place."

Ysbaddaden kept his eyes low, fidgeting one foot nervously on the ground, his voice a dry whisper. He hoped he wasn't overplaying his hand.

"I am the Mezzo-Sergeant of the Third Ward!" the pwca shouted. "Look at me when I'm speaking to you!"

Ysbaddaden looked up with what he hoped was an air of slack-jawed bewilderment.

"You are, sir? Oh my goodness, I had no idea, it is a great honor to be apprehended by one of your standing, sir."

The Mezzo-Sergeant bristled appreciatively.

"Why are you here, little one?" he shouted, his eyes bright with officious fervor.

Ysbaddaden yelped nervously but kept his eyes locked on the pwca's.

"I was sent with a delivery," he breathed in a barely audible whine.

The pwca leaned in close, his breath snorting hot over Ysbaddaden's face.

"What are you supposed to deliver?"

"Um...this," Ysbaddaden said as he slid his undamaged hand into his satchel and pulled out the first thing he touched, which happened to be another ladle.

"This?" shouted the pwca, grabbing the ladle and shaking it wildly in the air.

"Yes," Ysbaddaden whimpered.

"This ladle?" the pwca shouted in an even more agitated manner.

"Yes, that ladle."

"You were sent to deliver this tarnished, dented ladle direct to the Underminster's office?" the pwca shouted, towering ominously over Ysbaddaden's cowering frame.

"Yes."

"Oh, were you now?"

The pwca's eyes were practically glowing now in bureaucratic rage.

"Yes, I was."

"Oh really?"

Ysbaddaden only nodded.

"Very well, then! Delivery accomplished! Excellent work, tiny being!"

Ysbaddaden breathed a sigh of relief as the pwca turned away from him and set the ladle down gently on the enormous desk at the center of the room.

"Wait a second!"

The pwca whirled, charging back across the room and returning his thick, blunt finger to its previous position, pressing into Ysbaddaden's breastbone.

"How did you get in?" the pwca shouted.

"Opened the door, sir." The words tumbled out of him. "Turned the handle, opened it, walked in."

"It wasn't locked?"

"Not when I arrived, sir."

The pwca glared at him, then stepped back and assessed him, as if he hadn't actually bothered to look at Ysbaddaden in any appreciable manner before this moment.

"What's your status?" he shouted, a heavy accusation in the air.

"Ancillary Plenipotentiary, sir. Victuals and Vitals Division. Minor third."

The pwca stared at him for a long while. Ysbaddaden fidgeted and stared groundward in what he hoped was an innocent manner.

"Be on your way!" the pwca finally exclaimed. "I'll inform the Underminster that her ladle has arrived!"

"Yes, sir. Thank you, sir."

Ysbaddaden backed out of the room, bowing furiously, then wiped the sweat from his brow. Once he was sure he was out of sight, he let the glamour drop, grateful to have escaped with only a burn on his hand but with even less idea now of where his path should take him.

Chapter 21

Makayla was over at Brynn's house when her father returned. He wouldn't say where he had been (at least not while Brynn and Makayla were in the room), but his clothes were torn, his hair was full of burs, his shoes were gone, and he smelled vaguely of kerosene. He climbed in through the living room window and Makayla was surprised to see that no one else in the house found this at all unusual.

"I found him," he said, his voice weary but exhilarated. "I know where he is."

"That's amazing, Gaf!" Brynn's mother said as her husband sat down wearily on the couch. "Where?"

He looked at Brynn and Makayla, his mouth clenched.

"It's...quite...far," he said, after several moments of thought. "It would be a dangerous journey, and I...I don't think I can do it alone."

He looked significantly at his wife.

"I...I can't go, Gaf," his wife said, scoffing. "Brynn. The baby."

He continued looking at her significantly.

"You can't be serious. We have a baby and a teenage daughter and no one to look after them."

"If I thought there was any other way," Brynn's father said, "I wouldn't have come back. But you're the only one I know who can get us there."

"What do you mean?"

He whispered in her ear. Her eyes widened and she nodded, her hands beginning to shake.

"Yes, that would have to be me, wouldn't it?" she said, her voice trembling.

"What is going on?" Brynn interjected.

"Your father and I are going to find Conn," her mother said, getting to her feet, a picture of measured efficiency.

"What? You can't leave me here on my own!"

"It has to be both of us. I'm sorry. I can't explain now. It's...it's complicated."

"What about Hero?" Brynn hissed, gesturing upstairs to where the baby lay asleep.

"You're going to have to take care of her," her mother said.

"What? I'm fifteen. You can't leave a baby with me!"

"If we had family to call, we would," her father assured her. "But we don't because—"

"Yeah, I know, the rest of our family has been dead for hundreds of years and are buried in another dimension. I'm so sick of hearing that."

"You help out with Hero all the time," Brynn's mother said tenderly. "She loves you. She likes you better than me most of the time, I think."

"Can you at least tell me where you're going?" Brynn pleaded to her father.

"I can't. I only know where the trail is leading, not where it ends."

"Not on Earth, though, right?"

"Definitely not on Earth," he said, grimacing.

"Will you be okay?" Brynn asked her mother, her cheeks wet with tears.

Her mother held Brynn's face in her hands.

"We will. I promise you that. I've...well, you'd be surprised at some of the things I've been through and come out safe on the other side."

"Can't I come with you?"

"No, sweetie. This is one your father and I need to do by ourselves."

"You went to Annwfyn once, Brynn," her father said. "You barely made it out alive. I'm not letting you risk yourself again."

"But…"

"I'm sorry. This decision is final. Your mother and I know how to get there, we know how to get around there, and most importantly, we know how to get back. It should be a quick trip: follow the trail, locate Conn, swoop in and pick him up."

"Are you using 'swoop' in a literal or figurative sense there?" Brynn asked suspiciously.

Her father looked skyward.

"I'm not going to answer that right now." He turned to his wife. "We need to go. The doorway I used will be closing in less than an hour and it's not close."

Brynn's parents rushed upstairs and opened a secret panel in the back of their closet that neither Brynn nor Makayla had ever seen before. They filled their bags with supplies that Makayla mostly didn't recognize, but that might have been food or climbing equipment or weapons or woodworking tools or costumes or any and all of the above.

"And here's some money," Brynn's father said, handing her a huge stack of bills.

"Whoa. Where did this come from?"

"We should only be gone a few days. But you'll need food…essentials. Use your best judgment, okay?"

"Okay."

"And then there's this."

Her mother handed Brynn an ancient-looking sheet of paper that had been folded in a complicated manner and sealed with wax.

"Keep this close to you at all times," she said.

"Okay…" Brynn responded.

"Promise?"

"Yeah, but—"

"And only open it in an emergency."

"Only if things get bad," her father added.

"What is it?" Brynn asked, turning the very normal-looking sheet of paper over in her hands.

"Just...instructions," her father said. "In case things get too bad."

"How will I know if I should open it?"

"You'll know, sweetie," Brynn's mother told her. "We have to go."

Brynn's parents kissed her on the forehead, climbed out the second-story window with their bags, and were gone before Brynn or Makayla could even react to what had just happened.

"What just happened?" Brynn asked, her face and voice both blank.

"I don't know, dude. I think your parents just took off and left you in charge of a baby."

"Um, left *us* in charge of a baby, 'cause you're not going anywhere now."

As if to prove the point, at that moment, the baby wailed from the next room.

"Right on cue," Makayla said.

"Yeah. So what do we do?"

"Well...clean diaper, food, or love, that's all they ever want. Usually all three."

"I bet we've got all three of those things in the house."

Makayla smiled.

"I bet you're right."

Chapter 22

"What happened to your hand?" asked Lwmpyn as he sat down in their regular booth in the back corner of the bar.

"Nothing," Ysbaddaden said grumpily, cradling the bandaged limb against his chest. "Just made a mistake while I was cooking. And keep your voice down." He drained his glass of wine and asked for another.

"Why do you want me to keep my voice down?"

"Because I need to ask you a question. There's something fishy going on and I've run it over and over in my mind but all I hit are dead ends. Mentally speaking. I need a fresh perspective. Needless to say, this can't go beyond us."

"Needless, as you said. Although your secrecy has aroused my suspicions."

"Well, there's plenty of suspicions to go around right now." Ysbaddaden leaned closer to the rocky being across the table from him. "The Changeling Logbook has gone missing."

Lwmpyn's eyes went wide. He started to speak. Ysbaddaden put a finger up to silence him.

"Not my fault. Trust me. Someone made off with it. But they left a trail that took me all over the compound. I thought I found the book in the Underminster's office but it evaporated in my hands. It was a decoy. Why would someone want me to go there? Why would someone want me to find a fake book in the Underminster's office?"

Lwmpyn gave a puzzled frown, his eyes twinkling.

"Well, it's obvious," he said, "if you stopped to think for one moment. Whoever laid the trail wanted you, or whoever was following the trail, to get caught. They didn't want you in the office. They wanted you in the hands of the constables."

Ysbaddaden slammed his wooden cup down on the table, sloshing warm wine across his sleeve.

"Which would remove me from my search precipitously and semi-permanently."

Lwmpyn nodded while his companion fretted.

"Let's break this down," the rocky being began. "First, a series of increasingly confounding crises pull you from your work. Second—"

"Wait," Ysbaddaden interrupted. "What did you say?"

"I said, 'a series of increasingly confounding crises—'"

"No, no, no. Before that."

"Let's break this down?"

"Well, yes," Ysbaddaden said, steepling his fingers. "Yes, yes, yes."

"What do you mean? Yes what?"

"Well, if you really wanted to hide a book, that's what you'd do, wouldn't you?"

"What?"

"Break it down. A book is just the sum of its parts, after all. The parchment, the cover, the binding, the ink. If I wanted to hide a book, that's how I'd do it."

"You're not making any sense."

"Oh yes. Trust me, I am. Pay for this, would you?"

And he was out of the bar before Lwmpyn could object. The granite-faced being lifted his drink, drained it and called for another, wondering on the curious behavior of his diminutive companion.

Chapter 23

Makayla called her parents and asked them if she could stay at Brynn's for the weekend. They agreed, although she may have neglected to mention the fact that Brynn's parents were no longer in the same dimension. The girls used the wad of cash to make full use of Jeffersonville's delivery services. They ordered pizza and they ordered ice cream and they ordered diapers and hummus for the baby.

"What kind of baby's favorite food is hummus?" Makayla asked.

"This one, I guess," said Brynn.

On Monday, though, there was a decision to make. They had school, but now they also had a baby to take care of. They eventually landed on trying to drop Hero off at the daycare center down the street. It took them nearly half an hour to figure out the Ergo, but eventually they had Hero snugly worn on Brynn's chest and a bag packed with all her essentials: her bottles, her hummus, her diapers, her wipes, and her favorite stuffed dinosaur.

When they found the daycare center, they saw toddlers chasing each other furiously on the playground while teachers stood idly by, chatting and snacking. Inside, they walked through a room with cribs lining both walls. A teacher stood at the far end, scribbling on a large diagram that was tacked to a bulletin board. Brynn was just about to tap the woman on the shoulder when Makayla grabbed Brynn's hand and gestured toward the cribs. Each crib held an infant, and every single baby was standing upright and watching the girls silently and intently, without blinking. Makayla gave the barest shake of her head and the girls left without saying a word.

Taking the baby to school with them seemed to be the only remaining option. However, even before they got to the front doors, they could tell that something was wrong. In one room, they saw a small group of students setting fire to a pile of textbooks. In another, three teachers were having a knife fight with utensils stolen from the cafeteria. In the A/V room, the windows were broken out, and overhead projectors were being thrown out onto the grass.

While Brynn and Makayla were standing outside the school, trying to decide what to do, they heard the first bell. Only a moment later, their phones rang. They answered them together, and both girls heard the same voice, raspy, loud, and belligerent.

"It's time for school. Why aren't you inside yet?"

Neither girl answered.

"Go to your homeroom. Bring the baby with you."

Neither girl answered. There was a short pause, and then the voice on the other end of their phones began to scream.

"Stop dawdling! Get inside before we come out there and bring you in!"

They immediately hung up their phones and, without another word, turned on their heels and walked briskly away from the school, throwing nervous glances over their shoulder to make sure no one was following them.

"I think maybe we're not going back to school until your parents get back," Makayla panted.

"Yeah, I think that's probably right," Brynn agreed, and they made the trip back to Brynn's house faster than they ever had before.

Chapter 24

"Well, the first thing to do is find out if my theory is correct."

Ysbaddaden was talking to himself again, a bad habit he'd acquired after years and years of isolation, in a place barely touched by light or time, long before he took this form and this job.

"If the book has been unbound, rendered back into its component parts, and the components scattered who knows where, then the first thing is to try and recover one of the components. My sniffer is clearly unreliable. Luckily, I have some other tricks up my sleeve, even if they are long unused." He paused. "For that matter, I hope they're still where I left them. I haven't checked in centuries."

Fan was waiting outside his office door, a picture of barely-contained impatient fury. The scream was already beginning to escape her tiny mouth when he held up his finger to quiet her. He was almost surprised when she acquiesced.

"It doesn't matter, Fan," he said, with a stare that was striving for imperious but was willing to settle for overbearing. "Whatever it is, it doesn't matter. I'm going into my office now. You are under strict orders to allow no one inside until I come back out."

Still holding his finger up, he continued to stare at her until she closed her mouth and nodded slowly. He lowered his finger, slipped into his office, and locked the door. He moved a rug, slid aside a bookcase, and wiped away several runes of concealment. Then he reached into a small cubby in the farthest corner of his office and retrieved eight items, setting each of them carefully in a nearby basket.

A cup made of metal, battered but radiating ancient power.

The tusk of a boar, broken at one end, fearfully sharp on the other.

A wooden box filled with pungent earth.

A leather pouch with a small handful of seeds.

A pair of shears carved from bone.

A glittering comb wrought of obsidian and tourmaline.

A dusky cauldron, dull and pockmarked.

A small harp with strings cut from the wings of a zephyr.

All long-lost relics from a long-lost time of his life. He sighed as he looked them over. They'd been hidden here ever since he had taken over this office, a time so long ago that he could barely remember who he'd been when he'd last seen them.

He searched the desk to see if he could find any remnant of the book that had lain there for so many years. When he'd found one, a nearly microscopic fragment of the cover, he held it carefully pinched between thumb and forefinger. He retrieved the battered metal cup and nestled it into the spot where the Changeling Logbook had long rested. He opened the wooden box and scooped out a handful of dirt, then let it fall between his fingers into the cup and onto the desk beneath. He placed the fragment of cover into the cup along with a seed from the leather pouch. Then he watered the seed with the only liquid available, which turned out to be soup. He suspected it would serve. He'd made do with worse.

He murmured a few words and watched as the seed sprung from the dirt. It grew rapidly and sprouted leaves and petals of embossed leather. It gave off a distinct odor of oils, musk, and mystery, with a slight hint of parsley. Probably from the soup, he suspected.

His eyes twinkling with satisfaction, he whispered to the plant. When it whispered back, his eyes went wide and he nodded. He picked up the plant in its makeshift pot and opened the door.

"Fan! I'm going away. I don't know for how long."

"Where are you going?" she asked as she flitted into the room.

"Wherever this plant tells me to go."

Where the plant told him to go was to a tannery far outside the walls of the compound, under the sunless sky. The tannery looked as if it had been abandoned for years, if not decades or centuries. A thick layer of dust and grime covered every surface. Under the grime were streaks of blood, dark and clotted. Bones were piled in bins along the walls. In the corner was a rubbish bin, long untouched. And in the rubbish bin, he found the cover of the missing book.

Chapter 25

Brynn practically begged Makayla to keep staying over, although Makayla didn't need much convincing. She didn't want to leave Brynn and Hero alone with all the weird things that were going on in town. Her parents were surprisingly game about this, bordering on indifferent. She called every day, extending her sleepover at Brynn's by one more night, and the last time she called, her mother had agreed before she'd even finished asking the question. This seemed strange for parents who were usually much stricter about such things, but Makayla had no time to worry about whatever might be distracting her family. They'd be fine, she knew. They had two adults to take care of three boys. While at Brynn's, there were two teenagers struggling to take care of one baby.

Luckily, Hero was an easy baby. She was already sleeping through the night, ate plentifully and often, and spit up infrequently. (Makayla still shuddered when she remembered how often her little brothers had puked all over her shoulders.)

They managed nearly a week holed up inside Brynn's house, but eventually, they needed some things that delivery services could not provide. Like fresh air and the sight of anything that wasn't the inside of Brynn's house, along with some essentials like vegetables, laundry soap, and cupcakes. So, they strapped Hero back into the Ergo and headed to the grocery store.

As soon as they stepped inside, though, they realized that the strangeness infecting their town had made its way here as well. Many of the shelves were completely bare. All of the bins in the vegetable section had been filled with motor oil, some still in bottles, some not. The cereal had been moved to the laundry and dish soap section, and the laundry and dish soap had been moved to the cereal section. It was unclear to Brynn and Makayla whether the contents of the boxes had been switched as well, so they decided to leave those aisles alone.

When they tried to find some cupcakes in the freezer case, they saw a young girl behind the door. She was sitting cross-legged, eating a chocolate eclair. Empty plastic clamshell containers littered the inside of the case around her. Her hair and eyebrows were white with frost. When Brynn tried to let her out, she said she was fine, then pulled the door closed and continued eating.

As the store was mostly abandoned and didn't seem to be operational anymore, Brynn and Makayla grabbed the few things they needed off the shelves and left without paying. Makayla felt guilty about this, but Brynn assured her that if the store got back up and running again in any sort of normal fashion, they would come back and pay for what they'd taken.

Brynn handed Makayla a cupcake. She ate it. It was delicious, which helped with the guilt, but the knot in her stomach continued to grow—the knot of guilt, of panic, of fear—growing more quickly than any number of delicious cupcakes could assuage. She ate them anyway.

Chapter 26

Now that he had the cover of the Logbook in hand, Ysbaddaden set his sights on the pages, the reams of parchment that had once been stitched tightly inside it. He laid the cover down in a patch of dirt outside the tannery. With the broken tusk, he inscribed a circle in the dirt around the cover while he sang three lines of a forgotten ode.

Golden letters appeared on the cover, telling of a secret forest path. When he followed the path, he found a hollow. In the midst of the hollow was a tree, tall and slender. At the top of the tree, a tiny brass whistle hung from a branch. No sound was heard when he blew the whistle, but minutes later, a dustwine appeared, with wings darker than dusk and claws sharper than any knife. The dustwine bowed respectfully, grasped Ysbaddaden gently in its claws, and flew across the forest to an eyrie in the clouds, larger than a church, taller than the sky. The eyrie was filled, rim to rim, with pages of blank parchment, pages no bigger than his fingernail, pages which would dwarf the monstrous bird which brought him here, and every size and shape between.

Ysbaddaden sat in the midst of the piles of parchment. He pulled the shears of bone from his satchel and placed them on the cover of the book. He muttered a few words from a lullaby he had learned in his youth, eons ago, a lullaby that held more power than its singer had intended to teach him.

He cut one sheet of parchment in half with the shears and then did the same to another. He cut and cut and cut until he found a sheet that the shears would not sever. This sheet he set aside, then cut and cut and cut some more until he found another that the shears would not touch. He set this on the first and, as the hours went on, the pile of pages beside him grew, the pages which belonged to the Changeling Logbook.

For seven days, Ysbaddaden sat in the eyrie among the heaps of parchment. Each page he found he set atop his ever-growing stack. The rest he cut with his shears and threw the fragments into the air, where they fluttered and fell like rain, until they piled like dunes around him, and he sat within the parchment dunes, cutting, cutting, cutting.

Chapter 27

Makayla hadn't been home in over a week. She needed some fresh clothes and she thought it would be nice to see her family. She hated to admit it to herself, but she even missed her three brothers.

"Ma?" she called out as she opened the front door. There was no answer. She stepped inside, gesturing for Brynn and Hero to follow her. "Ma, I'm home! Boys? Anyone here?"

Her mother stepped out of the kitchen but did not respond.

"I'm still going to stay at Brynn's if that's okay," Makayla said. Her mother looked in her direction, but there was no emotion on her face. Makayla couldn't tell if she was listening or not. "I know it's been a while, but with everything her family's been going through," Makayla continued, speaking louder now, "I think it's a good idea if I...stay with her a few more days...and take up beekeeping—are you even listening to me?"

Her mother stood there placidly, her eyes barely focused on anything around her. She hadn't stepped out of the kitchen doorway. There was a strange smell in the air.

"What's going on in the kitchen?" Makayla asked.

Her mother didn't answer. Makayla tried to peek through the doorway, but her mother stepped to the side and blocked her. She tried again and her mother blocked her again. Makayla dodged around her and darted into the kitchen. A large portion of the floor had been ripped up and a hole had been dug beneath. Broken boards, chunks of concrete, and linoleum fragments were everywhere. A shovel rested in the hole and mounds of dirt were piled up in the corners, on the stove, under the dinner table. Makayla edged over and looked in. The hole was surprisingly deep.

In the yard, she saw her three brothers dismantling the wooden fence and hauling the boards into the center of the yard, which for some reason now held an assortment of power saws and pneumatic nail guns. The boys were working together in silent unison, ripping the boards from the fence, cutting them, and assembling them into what seemed to be some kind of massive humanoid creature.

"Ma? Ma, what are the boys doing? Are they using power tools?"

Instead of answering, her mother walked over to the hole, jumped into it, picked up the shovel, and continued to dig.

"I think maybe I should get going," Makayla said in the calmest voice she could muster. "Hey, Brynn, I think we should get going," she called a little louder.

As she backed out of the kitchen, away from her mother with the shovel and her brothers with the power tools, she stumbled over her father. He was kneeling on the ground, drilling holes into the hardwood floor with a battery-powered drill. Makayla regained her balance and looked at him with confusion.

"Dad?"

Her father didn't answer.

"Dad, what are you doing?"

He looked up at her briefly, but then resumed his work, drilling a series of evenly spaced holes across their living room floor. Brynn was standing with Hero just inside the front door. Her eyes were wide and her fists were clenched.

"Brynn, why don't you take Hero outside," Makayla said. "I'll be there in just a second."

Brynn opened the door and stepped out. Makayla turned back to her father.

"What is going on, Dad? Why is everyone being so weird? I'm sorry I haven't been here, but Brynn really needed my help." There was no response. "Dad? Dad?"

Her father only stared at her. His eyes looked strangely dark. Then, so rapidly that she could hardly follow the motion of his arm, he hurled the drill through the front window. The glass shattered. Makayla screamed. She ran out the front door, slammed it behind her and joined Brynn on the front lawn.

"What's going on?" Brynn shouted. "What happened to the window?"

"Come on," Makayla said, grabbing Brynn's hand. "We have to go. Whoever those people are, they aren't my family."

"What the hell?"

"I know. Something...something is very wrong."

Makayla looked back at her house. The wind was whipping the curtains, which were blowing freely out the shattered window. Inside, her father, her mother, and her three brothers stood together, unmoving, staring at her through the broken frame, staring with eyes grown strangely dark.

"This place isn't safe," Makayla said. "We have to keep moving."

"Where? Where can we go? What kind of place is safe for us now?"

"I don't know, but we need to find one."

They hurried away from Makayla's house. Shadows were scurrying along the sidewalk. The boy from the playground, still in his bow tie, still with his cohort of child followers, was approaching from the other end of the street. They could hear screams and they could smell bonfires.

"And we need to do it quick."

Chapter 28

Ysbaddaden pulled a handful of earth from the wooden box in his satchel and sprinkled it on the top sheet of parchment. Using two fingers, he drew seven runes in the sprinkled earth and then blew gently. As he blew, the fragments of earth jittered and bounced across the page, then settled themselves into a new pattern. Ysbaddaden studied this pattern and marked it in his memory, then followed this map (for so it was) across the length of Annwfyn until it led him to a loomery.

Within the loomery were miles of thread, acres of yarn, bushels of wool, barrels of silk, and a colony of bright-eyed birds nesting in the corners and in the rafters and hidden in the skeins and perched on the spinning jennies.

Ysbaddaden retrieved the obsidian comb from his satchel and wandered through the vast loomery, plying the comb along the threads already on the looms, teasing the comb through whorls of yarn still on the wheel. Again and again he combed, and occasionally the comb would catch on a length of thread. This thread he would carefully pluck out, then walk and comb some more, until he had uncovered all the threads that had once bound the book. Spying a tarnished copper needle, discarded in a corner, he took one of the threads and began the laborious process of sewing the empty pages of parchment back onto the cover. It took him several hours, but when he had finished, he no longer had parchment, thread, and hide. He had a book. A massive book. But the pages were still blank. The contents of the book were still missing.

Chapter 29

Brynn and Makayla fled the shadows, fled the bow-tied boy and his companions, fled the screams and the bonfires and the power tools. They tried a nearby fast food restaurant, hoping they'd be safe in a more public building. They were not. The teenage employees had somehow obtained welding equipment and were making alterations to the grill and the deep fryer, alterations whose intent was unclear. Brynn and Makayla tried to ask about food, but the workers only grunted and pointed toward a rotting pile of burgers and fries in the corner.

They tried the karate studio where Makayla had taken a class several years ago. Through the plate glass window, they saw students kicking one of the teachers until he fell down, then continuing to kick him in the head and stomach until he was unconscious and bloody. The students laughed and moved on to the next adult.

They tried the police station. Outside, the officers were filling the squad cars with propane and barbed wire. The girls turned around before they even got close to the door.

Chapter 30

Now that the Changeling Logbook was whole but empty, Ysbaddaden could practically feel it crying out for its own completion, yearning to be reunited with its contents. No fancy tricks were needed this time, no relics, no words of power. He just listened to the book calling out for the characters and figures that had covered its pages for so long, and once he listened hard enough, he knew where he needed to go.

He followed the book's call to a cave beneath a rolling moor. Within the cave, he found a tunnel that led him deep underground to a massive cavern dimly lit by glowing jewels. Within the cavern's walls were veins of glittering ore, veins of precious minerals, and veins of something darker.

Ysbaddaden smiled. He set the cauldron and the book upon the cavern's floor. He pulled the harp from his satchel and began to play. The strains of an ancient melody drew the veins of darkness from the cavern walls. They flowed across the floor and into the cauldron and once the flowing stopped, he had a cauldron full of ink.

Chapter 31

Inevitably, their path took them to the library. It was clear they were being followed, and if nothing else, the library was close by and had been empty the last time they were there. They avoided the shadows and the children and the screams and the bonfires and the darkness. They ran up the library steps and through the doors. When they called out, there was no answer, so they unbuckled Hero and let her crawl around on the floor. They flipped the locks closed and pushed any furniture they could move in front of the doors: benches, chairs, smaller tables.

Beyond the glass doors, men and women and children with dark, hollow eyes were massed so thick that Brynn and Makayla couldn't see the steps, couldn't see the street, couldn't see the sky. The thought that had been slowly building in Makayla's brain for the last few weeks finally came tumbling out of her mouth.

"Those...those things out there...those are definitely not people right?"

"Yeah, no, they're not," Brynn answered.

"So what happened to me last year, where I was taken away and that thing took my place. A thing that looked like me, that sounded like me, but most definitely wasn't me? Could that...is that happening again?"

"You mean, have some of those people out there been stolen away and replaced by a goblin or a fetch or a whatever?"

Brynn nodded nervously. "Yeah, I think that would be 'probably' verging on 'certainly.'"

"Except I don't think it's just some of them," Makayla said. "I think it might be *all* of them. And not just the ones here. What if it's happening all over town? What if all the weird things we've been seeing are happening because lots and lots of people got taken away and lots and lots of people got replaced? What if...what if the whole town is full of changelings now?"

"Jesus, Makayla," Brynn breathed, her voice thick with horror. "If that's true, do you know what that means?"

Chapter 32

Ysbaddaden heaved open the book to its very midpoint. The darkness within the ink-filled cauldron swirled and then bubbled. A single, quivering droplet of ink rose from the cauldron into the air. It wafted toward the book and set itself down gently upon the open page and where there had been blankness, there was now a single, quivering line. The first droplet was followed by another and then two more and then a veritable fountain of ink was flying from the cauldron into the pages of the book, recreating the numbers, the lines, the charts, the dates, the names, that had been ripped from it. The pages of the book fluttered back and forth and forth and back as the ink returned to where it had lain for so long.

It seemed to Ysbaddaden that the words of the book and the pages of the book sang a soft song to each other as they were reunited—for what is a book without its words, and how sorrowful for them to have been apart—but now they sang to each other as they nestled together, as the ink danced in the air and upon the pages. Moments later, or perhaps hours, the book was complete once more, and the cover closed with a sigh of contentment.

The journey back was far quicker than the journey out. When he returned to his office, he worked through the night, entering the towering stack of forms which had sat moldering on his desk for so long, entering them into the Changeling Logbook. As the stack dwindled, his suspicions grew.

He spread a stack of maps on his desk and started marking out the journeys. Each form he entered into the book represented the journey of a particular pair of changelings— a human child spirited away and one of the Tylwyth Teg set in their place. As he marked the journeys on the maps, a pattern began to emerge, the lines converging in a manner which should not have been possible, should not have been allowed.

"Well, this doesn't make any sense," he muttered. "Why would they be relocating this many changelings? Dozens a week for months and then dozens a day, hundreds a day. And all to the same place?"

He pulled out a scrap of parchment, did a long series of calculations, adding up all the changelings he had just tracked. Then he pulled another book from the shelf and looked up the population figures for Jeffersonville, Indiana, United States, Earth. When he compared the two figures, the furrow in his brow grew deeper than ever.

"Well, that...that can mean only one thing."

Chapter 33

"It means there are no people left in Jeffersonville," said Brynn.

Chapter 34

"It means there are no people left in Jeffersonville," said Ysbaddaden.

Chapter 35

"It's nothing but goblins and shadows," said Brynn.

Chapter 36

"It's nothing but coblyns and bwgans," said Ysbaddaden.

Chapter 37

"Wait." Ysbaddaden flipped through the book again. "That can't be right. Why have the bwgans been sent to Earth? They've never been authorized to travel out of Annwfyn in such numbers. And why have they been sent to the same place as the changelings?" Sudden realization struck him like an icicle in the heart. "Oh no. Oh by the saints of Senghennydd. I can't...who would have...how could they..."

He closed the book. He took a deep breath.

"I have to go."

Chapter 38

"Then where did the *people* go?" Makayla said. "Where's my family? Where are the bus drivers, where are the skater kids, where are the waiters and the grocery store baggers and the gas station attendants and the girls who ride around on their scooters?" She paused, her eyes wild. "Where are our teachers?" she shouted.

Brynn looked at her.

"I can't believe I'm worried about our teachers," Makayla said. "I hate our teachers."

"I know you do," Brynn said. "But you're still a person. You still have feelings. It's a weakness you humans have," she deadpanned.

"I'm glad you can joke while our town is being torn apart by goblins."

"Might not be goblins," Brynn said defensively.

Makayla arched her eyebrows.

"Okay. It's probably goblins," Brynn admitted. "But it's not *my* goblins. I know my father didn't do this."

"This time."

"Exactly. At least I know, for once, that my father wasn't the cause of the terrifying crap invading my life."

"So what do we do now?"

"We have to go," said Brynn, buckling the baby back into the carrier.

"We have to go where?"

"Well, we already know that your house isn't...safe," Brynn said as gently as possible. "The appliance store is gone. School is certainly out of the question. I think my house is the only option."

"It's not close," Makayla said.

"I know. We'll have to move fast."

"You're carrying a baby. How fast can you move?"

"Fast enough. Hopefully," Brynn said, glancing down at the baby cooing on her chest.

"Plus, there's also the question of, you know, that."

Makayla gestured to the front door. The library remained empty and dark, but outside, they could see the hungry, writhing mass of goblins and shadows pressed up against the glass.

"How the hell are we supposed to get through that?" Makayla asked.

As if on cue, a single fluorescent bulb flickered to life above their heads. As they looked upward, a table lamp came on at the circulation desk.

"Hello?" Brynn called gently. "Is there someone here?"

There was no answer. They walked cautiously to the desk but there was no one behind it. Makayla flipped the switch on the lamp, but the light did not turn off. She pulled the plug from the socket, but the light still did not turn off.

"Okay, what the hell is going on now?" she hissed.

In response, another light came to life, this time in the administrative offices. They walked to the office door, opened it slowly, and called inside.

"Hello?"

But there was still no response. They entered and closed the door behind them. The office held two desks and an assortment of chairs. On the far side of the room, a light flickered on in a hallway beyond a glass door. Unsure of what else to do, they followed the lights as they came to life and then darkened behind them. The lights led them through the hallway, down a stairway, into a basement, down a service elevator, into a sub-basement, and then into a tunnel. The lights led them down the tunnel and up a staircase at the far end. At the top of the staircase were a set of heavy metal cellar doors. When they pushed the doors open and climbed out, they found themselves next to the empty concrete lot where the appliance store had once stood.

As they stood there blinking in the sunlight, they noticed that (fortunately) they were only a few blocks from Brynn's house. However, they also noticed that (unfortunately) a throng of goblins and shadows were storming down the street in their direction.

"Well, what the hell do we do now?" Makayla shouted.

"What do you think? We run."

Chapter 39

They ran. They ran while shadows massed in the sky, blocking out the sun. They ran with a horde of goblins screaming behind them. They ran while baby Hero looked curiously around from her carrier on Brynn's chest, probably wondering what all the commotion was and whether it would delay her next feeding. They ran through the dark, lungs burning, legs straining, and somehow, they made it to Brynn's house without incident. They locked the door behind them and peered through the window. The goblins and shadows had slowed but had not stopped. They gathered on the lawn and the sidewalk. They pressed up against the house but made no move to enter.

"Are we safe?" Makayla panted.

"I think so," Brynn shrugged. "My parents said they used some kind of protections on the house. Whatever that means."

"Like mystical goblin stuff?"

"Yeah. I guess."

"Will it be enough?"

"I don't know. Hope so."

They checked the window again. The horde of goblins was growing with every passing second. The shadows were shrieking in the sky, blotting out the moon.

"Did you lock the door?" Makayla whispered.

"Yeah."

"What about that other lock?" Makayla said, pointing. "What's going on with that lock?"

Brynn scowled.

"I don't know. We never use that one."

"Well, use it! Your house is being attacked! If there was ever a time to use two locks, now is the time! Do you have the key?"

"Yeah, it's the one my parents insist I wear on a string around my neck."

"Well, get the key out!"

"I'm not wearing it on a string around my neck! I forgot it today! Just like every day!"

Brynn ran to her room, threw piles of dirty clothes into the air until she found the key, then ran back to the front door and inserted the key into the second lock. The effects were instantaneous.

The lock shone with a bright white glow. A loud whoosh ran through the whole house from top to bottom. Every door in the house slammed open and a fresh breeze, with the undeniable scent of new rain, cascaded around them. A wave of warmth and light passed across the windows and gathered on the glass in the front door. A faint humming sound emanated from the walls or possibly the floor or maybe even the sky. The entire house was filled with an aura of tranquility and security. The walls were slightly warm to the touch and the baby, who had crawled into the living room, sat up and giggled.

"Well, I guess that's those extra protections my parents were talking about."

They peered through the window in the front door. Whatever force had been activated had pushed the goblins and shadows away from the house and they were now gathered on the sidewalk and in the street. One impetuous goblin tried to reach across the mystical barrier and got his hand burned for his trouble. He shouted some words which were presumably goblin swears and sucked on his fingers.

"Well, that's cool," Makayla said. "How long do you think it will hold them?"

"I don't know. I have no idea what the hell it is. I'm just glad I found the key."

"Yeah. Me too."

Makayla took a deep breath, her face scrunched up in thought.

"Where are the real people?" she finally asked softly. "If those are...replacements?"

"Changelings."

"Whatever they are. If they're replacements, where are the people they replaced? Where's my family?"

"I don't know, Makayla. I'm sorry."

Suddenly realizing how exhausted they were, they stumbled to the living room, curled up next to the baby and fell immediately asleep.

Chapter 40

The goblins and shadows were clearly using every means at their disposal to try to breach the barrier surrounding Brynn's house. Spells were cast. Ramrods were assembled and discarded as the mystical field burned them up. Runes were scrawled on the sidewalk, on the fence and in the air. The girls didn't know how long the shield would last. It turned out the answer was three days.

Brynn and Makayla didn't see what happened, but they felt the light and warmth drain from the house and heard victorious screams from the street. Hundreds of goblin bodies slammed against the door, the windows, the walls outside.

The girls fled to the basement, but when they opened the door to the scorched den, the runes inscribed on the floor were burning with an unnatural blue flame and screeching an unholy song. They ran upstairs, away from the flames, away from the front door which already threatened to splinter under the weight of so many goblin bodies thrown against it. They fled to the upper floor, to Brynn's room, the baby screaming in Brynn's arms. When they looked out the window, they saw goblins and shadows everywhere, swarming around the house, flying overhead, climbing the walls.

Makayla tried to shout, "What do we do?" but she couldn't make herself heard over the tumult all around. The girls stared at each other, trying to come up with something, anything to escape what seemed an inescapable fate. They were just contemplating making a last stand in the living room when the window slammed open and all the air was sucked out of the house. The shadows in the sky were thrown asunder. They looked out of Brynn's bedroom window and saw the librarian walking across the sky, spectacles and argyle sweater and all. The goblins and shadows had not ceased their swarming, but the sound was muted now, as if whatever the librarian was doing had declared itself much more important than the frivolous act of trying to break down the door to a house. He walked across the air until he stood on the roof outside the window. He inclined his head slightly and politely asked, "May I come in?"

Brynn gestured for him to enter and he did, slipping gracefully into the room. He looked down at himself and his brow furrowed.

"Oh," he said softly, "there's no need for this anymore." He gestured casually. His body shimmered, then disappeared and reformed itself, and where the librarian had stood, there was now an old woman, a woman Brynn had met several times before but who was a stranger to Makayla.

"Who are you?" Makayla asked sternly.

"You may call me Cyrridwen, although others have styled me as the Cailleach Bheurach," the woman responded, smiling grimly.

"I don't know what that means," Makayla responded. "Are you a librarian?"

"I am not a librarian, though I take many forms when necessary."

"Okay..." Makayla frowned and spoke more slowly. "But who *are* you?"

"I have been known as Gwrach-y-Rhibyn."

"I don't know if you thought that would help, but it didn't."

"Some have worshipped me as Dôn."

"Don? Just Don?"

"Yes."

Makayla shook her head. Cyrridwen sighed.

"You may know me as the old woman from the appliance store."

Makayla's face brightened.

"Okay! Now we're getting somewhere."

There was a pause while Makayla just smiled.

"May we move on?" the old woman asked.

"Yep," Makayla said. "I'm good now."

The woman drew herself up to her full height, her eyes glinting, her hands gesturing grandly.

"I have uncovered the mystery!"

"The mystery?" Brynn asked.

"The mystery!" the woman responded.

"And...which mystery would that be?" Makayla asked.

The woman squinted at one girl and then the other.

"The runes. You asked me about the runes."

"But we didn't," Makayla began confusedly, "we asked the librarian." A lightbulb went off in her brain. "Oh, I get it. You were the librarian the whole time."

The old woman's eyes widened slightly, and she turned away from Makayla and spoke to Brynn.

"I have translated the runes you brought me. It's much, much worse than I feared. Your parents are in terrible danger. And so are you. You must stay away from Annwfyn. The whole world, perhaps the whole universe, depends on it!"

Brynn shook her head, trying to comprehend this.

"Wait. What?"

"Do not cross the threshold," the old woman continued. "Do not set foot in the land of the Tylwyth Teg. The consequences would be dire indeed."

"I almost hate to ask, but how dire?" Makayla asked, interjecting herself into the conversation. "Really dire? Or just kind of dire?"

"Unbelievably dire," the woman intoned.

"I'm sorry, I'm just trying to figure out what kind of scale we're working with here. This mystical stuff is still fairly new to me..." Makayla's voice trailed off as the old woman's eyes clouded with fury.

"I feel you are not taking my warnings as seriously as you should," Cyrridwen said. "Do. Not. Go. To. Annwfyn!"

"Why not?" Brynn asked defiantly.

"What you seek there shall not be what you find."

Brynn and Makayla glowered at her. The old woman tried again.

"Your very presence will cause all that you have sought to cure to descend into darkness."

Brynn and Makayla thrust their jaws out defiantly. The old woman tried yet again.

"A mirror shattered cannot be remade."

"No!" Brynn said sharply. "No, no, no! No riddles. No cryptic BS. We need to know things, actual fact-type things, so we can make decisions about other things. Got it? Only clear, unambiguous answers from here on out. What will happen if we go to Annwfyn?"

The old woman sighed and gave a surprisingly human shrug.

"A likely consequence, as far as has been revealed to me, is that your universe as you know it may cease to exist. All would return to darkness and evil would be victorious."

"Not cryptic," Makayla said. "Thank you. Terrifying but at least not cryptic."

"Okay," Brynn said. "'We shouldn't go to Annwfyn. We clearly can't stay here."

"Yeah, I don't think Jeffersonville is safe anymore," Makayla said. "Our Normal American Midwestern Town appears to have become A Dangerous Hellscape Unsuitable For Children Of All Ages."

"Do not stay here," the old woman said, her voice soft and resolute now. "Do not venture into Annwfyn. Find Gwenllian. She will help you."

"What about the shadows?" Brynn asked in desperation. "What about the creepy-ass residents of this creepy-ass town?"

"There is nothing else I can offer now. My attentions are needed elsewhere."

"No, wait!" Makayla shouted. "Can't you help us? We're teenagers! We're being attacked!"

"I'm sorry. My time with you is at an end. You took a dangerous journey once before, Branwen the Coblyn. You shall have to do so again."

Her head twisted subtly, as if she heard something far off in the distance, and then, without another word, she climbed out the window and walked off across the sky. Within moments, she was lost to their view.

Brynn and Makayla stared after her, and the noise and chaos around them roared back to life. Splintering wood, shrieks and howls, and other sounds too terrifying to contemplate assaulted their ears. The girls could barely find words to describe what had just happened, much less make sense of the apocalypse threatening to engulf their house, their town, their lives. Even the baby was merely staring silently into the night, at the mysteries above and the destruction below.

"This is...this is insanely terrible, B. What the hell do we do? Where the hell do we go?"

Brynn did not respond. She was lost in thought, her eyes vacant, her mouth taut, her hands shaking with terror.

"Yo. B! Snap out of it. We have very few minutes to make a decision here, like probably less than one."

Brynn shook her head and opened her mouth to speak, but before the words could escape her lips, she jumped and winced in pain.

"Ouch," she yelped. "Jesus Christ. Something just bit me!"

"What do you mean something bit you?"

"Something bit me! On my leg."

"There's nothing there," Makayla insisted as Brynn hopped around wildly, digging in her pockets.

"I think it was this!"

She pulled out the ancient-looking piece of paper her parents had given her before they left. It twitched in her hands. Brynn tried to hold onto it but the paper resisted her efforts and leapt from her hand, landing as sprightly as a folded piece of paper could on the nearby dresser. The wax seal popped off the paper and then, as Brynn and Makayla watched in amazement, the folded paper square unfolded itself and promptly refolded itself into the shape of a tiny paper person who promptly picked up the wax seal and promptly set it upon its shoulders where a head should be.

The tiny paper person did a tiny paper dance and pulled out a tiny paper sword from its tiny paper belt and then proceeded to use the sword to chop itself apart into pieces no bigger than confetti. But before the wax seal could even hit the dresser, the confetti reassembled itself into a square, folded piece of paper that was exactly the same size and shape it had been before Brynn pulled it from her pocket. The wax seal waddled over and settled itself back into its previous place and then the paper was still. The entire routine had taken no more than thirty seconds.

"What the hell?" Makayla shouted.

"It's the same note," Brynn said, picking up the piece of paper. "Look, same shape, same seal, same everything."

"No. It's not," Makayla said, examining the paper in Brynn's hand. "Look at the back. All the cuts that the little paper dude made with his little paper sword are still there. You can still see them. Lines running everywhere, around and through each other."

Brynn held the paper up to the light.

"You're right. But I can hardly see them. Are there words there?"

"I think so."

"But then what is it now? What the hell did my parents leave me?"

In a flash of realization, Makayla realized where she had seen lines like that before.

"I think it's a map."

Chapter 41

Brynn was writing on the hallway wall with a thick red magic marker. She wanted to leave a message for her parents and it was the best solution she could come up with in the last few moments they had before the goblins broke down the door.

I hope you don't come back, she wrote.

Too dangerous here

M and I are gone

Taking Hero somewhere safe

Brynn thought for a minute, then added:

Once things have quieted down we'll meet you at the old house

"Old house?" Makayla asked.

"Yeah. The place we lived before Jeffersonville. They'll know what I mean."

"Shouldn't we just go there first?"

"I don't think so," Brynn said. "We're supposed to find Gwenllian, right? Plus my parents said the goblins found the old house, even though they shouldn't have been able to. Which is why we came to Jeff in the first place. If the goblins wanted to find us, that's the first place they'd look."

"Well, second probably. This would be the first place."

"Yeah, but they already found this place."

They slipped on their backpacks (hastily packed with clothes, food and baby supplies) and Brynn picked up the baby.

"We need to go," she said as the noises of invasion from downstairs increased sharply.

"Yeah, we do. Bye, Jeff! It's been real!" Makayla called to the world at large.

"Ouch," Brynn cried suddenly. "That piece of paper bit me again!"

She pulled the paper out of her pocket. On the formerly blank exterior were written two words, scrawled in the same blood red she'd used to write on the walls:

RUN

NOW

They heard a crash from the living room, a window breaking, and a loud cracking and splintering which was clearly the front door giving way—whatever mystical protections had been embedded in it had finally fallen to the goblins' relentless onslaught.

"Well, the front door's out," Makayla shouted. "The basement is still on fire, presumably. Back door?"

Brynn ran to look out the window at the end of the hallway.

"Nope. Tons of them out there too."

"Then...what?"

"In here," Brynn said.

They ran into Brynn's room and slammed the door behind them. Out the window, they saw swarms of goblins and shadows with more arriving by the minute. Brynn took only a second to make her decision.

"You wear both backpacks," she said, handing hers to Makayla, who awkwardly adjusted it over her own. "I'll wear Hero." They strapped the surprisingly calm baby into the Ergo on Brynn's chest. "Okay, there we go." She jerked her thumb toward the window. "Out this way."

"The roof?" Makayla asked nervously.

"Yep."

The two girls climbed out onto the roof, one confidently, one with much trepidation.

"Do you trust me?" Brynn asked.

Makayla gulped and nodded. Brynn's body shimmered and shifted into her goblin form. She lifted her green, sinewy arms away from her body.

"Hop on," the goblin said.

"Wha…"

"Hop on, Makayla. Hurry!"

"You want to give me a piggyback ride? This may not be the best time!"

"Jesus, Makayla, they're going to be on top of us any second!"

Makayla shook her head at the insanity of this and every other crazy thing that had happened to her life over the last few weeks but had no better options to offer. She hopped onto Brynn's back and wrapped her arms around her neck.

"I'm way stronger like this," Brynn said. "Trust me."

With Makayla on her back and Hero on her front, Brynn ran to the edge of the roof and leapt over the goblins and the shadows below. The trio sailed through the air, landing cleanly on the roof of the next house over, at least a twenty-foot jump. Brynn was not even winded.

"See," she grinned.

"I'm duly impressed," Makayla said. "But we probably shouldn't stop moooooving!"

As soon as Brynn jumped, the goblins swarmed to the next house and were already climbing up on to the roof. The smallest goblin grabbed Makayla's ankle, but she quickly kicked it off.

"I think you're right," Brynn said. "Hold tight!"

Brynn ran again and jumped to the next roof, then kept running. The goblins were close behind, running, jumping, climbing up and around the houses, with more swarming to their location from the side streets. Brynn jumped to another roof and then to another, again and again.

At the end of the block, though, they ran out of roofs. Brynn jumped down to street level. Makayla disentangled herself and hopped off. The goblins were a few houses back. They had gained ground but not much, a few seconds at best.

"Now what?" Makayla asked.

"Now we run," Brynn said, gripping her friend's hand briefly. "Again."

They ran through the night, shadows caterwauling through the sky, goblins close on their heels, fear cascading from their pores. They ran, holding tight to the baby, to their meager supplies, to each other.

"I had a good look at the map while you were loading up our supplies," Brynn panted as they ran. "I think I know where we're going. It's a place my parents used to take us."

"How far?" Makayla panted, already winded. "'Cause I think they're gaining on us."

"Only a few miles," said Brynn.

"Miles?" Makayla shrieked.

Brynn scanned the street, the sky, the houses around them, looking for anything that could help.

"What about that?" she said, pointing to a truck in the next block. It looked like an antique, but it also looked like it might be running, idling in the street, abandoned by whatever person or goblin or creature had been using it. "Is that truck empty?"

"Looks it."

"Do you know how to drive?"

"Sort of. I don't have my license yet, though."

"Yeah, I don't think anyone's going to be checking those tonight. Give it a shot?"

"Better than the alternative."

They skidded to a halt when they reached the truck, threw the doors open and jumped inside. Makayla found the steering wheel, the gas pedal, the brake, then grimaced when she saw a third pedal beside them.

"Damn it!" she shouted. "It's a stick shift!"

"What does that mean?"

"It means I'm going to be really bad at this, B. Really bad."

"Doesn't matter how bad you are, just get us moving!"

Makayla pressed in the clutch and yanked at the gear stick, causing a deafening screeching. It took her several tries to get it in gear, but she finally did and the truck lurched slowly down the street.

"I've only driven a stick shift once before! It's the worst!"

"Just drive!"

The goblins were almost upon them. Brynn and Makayla pounded the locks shut. The goblins pulled at the doors and banged on the windows as the truck inched slowly forward. Hero began to howl and Brynn did her best to comfort her. Two of the larger goblins were running at the truck with a garbage can, preparing to smash in the windows when

Makayla shouted, "Holy crap, I think I figured it out!" and the truck took off down the street, the nails of the goblins screeching against the metal, their cries nearly deafening as they realized their prey had escaped.

Makayla gave a whoop of relief and Brynn allowed herself a brief smile before she pulled the paper from her pocket and gave Makayla directions. The map took them out of town and into the hills, to a rural road, then a gravel road, to a narrow dirt track through the trees and eventually to a bluff overlooking the town. A ramshackle cabin sat off to one side near the trees. Although "cabin" might be generous, Makayla thought. "Shack" might be more accurate and "decrepit shack" even more so.

"I think that's where we're going," Brynn said.

"There? That shack?"

Brynn checked the map and gave a quick, "Yup."

"Okay. We're almost out of gas anyway."

Brynn's head snapped around.

"Crap."

"What?"

"You know how we left the goblins behind and that was really exciting and we were relieved and all that?"

"Yeeeeeessss."

"Yeah, it looks like the goblins stopped but the shadows kept coming."

A tidal wave of shadows was pouring up the dirt path, through the trees, onto the bluff.

"What do we do?" Makayla shouted. "What do we do now?"

"Into the shack, Makayla! We need to get into that shack! Stop the truck!"

Makayla smashed her foot down on the brake and the engine ground to a halt. The girls ran to the shack, pulled the door open, and made it inside just before the shadows reached them. They slammed the door shut and were answered by howls of fury from outside as the shadows keened their anger into the night. Hand in hand, the girls slumped against the wall, sobbing, exhausted, filthy, lost. They were in a cold wooden shack, the baby was crying, and they only had enough food to last them a few days. But they appeared to be safe. At least for now.

Chapter 42

The goblins arrived several hours later and with the arrival of reinforcements, the creatures began their assault in earnest. Brynn and Makayla, though, found the shack to be sturdier and better equipped than it had first appeared. They barred the door. They closed heavy metal shutters over the windows and barred those as well. The beings simply threw themselves at the shack's walls for the first hour, claws attempting to rip through the wood and through the metal, but to no avail. After that, the ground began to shake, a low, rhythmic thumping which went on for another hour. When that had subsided, the lightning began, and then thunder and hail, which rattled the metal roof ceaselessly, making the baby wail, although she hadn't really stopped since they left Brynn's house.

Eventually, after several hours of this, the noises outside subsided, the howls faded away, the hail ceased its battering, and they were able to calm Hero down and lay her to sleep on the cot in the corner of the shack.

Despite their exhaustion, however, the girls could not sleep. They tossed and turned and tried to make themselves comfortable with backpacks for pillows and sweatshirts for blankets, but nothing seemed to work.

"You asleep yet?" Brynn whispered.

"Nope," Makayla answered. "Are you?"

"Indeed I am."

"Good for you. I admire your ability to sleep in a decrepit shack which is about to be torn apart by magical shadows."

There was a long silence before Brynn spoke again.

"Hey, Makayla?"

"Yeah?"

"Where have you been lately?"

"In Jeffersonville. With you. Trying to not get killed."

"No, I mean before," Brynn said nervously. "I tried to hang out with you and you said you were busy. I waited for you so we could walk home after school and you wouldn't show. It's...it's been weird. It just seems like...you're not like you were before."

"Nothing's like it was before."

"Well, yeah, but—"

"No, B, I mean it," Makayla said. "Nothing is the same. Everything has changed. You've changed. Jeff's changed. The whole world has changed. And I...I've changed. But..." And this was the hardest part to admit to anyone, but especially to her best friend. "But the main thing that I think has changed about me...or that I *know* has changed about me—because I've had to talk to way too many people about it—is...is my brain. I guess."

"What do you mean? How has your brain changed?"

"It...might not work as well as it used to, I suppose is one way of saying it."

"I don't..."

Makayla sighed.

"Therapy, B. I've been going to therapy."

"Why?"

"Oh my god, how do I even start to answer that question. Well, after...after everything that happened last year—

getting kidnapped into another dimension and getting replaced by the evil enchanted version of me and you telling me you're a goblin and us riding on the back of a giant bug and just in general finding out that everything I thought I knew about the world was mostly inaccurate—I guess my brain went on the fritz a bit."

Makayla stared at the walls of the shack and clenched her jaw.

"I have...I have these spells where I just feel really, really wrong, like my body and brain are just not running how they're supposed to."

"What does that mean?"

"I don't know," Makayla said. "My chest gets tight. My head gets fuzzy. My neck and head and chest get really hot and I feel like I've got a fever but I don't have a fever and I've been...I've been crying a lot." She shrugged and grimaced. "Not just crying. Bawling."

"But you...you never cry."

"I know! But lately it has been making up a significant portion of my daily routine. I was having a hard time just getting through the day and I didn't want to tell anyone, but my Ma..." Makayla blew out her cheeks. "My Ma started seeing it, and it took her forever to convince me, but she finally...she just said, go to this place, just talk to someone in the office, and see what happens."

"So I went in," Makayla continued. "I couldn't even look anyone in the eye, and the lady behind the glass at the front counter barely even talked to me, which meant I knew she thought I was weird and I almost left. But I forced my damn feet to walk into that lobby and I waited for them to call my name and this nice older lady called me into her office." She shook her head. "I couldn't even deal. I couldn't look at her. I...I literally laid down on the floor and stared at the ceiling. And she didn't say anything for a while. So I cried. I cried a lot. And then she said, 'Good. Now do you want to tell me what's wrong?' And I told her as much as I could. I mean, I didn't tell her about goblins or getting hauled off into another dimension, but I told her about how I didn't know how to handle anything going on around me anymore and how everything felt different. And I talked and I talked and I talked and I don't think I've ever talked so freaking much in my whole damn life but finally the words ran out. And I cried a little more. Then she sat down on a chair next to me and she said, 'You came to the right place. We're going to get you the help you need.' And she did. Since then, I've been back there twice a week."

"Is it helping?"

"A bit. I think," Makayla said, biting the inside of her cheek. "They set me up with this...she's a counselor, I guess, although she's not really that much older than me. I talk to her and she asks me questions, and I tell her how my body feels when I freak out, and she gives me...suggestions on what to do when it happens."

"Like what?"

"Like find something solid and hold onto it. Concentrate on that for a minute. Notice the things around me, the really normal things around me and think about those instead of the weird things that are trying to happen in my head. Let the normal things around me, the sound of the clock ticking, the table, a lightbulb, let those things push the darkness away."

Makayla reached into her pocket and pulled out the small smooth stone she'd been keeping there for the last few months.

"And if I need to," she said, "I use this."

"What is it?"

"It's a rock."

"A rock?"

"Yep. Just a rock. But I can hold onto it and I can feel it. It's just hard and smooth and cold and those are familiar feelings and sometimes I just need to feel something familiar. Because, damn it, B, there's things going on that don't feel familiar in any way, shape or form and I just really, really need to hold onto something that I understand, because otherwise… otherwise I think I might get lost inside the fear and I'm not sure I'd know how to come back."

Brynn scooched closer to Makayla and took her hand.

"I'm not going to let you get lost, Makayla. I love you. Even the broken parts of you."

Makayla let herself cry then. She buried her face in Brynn's shoulder and cried, and Brynn held her until she fell asleep.

Chapter 43

When Makayla awoke, she found she was curled up on the floor, covered in Brynn's sweatshirt. She shivered and stretched and saw that Brynn was already awake and standing by the window, trying to peer through the cracks in the shutters.

"Hey."

"Hey," Brynn answered softly without turning around.

"Anything out there?"

"I can't tell."

"The baby's still asleep?"

"Yeah," Brynn said. "She's a crazy good sleeper. My mom said not to tell anyone else what a good sleeper she is because they'd only think I was lying."

Makayla rose and stood next to Brynn.

"It's quiet."

"Too quiet," Brynn said dramatically, arching her eyebrows skyward.

"Really? You think it's too quiet out there?"

"Nah. I think it's exactly the right amount of quiet, I've just always wanted to say that."

"Safe to open the shutters, do you think?"

"I don't know if it's safe, but I think we need to see what's going on."

They pulled the thick metal shutters aside and blinked into the sunlight that poured into the room. Hero woke from her sleep and cooed happily.

"Well, no monsters out there anyway," said Brynn.

"No monsters, but look at Jeff."

From their vantage point in the shack on top of the bluff, they could see the city below. It was in chaos. What wasn't on fire seemed likely to be so soon. If there had been any doubt remaining in their minds, it was now extinguished: their town was gone.

"We can't stay here, can we?" Makayla asked.

"No. We have to go."

"But where?"

"To find Gwenllian, I guess." Brynn grimaced. "That's what the old woman told us to do, and she's...well, I'm not sure she's the only one who knows what's going on, but she's the only one who's told us anything about what's going on."

"And what then?"

"What do you mean?"

"After we find Gwenllian. *If* we find Gwenllian. What do we do then?"

"We do what we said we were going to do. We get Hero somewhere safe. That's the most important thing."

"But where is safe?" Makayla asked. "Where is there a place that the goblins and shadows can't get to?"

"I don't know."

"The place in California? Is that safe?"

"I don't know."

They packed slowly, putting away the few things they'd retrieved from their backpacks. They changed and fed Hero and ate a little themselves. When they were ready, Brynn slipped Hero into the Ergo and they both slung on their backpacks. Brynn gave Makayla a nod, and then Makayla unbarred the door and pulled it open.

On the other side of the door stood a tall slender being with gray skin, pointed ears, and a fancifully appointed outfit, richly embroidered with silk and lace in abundance. She wore leather shoes with silver buckles and pointed toes. Her hand was raised as if she were about to knock. The girls, the baby, and the new arrival did nothing but stare at each other for several moments before the being outside the door finally cleared her throat and spoke.

"Oh, hello," she said cheerfully. "Brynn? Makayla?"

The girls nodded confusedly.

"Hi! I'm Heddwyn."

"Heddwyn?" Brynn asked.

"Yes. But you can call me Winnie."

"Okaaaaay," Brynn responded.

"And…" Makayla added.

"And what?" Winnie asked nonchalantly. The girls just stared at her. "Oh. Yes. I'm here to help you."

"You're…what?"

"Here to help you. On your journey."

"Our…journey?"

"Yes, of course. You don't want to stay here, do you?"

The girls shook their heads in unison.

"Then a journey it is," Winnie said brightly. "Come on! It'll be fun!"

ACT 3: JOURNEY

Chapter 44

Brynn was clearly struggling to keep herself airborne. Once she'd changed into her white raven form, they had somehow managed to attach the Ergo to her wings and neck, but the additional weight of her baby sister threw her off balance and her path through the air wobbled in the wind. Makayla had her own things to worry about, however, in the arms of the slender, gray-skinned woman, who apparently had enormous wings tucked under her fancy coat. Makayla had nearly jumped out of her skin when the woman picked her up and launched into the air, but quickly learned that the woman was far stronger than she looked.

The curious foursome flew over Jeffersonville on their way to a place that Makayla had been alarmed to learn was called the Devil's Backbone. Brynn had assured her that she'd been there before, and that it was nothing to worry about, but Makayla had known Brynn long enough to figure out when she wasn't telling the truth. Or the whole truth, anyway.

Makayla tried to ignore the fact that the Jeffersonville she knew was clearly gone. Huge swaths of the town were on fire and the portions that were not aflame were so overrun by goblins or covered by shadows that she couldn't make out the buildings beneath. Towering wooden structures now rose from various yards and parking lots, but what their purpose might be, Makayla couldn't even guess at.

Eventually, the destruction grew too much for her and she allowed her eyes to fall closed. She felt the wind rushing past. Her skin prickled and she let the powerful arms of the winged woman hold her and warm her. She wasn't entirely sure, but she might have fallen asleep for a few minutes. In any event, when she next opened her eyes, they were descending through the treetops onto a bony ridge in the middle of the river. The ground was covered with a soft layer of underbrush and dotted by overgrown earthen mounds.

The white raven that was also Brynn landed gently next to them, shimmered and changed into human form, and picked up the cooing baby she had carried as she flew. Winnie tucked her enormous wings back under her impeccable bodice or jacket or kirtle or whatever the embroidered lacy thing she was wearing should be called.

"Well, here we are!" Winnie said with an extravagant gesture that showed off all her best features. "We have arrived at the Devil's Backbone. Call to adventure complete." She gave a sly wink. "Now to find the threshold."

"Threshold?" Makayla asked, confused.

"We're looking for a door," Brynn explained. "This is how I got to Annwfyn last time."

"But we're not supposed to go to Annwfyn."

"We're not going to Annwfyn," Winnie assured them. "But we are going."

"Going where?"

"I told you," Winnie said. "On a journey. And journeys start with doors. For further information, see 'thresholds comma the crossing thereof.'"

"Where are we going to find a door out here?" Makayla asked. "All I see is a bunch of trees and a bunch of piles of rocks and dirt."

"Burial mounds," Brynn answered with a grimace.

"I'm sorry, what?"

"They're burial mounds," Brynn repeated. "The piles of rocks and dirt are burial mounds."

"Who is burying all these people out in the middle of the river?" Makayla asked in alarm.

"Only a few people. And it happened centuries ago."

"Is that supposed to make me feel better? Jeff is on fire and we're hanging out in a prehistoric cemetery?"

"Not prehistoric," Brynn continued. "Twelfth century. But we're getting off track. This is the one I used last time." She pointed at one of the mounds and shouted to Winnie, who was traipsing along the ridge far ahead of them. "Hey! Isn't this the one we want?"

"That's the third one and that would take us back to Annwfyn," Winnie trilled, "and you said you most certainly do not want to go there and I most certainly agree with you. Our journey today requires the seventh mound."

Brynn and Makayla shouldered their backpacks and joined Winnie at the end of the ridge, at the final burial mound. It was smaller than the others and, if possible, even more ancient-looking. A few sickly saplings were growing between the flat moss-crusted rocks which covered it.

"Well, here we are," Winnie said, patting the mound affectionately.

"There's no door here," Makayla groused. "Just dirt. Dirt is not a door."

"It will be," Winnie assured her.

"The dirt will be a door? That doesn't make any sense."

Brynn shushed Makayla and she grumpily acquiesced. Winnie hummed to herself as she unfurled her wings and fluttered slowly around the mound, her feet barely touching the ground, her wings keeping her almost aloft, just on the cusp between the land and the sky. She circled the mound seven times, then turned to the girls and pressed her finger to her lips with a winsome smile. Hero, in Brynn's arms, giggled and repeated the gesture.

Makayla stared at the mound of rocks and dirt, but nothing happened. She stared at Winnie, who just kept smiling and humming to herself. She stared at Hero, who had once again fallen asleep. She stared at the burial mound again for what seemed like an insanely long time and was just about to burst and finally say something when, with a loud pop and a blast of cold air, a door appeared in the midst of the rocks where there hadn't been a door seconds before and Makayla was a bit concerned that Winnie and Brynn were acting like it was no big deal.

She gave a grunt of frustration at the fact that everyone around was so blasé about the suspension of the normal laws of reality but as there didn't seem to be anything she could do about their attitudes, she turned her attention back to the impossible door.

It resembled a cellar door, in that there were two wooden panels set at an angle into the ground, but these panels would have not appeared in any cellar doors on Earth. They were finely wrought and heavily engraved and inlaid with what appeared to be gold. The lines etched on them reminded Makayla of the runes she had seen in Brynn's basement, but where those had made her feel decidedly uncomfortable, these runes made her skin tingle and her feet itch, like they wanted to jump or dance or cartwheel or spin and Makayla was seriously considering giving in to these impulses.

"At least there were no snakes this time," Brynn said, which shook Makayla from her reverie.

"There were snakes before?"

"You don't even want to know. So many snakes."

Winnie was looking at them with festive impatience.

"Well then. Shall we?"

"Shall we what?" Makayla responded.

"Proceed," Winnie said. "Enter the door. Cross the threshold. Commence our journey."

There were handles of rope set into the door, white twisted with gold, and when Winnie pulled upon them, the doors opened easily. On the other side, there was nothing but darkness. At the first glimpse of the nothingness that lay just on the other side of the threshold, a familiar tightness took hold of Makayla's chest and a familiar fevered heat poured across her neck.

"I'm...I'm not sure I can do this, B," she said, her voice a hoarse croak.

"Of course you can, Makayla."

Makayla only shook her head.

"We can't go back," Brynn went on. "I'm sorry, but we can't. There's nothing left. The only way out is through which I know is trite but seriously, the only way for us to figure out what's going on around here is to go through that door."

Makayla knew this was true but she also knew that the darkness beyond the doorway was screaming at her and telling her to stay away.

"I can't. I can't go through that door. B, that door just appeared out of nowhere and we don't know where it goes and there is no part of me that thinks I can actually go in there...into that...that darkness..."

Brynn looked at Makayla and her mouth crinkled in concern. She turned to Winnie.

"You go ahead. I'll be right there."

Brynn handed the sleeping baby to Winnie, who fluttered downward through the doorway and disappeared into the darkness. Makayla felt Brynn take her hand and lead her forward, and somehow, despite the claws grasping at her heart, her feet managed to take her to the edge of the doorway and when Makayla was there, standing on the threshold, looking into the nothingness, that was where it hit her for the first time.

It was like she was back in the Swallowed Hall again, back in Annwfyn, back in the room where Brynn rescued her, before they fled from Efnysien and found their way home.

It smelled like rot and death.

The memory of it came flooding back. When she woke up in that crumbling hall full of rotting wood and dead bodies and blood and maggots, before she even opened her eyes, the smell told her that something was wrong and it was that same smell that filled her brain now—the pungent, earthy odor of rotting wood, the sickly, sweet smell of decaying flesh, the sharp, metallic smell of blood all around her—and even though she knew it was just a memory, even though she knew she wasn't back in the Swallowed Hall, she couldn't escape it, couldn't escape how real it felt. Her body trembled and her hands shook and she felt the sound welling up deep inside her, building from the tips of her fingers and the tips of her toes, before it escaped in a scream that was sharper and harder than she had ever imagined she could make.

"I can't, Brynn! I can't go through that door! I just can't!"

"You can do it, Makayla. You have to."

"I can't, I'm sorry, Brynn, I can't, it's too hard, I can't, I can't, I can't…"

"Come on, you can," Brynn pleaded. "I know you can, we have to. My sister is in there. My parents are gone. Your parents too. My brother is missing. We can't stay here anymore. We have to go."

Makayla was screaming and she was standing right on the threshold of the doorway that led nowhere, that led into darkness, and the smell of death and rot was still filling her brain, and tears were streaming down her face and she was screaming.

"You have to push me through, Brynn! It's the only way!"

"No, Makayla, just take a step!"

"I can't!"

"You have to! We have to go!"

"I can't!"

Brynn grabbed Makayla's hand.

"I'll be with you! The whole time!"

"I can't Brynn, I'm sorry!"

Makayla closed her eyes, trying to shut out the world around her, trying to shut out the smell of death that filled her brain, trying to shut it all out, and then she felt a pair of strong arms around her, holding her, enclosing her, and then she felt two strong legs leap and the two girls fell together, across the threshold, into the darkness, into the unknown.

Chapter 45

When Makayla opened her eyes, they were in a very dark, very cold cave. There was no sign of the doorway that brought them here, and now that it was gone, the smell of death no longer filled her thoughts. The fear went out of her. Her chest unclenched and the feverish heat faded.

The cave looked out over a field dusted with snow. Bands of pink and blue light cut through the darkness in the sky above and Makayla wondered if they were the northern lights, which she had never seen before. Then it occurred to her that the northern lights were something that happened on Earth, and then she realized they might not be on Earth anymore, and then her head started to hurt so she moved on.

In the center of the cave, Winnie was sitting next to a roaring fire, smiling and singing to the baby, who was giggling in her arms. A pot was hanging over the flames and the smell of cooking food filled the air. A large tent made of lavender canvas with spiraling trim in a pearly silver stood nearby.

"Where did she get that tent from?" Makayla hissed to Brynn.

"I have no idea."

Winnie smiled up at them as they approached and told them that dinner was ready. The food was unidentifiable but delicious, and Makayla ate at least three bowls full, but she may have lost track. When they had all eaten their fill (including Hero, who nibbled on soft chunks that Winnie pulled from the pot), they sat around the fire, full and sated.

"I've been meaning to ask," Brynn said quietly to Winnie, as they stared at the fire. "We appreciate your help, and we didn't really seem to have any choice other than to let you help us, but..."

"Yes?"

"Well, where...where did you come from?"

"You mean, where was I born?"

"No. I mean, why are you helping us? Why did you show up at that shack in the middle of nowhere and offer to help us?"

"Oh! That's easy," Winnie answered with a grin. "Llyn Llyw sent me. He thought you might need some help."

"Who sent you?"

"Llyn Llyw."

Makayla's brows knitted. "I don't...I don't really understand what you're saying. Could you write it down for me?"

Winnie traced the letters in a patch of dirt beside the fire:

L L Y N

L L Y W

"Where are the vowels?" Makayla said, throwing her hands up. "Why don't you people have more vowels? They cost nothing!"

Winnie just shrugged.

"Of course, his proper name is The Salmon of Llyn Llyw," she said, "but we usually just call him Llyn Llyw."

"The Salmon sent you?" Brynn asked.

Winnie nodded.

"Who?" Makayla asked.

"The guy from the fish restaurant," Brynn said, "in the fish costume. We talked to him, remember?"

"The fish guy sent you?" Makayla asked Winnie. She nodded. "Okay, well, that's weird, but if I have to refer to him, I'm not going to try to say his name. I'm just going to call him the fish guy. Deal?"

"Deal," Winnie said with a yawn. "Speaking of deals, I'm going to go make a deal with a cot." She paused. "That's a thing you guys say on Earth, right?"

"Not really."

"Well, anyway, I'm tired and I'm going to bed. Should I take the baby with me?"

"Yeah," Brynn said. "Thanks."

Winnie picked up Hero, who was already nearly asleep, and disappeared into the massive, gaudy tent. Brynn and Makayla stared into the fire, each lost in their own thoughts, lost in the sounds of the fire and the sounds of the night that filled the cave. After a long period of companionable silence, Brynn's brow furrowed and she cleared her throat.

"So...I feel like I should ask you about what happened back there," she said. "When the door opened and you...you kind of started screaming. A bunch."

"I don't know, man," Makayla said, shaking her head. "It was just like...I saw that door, and I knew it went somewhere else. Probably somewhere strange. And all of a sudden I was remembering the last time I ended up somewhere strange, when I woke up in Annwfyn and you were rescuing me. I remembered that, except it was like it wasn't just a memory, it almost...it almost felt like I was really there again. And I kind of...I kind of freaked out."

"Yeah. You did. It scared me."

"Sorry, B."

"You pulled through, though, right? I mean, you ended up coming through the door."

"Well, you carried me through," Makayla said. "I'm not sure it really counts."

Brynn gave a small smile.

"I think it counts."

"Okay. We'll count it then."

They sat again in silence for a while, which finally broken by a sound from somewhere in the region of Makayla's stomach. Brynn chortled.

"What was that?"

"Sorry," Makayla grumbled. "I don't know what that food was that Winnie gave us, but either it wasn't very filling or I'm way hungrier than I thought I was."

"Maybe both."

"Yeah, maybe both."

"Or maybe traveling through interdimensional doorways to strange caves really takes it out of one."

"Yes, I think that's correct," Makayla agreed. "Whatever it is, I'll tell you something, I would just about kill for a hamburger right now."

"Kill? You would kill?"

"Yes, Brynn. I would literally kill a human being in order to obtain a hamburger right now." Brynn grinned. "Wait a second. Your goblin powers!"

"What about them?" Brynn said suspiciously.

"Didn't you tell me that one of your powers is to grant wishes?"

"Well, yes," Brynn said slowly, "but—"

"I wish for a hamburger!" Makayla burst out. Her head spun madly around as she searched for the hamburger she assumed would appear, but no hamburgers materialized. "What the hell," she muttered sadly.

"It doesn't work like that," Brynn said softly with a small smile.

"Well, how does it work then? I really want to wish for a hamburger."

"I mean, it's complicated, and I don't totally get it, and...and it only happened to me once, but I know for the wish to be granted, it has to be wisher's fondest desire."

"Oh. It is."

"No," Brynn said, "I mean, it has to be your innermost, deepest, biggest wish, your heart's desire. The thing you want most in the world, out of all the things in the world."

"I don't think you understand how much I want this burger."

Brynn rolled her eyes.

"No, for real," she said. "It's massively complicated. Even my mom says there's tons about it she doesn't know. There's all kinds of conditions—it has to be your deepest desire, I have to owe you a boon—"

"A what?"

"A boon," Brynn said, enunciating carefully.

"What the hell is a boon?"

"Like...a favor. Like you did something for me, and now I have to pay you back—"

"Oh my god," Makayla said, in mock alarm. "Brynn!"

"What?"

"Dude. Your shoe's untied."

Makayla reached over, tied Brynn's shoelace, and then, as quickly as she could, she said, "There I did you a favor you owe me a boon and I really really really wish I had a hamburger!"

Instantly, Brynn's body filled up with a bright white light, which then poured out of her, from her eyes, her mouth, her fingers. The light lifted her in the air and held her suspended there, glowing, energy pouring from her, and then suddenly, there was a sharp snap, the light disappeared and Brynn landed gently on the ground. With a small poof, a hamburger appeared in front of her, warm and juicy, sitting on a cracked china plate.

"Holy crap!" Makayla said. "It worked." She reached for the hamburger, held it in front of her nose and took a deep bite, savoring it as the delicious beef almost melted in her mouth. She glanced up at Brynn. "You okay?" Brynn glared at her. "You went all glowy and stuff."

"Yeah, I did," Brynn said with a sigh. "Let's not make a habit of this, yeah?"

"Yeah," Makayla agreed. "Okay. Really good burger, though."

Chapter 46

When they had gone into the tent and were falling asleep on their surprisingly comfortable cots, Makayla realized that Winnie was singing. Afterward, when she thought about it, she was never quite sure whether Winnie was singing in English or some entirely different language or whether she dreamed the whole thing, but in any case, Winnie sang and Makayla understood the words and this was the song that she heard.

> *For they walked alone*
> *Before time was young,*
> *The Shining Lion*
> *And the Summer Song.*
>> *And from the darkness,*
>> *The Maker of all*
>> *Saw they were lonesome,*
>> *And the peoples did call.*
> *The Maker's gift to the Lion and Song*
> *Was to care for all those who fell from above,*
> *And the Maker's whisper to the growing throng*
> *Told them Lion and Song were theirs to love.*
>>> *In the great above, the stars beyond*
>>> *Found the water for their bed,*
>>> *And the stars they slept,*
>>> *Their light grown fond,*
>>> *And the water waits for her, for her,*

And the water waits for her.
But soon jealousy
In two hearts grew strong,
In the Shining Lion
And the Summer Song.

 For the Lion, he sought
 All peoples in his thrall,
 And the Song, she yearned
 To be sung by all.

The strife between split the peoples asunder,
From a roar and refrain new lands were unfurled,
And the Song took nine to a world grown under,
The Lion took the rest to the Otherworld.

  The water flowed into the lands
  Made by the Lion and Song,
  And the stars, they held her in their hands
  And the water waits for her, for her,
  And the water waits for her.

 Long years the Shining One whithered and strayed
 Across and through the land he had made,
  And though he did not walk alone,
  He longed for one to call his own.

He wished for a wife,
He wished for a daughter,
And his tears and his steps
Brought him to the water.

 He came to the Lake
 To speak of his sorrow,
 The Lake called to him,
 'Come again on the morrow.'

When he returned, the Lake spoke of her longing,

For the stars and the water she could not forsake,
But sweet honeyed words promised joys from belonging,
And the Lady stepped forth and did leave the Lake.

> The stars they watched as their Lady left
> The waters now untended,
> And as they slept, the stars they wept,
> And the water waits for her, for her,
> And the water waits for her.

O, full joyful then
Were the Lion's eyes,
As he made a home
For his joyful bride.

> And given to them,
> Four sons and a daughter,
> For the Shining Lion
> And she from the water.

Years passed, shadows lengthened,
The children they grew,
The four sons whispered and did conspire,
Hearts black as coal, their father they slew,
For their father's realm they did desire.

> With rage unquenched, with heart unfilled,
> The Lady returned to the Lake,
> Within the water, she sleeps there still,
> And the water waits for her, for her
> And the water waits for her.

Chapter 47

When Brynn and Makayla emerged from the tent, Hero was sitting happily on the ground, playing with some smooth round rocks. Winnie had already prepared another meal and was ladling it into shallow earthenware bowls. As the four sat and ate, they looked from the mouth of the cave at the land around them, where the sun was already beginning to melt the night's frost. The cave opened onto the floor of a large canyon, and in the middle of the canyon, dividing it neatly in two, was a towering rock formation. Snow-dusted trees covered the ground around them, but little seemed to grow on the island of rock or on the cliff walls that hemmed in the canyon's floor.

"So where are we anyway?" Makayla asked at last, unsure if she actually wanted to know the answer.

"Excellent question," Winnie answered. "We are on Earth. For the moment."

"Good to know. Little more specific, please."

"Ah. Yes. We are currently in the fair land of Garðarshólmur."

"Come again?" Makayla said.

"Garðarshólmur."

"Still not getting it."

"It is also sometimes called Snæland," Winnie said with a wistful smile.

"What?"

"Snæland."

"I don't…what…what are you saying?" Makayla said, throwing her hands in the air.

"English maybe?" Brynn added.

"You want me to tell you where we are in *your* language, instead of the language of the inhabitants?" Winnie sniffed, arching her eyebrows. "You want to know what people in America call this place, instead of what the people who live in this place call this place?"

Brynn and Makayla squinted at Winnie.

"Iceland," Winnie said, rolling her eyes. "Okay? We're in Iceland."

"Iceland?" Makayla asked.

"Yes, Iceland."

"Now we're getting somewhere." Makayla waved her arms toward the canyon outside the cave. "And what are we looking at here?"

Winnie smiled.

"We currently sit at the bottom of the canyon of Ásbyrgi, also called Sleipnir's Footprint, home to the hidden people of Iceland, the Huldufólk."

"And what's that?" Makayla asked, pointing at the towering island of rock.

"That…that is Eyjan."

"And I almost hate to ask this, but where are we going next?"

"To the top," Winnie said.

"The top?"

"Of Eyjan." Winnie grinned. "There is a doorway there. The only doorway on this world that can take us where we need to go."

Getting to the top was much easier than Makayla had expected it to be. Winnie packed away their campsite in barely an instant, although neither of the girls were able to see where she had packed it away to. The weather was warmer than it seemed, and the trail that led to the top of Eyjan was an easy walk, even with their backpacks still crammed with diapers and baby supplies. Barely two hours after they left the cave, they arrived at the top of the rock, which turned out to be covered with haphazard growths of stunted trees and was pockmarked throughout with tiny pools and ponds. Brynn wore Hero close against her chest as they hiked, and the baby barely made a peep, clearly entranced by the view.

"So...what are we looking for?" Brynn asked, looking around curiously. "Burial mound again? Trap door? Ladder?"

"No. None of those," Winnie said. "Just this."

She gestured to a small pond. It was as non-descript as the dozens of other small ponds they could see, shallow and ringed with brush and saplings. There was a large birch growing at the shore, the largest tree to be seen on the island of rock. Winnie collected five leaves that had fallen around its trunk and laid them gently on the water. The leaves flashed briefly, and Makayla thought she heard a faint voice singing, yearning, wandering. In the midst of the leaves, the water grew bright and a circular ripple flowed softly outward.

"What...what's that?" Makayla asked.

"That's our door," Winnie answered.

As soon as she recognized it for what it was, Makayla's chest tightened and her hands clenched. The smell of death and rot filled her nostrils and she felt a scream beginning to rise in her throat, or maybe it was a sob, or maybe she just needed to run far, far away, but before any of those things could happen, a pair of strong arms wrapped around her waist and a sinewy tail wrapped around her legs. A face with green skin and pointed ears, which she knew was Brynn's but also wasn't, swam before her eyes.

"Sorry, M, but we need to keep moving," a voice said, a voice that was a million miles away but that also whispered gently in her ear. Makayla knew this was true and even though she didn't want to, even though every fiber of her being was screaming at her to escape, to run, to curl up and let it all fade away, she managed to look at the face in front of her and nod, and then she closed her eyes, closed them as hard as she could.

The strong arms picked her up and the powerful legs leaped and then the two of them were in the water. They were falling, falling, falling, and it was bright. It was so bright that she could see how bright it was even with her eyes shut so tight that not even her tears could escape. Then suddenly, it all stopped.

"You can open your eyes now, Makayla," a voice said gently. "It's all over."

Makayla opened her eyes slowly, first one and then the other, and as her eyes came back into focus, the first thing she saw was Brynn and then all she could see was Brynn.

"You okay?" Brynn asked.

Makayla nodded.

"Hope that was alright," Brynn said. "Thought I'd try to head whatever was happening with you off at the pass and just get you through the doorway."

"Good idea," Makayla said, her voice a raspy whisper. Her head snapped around as she finally noticed her surroundings, which were distinctly un-Earthlike. "Whoa, whoa, whoa,

whoa! Are we in Annwfyn? 'Cause we're really not supposed to go to Annwfyn."

"We are not in Annwfyn," Winnie said, who Makayla now noticed was holding Hero and sitting cross-legged a few feet away.

"Are we on Earth? 'Cause this *really* does not look like Earth."

Makayla couldn't figure out exactly what this place did look like, though, despite her confidence that it was nowhere on Earth. Whenever she tried to identify any details, she found it was hard to focus on any one specific thing. Her eyes kept sliding off and her brain refused to dwell on it, as if everything around her was so mundane that her eyes just didn't care what they were looking at. Or perhaps everything around her was so extraordinary and unlike anything she'd ever seen before that her brain just refused to accept it. Or perhaps it was some combination of the two.

"We are not on Earth," Winnie assured her.

"So where are we?" Brynn asked.

"This place," Winnie said, wrinkling her brow, "well, this place...where we are...is kind of hard to explain."

"Maybe give it a shot, though?" Makayla suggested.

"This place...where we're standing...or sitting...it's not really anywhere."

"That's a really bad explanation."

"I told you it was hard to explain," said Winnie.

"Yeah, but I kind of feel like you didn't even try."

"I agree," Brynn said. "However, I think maybe where we are exactly is less important than *that*."

"That?" Makayla asked.

"Yes, *that*." Brynn pointed at something in the distance that Makayla's eyes couldn't quite comprehend. "What's that?"

"That's her house," Winnie said brightly.

"Her?" Brynn asked.

"Yes. Gwenllian. That's where she lives. Sometimes. Somewhens."

"So, Gwenllian has a house here," Makayla said, "in a place I guess we're now calling Not Really Anywhere?"

"Sure," Brynn agreed, joining Makayla as they tried to focus on the object in the distance.

"And also," Makayla said, "now that I look at it, 'house' may not be the right word."

"Tree?" Brynn suggested.

"Tower?"

"Flower?"

"Gem-encrusted sword pavilion?" Makayla pondered.

"She does like swords."

"You think she's home?"

"Only one way to find out."

Chapter 48

Minutes later, they were standing in front of what Makayla insisted they call the Gem-Encrusted Sword Pavilion in the Land of Not Really Anywhere.

"Is this a door?" Brynn asked, walking up to a segment of the pavilion that might have been a door or might have been something else entirely. Makayla shrugged. Brynn tried to knock but wasn't entirely successful.

"It's squishy," she said.

"Not a door then," Makayla said.

"No?"

"Yeah, I think that's a rule about doors. They can't be squishy."

"I didn't know doors had rules," Brynn said.

Makayla shrugged.

"Try another one," she suggested.

Brynn tried knocking on another section of the pavilion.

"Squishy?" Makayla asked.

"Nope."

"Might be a door."

After a few moments of quiet waiting, the solid panel that Brynn had knocked on split softly into several sections and curled outward like a flower blooming, revealing a bright room beyond.

"Huh," Makayla said.

"Sort of a door," Brynn said.

"Yeah, sort of."

Once the door-like aperture had finished opening or blooming or whatever it had done, a figure stepped into the light. It was the woman who had stalked Brynn, tried to kill her and then fought at her side, who had been imprisoned along with Makayla in the Swallowed Hall, who had saved the life of Brynn and her family when Efnysien tried to kill them. It was Gwenllian, the warrior princess, but not as they had ever seen her before. She wore no armor, bore no sword, and her long blond hair was undone and flowing freely down her back.

Gwenllian looked curiously at the group that had arrived at her door, inspecting each one in turn, a small smile hiding at the corners of her mouth. Finally, she nodded sagely at them and spoke and though her appearance had changed, her voice was not. It was still full of melodious resolve, a voice that sounded like nothing so much as velvet wrapped in steel.

"Hello, coblyn child," she said to Brynn and then turned to the rest in turn. "Human. Bwbach. And," she peered at the baby in Winnie's arms, "coblyn baby." She waggled her eyebrows in a way which seemed unbefitting a fierce warrior princess. "Hello, coblyn baby."

"Hi, um, Gwenllian," Brynn said finally, bucking up her courage.

"Greetings," Gwenllian said warmly.

"So, I know this is probably really weird," Brynn said, "that we just kind of showed up on your doorstep—"

"Even though there's not really a door or a step, per se—" Makayla interjected.

"But we're in a lot of trouble and we don't know where else to go, and Cyrridwen told us to come find you, and Winnie here helped us do that—"

"Hello!" Winnie chimed in.

"And Jeffersonville has sort of been destroyed for the most part," Brynn continued. "All the people there are gone and now it's full of goblins—"

"And shadows too—" Makayla added.

"Yeah, and shadow things, and also we kind of think that maybe the universe is in danger of being destroyed."

Gwenllian stared at them calmly, her eyebrows raised.

"So...do you think," Brynn asked in a nervous whisper, "maybe...maybe you could help us?"

Gwenllian stared at them again for a long moment before speaking one word.

"No," she said.

And then she slammed the door.

Chapter 49

The door immediately bloomed open again, revealing Gwenllian with a small smirk on her face.

"I jest," she said. "Obviously, I jest. Please enter."

They did.

Chapter 50

The house they entered was much more normal inside than it appeared on the outside and also much larger. It was furnished with objects that would have seemed at home in suburban America and objects that might have come straight out of a medieval castle, and Makayla guessed that the ratio was about fifty-fifty. Gwenllian led them through the entryway and down several long corridors, and in the halls and rooms they passed, Makayla saw tapestries and televisions, mirrors and manuscripts, frescoes and futons.

They ended up in a large chamber with a vaulted ceiling, walls of white stucco, and dozens of skylights, each with their own sun, or moon, or night-time sky. Makayla wondered if all the light came from the same world or whether she was looking out at stars from across the multiverse.

The room was dotted with overstuffed sofas and thick, colorful woven carpets. Pots along the walls held a variety of flowering plants Makayla didn't recognize but that filled the room with a scent that was somehow both pungent and comforting.

The travelers settled themselves onto the couches, Brynn holding Hero on one, Makayla sitting nearby, and Winnie stretching out full-length on another. Gwenllian fetched food and drink for them (exotic and unfamiliar but nourishing and delicious) and once they had all sated themselves, Gwenllian turned to Brynn and examined the baby in her arms.

"Is this thy sister?" she asked.

"Yeah."

"She hath grown much. How long hath it been in thy world since last I saw thee?"

"One year."

Gwenllian waggled her eyebrows at the baby again, then turned and looked at the other faces around her.

"I do see from your visages that your matter is pressing," she said. "And although time hath less meaning here than in other places, I will not keep you from it. Come. Tell me your tale."

They told Gwenllian all that had happened—how their town had been taken over by goblins and shadows, how Conn went missing and Brynn's parents went searching for him, how they escaped and fled through the night. And they told her of the old woman who warned them against traveling to Annwfyn under any circumstances.

"Ah!" Gwenllian chuckled. "The Cailleach Bheurach meddles yet again, does she?"

"Yes," Brynn answered, "the old woman is involved again, but we're still not sure exactly who she is."

"Although we think she might be a librarian sometimes," Makayla added.

"So mainly," Brynn continued, "we need to start by getting the baby someplace safe. And after that...I guess we need to look for my parents. They went to find Conn. They might have figured out what's going on."

Gwenllian nodded sagely.

"Thou speakst sooth, this is clear," she said melodiously. "We must needs find a safe refuge for thy infant sister."

"What about here?" Makayla asked. "This place seems safe."

"Indeed, it is so," Gwenllian answered. "While I am here, it is a place of exceeding safety."

"What happens when you're not here?"

"It ceases to be a place. It is...difficult to explain."

"I told you," sang Winnie.

"And if I am to pursue thy missing family," Gwenllian said, "I must needs leave this place, and when I leave this place—"

"It's not a place anymore," Makayla said. "Right. Makes total sense. Not confusing at all."

"So, a safe refuge must be found for a coblyn youth, a coblyn baby, and a—" she turned to Makayla. "You are human, correct?"

"Yep. Still human. Quite."

"Very well. That does limit our options."

"But there are options?" Brynn asked.

"There are, indeed," Gwenllian said. "And I will find an appropriate sanctuary for you. For all of you. On that, you have my word."

"Even though you hate goblins," Brynn said, a slight edge in her voice.

"I must tell thee, little one," Gwenllian said with a soft chuckle, "my encounters with thee have changed me more than thou canst guess at."

"So you're going to stash us somewhere safe," Makayla said, "and then head out and find Brynn's family?"

"I shall do this, yes. I have said so."

"But what..." Makayla shook her head, trying to ward off the tears. "What about *my* family? What about everyone else in Jeffersonville? What about the bus drivers and the mayor and the grocery store clerks and the lady who does my mom's nails? What about *them*?"

Gwenllian paused.

"Once the coblyns have been accounted for," she said softly to Makayla, "we can essay the mystery of how an entire human city hath been replaced. Thy family will be found, if it is within my power to find them. I give thee my word. But no families can be found tonight. I can see that you are weary. You shall sleep and I shall prepare. In the morning, we depart."

Gwenllian led them to a large room with several beds. The skylights here showed nothing but starlight. As they were falling asleep, Winnie sang to them again, but this time, Makayla either couldn't understand the words or didn't remember them afterward. That night, she dreamt of a burnt land, of a journey through fire, of a blood red sky seen through a broken glass.

Chapter 51

When they arose (in what may or may not have been the next morning), the skylights above their beds now shone with the lights from a dozen different suns. They made their way back to the room where they had eaten the previous night and found Gwenllian waiting for them. She looked more familiar now, dressed in light armor, jacket and boots, a long blond braid, and her (presumably magic) dragon-pommeled sword strapped to her back. Her aviator sunglasses were perched atop her head. She fed them again and the food was just as delicious as the night before and just as unidentifiable. When the dishes had been cleared away, they prepared to depart. Gwenllian had a small satchel that she slung across her hip. Winnie strapped the Ergo over her gown and Hero snuggled up safely inside and promptly fell asleep.

"Where are we going?" Brynn asked, as she and Makayla slipped their backpacks on.

"To an island," Gwenllian answered, "in the Atlantic Ocean, back on Earth."

"How do we get there?"

"We walk out the door of my house."

"We've been outside your house," Makayla said. "There's no island there."

"The door of my house opens onto many places. Most places, to say it true. Are you ready?"

Brynn and Winnie nodded, but Makayla only clenched her jaw, already terrified by what the sight of yet another door might do to her. She turned to Brynn, whispered in a strangled voice, "I don't even want to see it," and clenched her eyes shut as tightly as she could when Gwenllian turned to open the door. Despite this, when the sound of the door hit her ears, the smell of rot and death flooded her brain and the memory of the Swallowed Hall threatened to overtake her. But just as her chest tightened and her head went fuzzy, she felt Brynn's arms wrap around her, lift her and carry her through.

When she opened her eyes again and the tendrils of fear withdrew from her senses, she saw an ocean and a small village. The smell of salt was on the air. The land around was grassy and dotted with rocks. Several flocks of sheep could be seen in the distance.

"Welcome to the Faeroe Islands," Gwenllian said. "One of the most beautiful places in this realm or any other."

"The door we need is here?" Brynn asked.

"It is, indeed."

"Down in that village?"

"Nay. Not down. Our path takes us up." She pointed behind them, to a grassy mountain with a flat summit. "Up to the top of Slættaratindur." Without another word, she turned her feet to a well-traveled path which led to the foot of the mountain. The others followed.

"Lot of climbing on this trip, B," Makayla whispered to Brynn.

"Yeah, I noticed. Next time interdimensional creeps take over our city, I'll make sure the escape route involves motorized transportation."

"Deal."

This climb was harder than their previous and took them several hours. Winnie provided drinks and light refreshments along the way, though where she provided them from, Makayla and Brynn were never able to tell. By the time they reached the summit, the girls were exhausted and sweaty. Gwenllian and Winnie, however, looked as if they weren't even winded, and Makayla hated them both for the briefest of moments. Gwenllian halted them at a moss-covered mound, a dozen yards from the mountain's highest point.

"Burial mound again this time?" Makayla said to Brynn.

"Looks like it."

"It is indeed," Gwenllian told them. "We stand at the burial place of Grímr Kamban, the first human to set foot on the Faeroe Islands."

"We won't be meeting Mr. Kamban, will we?" Brynn asked.

Makayla looked alarmed at this prospect but Gwenllian quickly reassured them. "We shall not. His sleep endures. We shall merely be using his final resting place for our departure from this realm." She pulled a slender, silver knife from her boot and inscribed a small X in the moss atop the burial mound. Then she sprinkled a pinch of acrid dust into the center of the mark she had made.

Makayla braced herself for the appearance of a doorway, for the terror she knew would flood her veins at the sight of it. She clenched her eyes shut and waited. She waited some more. After a minute of two of this, she opened one eye ever so slightly and whispered to Brynn out of the corner of her mouth.

"What's happening? Is the door here yet?"

"No. Nothing's happening. Gwenllian's just standing there."

Makayla opened her eyes the rest of the way and saw Gwenllian just standing there, a blossom of concern spreading across her face. The warrior princess leaned close to the burial mound and inhaled deeply.

"Something...something is wrong," she said as she wafted further fragrance toward her nose.

"You can tell that by sniffing a gravesite?" Makayla asked dubiously.

"If allowed," Gwenllian assured Makayla quietly, "the senses given us, those ill-understood intermediaries between body and brain, can alert us to a great many things, visible and not. Even thy human senses, should thou deign to free them, could open up a vast unseen dominion that few of this world ken."

"I'll, uh...I'll keep that in mind," Makayla said as Gwenllian returned to her investigation.

At last, the sword-bearing woman straightened, her jaw clenched and her eyes tight.

"The portal is here no longer. It hath been removed."

"Removed?" Brynn asked.

"In sooth. I thought at first that perhaps the bindings had simply decayed with time or usage. But this is not the case. The gate hath been removed and humans are not responsible."

"Okay, wait," Brynn said, her voice rising in alarm, "so the safe place you wanted to take us to, it...it's gone?"

"Nay. That realm hath not been dismantled, so far as I can discern. The doorway, however," Gwenllian said, looking with concern upon the burial mound, "is certainly taken from us."

Brynn collapsed wearily to the ground, nearly in tears. Gwenllian sat next to her and laid a surprisingly gentle arm across her shoulders.

"Do not fear. There are other options, other realms, other doorways. This is not the end of our journey."

Chapter 52

Only a few minutes after they left the burial mound behind, they found themselves walking out of a forest toward a train station surrounded by trees and wooded hills. A shiny steam engine sat on the tracks belching smoke, passenger cars trailing behind it.

There was a chill in the air and Makayla found herself shivering. She wasn't sure where they were and, for that matter, she wasn't entirely sure how they had arrived here. One minute, they had been walking along the summit of a mountain and the next, they were approaching a train station. Somewhere in between, Makayla was pretty sure Gwenllian had made some strange gestures that might have involved her sword, but the memory had already grown surprisingly hazy and trying to probe her recollection any further made her head hurt. So she left off trying to figure out how they had gotten here and tried to figure out just exactly where "here" was.

Aside from the train, the station, and the trees, there wasn't much to see, but she did notice that all the signs were in Spanish. Considering the landscape and the weather, she was guessing they were somewhere in South America, but this was mostly based on a geography class that she hadn't paid much attention to. Gwenllian was keeping a brisk pace and Brynn had to jog to pluck her by the sleeve.

"Where are we going now?"

Gwenllian pointed at the mostly empty passenger train.

"The doorway is on a train?" Brynn asked.

Gwenllian nodded and said, "Not just any train," as she gestured to a bright wooden sign.

"El Tren del Fin del Mundo," Brynn read quietly.

"The Train at the End of the World?" Makayla said archly. "That's a little on the nose, isn't it?"

Gwenllian obtained tickets for them, speaking flawless Spanish, although no money seemed to exchange hands when she did so. Moments later, they were boarding the train. The cars were surprisingly small and surprisingly comfortable.

"What now?" Makayla asked.

Gwenllian gave a nonchalant wave of her hand.

"We have boarded a train," she said. "Now we ride it."

As they settled into their seats, Makayla noticed that there were no other passengers on the train, even though there had been plenty milling around at the station, and she wondered how Gwenllian had been able to manage this.

With a clang of the bell and a billow of smoke, the train pulled away from the station and moved slowly down the track. Makayla was hoping to settle back in her seat and maybe even have a quick snooze—the hike earlier in the day had taken more out of her than she had realized—but only a few minutes after the train departed, Gwenllian urged them to their feet.

Makayla looked out the window and saw that the train was approaching a wooden bridge. Gwenllian took up position, grasping the handle of the door separating the cars. As the train pulled onto the wooden bridge, she muttered some words under her breath, sharp and melodic, and opened the door. Nothing unusual happened. Just a door opening between two train cars on a wooden bridge over a canyon. Gwenllian closed the door, muttered the same words, and pulled the door open again, with similar results. After a third try, she gave up her efforts and slammed the door closed.

"I do not understand how this hath transpired. This portal is known to almost none other than me."

Clearly discouraged, she slumped into a nearby seat, and the train car sank into silence. At the end of an hour-long ride, they disembarked at a smaller station in the middle of a forest and Gwenllian purchased empanadas for them from a vendor at a food cart.

"We didn't find the doorway, I guess," said Brynn as they sat down to eat.

"We did get to take an astonishingly beautiful train ride, though," Makayla said, trying to lighten the mood. "And eat delicious empanadas."

Brynn nodded, still chewing. "Do you have any other ideas?" she asked, turning to Gwenllian.

"I do," the woman said. "There are other doorways we can use, that can take thee to a safe location. I will find one. I have promised this."

For just a moment, Makayla thought she might have seen something in Gwenllian's eyes she never imagined she would see there: a hint of doubt.

"Just give me a minute," Gwenllian said, and took another bite of her empanada.

Chapter 53

They were standing in the middle of a rooftop garden. Once again, Makayla wasn't exactly sure how they'd arrived. She had tried to ask Gwenllian about it, but the answer involved the words 'folding space' and then a bunch of other words that might have been Welsh or archaic English and at that point, Makayla decided she didn't care anymore.

The building that stretched below them was so tall that Makayla thought they might be among the clouds. The air was thick and warm, and the sun shone brightly overhead. The roof was covered with green: neat rows of hedge, clusters of short trees, flowering vines, wide round shrubs. Where they stood it was quiet and still, but far below, they could faintly hear the noises of a bustling city.

"At least it's warm," Makayla muttered to herself.

"So where's the doorway?" Brynn asked.

Gwenllian said nothing as she moved toward the largest cluster of trees, but after only a few steps, she dropped into a defensive crouch and halted the others, bringing a finger to her lips. She cocked her head and listened to the wind.

"Wait," she said quietly. "Something's not right."

The words were barely out of her mouth when a dozen green-skinned shapes came hurtling at them from all directions. Almost instantly, the sword was in Gwenllian's hands, Brynn had shifted into her goblin form, and Winnie had unfurled her wings and carried Hero into the air, away from gnashing teeth and slashing claws.

"Run!" Gwenllian shouted to the others as her sword whirled and slashed, decapitating one of the goblins and delegging another.

"Run where?" Brynn shouted back as she kicked a goblin in the chest with such force that it flew across the rooftop and crashed with a sickening crunch into the nearest tree trunk.

"There!" Gwenllian responded, pointing with her sword to the nearest roof edge, before flipping the sword and thrusting behind her, impaling the goblin who had been about to land on her back.

Brynn punched a goblin in the face, grabbed Makayla's hand, and they ran. Gwenllian was still behind them, cutting, thrusting, leaping, already spattered with blood of several different colors.

"What do we do now?" Brynn shouted as they approached the edge of the roof.

"Jump!" Gwenllian yelled to them. "You must needs jump!" She ducked under a pair of daggers thrown by one of the larger goblins and slashed another across the chest. The first goblin reloaded and the second collapsed onto a shrub.

"You have got to be kidding me!" Makayla wheezed to Brynn, her breath spent. "I am not jumping off a building! That's insane!"

"I'm sorry," Brynn said to her, "there's no time to discuss this."

Without losing a beat, Brynn wrapped her arms around Makayla and jumped off the edge of the building.

"Whaaaaaaaaaat the hellllllllllllll, Brynn!"

The air was rushing past Makayla's ears and the ground was so far away but coming closer at an alarming rate, and it was hard to hear, to think, to see, to move. There was a sound louder than the wind, though, and Makayla craned her neck to see what it was. She saw three hissing, snarling goblins falling above them, their fingers grasping and claws outstretched, so close that she could smell their fetid breath.

"Did those...did those dudes just throw themselves off the building?" Makayla shouted. "To try and catch us?"

"I think so, yeah," Brynn answered, her goblin tail thrashing as they fell.

The pursuing goblins were near enough that sharp fingers raked at Makayla's ankle, drawing blood.

"Fall faster!" she shouted to Brynn.

"I can't! Gravity works the same for them as it does for us!" Brynn's eyes lit up. "Wait a second!"

"What?"

"Bad luck powers...I have bad luck powers!"

"I don't know what that means!"

"I've never used them before, but..." Brynn twisted her face up in concentration. "Bad luck...bad luck...bad luck for the goblins..."

Makayla felt Brynn's legs clench and saw something dark happen in Brynn's eyes. Suddenly, a largish pigeon collided with the nearest goblin, throwing it ever so slightly into a spin. It collided with an outcropping on the building and let out a yowl of pain before it collapsed onto a nearby balcony and was still. A second goblin bounced off an outthrust flagpole with a sproing that would not have been out of place in a slapstick cartoon and tumbled away screaming.

"Surprisingly effective, B."

Brynn nodded in grim satisfaction. Above them, Makayla saw that Gwenllian had thrown herself off the edge of the building as well. She dove through the air, head first, arms tight against her sides. She came aside the third goblin, raised one leg and kicked it in the ribs, causing it to collide with the building and spin away from them.

Now that the pursuing goblins were dispatched, Gwenllian shouted a few guttural words that made Makayla's guts clench and her throat tighten. Makayla saw a dark portal open far below them. Gravity would have them inside it in mere seconds.

Makayla shouted, "No!" as the fear overtook her. She was lost in the memory, back in the Swallowed Hall but also falling to what she was sure was her certain death. Through the haze of memory and terror, she saw Winnie, carrying Hero, fly into the dark portal. She felt Brynn's arms wrap around her and she clenched her eyes as tight as she could, shutting out everything: the goblins, the air whistling past her ears, the churning smell of rot and death, the memory of the dead bodies all around her.

Suddenly, they weren't falling anymore but rising. They bobbed upward and Makayla realized they weren't in the air anymore, they were in the water. She sputtered and opened her eyes.

They were near a sandy beach on a small rocky island. The saltwater was so warm they might as well have been taking a bath. Brynn released Makayla, shifted back to her human form, and together they staggered through the water and collapsed on the beach.

Winnie was already out of the water and Hero was crawling in the sand, chasing a small crab. Gwenllian joined them shortly after, threw her sword to the sand in frustration and pulled off her shirt of mail, allowing her undershirt to dry in the sun. They lay there in silence for some time, until their breathing slowed and the adrenaline faded.

"Where...where are we now?" Brynn asked, her eyes still closed, her body still prone.

"Thailand," answered Gwenllian.

"Thailand?"

"Thailand. A small islet in the Andaman Sea."

There was a long silence again as the adults soaked in the sun, allowing it to soothe their aching bodies, and as the baby turned her attention from the crab and began to dig a hole in the warm sand.

"So...that last door didn't really work out then?" Makayla said eventually.

"Indeed," Gwenllian replied. "I ken not how those foul coblyn fiends—no offense—"

"None taken," Brynn said.

"How they had the foresight to lie in wait at that particular doorway at that particular moment. It defies logic."

"But, I mean...the goblins are gone, right?" Makayla said. "You and Brynn kicked their butts. Can't we just go back and use that doorway now?"

Gwenllian shook her head.

"I fear not. Even amidst the furor of the battle, I could sense that the rooftop doorway was destroyed, selfsame as the others. The Faeroe Islands, Tierra del Fuego, and now this. One destroyed gate could be bad luck. Two could be coincidence. Three gates destroyed...three gates that could deliver thee and thy companions to safety and away from

Annwfyn? This seems less like coincidence, more like ill favor. I confess...I may be out of ideas."

"There have to be other gates we can use," Brynn insisted.

"There *are* other gates," Gwenllian agreed, "but considering this chain of failures...even were we to seek them out, I find it unlikely that we would happen upon anything other than a broken gate or an ambush or both. And now that this particular cadre of assassins hath failed, the next batch we encounter will likely be larger, fiercer, and better equipped."

"Well, what the hell are we supposed to do now?" Brynn shouted, which startled Hero, but she soon returned to digging her hole. "We can't go back to Jeffersonville. We can't go to Annwfyn. My parents are still missing. My brother is still missing. Makayla's family and the entire freaking city of Jeffersonville are still missing! I don't think staying here is an option—"

"'Tis warm and beautiful, to be sure," Gwenllian said, "but no, staying here more than an hour or two is likely unwise. We could return to my home. We would be safe there, but that would not solve any of the larger problems at hand."

"Well, I'm going to return to my first question then," Brynn said, a strident edge to her voice, "which is: what the hell are we supposed to do now?"

Makayla gulped.

"Well...what about..." She looked at Brynn. "What about California? I know you said that going there wouldn't be your first choice, but our first run of choices do *not* seem to have panned out."

"California?" Gwenllian asked. Brynn nodded. "What, pray tell, is in California?"

"There's a house," Brynn said slowly, "out in California. It's where my family and I used to live. My parents said the way they built it…they said it protected us and made us really hard to find."

"A family of coblyns was living in California? For how long?"

"I have no idea. I know they were living there for a long time before I was born. Decades? Maybe centuries? They've been pretty tight-lipped about what happened before they had kids."

"I've spent countless years on this planet searching for the Tylwyth Teg," Gwenllian said curiously, "and never once did I detect coblyns in California. The wards on this house must be strong indeed."

Brynn nodded.

"Yeah," she said. "I just…I think…I don't know if California is the best choice. I mean, if they were waiting for us on that random rooftop, they've got to be watching my old house, don't they? Whoever 'they' are…"

Gwenllian thought on this for a few moments.

"The ways may be watched," she said, "thou art correct. But as our options are rapidly being whittled down to nought, I do think that this house of thine may be our next best option."

Brynn clenched her jaw.

"Makayla?" she asked.

"I don't know, man…the only thing I know about your old house is that you and your parents said it was super-safe. If you and Gwen here—"

"Never call me Gwen."

"Got it. I know there may be trouble waiting for us there. But I think if there's safety on the other side of the trouble...I think we have to take that chance."

"Winnie?" Brynn asked.

"I want to keep you two safe," the winged woman said. "I want to keep the baby safe. Let's go somewhere safe."

Brynn looked at the others: at her friend, at her companion, at her sometime nemesis, at her sister. A small smile appeared in her eyes.

"So," she said, "I guess we're going to California."

Chapter 54

The journey to California was surprisingly uneventful. They walked into the ocean, Gwenllian gestured with her sword as she had before, and moments later, they found themselves on the outskirts of a small town. Gwenllian sniffed and scouted but said she found no sign of any lurkers lying in wait for them.

They rode in the back of a pickup truck driven by someone Winnie met in a feed shop. ("My parents would kill me if they knew that I let Hero ride in the back of a truck," Brynn groused.) The pickup took them on a long, winding road through a forest and dropped them off in a place that seemed to be the middle of nowhere but that Brynn assured them was not. She lifted open a gate that was cleverly disguised as logs lying by the side of the road, which revealed a gravel driveway that twisted and turned between the trees. After about a mile, the driveway ended at a grassy meadow ringed by a split-rail fence, in the middle of which sat an ancient red barn. Gwenllian brought them to a silent halt and poked around for a bit but still found no sign of an ambush. Brynn smiled. They had apparently arrived.

"Ta da!" Brynn said triumphantly. "No trouble at all to get here. And you were all so worried."

Makayla looked from her friend to the barn and back again. And then looked back to the barn once more.

"Um...not to be a downer, but...where's the house? You said we were coming to a house. There's no house."

"There is a house," Brynn said.

"What do you mean, there's a house? There's no house. Fence. Grass. Trees. Barn."

"There is a house. It's just sort of not actually in this dimension."

"It's not in this dimension?" Makayla asked, her brows furrowed.

"It's *sort of* not in this dimension," Brynn said.

"Sort of not? So it's not on Earth?"

"It's *sort of* not on Earth."

"Sort of?"

"Sort of not. But it sort of is."

"This house needs to make up its damn mind," Makayla grumbled.

"I wish my dad was here," Brynn said, staring wistfully at the barn. "He could explain it way better than I could."

"Well, I doubt he could do it worse," Makayla muttered.

"Unkind," Brynn responded with a frown.

"Sorry."

"I wish he was here. For that among other reasons."

"Sorry, B."

"It's okay."

"So, the house is sort of here but sort of not," Makayla said, trying to piece it all together. "If it's only sort of here, how do we get to it? I mean, it's The Safe Place, right? It's the Emerald City at the end of this crazy-ass yellow brick road that we've been skipping down, right?"

"Wait," Brynn said with wide eyes. "Does that make me Dorothy?"

"No, dude. I'm Dorothy."

"Who's Gwenllian?" Brynn asked.

"Tin Woodman."

"Winnie?"

"Scarecrow."

"Hero?"

"I don't know," Makayla shrugged. "The Cowardly Lion? She makes a lot of noise. Yawns a lot. Seems like she's trying to roar sometimes but can't quite figure out how."

"So...I'm Toto?" Brynn asked with a frown.

"Yep."

"I have many things to say about this but we should probably keep moving."

"Yeah," Makayla said, "I was just BS'ing 'cause I'm nervous."

"Okay. Let's go."

Brynn walked up to the barn and lifted a heavy, tarnished latch. She heaved the doors open. The interior of the wooden barn was long and vaulted and musty. Through the other set of doors at the far end of the barn, they saw no forest, no meadow, just rolling hills alive with grass, a gentle stream with willows growing along its banks, a sunny sky, and in the midst of it all, a tall farm house, with warm yellow paint and white shuttered windows and a low picket fence around a well-kept yard.

"House," Brynn said, her voice full of longing. "I told you so." She smiled at Makayla and Makayla smiled back.

Gwenllian, Makayla, and Winnie, still carrying Hero, joined Brynn at the barn doors. After so many misfires, so much doubt, so much uncertainty, their safe place was finally here at hand.

"Come on, let's go!" Brynn squealed, barely able to contain herself, her feet already moving toward the barn. She grabbed Makayla's hand and they ran. They were halfway through the barn when they heard Gwenllian's voice.

"Wait! Come back!"

The two girls turned, wondering what was wrong, and saw that it was everything. The entire barn around them was twisting, the boards warping and bending, the ceiling bubbling and spinning. It was as if the fabric of the barn and also reality was being torn apart, the threads shredding, the fibers tattering, and in the world beyond, it looked as though a seam ripper was slicing through the sun.

"No!" Brynn shouted.

They tried to run back toward Gwenllian and Winnie and Hero, but the wood beneath their feet was losing coherence, was no longer holding them up, was ceasing to be wood, was ceasing to be anything. They saw Winnie's wings unfurl, they saw her try to fly away, to take the baby to safety, but she didn't seem to be moving. They saw Gwenllian draw her sword, saw her swing it against an unseen threat, but the sword was ripped from her hand and was lost among the rapidly shredding threads of reality. They tried to run out of the barn, back toward their friends and away from the world collapsing around them, but the very concepts of "barn," "out," "toward," and "world" were losing all meaning. The faster they tried to run, the farther they got from their goal.

"We're not getting anywhere," Makayla shouted to Brynn. "What's happening?"

"I don't know."

The visible world was now nothing but threads and the nothingness was growing as the threads decayed and dissolved until there was little left but two fifteen-year-old girls in the midst of the void.

"Everything's collapsing!" Makayla shouted as the last shreds of reality were crumbling around them.

"Grab my hand!" Brynn screamed, extending her arm through the nothingness.

"What is going on?" Makayla screamed.

"I don't know, but I don't want to be alone. Grab my hand!"

"Screw that," Makayla said, lunging forward. "I don't want to be alone either. I'm taking more than a hand."

She grabbed Brynn around the waist and closed her eyes. Reality shrieked. Makayla felt as though her insides were shredding just like the barn did and she tried to scream but there was no sound, or maybe all there was now was sound, or maybe the scream dissolved before she could even think of its name. Chaos overwhelmed her and there was nothing for a long time, not thought, not substance, not even memory.

After what may have been hours or days or merely seconds, thought and feeling returned to Makayla's body and she felt some semblance of a world around her, although all remained dark. Her arms were still clasped tight around Brynn's waist and trembled as she released them, her muscles weak after long use, her fingers sore. She stood on her feet and tried to speak and found she could, though her voice sounded croaky and hoarse.

"We're alive?" she asked. "Brynn, are we alive? I think we're alive." She stamped her foot on the ground. "We're standing on...something. Definitely standing upright on something. Gravity seems to exist."

"Open your eyes," Brynn said, and her voice sounded shaky as well.

It was not until this moment that Makayla realized that the reason it was still dark was because her eyes were still closed. Despite this, she felt no compelling impulse to change the situation.

"Why?" she asked.

"We're...somewhere, right?" Brynn said, trying to sound breezy. "Open your eyes. Check it out."

"Why? Is it interesting? Terrifying? Is it heaven? Are we dead?"

"Open your eyes, Makayla!"

"Why? What is it?"

"I don't know! My eyes are still closed because I'm terrified!"

There was a brief pause.

"Okay," Makayla said slowly, "so both our eyes are closed."

"Yes."

"One of us should perhaps open our eyes before we get, I don't know, eaten by something."

"Okay," Brynn agreed. "You first."

"You first."

"You first."

"How about you?" Brynn insisted.

"How about nope."

"Together?"

"I guess," Makayla groaned.

"Okay," Brynn said. "Ready? One...two...three...open!"

Makayla opened her eyes but nothing seemed to change—she was still surrounded by complete darkness.

"I can't see anything," Makayla said.

"Me neither. Are we sure our eyes are open?"

"Let me check," Makayla said. She did so and then yelped in pain. "Ow!"

"What happened?"

"I poked myself in the eye, what do you think!"

"Wait a second. I think I feel something."

Makayla heard a soft metallic sound.

"I think it's a door," Brynn said.

A thin line of the brightest light Makayla could imagine appeared in the darkness. The line widened and grew into a doorway and beyond that was a dappled field with mountains in the distance. The girls looked at each other and squinted in the sudden light. Brynn gestured with a twitch of her head and Makayla nodded. Together, they walked across the threshold and into the world outside.

There were vast, rolling fields of yellow that might have been covered in wheat or daisies. An enormous forest lay in the distance, and beyond that, forked, spiring mountains, like jagged teeth against the sky. Dark lines that could be rivers or could be roads wound through the fields and ran off to the horizon. The sky was blue and the air was warm. But there were no clouds and there was no sun.

"I know where we are," Brynn said in a hushed voice. "This isn't Earth. This isn't Iceland or Argentina or California. It's Annwfyn."

"But didn't that old woman say that if we came to Annwfyn, the universe would get destroyed?" Makayla asked.

"Yep. Yep she did."

"Well, this is not good then."

"Nope."

ACT 4: OTHERWORLD

Chapter 55

Brynn and Makayla were sitting on a hill in the Land of Annwfyn, home to goblins and pwca and a host of other strange creatures. They still weren't sure exactly how they got here and they hoped they hadn't inadvertently destroyed the universe in the process. The hill they sat on was covered in rocks and moss. Behind them stood the windowless wooden shack they'd arrived in. At the bottom of the hill was a crossroads, where three roads ran off in different directions. One road ran toward a forest, one toward the foothills of the nearest mountains, and one downward into a shallow valley and a wetland beyond. There was a signpost at the crossing, but the language was not one that either of them could read.

"So...are you...are you okay?" Brynn finally asked.

Makayla tried to give a confident smile and a thumbs-up, but it ended up as more of a grimace and a flail.

"I mean...it's okay if you need to freak out for a bit," Brynn said. "Or yell. Or cry. Or whatever. I don't think there's anyone around for miles. Just us and an empty shack." Makayla did not respond. "Do you want to yell at the shack? Huh? Do you? Come on...shack-yelling, our favorite pastime. Loved by teenagers near and far, in this realm and many others."

Makayla wanted to smile but couldn't.

"Sorry," Brynn said. "Just trying to lighten the mood."

"I'll be fine, just...just give me a minute," Makayla said after a ragged sigh. "This is a lot to deal with, you know? I mean, we're not on Earth, we don't know how we got here or why and our existence in this dimension may or may not be catastrophic for everyone we know."

"And perhaps even those we don't."

"Exactly! So I just...I just need a minute."

"Is there anything I can do?" Brynn asked gently.

Makayla shook her head.

"How about your rock?" Brynn said. "Couldn't you use that?"

"My what?"

"Your rock, the little rock your doctor gave you. Where is it?"

"I don't know, Brynn! Somewhere back on Earth, probably! Maybe Iceland or Argentina or maybe in Gwenllian's crazy flower-sword house! If I had it, I would be using it, because I would absolutely like to be thinking about anything other than where we are right now!"

"Okay, right. Sorry, sorry." Brynn fumbled in her pockets. "What about this?" She offered a slim metal tube to Makayla, the laser pointer that had been given to her by the old woman in the appliance shop, so long ago, back before her first trip to Annwfyn.

"Yeah, maybe."

Makayla took the laser pointer from Brynn and wrapped her hand around it, feeling its coolness, its smoothness, its solidity.

"Does that help?" Brynn asked.

"A bit, yeah. Thanks."

They sat in silence again for a while, until Makayla had calmed down enough to ask the obvious question.

"So what do we do now?"

They decided to start by checking out the shack, whose inside was as bleak as the outside, dark, barren and musty. There was a trap door in the center of the floor, but when they opened it, there was nothing but darkness and a dank fetid smell that made them retch. The only other thing they found in the room, tossed in a corner and barely visible, was Gwenllian's dragon-pommeled sword and scabbard, which must have been thrown into this dimension alongside them. Brynn picked it up and carried it carefully out into the light.

"It's her...her sword," she said, a note of panic in her voice. "Gwenllian's sword is here. But she's with Hero. She has to protect Hero. How will she protect Hero without her sword?"

Makayla looked at her quizzically.

"Have you ever met that chick?" she said. "She will be fine. She could be naked on a rooftop during a thunderstorm with a sprained ankle and a bad case of the bends and she would still be more qualified to protect that baby than any other person in the world. Or universe, I suppose."

"Multiverse," Brynn muttered.

"Your sister is going to be fine."

"Yeah," Brynn said with a sniffle, "I suppose you're right."

She offered the sword to Makayla.

"You want to carry it?"

"I'm not carrying that thing. It looks sharp and magicky. All you."

It took them quite a while to figure it out, but eventually, they were able to strap the sword to Brynn's back, the way they had seen Gwenllian carrying it. Then they combined what few supplies they had into one backpack, which Makayla wore. The baby food and diapers were nearly gone by this point, and what little was left they dumped in the shack, figuring they could obtain more if and when they were reunited with Brynn's sister.

"So we need to get out of this place," Makayla said, once they were loaded up.

"Well, yeah. We don't want to be the cause of the universe's destruction."

"Sure. I mean, if everything gets destroyed, everything gets destroyed, but we certainly don't want it to be our fault."

"Exactly," Brynn agreed.

"So we need to get out of Annwfyn."

"Yeah."

"And...how do we do that...exactly?" Makayla asked with a frown.

"Well, when we did it before—"

"We flew on the back of a giant bug into an enormous metal anemone and snuck into a room full of ladders and climbed out through a manhole."

"Hmm. Yeah. You see any of those things lying around anywhere?"

Makayla scanned the horizon quickly.

"Nope. Fresh out of gigantic metal sea creatures and manholes," she said. "So where do we go? To get out?"

"I don't know. I mean, there's that trapdoor in there. And there's here, outside. So...I guess the first choice is in or out? Go back in and explore whatever's past the trapdoor...or stay out."

"Out," Makayla stated definitively. "Not back into the dark."

"Good," Brynn nodded. "That's a decision. So there's this whole world out here. Which way?"

"Your choice."

Brynn closed her eyes, spun, and then randomly pointed toward one of the roads at the bottom of the hill, the one toward the valley and the wetland beyond.

"That way," Brynn said. "Shall we?"

"You first."

"Together."

Chapter 56

Makayla was used to roads leading somewhere but this one did a whole lot of not doing that. It meandered through the yellow fields, twisting and turning but never seeming to get anywhere. They saw no other beings, no other animals while they walked. A few times, they thought they heard something scurrying in the brush on the side of the road, but they never caught a glimpse of whatever it was.

The road was cobbled in a light brown stone which was surprisingly easy on their feet, and it inclined slightly downward as it headed vaguely toward the valley they had seen, so the walking was relatively easy.

They crossed over several quaint wooden bridges adorned with charming figural carvings and intricate silver filigree. The streams beneath were clear and clean, and eventually their thirst compelled them to take the risk of drinking from one. To their relief, they found the water cool and refreshing and they suffered no ill effects after they drank their fill.

But they found nothing to eat and weren't even really sure how they would go about looking for food in this strange land. Hunting didn't seem to be an option with no animals around, even if either of them knew how to capture an animal, which they didn't. Plus, they didn't have a firm grasp on how the laws of nature worked here, and worried that even if they captured an animal, it might start talking to them or something, which was too horrifying to contemplate. Foraging seemed risky as well. Neither of them would have been able to identify poisonous plants back on Earth and the vegetation here was even less identifiable. Halfway through the day, they split a lonely, shriveled granola bar they found in the bottom of the backpack, which took the edge off their hunger, but only barely.

After they'd been wandering down the road for what seemed like hours, it grew dark. Night was apparently falling, which seemed strange in a world with no sun, but they were too tired from walking to worry about the mechanics of it. They found a secluded spot away from the road, under the boughs of a copse of low-hanging trees that resembled willows (if willows flowered in a kaleidoscope of hues), and decided it was as good a place as any to make camp for the night.

They were discouraged and scared and tired. They were fearful for the fate of their families and their friends and the universe at large. They had no clear destination in mind and weren't sure what dangers might lurk here at night, but they knew they needed sleep. As they bundled up piles of fallen crimson leaves to cushion their rest, Makayla's hunger made itself known.

"Was that your stomach?" Brynn asked.

Makayla shrugged.

"I could really go for a hamburger," she said softly. "Brynn? Huh? What do you think? Should we wish for a hamburger? Maybe two?"

Brynn just glared at her.

"Okay. Jeez," Makayla said. "You have these superpowers and we can't even use them."

"We can use them," Brynn said as they made themselves comfortable on their bed of leaves. "We'll probably *need* to use them. Just not that one. Not if we can help it."

Chapter 57

Despite their fears of what might lurk in the dark in this unfamiliar place, the night passed uneventfully. If there was anything out there, it did not come upon them or did not disturb them if it did. After rising, they refreshed themselves in a nearby stream and put their feet back to the road. Only an hour or two later, they came to a fork. One way led toward a pass between snow-covered mountains. Near the pass, a dark glistening tower could be seen. The other way followed a winding river and led farther down into the valley.

It took little thought for them to decide against the uphill path toward an ominous tower and to turn instead onto the road that took an easy downward slope and had access to fresh water. As the day wore on and they descended into the valley, they saw a settlement ahead and began to move more cautiously. They skirted along the edge of the road, under the overhanging trees, in case they needed to dart into the underbrush. For the first time since they'd arrived in Annwfyn, they heard birdsong and saw brightly colored winged creatures flitting among the branches.

Eventually, they left the road entirely and found a tall hill in the midst of the trees which gave them a clear vantage of the town in the distance. They saw farms with cultivated fields and fences around low wooden houses. They saw mills and markets and a couple of longer buildings that could have been schools. Most of the structures had only one or two floors, made of stone and wood with thatched roofs, but there was a larger building in a central square, entirely of stone, that must have stood six or seven stories tall.

There was a wide river flowing through the middle of the town. Men and women walked briskly through the lanes and children played in the grass. For the most part, the inhabitants were tall, with golden eyes and horse-like ears. Many had long hair falling down their back like a thick mane, and all had long tails of wiry hair.

"I met someone like this last year," Brynn said with surprise, "when I was here before. They're called pwca."

"Puh-what-now?"

"Poo. Kuh," Brynn said, drawing the syllables out. "The one I met was running a kitchen."

"Does...does that mean there might be food here?" Makayla asked with excitement. "If they have kitchens, then they cook, and if they cook, then there's food here, right? Please, Brynn, please say there's food here."

"There's got to be food. I mean, it's a whole village, right? They've got to eat something."

"And how do you think we might get some of that food? 'Cause I am more than willing to eat the food of the horse-people. If we can find a way to get some without, you know, dying."

"Well...we don't have money...so..."

"Yeah, I didn't think we were going to stroll on into a horse-person store," Makayla said. "So...we're thinking about a little end-justifies-the-means food theft then. But how do we even manage something like that?"

Brynn shrugged.

"Find some food," she said. "Take it. Don't get caught."

"All three steps sound a little dubious to me."

"Ah. But you forget. We have something they don't."

"Backpack full of nothing?" Makayla suggested. "Laser pointer? Magic sword?" Her eyes went wide. "We…we're not going to try to fight them for the food, are we, Brynn?"

"No, doofus. We have my goblin powers. Which include, in case you've forgotten, the ability to turn invisible."

"Riiiight…so *you'd* be invisible and I'd be trampled to death by angry horse-people."

"No, remember what Chwilen did last time we were here? He could make a bunch of people invisible at the same time. He's a goblin, I'm a goblin. We're about the same age, I think. So I should be able to do that too. I just have to figure out how…"

This took them the better part of an hour. Brynn had long had a good grasp on her power of disappearing and could blink her own body in and out of visibility at will. But it turned out that adding anyone else into the equation took a significantly greater amount of energy and concentration. However, after a number of false starts and a number of breaks to curse and kick a tree in frustration, she managed to disappear Makayla's hand while she was holding on to it. She then proceeded, on subsequent tries, to add limbs and then torso and then head, until both girls were as insubstantial as the wind.

Makayla held her hand up in front of her face, astonished to be looking directly through it at the village down the hill.

"This is…this is crazy, B. This may be the weirdest thing I've ever done and I once smacked a magical replica of myself in the face with a baseball bat." She held her hand up to the sunless sky. "How long do you think you can hold it for?"

Brynn released Makayla's hand and shuddered as they both flickered back to visibility.

"I don't know," she gasped, "that one really took it out of me. How long was that? Ten minutes? Fifteen?"

"Um...maybe three," Makayla said nervously, though she thought even this might be stretching it.

"Okay," Brynn said as she caught her breath. "I'll be okay. I can do it, I'm sure I can. It'll get easier, right?" She plopped down onto the grass and muttered, "I mean, it can't get much harder."

After a brief rest, they decided, for better or for worse, it was time to make their attempt. Makayla pulled her backpack on and Brynn strapped on the sword, which, although she'd only done it a few times, she could now manage with ease. Makayla smiled.

"You know, you actually look pretty cool with that sword strapped to your back."

"Yeah?"

"Yeah," Makayla said. "Brynn McAwber: Battle Goblin."

"Really?"

"Yeah."

"Maybe not."

Makayla shrugged.

"It's just...I mean, we've never really talked that much about you being...you know, being a goblin," Makayla said hesitantly. "You still look like a person."

"Most of the time."

"I still think of you as a person."

"Good. I guess," Brynn said, then added with a smile, "I also think of *you* as a person."

"Because I *am* a person."

They grinned nervously at each other.

"You ready?" Makayla asked.

"Yeah. Let's go steal some food."

Chapter 58

They took hands, Brynn squinted her eyes in concentration, and the girls shimmered out of visibility. On their hike up the hill, they had spied a walking path running parallel to the road, and it was along this path that they made their way toward the town.

They met no others on the way and, once they crossed into the village, they stuck to the less-traveled streets, skirting along the edges, giving wide berth whenever they encountered one of the residents, who towered over them with their shining golden eyes. They had only been in town for a matter of seconds before they realized that there was food all around them: vegetables and fish and breads and cheeses being sold in market stalls, being eaten at tables, being loaded into carts, being packed into jars. Their stomachs rumbled so loudly they were amazed that they weren't discovered. Everything they saw seemed edible and appetizing but all of it was either being watched or actively eaten.

They kept looking.

As they wandered cautiously through the streets of the pwca village, they passed houses and shops, a metalsmith, a dance. They saw an elderly pwca fashioning a magnificent tapestry on a loom, and a bookbinder embellishing a volume as wide as he was tall. They saw a school with dozens of small pwca sitting at carved wooden desks and a jeweler working on a pendant, setting a silvery butterfly within, which fluttered its wings as he worked. They saw a spinning wheel, where a thin pwca was spinning a dusky fiber into piles of glittering thread that sang softly to them as they passed.

On a side street, Brynn and Makayla came upon a pwca dressed more elegantly than the others they had seen, with a low collar exposing an elegant alabaster neck and slashes in the sleeves exposing smooth toned arms. As the girls clung close to the wall and allowed the pwca to pass, Brynn's head turned to follow with her eyes, and then her body turned as well, until she was walking backward as she stared. Makayla tugged her onward.

"What the hell, Brynn," she hissed.

"Dude. He was hot."

Makayla looked back at the attractive pwca, who was about to turn a corner onto another street.

"Um...he?" Makayla questioned.

"Yeah, now that you say that, I'm not so sure," Brynn said, her gaze still fixed on the pwca. "Still hot, though."

Makayla groaned.

"Come on, we've got to keep moving. You can stare at hot humanoids later."

Two streets later, behind a baker's shop, they spotted some hot hand pies cooling on a bench, along with a loaf of bread and several whole dried, salted fish.

After double-checking to make sure that no one was watching, Makayla began filling her backpack, which was difficult to do, as one of her hands needed to remain in contact with Brynn at all times to maintain her invisibility. She had to switch hands a couple times to slip off the backpack, then use her teeth to open it, and then hold it between her knees to load it up with food.

All was going smoothly until she tried to retrieve the salted fish from where they hung drying in the air. Dislodging the fish set adrift some unfamiliar spices that tickled Makayla's nose and made her eyes water. But they had an even stronger effect on Brynn. Although she could not see her, Makayla heard Brynn gasp.

"Oh, no...oh god," she said. "Makayla...I think...I think I'm going to sneeze!"

"No, no, no, no, no, hold it in, B, come on, I'm almost done."

But her protestations did no good. Brynn's hands flew to her face as she let forth a massive, phlegmy sneeze. Her concentration and her connection with Makayla now broken, both girls flickered back to visibility. They pressed themselves up against the wooden wall of the bakery and scanned quickly up and down the small street.

"Did anyone see us?" Brynn whispered.

"I don't think so," Makayla replied.

They heard a slight cough behind them, and it was only then that they realized they were standing in front of a window. They turned slowly and saw two pwca through the glass: the baker and her assistant. Makayla was still holding two fish in her hand. Brynn grabbed Makayla's arm and tried to concentrate, tried to disappear, but it was too late. The baker screamed, raising an alarm. Almost immediately, they heard responses from all across the town, shouts and cries and feet moving in their direction.

"Let's go, Makayla, we have to go!"

Makayla stuffed the fish into the backpack and zipped it up and slipped it on. She grabbed Brynn's hand and Brynn, as exhausted as she already was, managed to make both of them disappear as they ran.

They headed for the main thoroughfare, hoping to use it to get out of town as quickly as possible before they were seen by anyone else. In the central square, they saw a trio of pwca in uniforms, dark tunics with bright badges on their chests. Some kind of local police or soldiers, Makayla guessed. They were armed with short curved swords and wore strange metal goggles with multi-faceted lenses that shimmered with reflected light. One of them snapped his head around, adjusted the goggles with one hand and pointed directly at Brynn and Makayla with the other.

"Brynn!" Makayla shouted as they ran with invisible legs, away from the swords, away from the officers. "I think those dudes can see us!"

"Yeah, I got that."

"What do we do?"

"Run faster!"

So they ran and there was a whole host of pwca chasing them now. More with the goggles that apparently allowed them to spot invisible goblins. More of the soldiers with the curved swords. More normal townsfolk who were now carrying weapons too—pitchforks and rolling pins and carving knives and metal shears.

They ran out of the village. They ran away from the road. They ran between the trees and the villagers fell farther behind the deeper they got into the woods. Then they realized they weren't really running into a forest—they were running into a swamp, the wetland they had seen when they first arrived. They crossed one streamlet and then another, their feet splashing in the muddy water, but the next one was too deep for them to ford, so they turned and ran alongside it. When they came across another, even deeper, they turned again.

It didn't take too long before they realized they had no idea where they were, no idea where they had come from, no idea which direction (if any) would be a good way to go, to either find the road again, or to stay away from the pwca village.

In the end, it didn't really matter, as utter exhaustion took hold and running was no longer an option. They found a dry hillock and dug out the food they had swiped. The pies were mildly crushed but they were still warm and filled with luscious, unidentifiable fruit. They ate in silence for some time, licking the juice from their fingers when it dripped down.

"Brynn..." Makayla said in between bites, but Brynn didn't answer as she was too busy eating. "Brynn..." Makayla said again, but still received no response. "Brynn..." Makayla said again.

"What, Makayla?" Brynn said, pretending to be exasperated, but too full of delicious food to be anything but happy.

"Brynn, this may be the best pie I've ever had."

Brynn smiled.

"Yeah," she said. "Me too."

"Want another one?"

Brynn thought about it for almost a full second.

"Yes. Yes, I do."

Chapter 59

They desperately wanted a longer rest, but they heard noises moving through the swamp. With a groan, they pulled themselves to their feet, slipped on sword and pack, and headed out once more.

They kept a steady pace until whatever it was that had been closing in on them could no longer be heard. They were in the thick of the swamp now and had to move carefully to avoid the swaths of muck and the patches of brambles and the pools of dark water that were much deeper than they seemed at first glance. The swamp's odor was growing progressively fouler. Makayla pinched her nose closed and made a gagging nose to Brynn who nodded in agreement.

They spotted a cluster of trees that allowed more light through than the others and, thinking this might lead them back toward the road, they tried to make their way in that direction. But in the tangle of the swamp, every move they made toward the light seemed to require two moves away. The trees were getting darker and more gnarled and the walkable areas of land were getting fewer and farther between.

Finally, the tortuous path came to a dead end with only thick, bubbling muck in front of them. The smell was now nearly unbearable. They tried to backtrack, to find another branching they might take, but they could no longer find the path they came in on. There were no footprints behind them, no water disturbed, no branches bent. The path had simply disappeared. They were stuck on an islet of red clayey soil in the middle of a dank, foul-smelling swamp and there was nowhere left to turn.

They were just contemplating jumping in and swimming through the muck when a huge beast climbed out of the water and took up position on the next islet over. It was part fish and part cat, and the cat parts and the fish parts seemed to be fighting for dominance, leaving a vast scarred battlefield behind. The head was more cat than fish and the tail was more fish than cat but everything in between was a patchwork mixture of both.

The beast was so dark it could barely be said to have any color at all. The scales were rough and the fur was matted. The ears (one of the only parts that clearly resembled a cat with no influence of fish at all), were dark and whorled and one had a large chunk bitten out of it. Its teeth, yellow and sharp (at least the ones that weren't cracked in half or broken off entirely), were as long as Makayla's arm. The claws on its fins and paws were thick and stained. The eyes were the brightest thing about the beast, the only part of it that didn't resemble clotted blood or burnt earth. They were huge and yellow and glowed with a malevolent light.

The beast stared at them for quite a while, as if daring them to challenge it or hide or flee, but Brynn and Makayla did neither. Finally it spoke and for some reason, Makayla was not surprised by this. Its voice was low and guttural but with a hint of melody behind it, as if a bullfrog had swallowed a myna bird.

"Two little ducks as frail as milk
Ventured into my swamp.

'Tis past a week since last I ate,
I long their tails to chomp."

"I don't know what the hell that thing is," Makayla said quietly to Brynn, "but is it...is it rhyming?"

"Yeah, I was wondering that too."

"And did it say it wanted to eat us?"

"Yeah, I think so." Brynn cleared her throat and spoke loudly to the fish-cat. "We're no one important, I assure you, and we're really sorry to have disturbed this lovely, um, swamp you have here. We'll let you get back to looking for some food—"

"Which we are definitely not—" Makayla interjected.

"And we'll...just...go..."

"Leave you shall not, for I rule all
That come into this land,
My interest now is fully piqued,
Your names I do demand!"

Brynn and Makayla looked at each other, then turned slowly back to the beast.

"My name is Brynn...ifer," said Brynn. "Brynnifer. Is my name. Yes."

Makayla looked at Brynn, confused.

"We're giving fake names?" she whispered out of the side of her mouth.

"I guess," Brynn whispered back with a hint of a shrug. "I kind of panicked."

"Okay," Makayla said, then turned to the beast. "My name is Junkyard McLotterysnozzle."

"Really, Makayla?" hissed Brynn, discreetly throwing up her hands in disbelief. "Really?"

"That thing is half fish, half cat, lives in a different dimension than us and talks in bad rhyme. I doubt that discerning the plausibility level of names from Earth is one of its strengths."

Whether this was true or not, the fish-cat seemed pleased with their answers.

"Fine names you have, I do confess,
Fit for coblyn or for bug,
And as for me, you may have guessed,
I'm the only Cath Palug!"

The beast gave a grand gesture with one of its fin-paws and a haughty shake of its head. It clearly seemed to think they should know of it and was clearly waiting for Brynn or Makayla to say something in recognition.

"Our apologies, Mr. Palug," Brynn said, "but we…"

"We don't know who you are…"

"But you seem like a very nice…cat?"

"Or fish?"

"I'm sorry, we're not quite sure how to address you."

"Are you…are you a cat or a fish? Or both?"

The gigantic fish-cat shook its head in disbelief, twirled its scaly whiskers between two long claws, then spoke again.

"Cath Palug my name it be,
My story I'll unwind,
Another tale full grand as this,
Sooth, 'twould be hard to find.
    My mother true was Henwen the sow,
    In color purest white,
    Children had she numbered six,
    Different as day and night.
My brothers were a grain of wheat,

An eaglet, and a bee,
My sisters a wolf cub, a kitten, a grain
Of rye, they numbered three.
>*I was the seventh child born.*
>*After one look at me,*
>*My mother gave a sickly shriek,*
>*And cast me into the sea."*

As the beast paused for breath, Brynn and Makayla gave each other a quick glance.

"This thing is going to eat us, Brynn! How do we get out of here?"

"I don't know! I mean, it seems to really like talking about itself so maybe we should try to keep that going!"

"How do we do that?"

Brynn turned to the fish-cat and gave a sickly-sweet smile.

"That's very interesting, Mr. Palug," she said in an awed voice. "What happened next?"

The beast gave a shiver of excitement and continued.

"For years I lived beneath the sea,
I ate, I grew, I roamed,
Until a fisherman caught me
And took me to his home.
>*My hunger swelled, the fool indulged,*
>*I grew fat as can be,*
>*Then I ate the fisher, I ate his wife,*
>*And his whole family.*
And then I went into the town,
Their home was now my lair,
From shore to shore the island I plagued,
Scourge of all who lived there.

> *They came with cannons, they came with swords,*
> *With wizards, with soldiers tall,*
> *I shrugged off their spells, their soldiers I slew,*
> *More came, I fought them all.*
> *And finally, they sent a King,*
> *I killed the King as well,*
> *I devoured him along with his crown,*
> *My innards now his cell.*
> *I slew the greatest King of all,*
> *Slaughtered his closest brother,*
> *Full nine score warriors to their graves,*
> *But then they sent my mother.*
> *The only one I could not face,*
> *She stood there, did not speak,*
> *I slunk away, did not return,*
> *My ferocity now meek.*
> *From that island was Cath Palug*
> *Driven out by his mother,*
> *And now this swamp I call my home,*
> *I wait, I rest, I hunger."*

The beast, now finished with its tale, gave them a look that might have been called a smile, a sinister fishy smile. It took one step toward them, its scaly paw slipping easily through the muck. It took another step forward.

Brynn and Makayla retreated as far back as they could on the hillock of mud, but there was barely anywhere to go. Behind them, the muck burbled and popped. Makayla stuck one foot into the sludge to test an escape route. Her foot sank in up to the knee. She did not find the bottom and almost lost her shoe.

"What do we do?" she said to Brynn.

"I don't know."

The fish-cat took another two steps forward. It licked its lips. With no other options presenting themselves, Brynn reached for the sword on her back and attempted (as best she could) to imitate the fighting stance she had seen Gwenllian use. But even before the sword was drawn, the beast leapt at Brynn. Its mouth wrapped around her torso, immobilizing her. Brynn tried to scream but the fish-cat's jaws were holding her too tightly.

"Brynn!" Makayla shouted and tried to lunge for the beast, but her leg was still half stuck in the muck. By the time she removed it, the beast had scrambled away with Brynn in its mouth. It was now running through the swamp, its gait surprisingly light for a massive fish monster. Makayla tried to follow them but realized almost immediately that she would never be able to keep up.

"You're bad at poetry," she screamed at Cath Palug, in a last-ditch attempt to get the monster's attention, but it did no good.

She followed the creature's path as best she could, through brambles, through streams, through muck up to her waist, but eventually the sound of the fish-cat was lost to her. She stood there in the middle of the swamp and realized that she was on her own, in another world, with no friend, no path, no way to defend herself, and no one to guide her. She knew almost nothing about this world, didn't know where she was or where she should go. She was too tired, too full of despair, too lost, to panic or cry or even eat.

She waded through the muck to the largest piece of dry ground she could find and curled up at the base of a tree. Darkness fell. A thousand iridescent lights rose from the trees and floated in the air, swirling and eddying, cascading inward and outward and spiraling again, and Makayla wondered if they were something like fireflies. They didn't seem to be bothering her, whatever they were, and with the lights circling gently around her, Makayla closed her eyes. The exhaustion took her into the darkness and she slept.

Chapter 60

Makayla was moving through the swamp. She'd been moving all day. She had no clear idea which direction to go, but she wasn't going to let that stop her. She would search the swamp as best she could until she found Brynn or until...well, she wasn't quite sure what the "or until" would entail and she didn't want to waste her time worrying about it.

She was holding the laser pointer in her hand. Her fingers were wrapped tight around it, feeling its weight, its solidity, letting it keep her connected to the world, willing that tiny metal tube to keep her from spiraling into panic. Panic was not an option. She'd been telling herself that all day, step after weary step. Brynn was counting on her and she had no time for panic or tears or despair or any other inconvenient emotions.

After a few hours of fruitless searching, she came across a wide stream, the clearest she has seen so far in the murky swamp. She wasn't sure about the safety of the water, but she knew she needed to risk it if she was going to survive. She had several long drinks and ate the last of the stale bread.

While she was finishing up her food, a woman with translucent skin rose out of the water. Her entire body shimmered like a pond in a gentle breeze and Makayla wasn't sure where the water ended and where the woman began. She couldn't tell whether the woman was wearing water-colored clothes, or clothes made from water, or no clothes at all, and she hoped she hadn't been staring, but in the end, she decided the best course of action was to keep her eyes directly on the water woman's face.

The shimmering woman smiled and greeted Makayla, and Makayla was only about eighty percent sure that the woman was speaking English, but in any case, she understood the intent behind the words.

"Precious one, you look tired and hungry," the woman said (or words to that effect). "Come. I have solace for your body. I have comfort for your soul. Your hunger and your thirst shall be sated if you will but take my hand and join me."

The woman held out her hand, but Makayla did not move.

"Do not fear. I have a home in this river, close to the bank, with food and drink and many other comforts besides. You will be safe. Come join me in my home under the water."

Makayla found herself strangely tempted by the idea, but she shook it off.

"That sounds really nice and all," she said, "but I can't...I can't actually breathe in the water so I'm not sure if that's a great idea for me..."

"You have no cause for fear," the woman said, "I assure you. I will care for you." The woman made of water reached out a gentle hand and laid it on Makayla's cheek. The hand was surprisingly warm and surprisingly solid. "Your life is safe in my hands."

Something about this whole situation was starting to strike Makayla as decidedly unhealthy. Keeping her eyes fixed on the woman in front of her, she backed away, running directly into another woman standing behind her. The second woman placed her hands on Makayla's shoulders and held her tight. Makayla struggled but it was no use. The woman was clearly far stronger than her watery consistency would suggest.

The first woman was now striding up the bank toward her, and Makayla saw a third woman emerging from the river as well. And she wasn't sure exactly when it started, but the women made of water were singing now, and Makayla knew for sure that this time their words were not in English but, once again, their meaning was clear.

Their song captivated her, entranced her, made her want to spin and flutter across the floor, but most of all, it parched her. She thirsted as she had never thirsted before and her desire for a drink, a single drink of anything, was growing and growing until it was enough to drive her mad. The only thing she wanted in this entire world, or any world for that matter, was to join the translucent women in their river and drink and drink and drink, drink her fill, quench her unquenchable thirst.

Their song was stronger now and where before it had captivated, it now insisted, and where it had entranced, it now compelled. The women were beckoning her, and Makayla felt the hands release her, and she found herself walking toward the water and then her feet were in the water and then she was in the river up to her knees. She could see their home far beneath the water and the woman was right, she saw food and drink there and she knew that if she went there, she could sleep, she was so tired, she could sleep there, sleep for days, sleep forever.

Makayla slipped off her backpack to throw it aside—she knew she wouldn't need it where she was going—but the feel of it in her hands reminded her of where she'd been and why she was here. Through the song's hazy fog, she realized that if she went with these women, if she slept in their home, Brynn would be left on her own in the clutches of the horrifying fish-cat. The memory of Brynn's face and the memory of the horrifying monster that had her friend in its clutches shook her from her the song's power and she clutched the strap of the backpack in her hands, clutched it so hard it hurt.

She saw the three women around her still singing, still beckoning her into the water toward their home, and she did the first thing that came into her mind. She swung the backpack through the air as hard as she could. It connected with the face of one of the women, and although there wasn't much in the backpack, just some dried fish and some clothes, it was enough to knock the watery woman off-balance.

The woman stumbled and the song was broken and Makayla's head began to clear. She swung the backpack again, harder this time, but it did not connect. The three women circled her. They were snarling and they were no longer beautiful. Their watery fingers grasped at her, threatening to take her to their lair by force. Makayla spun and swung and tried to run but slipped on the slick earth. She was on the ground now and one of the women had hold of her ankle. Makayla kicked, swung the backpack again, and she was free.

She scrambled to her feet and spun the backpack in a wide arc that connected with another of the women, throwing her off balance. The woman fell to the ground but landed nimbly, balanced on pointed toes and tensed fingertips. But this was enough of a window for Makayla to make a break for it and that's just what she did.

She ran away from the river as fast as she could. She felt fingers grasping at her as she escaped, but none were able to grab hold. The women did not follow, and Makayla wondered if they could travel farther into the swamp or if they were tied to the water that held their home. In the end it didn't really matter, she decided. She was away and had somehow escaped with no wounds other than the blow to her pride from the discovery that it had been so easy to pull her from her task when her friend needed her.

She wandered again, searching for any sign of Cath Palug, but her energy quickly flagged and, sensing no sign of the watery women, she rested beneath a tall tree with spiky yellow leaves. She clasped her knees against her chest and let her head fall against them. She was exhausted and frustrated. There was no clear path ahead and unknown dangers seemed to lurk around every bend. Her eyes were still closed when a chirpy voice spoke from somewhere nearby.

"Tough day?" the voice asked.

Makayla looked up and saw a very tiny woman sitting on a nearby branch. She had skin the color of burnt honey, hair the color of autumn leaves, and iridescent wings springing from her back. She was about as tall as a housecat, Makayla guessed, and could have sat comfortably on her shoulder. As the woman on the branch didn't seem to present any immediate danger, and with exhaustion running rampant through her limbs, Makayla decided that conversation seemed like a sensible course of action.

"You could say that," she said. "I ran into these three...well, they were like women but they were kind of made of water. They tried to get me to go to their underwater house, and I don't know, I think it was the song they were singing or something, but I...I almost went with them..."

The small woman nodded knowingly and whistled.

"Wow! You got off lucky," she said. "Those three are jerks. I think living in the swamplands for so long has addled their brains. I mean, all the gwragedd are a bit wacky, but most of them aren't really dangerous, they just like to mess with humans. You are a human, right?"

"I am, yeah," Makayla said cautiously.

"Yeah, the gwragedd kind of have a thing for humans. But I would have thought that even the ones in the swamp would leave you alone. I mean, you're just a kid! You are just a kid, right?"

"Yes, I am."

"Sorry, I'm not super-good with humans, you're all just so big and clunky."

"What...what would they have done if I went with them?" Makayla asked.

"Oh, they would have eaten you."

"Seriously?"

"Yeah, it's a thing," the tiny woman said with a tiny shrug. "For those three especially. They're still talking about this one human who wandered into the swamp a couple hundred years ago. They ate him, all the edible parts, made jewelry from the rest. And then spent *decades* bragging about it. Seriously, they would not shut up about it."

"What the hell," Makayla said, sitting up, her exhaustion now vanished. "This is literally the second time I've almost been eaten in the last couple days!"

"Who else did you run into?"

"Some big half-fish half-cat thing. It stole my best friend. I'm trying to find her."

"Cath Palug? Holy crackers, that thing is the worst. Did it...did it make you listen to its whole story?"

"It did!"

"Oh, just the worst," the little woman said, shaking her head.

"It was!"

"And it's so proud of it, that's the sad thing."

"Is it true?" Makayla asked.

"Its story? I doubt it."

"Do you know where it is?"

"Cath Palug?"

"Yeah. It's got my friend and I need...I need to find her."

"Oh," the woman said with a frown, "I hate to be the one to tell you this, but it...it probably ate her already. And even if it didn't...well, it's only a matter of time. If you try to find her, it'll just end up with two meals instead of one. That thing's a dope, but it's a powerful dope."

"I have to, though," Makayla said quietly. "I have to."

"Are you sure?"

"Yeah. She'd do the same for me. She already has, in fact. She saved me. Rescued me from...from the worst place imaginable. And even if she hadn't done that...she's still my friend, you know? And she's also the only person in this entire world who hasn't tried to eat me or kill me. Present company excepted. So, yeah. I'm sure."

The tiny woman gave a sad smile.

"Well...I think this is a terrible idea," she said, "just so we're clear on that. But if you really want to find the lair of Cath Palug—"

"I do."

"Then come on."

The tiny woman's wings fluttered and she took off between two shrubs. Makayla followed, and ten minutes later, they were standing outside a large ring of thick, twisted, ominous trees.

"This is it," the woman said quietly, fluttering in the air. "Its lair."

Makayla sighed nervously as she peered between the trees.

"I can't go with you," the woman said.

"I know. I wouldn't ask you to."

"But...take this."

She pulled out a small nut, about the size of Makayla's fingernail, and handed it to her.

"What do I do with it?" Makayla asked, holding it carefully.

The small woman smiled.

"You'll know," she said. "When the time comes, you'll know."

She flew away but turned around just before Makayla lost sight of her.

"I'm Seren."

"Makayla."

"Good luck, Makayla."

And she fluttered off between the trees.

Chapter 61

Makayla stepped between the trunks of the blackened trees and into Cath Palug's lair. Inside, she found a swath of mucky ground that might have been fifty yards across, surrounded by gnarled, ancient trees with bare branches and cracked trunks. Littered across the ground were stumps torn from the earth and jagged limbs torn from the trees, alongside skeletons of creatures long dead, their bones bleached white by the sun and stained green by the swamp. The trees that ringed the circle intertwined overhead, allowing little light to penetrate from above. The air was dank and dim. There was no sign of Cath Palug, but the foul smell that accompanied it still lingered, and Makayla guessed that this meant it was close. The whole place made her feel ill.

It took her a few seconds to spot Brynn, who was pinned to an algae-covered stump by thick strands of brambles. Her clothes were torn and covered in blood. Her eyes were closed. She wasn't moving. Makayla couldn't tell if she was alive or not. She ran to her and shook her gently. A low moan escaped from Brynn's throat and her eyes fluttered. A wave of relief washed over Makayla. She tried to free Brynn, but the brambles were too thick, the thorns too sharp. Within seconds, Makayla's hands were a mass of blood. She stood up, wondering if she could pull the sword from Brynn's back to hack the restraints apart, but before she could do it, she heard a noise behind her, a low chuckle as the massive beast re-entered its lair.

"Well, look, the other duck returns
To my abode so humble,
My dinner's now fit for a king,
To quell my stomach's grumble!"

Makayla turned to face the monster. A wide grin was plastered on its face, revealing the cracked and jagged teeth within. Its eyes glinted with hunger.

"You can't have my friend!" Makayla shouted.

"O pish, O posh, I shall have her,
And then I'll have you too!
I'll strip the flesh from off your bones
And eat little duckie stew."

A quiet fury built within Makayla. She was just one girl standing in the middle of a swamp on another world, facing off against the most dangerous monster she could imagine. But if there was anything, anything at all, that she could do to save her best friend, she'd do it. She moved slowly away from Brynn, trying to draw the beast's attention.

"I'll say it again," she shouted. "Your poetry is bad and you can't have my friend!"

This time, Cath Palug just growled. It licked its lips, shifting its weight from one foreleg to the other as if waiting for the right moment to pounce. Makayla slipped her backpack off and threw it to the ground. It had been heavy enough to knock one of those water women off balance, but she knew it wouldn't be any use against something as big as the monstrous fish-cat.

The beast let loose a mighty roar that nearly deafened her and the stench of it made her gag. She felt quickly in her pockets, wondering if she had anything that might help defeat a monster that was likely to devour her at any moment. There wasn't much: loose change, lip balm, house keys, laser pointer, and the small nut that Seren had given her.

"I can't believe I didn't think of this before," she said quietly to herself as she carefully pulled the tiny nut from her pocket. She held it up to her eye between thumb and forefinger. "She said I'd know. When the times comes, she said I'd know." She looked at the beast, growling, gnashing its teeth, pawing at the ground. "This has to be the time, right?" She grinned and held the nut aloft. "Hey fish-cat!" she shouted. "Try this on for size!" It was the coolest line she could think of.

Cath Palug looked at her curiously as Makayla wound up and threw the nut as hard as she could. She watched breathlessly, wondering what kind of magic would unfold, wondering what kind of spectacle she was in store for, whether it would simply kill the monster, or transform it, or send it into a deep sleep, or maybe even cleanse the entire swamp of darkness and evil.

The nut flew through the air in a high arc. It glinted in a shaft of sunlight that broke through the thick branches above. It hit Cath Palug, bounced off, and landed on the damp ground with a barely audible plop. Makayla waited but nothing else happened.

"God freaking cryptic magical bullcrap!" she shouted.

"What the hell was that, Makayla?" Brynn asked groggily, apparently having just come to.

"I don't know!" Makayla responded, too furious at the abject failure of the purportedly magical nut to find any joy at the awakening of her friend. "I met this little tiny winged woman and she gave me this magical nut and she said I'd know when to use it, but it didn't...it didn't freaking do *anything*!"

"I can see that," Brynn said, but Makayla had no time to respond.

The gigantic fish-cat reared back and sprang, its mouth open wide, ready to devour her. Makayla dived aside and barely avoided the attack. Scrambling back to her feet, she reached into her pockets again and pulled out the first thing her fingers landed on: the laser pointer.

"Wait a second," she gasped, a desperate thought coming to her. "Well, it's worth a shot." She held the laser pointer out in front of her.

"What are you doing?" Brynn shouted hoarsely.

"I don't know!" Makayla answered. "I mean, this thing's a cat. Sort of. This is a laser pointer. Cats like laser pointers, right?" She turned to Cath Palug and shouted, "Kitty kitty! Hey there, kitty kitty. Look at this!"

She pressed the button on the side of the laser pointer and a massive fireball erupted forth. It hit Cath Palug who was instantly reduced to ash.

"Well, that was...unexpected," Brynn said after a long silence, as cinders from the disintegrated monster fell softly to the ground.

"That was a fireball," Makayla said in an awed voice.

"I know."

"A fireball just came out of this thing!" Makayla said, holding the laser pointer carefully in front of her.

"I saw."

"You've been playing with this thing for like a year. Has that ever happened before?"

"Not to me."

"We should be careful with this thing," Makayla said.

"Yeah."

Makayla immediately pressed the button again, but no fireball came forth.

"Man…" she said, disappointed.

"How about you leave that thing alone and get me out of here," Brynn said.

"Right."

Makayla gently pulled the sword from the scabbard that was still buckled to Brynn's back. Once she had the sword in hand, it took her only a few seconds to slice through the brambles and then Brynn was free. She was heavily wounded, but she said that she could walk.

"Just give me a second," Brynn said. She closed her eyes, concentrated, and her body shimmered and changed, pale skin shifting to green, slender ears shifting to long and pointed. Fingers and toes lengthened. A tail sprouted and grew. Eyes turned small and bright. She breathed a sigh of relief. "That feels better. I heal way faster in this form," she said, which was clearly true, as her bleeding was slowing even as Makayla watched. "Let's get out of here, yeah?"

"Yeah."

Makayla slipped her backpack on and Brynn slid the sword back into the scabbard. They were just about to leave the lair when Makayla remembered the nut she had thrown. She retrieved it from where it had fallen to the ground and slipped it in her pocket.

"Really?" Brynn asked.

"Well…maybe it *is* magic…maybe I just didn't choose the right time to use it."

They slipped out between two of the blackened tree trunks and then they were in the midst of the swamp once again.

"What now?" Makayla asked.

"What now is we get the hell out of this swamp and never come back."

"Yeah. This place sucks."

Chapter 62

Whether it was their newfound determination to escape this place before anything else tried to kill and/or eat them, or maybe just sheer luck, it was unclear, but it took them only a few hours to find their way out of the swamp. They emerged, bedraggled and blinking in the brighter light, onto a different section of the road than they had traveled before.

The pwca village was nowhere nearby. They saw rambling fields of yellow grain and a nearby forest, full of tall trees, sharp points against the sky with richly colored leaves in reds and browns. Far in the distance, they saw the jagged mountains and the dark, sparkling tower.

As they were standing in the road, trying to decide on their next course of action, a light drizzling rain started to fall. It was not cold, but once their clothes were soaked through, they could not stop shivering. A nearby outcropping of rock seemed as if it might offer some shelter. As night began to fall, they collapsed beneath it, exhausted and damp and bloody, and were asleep almost instantly.

The rain did not let up until morning. When they awoke, cold and haggard, they found that all they had left in the backpack was the dried fish, which they forced themselves to eat, despite the foul taste. They argued (something they rarely did) over which way they should go next but couldn't come to a decision. They were both in ill tempers, angry at the world they found themselves in, at the weather, at each other.

"What the hell are we going to do, Brynn?" Makayla grumbled, throwing the remains of her fish into the grass. "We have no freaking clue what we're doing. We have made precisely zero headway in getting out of here, in finding our families, in figuring out what the hell is going on. We did, however, make significant progress in almost getting eaten!" She held up her fingers. "Twice! This is insane. This entire situation is absolutely insane. All I want is just any...any tiny minuscule scrap of information about what is going on! Just something. Anything. Any kind of hint at what our next step should be!" She slumped to the ground. "I wish...I just wish we knew where we needed to go, that's all."

Immediately, Brynn's body began to glow and she rose into the air.

"Damn it, Makayla! What the hell!"

"Oh, crap. I guess that was a pretty big favor I did you yesterday when I saved you from the giant fish-cat monster and then just now, I said...oh no, I used the 'W' word!"

"You can't do that!"

"I know, I'm sorry!"

Light filled Brynn's body and poured out of her mouth, her eyes, her fingertips as she floated in the air. Her body went rigid and her right arm stuck straight out, pointing directly at the tower near the mountains. She tried to pull her right arm down with her left, but it would not move. She yanked and yanked, but the arm stayed resolutely still, thrust out stiffly toward the horizon. Eventually, Brynn gave in and waited. After several minutes, the light slowly left her body and she descended to the ground.

Makayla looked regretfully at Brynn, who was clearly shaken and exhausted.

"I'm sorry, B."

Brynn shook her head.

"It's okay," she said. "I—"

She tried to take a step toward Makayla but her feet seemed unwilling to move. She tried again, straining against whatever force was keeping her back.

"What are you doing?" Makayla asked.

"I'm trying to come over to you," Brynn said, her feet flailing desperately, "so I can...unnh...talk to you or maybe even...urrrgh...get a hug." She was pushing against the unknown force with each syllable. "But... my... feet... won't... move... in... that... di... rec... tion."

She gave up and let out a brief scream, punching the air in frustration. She backed up a few steps, then tried to run toward Makayla, but the unseen force stopped her short and twisted her around until she was facing away from Makayla, toward the road that led off to the mountains in the distance. She crouched down and jumped, but her body twisted in midair until she was facing away from Makayla again, and her leap took her several feet in the opposite direction.

Brynn gritted her teeth. She tried to take a step toward the swamp but her foot resisted her. She tried to take a step toward the forest but couldn't move. She tried to take a step toward Makayla and her foot was again held in place by the mysterious force. She turned and took a tentative step toward the mountains and then another. Whatever power was compelling her movements seemed to have no problem with her traveling in that direction.

"What the hell!" Brynn shouted.

"What's going on?"

"You made that stupid wish that we would know where we needed to go and now my body won't do anything except move us toward that!"

Brynn pointed to the horizon.

"You mean that big scary tower we've been avoiding?" Makayla asked.

"Yeah!"

"That's where we need to go?"

"Yeah."

"You're sure?"

"Yes!" Brynn snapped. "You saved us from the giant fish-cat monster and then you wished and my stupid powers kicked in and I floated in the air and now my feet won't move in any other direction."

"Seriously?"

"Yes! Watch!"

Brynn tried to walk toward the forest. Her body convulsed and twisted, almost inhumanly, until she was walking toward the tower. She tried to walk toward the swamp. Her head snapped around like a puppet, and then her torso, and then her legs, until she was once again walking toward the dark, scintillating tower.

She tried to change forms—into a goblin, into a raven—but no sooner had her body started to shimmer and shift than the unseen force squished her back into her human shape. She tried to disappear and wasn't even able to achieve vague transparency. Walking down the road in her human form toward the tower seemed to be the only thing her body would allow her to do.

"Well, I guess we don't have much choice then."

"No, Makayla, we don't!"

"I'm sorry, dude. I don't really get how your powers work. I didn't mean to do...whatever is happening right now."

Brynn sighed.

"I know," she said. "I know you didn't. This is just a...a really, really uncomfortable feeling."

"I mean...at least we know where we're going now, right?"

"Yeah. At least there's that."

Chapter 63

As there seemed to be only one path forward for them now, they took it. The road was smooth and clean, paved with the same light brown stone they had seen before. This was good, since whenever they wanted to rest, they had to sit down on the road itself. Whatever force was controlling Brynn's body allowed her to move forward on the road and nowhere else. Even an attempt at a slight detour to sit on a nearby stump contorted her body like a mannequin and forced her back onto the road.

After a few hours of walking, their path took them into a forest, and Makayla spotted a figure she recognized sitting on a curved branch, a tiny figure with iridescent wings and skin the color of burnt honey.

"Hey, human," the tiny woman said to Makayla. "Where you going?"

"Oh...hey, Seren," Makayla answered. "What are you doing here?"

"Getting some work done. I have a job, you know. I don't just hang around in swamps all day."

"You know her?" Brynn asked Makayla.

"Yeah, we met in the swamp."

"Your best friend is a coblyn?" Seren asked Makayla.

Makayla nodded.

"That's craaazy," the tiny woman said. "You...you know what coblyns do to humans, right?"

Makayla raised her eyebrows and nodded again.

"Yeah, she does," Brynn said, calmly but forcefully. "Not me, though. Not my family."

"Okay. Whatever."

"I'm Brynn, by the way. The coblyn."

"Seren. The ellyll. Where you going now?"

"There," Makayla said, pointing to the tower on the horizon. "I guess."

Seren whistled.

"Damn. Taking on Cath Palug and now trying to get into Caer Wydr. You two are either monumentally foolhardy or a little short in the marble department."

"Maybe both," Brynn suggested.

"Maybe!" said Seren brightly. "Nice job annihilating Cath Palug, by the way."

"Thanks," Makayla said. "Although that little nut of yours was no help."

Seren shrugged.

"They can't all be winners." She looked at the shadows falling on the road. "Whoa! I'm late! See you two later." Then she flew off before they could say another word.

"So that tower...is called..."

"Caer Wydr," Brynn supplied.

"Do we have any idea what that means?"

"Nope."

"Oh man, I don't like that name at all," Makayla said nervously.

"Maybe the tower doesn't like your name either."

"You're a dork."

Chapter 64

The tower wasn't as far away as they had first thought and, by nightfall, they were standing at its base, nestled in the foothills of a jagged mountain range. The road stopped a few feet from the tower wall and all around grew a soft fragrant grass dotted with small bright flowers that had yellow stems and azure petals. They could see snow-frosted trees on the mountainsides, but here, the air was warm and a soft breeze blew. A small stream flowed nearby.

The walls of the tower were as smooth as glass and, upon closer examination, appeared to actually be made of glass, just a glass so dark that nothing could be seen through it. The tower was circular and wide, perhaps twenty or thirty yards across, and so tall that the top could not be seen from where they stood.

There was no door. They searched all around the base of the tower, but there were no cracks in the glass, no slight slivers that might indicate the presence of an unseen entrance. The entire tower was smooth and impenetrable and obscure. They saw one window high above, but there was no way to reach it. The glass walls would be impossible to climb.

They had found their goal. They had reached the tower. But they had no idea how to enter it.

"You know what we could really use right now?" Brynn asked, staring at the window far above them.

"What?"

"Someone with wings."

"Yeah," said Makayla. "And the weird thing is that we actually know several people with wings now."

"We seem to have lost them, though."

"Yeah. Any chance your wings are working again?"

With a brief burst of concentration, Brynn tried to bring out her raven form, but whatever force had compelled her on the journey to the tower seemed to still be fully in control. She shook her head and sighed.

Night was falling and they decided there was nothing else they could do in the dark. They ate the last of the fish, which was also the last of their food, and slept at the foot of the tower, hoping a solution might present itself in the morning. While they slept, Makayla dreamt the most vivid dream she'd had since arriving in this strange land.

In her dream, she climbed down a spider's web into a burnt and desiccated garden, and the sight of all the death around her made her weep. As she cried in the garden, she found that the garden was dead no longer. There were tendrils climbing up her legs, grasping at her, spreading onto her arms and up to her neck and they clutched her so tightly that she couldn't breathe. But then the green tendrils were carrying her and lowering her to the ground and now the garden was alive all around her. She rested on the bed of green that flowed beneath her and it soothed her mind and comforted her body. Then she rolled over and the garden, lying next to her, opened its eyes and smiled at her, and she was just about to ask the garden what she should do next when she woke up.

Chapter 65

In the morning, nothing had changed. The tower was still impenetrable and there was still no door. They stared up at the window, high above, as it seemed to be the only way to get inside.

"I have a...I have an idea," Makayla said. "I had this weird dream last night. I'm sure it won't work but I guess...I guess we've got to try something, right?"

She pulled the small nut from her pocket, the one Seren had given her outside of Cath Palug's lair. She pushed the nut gently into the ground beside the tower and covered it with earth. The only other thing she needed was tears.

She'd been working so hard for so long to keep the terror at bay, to fend off the memories of the Swallowed Hall, the sights and sounds of the dead bodies and the decaying wood and the pools of blood and the rotting flesh. But here with Brynn, with no one else around, it was as safe a place as any in this strange world to let her guard down. If she had to. If it might help her find her family.

She closed her eyes. She took a deep breath. And she let it in. She let in the terror and she let in the memories and she let in the fear. The smell consumed her brain, the stench of rot and death, and the memory took hold and she felt the tears come and she let them fall upon the ground beneath.

Her tears watered the earth where she had planted the nut. The terror washed through her. For long minutes, nothing happened, then slowly, so slowly that she could barely tell what was happening, a thin crack appeared in the earth, and then another. A tiny green sprout, no thicker than a hair, pushed out of the crack. An hour later, the plant was as tall as her thumb. By mid-afternoon, it was up to her waist.

The plant grew and lengthened, becoming a vine that twisted around itself as it climbed, clinging to the glass walls of the tower. The base of the vine grew wider and wider as the tendrils at its tips grew ever upward. Makayla and Brynn sat and watched as there didn't seem to be anything better to do. It grew a few inches an hour. Quickly enough to notice, but still very slowly compared to the height of the tower.

As the shadows began to lengthen, a few buds appeared on the vines, and just as night fell, three of the buds flowered, opening with large petals of deep red streaked with yellow and white.

"I feel like Jack didn't have to actually sit around and watch his beanstalk grow," Makayla said as they prepared to bed down for the night.

"Maybe the action was compressed for dramatic effect."

"Yeah, maybe."

"I mean, when you think about it, it is moving pretty fast."

"Yeah. You never know. Maybe it'll be up to the window by morning."

Chapter 66

It took a week. They stayed by the tower of glass and the plant continued to grow at the same pace, a few inches an hour. As they remained, the force that had compelled Brynn's feet to move toward the tower dissipated. Eventually, she could change forms again and move freely, but they stayed by the tower anyway. No other creatures approached, and they never saw any in the distance, so they felt safe. Every morning, the flowers on the plant grew fruit that was delicious and filling, so they were no longer hungry.

After seven days, when they awoke, the flowering ivy growing up the tower of glass reached all the way to the window far above. They had discovered several days earlier that the flowers were much sturdier than they appeared and were strong enough to hold their weight. They plucked as much of the fruit as they could carry and loaded it into the backpack.

They climbed the ladder of flowers, holding tightly to the petals of red and white. They climbed until they reached the window that had barely been visible from the ground below. There were no bars on the window and no shutters, so they climbed through into a room with glass walls and a glass floor and a wooden door on the far wall. A hanging lantern was aflame, and a wooden chair and a basin of water sat in a corner. Other than that, the room was empty.

Brynn and Makayla stood there, catching their breath after their long climb. They were inside Caer Wydr. They had entered the tower of glass.

Chapter 67

They lifted the door's latch and slipped out into the tower. They saw a circular room with three other doors, all standing open, and a spiral staircase in the center. Through the other doorways, they found rooms nearly identical to the one they had arrived in, albeit without windows. Each room was lit by a single lantern that burned with a cold blue flame and had no visible source of fuel. The entire tower was eerily silent.

The spiral staircase was made of the same dark glass as the rest of the tower and extended upward and downward as far as they could see. They listened carefully but heard no sounds in either direction. Brynn gave a questioning look to Makayla, who only shook her head. They hadn't discussed it but had both come to the same conclusion that here, in the tower of glass, silence was the best option. Brynn squinted her eyes shut and concentrated, cocking her head slowly from side to side as she tried to make a decision. Finally, she opened her eyes and shrugged, then pointed up. It seemed as good a direction as any, so Makayla nodded and they began to climb.

The spiral staircase went on and on. Occasionally, they would come to a landing and a circular room with four doors and the now-ubiquitous blue-flamed lanterns. On each landing, the doors stood open to rooms just like the ones they had already seen. They found nothing alive: no humans, no creatures, no animals, not even a spiderweb. There was nothing to hear but their own footfalls, and they dared not speak for fear of alerting whatever unseen beings they felt must reside somewhere within.

After they passed a dozen or so identical circular landings with the identically open doors, they finally found one that was different. Brynn raised her finger to her lips and gestured to Makayla, pointing at the single closed door. They padded softly over to the door and pressed their ears to it. For the first time since they entered the tower, they heard a sound. The noise they heard was low and metallic. It sounded like a raspy whisper heard through static or like wind through a metal fence.

Brynn pointed at the door handle and raised her eyebrows questioningly. Makayla nodded. Brynn lifted the handle as quietly as she could and eased open the door. Within, they saw a room full of shadows. The shadows were impossibly tall, with thin, grasping hands and cloaks floating behind them in a wind that wasn't blowing. They were gathered around a heavy wooden table covered in glowing runes.

Brynn and Makayla had only a sliver of a second to take in this sight before the shadows reacted. Their heads snapped around and their ghostly mouths opened wide and they screamed. The scream filled Makayla's head with static and clouded her thoughts and made stars dance in front of her eyes and made her breath falter.

Brynn grabbed Makayla's hand and pulled her flat against the wall. Makayla felt the slightest of shivers pass between them and she knew they had disappeared. The girls didn't move, didn't blink, didn't breathe as the mass of shadows rushed from the room out onto the landing.

One of the shadows was inches from Makayla's face. She felt terror rising inside her and felt a scream rising in her throat. Her heart was beating so hard she was amazed it couldn't be heard, but the shadows clearly couldn't find the two girls pinned silently up against the cold glass wall. They floated all around the landing, scanning in every direction, peering through the doorways, looking up and down the staircase. After a few minutes, they gave up their search, drifted back into the room, and slammed the door behind them.

Brynn and Makayla slunk to the stairway as quickly as they could and climbed upward as quietly as they could, still hand in hand, invisible to all outside eyes. When they arrived at the next landing and saw that it was empty, they finally let themselves rest, though their hearts were still pounding and their hands still shook. They slumped against the glass wall and let the panic fade. Makayla leaned her head close to Brynn's and whispered.

"I guess the shadows can't see us when we're invisible?"

"Guess not."

"That noise we heard when we were listening outside the door...was that the shadows talking?"

"I think so," Brynn said.

"I don't like the idea that those things are communicating with each other."

"Yeah. Me neither."

After resting for a few minutes, they kept climbing, their task more pressing now that they knew there were hostile beings within the tower. They passed dozens of landings. Some held shadows and some did not, but other than this, the landings remained identical to those they had passed below. They held hands and disappeared as they approached each new set of rooms, and in so doing, passed by all of the shadows in safety.

Finally, after several hours of climbing, and after several long rest stops at empty landings (where they refreshed themselves with the fruit they had plucked from the ivy they had climbed), they reached the top of the stairway. After checking to make sure there weren't any shadows around, they released hands and their bodies became visible once more. Circular windows ringed the room and they saw that they were now above the clouds. The landing here was larger than the others and there was only one door, wooden and dark, with a barred window set high. Brynn disappeared, stood on tiptoes and peered through the window, then pulled back.

"There's a bunch of shadows in there," she said to Makayla. "More than we've seen so far. Like, a bunch a bunch."

"Okay, so there's a bunch of shadows, not great," Makayla said. "What else?"

Brynn looked again, but when she pulled back this time, her concentration faltered and she slipped back into visibility. Her face was white and her eyes were wide.

"What is it? Brynn, who else is in there?"

Brynn turned to Makayla. Her voice shook as she answered.

"My parents."

Chapter 68

They sat in silence for several minutes, disbelief awash across their faces.

"What do we do?" Makayla asked weakly.

"I'm not sure we have a choice. They're in there, we're out here. Opening the door seems to be our only option."

"I know that, Brynn. I mean, what do we do *after* we open the door?"

"I don't know. Improvise?"

"That's a terrible plan!" Makayla hissed. "Haven't you ever seen a movie? Improvising an attack against a powerful monster or sorcerer or alien is always a terrible plan!"

"Okay. What's your idea?"

Makayla thought about it for several seconds, then scowled.

"Fine. We'll improvise."

Brynn drew the sword from her back and Makayla slipped off the backpack and pulled out the laser pointer.

"Okay," Makayla said, bouncing on the balls of her feet. "Let's count down from ten. On seven, we'll clear our minds. On three, we'll get into fighting stances. On zero, we'll open the door. Ready? Ten!"

"You, clearly, have watched too *many* movies," Brynn said as she pulled open the door.

Instantly, the shadows within began to shriek, and Makayla's head once again filled with static and with noise. At least a dozen shadows flew from the room in fury. One flew directly at Makayla and then passed inside her and the world went dark. Her stomach heaved and her head filled with pressure and ice. Then the shadow came out the other side of her body and she nearly collapsed to the ground, shivering and raw. Gritting her teeth, she gathered her strength and held her arm straight out, aiming the laser pointer at the shadow. She pressed the button. The light passed through the shadow and a small red dot appeared on the far wall.

"Stupid inconsistent magic," she muttered.

Meanwhile, Brynn raised the dragon-pommeled sword above her head and swung it at the first shadow that appeared before her. To her clear surprise, the sword sliced it in half with a sound like sandpaper being ripped in half, amplified through a corroded speaker. The shadow glowed brightly where it had been severed then dissipated into oily nothingness. Now that Brynn had put the sword into action, it seemed to move with a mind all its own. It swung and swung and swung again, each time slicing a shadow neatly in half. Brynn did nothing more than hold on as best she could while the sword slashed and twirled and thrust, dispatching one shadow and then another, until suddenly, as quickly as it had begun, the battle was over. Brynn and Makayla were left panting and shocked as they stood among the remains of the shadows, oily puddles that were already disappearing, evaporating into the air and floating away on the wind.

"That's quite a sword," Makayla said.

"Yeah," Brynn said, still catching her breath. "Yeah, it is."

After making sure that every single shadow was indeed gone, they stepped through the doorway. The room beyond was round and windowless. A dais of the darkest glass they had yet seen stood on the far side. Above it rose two bright pillars of light, white streaked with flashes of blue. Within the pillars of light, two figures were suspended motionless: Brynn's mother and father. Their eyes were closed and they floated gently in the light. Brynn looked at them wistfully.

"This is just how you looked when I found you in the Swallowed Hall, Makayla."

"But who did this to your parents, Brynn? Who put them here?"

"I don't know, but let's get them out of there."

Brynn lifted her father out of the pillar of light, and Makayla lifted Brynn's mother. As soon as the adults crossed the edges of the light, their bodies returned to movement and to life. They blinked and sputtered, clearly disoriented.

"Brynn?" her mother said, blinking in the bright light given off by the pillars.

"Makayla?" her father said.

"What are you doing here?"

"Where are we?"

"Where's Hero?" Brynn's mother asked, her eyes wide with alarm.

"Don't worry," Brynn said. "She's safe. We're pretty sure."

"You're pretty sure?" asked her father. "What is going on? And why do you have a sword?"

Brynn and Makayla did their best to explain. How Jeffersonville had been invaded and how they had fled. How Gwenllian had tried to take them to a safe place and how all the gates had been destroyed. How they had been separated from the others in California and ended up in Annwfyn. And how they had been lost and almost eaten and almost eaten again but had then found their way here to the tower of glass.

Brynn's parents sat and took it all in, occasionally gasping and sharing worried looks with each other. Finally, when the tale was done, Brynn's mother clenched her jaw and spoke.

"So, our baby is with that...that goblin-killer?"

"You're just going to have to trust me, Mama," Brynn said. "She's changed. She helped us, protected us. She's the only reason we're alive right now."

"Well, it sounds like you two might have done a bit of that on your own, actually," Brynn's father said with admiration.

"So...what now?" Makayla asked.

"Good question, Makayla," Brynn's father said. "What now, indeed." He paused thoughtfully. "To answer your question, I'd like to ask a question of my own." Brynn and Makayla waited expectantly. "By any chance, do you have any food on you?"

The girls smiled and led the adults into the outer room, where they retrieved the backpack and shared what food they had. The four of them chatted and relaxed and ate succulent fruit at the top of the glass tower, above the clouds. For the first time in months, Makayla almost felt like everything might just turn out all right. Almost.

Chapter 69

"So, we've told you *our* story," Brynn said, after they'd eaten their fill. "And I think the pressing question on everyone's minds now is 'how exactly did *you* get here?'"

"Well...that's a very good question," her mother answered.

"And I guess the answer is that we don't really know," her father added.

"What do you mean you don't know? You left us alone in Jeffersonville *weeks* ago!"

"Well, we remember what happened after we left home," her father said.

"We just don't exactly know how we got here to this tower."

"Maybe you should start closer to the beginning," Brynn suggested, arching her eyebrows.

"Maybe," her mother sighed. "We knew Conn wasn't on Earth, of course, and the information your father found clearly indicated we needed to come back to Annwfyn."

"So we came through one of the gates," her father said.

"And no, not the one on the Devil's Backbone—"

"That one's terribly dangerous—"

"I still can't believe you used it—"

"Twice!"

Brynn shrugged.

"And once we got here," her father continued, "we spent days and days searching, trying to wheedle information out of anyone who might possibly have any idea where Conn could have gone."

"Of course," her mother said, "we had to be in disguise—"

"And we couldn't use our real names—"

"Because...well, our departure from Annwfyn wasn't exactly on the best of terms."

"And there might be those who would still...hold a grudge."

There was a pregnant silence.

"Yeah, I know you guys left Annwfyn and moved to California and there was clearly some huge reason for it," Brynn said dryly. "You will tell me why someday, right? Or how long ago it happened? Maybe even just name the century?"

"Sure. Someday," her father said with a slight grimace. There was another brief pause. "Anyway," he continued, "after days and days of searching and talking and searching and talking, we ended up in a cave in a mountain in a tucked-away little corner of Annwfyn that not many visit—"

"Or even know about—"

"And we talked to one of the cewri—"

"A giant—"

"Who said she'd been out traveling with her winds and had seen an unusual...vortex."

"She said it could have been a portal or a void or maybe even a dimensional bubble."

"I should also say that this conversation was pretty difficult," Brynn's father said, "and we might not have been gleaning her exact meaning—"

"Her dialect was obscure—"

"But she saw a spark of chaos that she hadn't seen in Annwfyn before—"

"Or at least not for eons and eons—"

"But standing by this vortex, she saw a young coblyn—"

"At least, we're pretty sure she said 'coblyn'—"

"Might have been 'changeling'—"

"Or possibly 'cinnamon roll'—"

"Like I said," Brynn's mother continued, "we didn't have the best grasp on the nuances of her speech—"

"But we were able to pin down the location she was talking about—"

"And were getting ready to journey there—"

"When…I guess we were attacked. I'm not sure," Brynn's father said, turning to his wife. "Do you remember?"

"I don't. One moment we were slipping on our shoes and the next moment we woke up here."

"That's disturbing," Brynn said quietly.

"Yeah. But it seems like it worked out okay." Her father smiled proudly. "My daughter saved us."

Makayla scoffed and cleared her throat.

"Sorry. My daughter and her best friend."

"Okay," Brynn said, her voice rising with excitement, "that's a crazy story but it's good, right? I mean, we found you, we're all together and you know where Conn is! We know where to go!"

"We have an *idea* of where to go," her father said.

"It might not be Conn," her mother said.

"But it might be," Brynn insisted. "And you said so yourself: it's our best lead. So, we're going, right? All of us?"

This provoked a long discussion. Makayla hesitated to call it an argument since Brynn's family were all so unflaggingly civil with each other, even when they were angry or when they disagreed. Brynn's mother, Llwynog, made the point that Annwfyn was a dangerous place and that everything she'd done had been to try to keep Brynn and her siblings safe. Brynn's father, Gafr, made the point that the safest choice would be for Brynn and Makayla to leave Annwfyn as quickly as possible. Brynn made the point that she and Makayla been trying desperately to leave for quite a while now and it had only led to them almost getting eaten several times.

In the end, they decided as a group that the best plan was for all four of them to stay together. Whatever risk Brynn and Makayla's presence in Annwfyn posed to the universe's existence, the damage was probably already done. Hero was as safe with Gwenllian and Winnie as she would be anywhere else, and the sooner that Conn could be tracked down, the sooner they could all get back to Earth and back to the rest of their families.

The first thing they had to do was get out of the tower. Brynn and Makayla explained that there was no door, or if there was a door, they hadn't been able to find it, so they'd have to climb out the window. Descending the tower's interminable stairway was much easier than the trip up had been. The few shadows they encountered fled the instant Brynn drew the sword from her back. They found the room with the open window, climbed down the ladder of flowers, and shortly after, they were all standing on the ground below. They took a few moments to refill their bags with fruit from the flowering ivy and then it was time to begin their journey.

Whenever she remembered it afterward, this next part seemed to Makayla like a dream. Brynn's parents knew this land well and knew how to travel in it easily. They knew which beings to avoid, which to ask for food, which to barter with, which to ply with courtesy and humor.

The four of them traveled across fields and through forests. They rafted down rivers and navigated their way through mountains. They took back roads through villages and skirted around the edges of massive fortresses. At the end of the twelfth day, they stood in front of a wooden, windowless shack on a rocky hillside. All the information that Brynn's parents had found led to this place, to a solitary shack standing on a solitary hill, a shack that could have been a twin to the one Brynn and Makayla had arrived in, what seemed like so long ago, but which really had only been a few weeks.

When Brynn and Makayla had stood there on their first day in Annwfyn, they'd had to decide whether to go through the shack into the tunnels below or to move through the world outside. This time, however, they knew there was only one option: to enter the shack and find out what lay beyond.

Chapter 70

"You ready?" Brynn's father asked, just as dusk was falling.

Brynn nodded. They had discussed waiting until morning to find out what lay beneath the shack, but they were all anxious to keep moving.

"How about you?" Brynn's mother asked Makayla.

"As ready as I'll ever be, I suppose," Makayla answered, with a bit more confidence than she actually felt. But just as Brynn's father was about to open the door, a surprisingly familiar voice called out to them.

"Well, look who finally made it all the way here. Makayla the human and her best friend, the coblyn." Seren, the tiny woman Makayla had met in the swamp, was sitting on the edge of the shack's roof. Her wings were folded primly behind her and her legs were crossed. "Oh," she added in mock surprise, "and you found the others, did you?"

"What are you doing here?" Makayla asked, knitting her brow.

"I told you," the tiny woman said simply. "I have a job to do."

"A job? What, your job is to wait for us in random places around Annwfyn?"

"Well, no," Seren said impishly, with a toss of her hair, "or not entirely, anyway. It's a little more serious than that." She smiled. "I mean…you didn't think you were actually going to make it out of here alive, did you?"

"You're here to kill us?"

"Well, yeah. Why else would I be following you around?"

"Then why did you give me that magic nut?"

"Magic nut?" Seren made a gagging sound and stuck out her tongue. "I didn't give you a magic nut. That was just an ordinary nut! I was worried you might outsmart Cath Palug. That thing's pretty dumb, so I thought the nut would be a good distraction, give the big dope a chance to eat you. It obviously failed. Ah well, try and try again, as the saying goes," she said, stretching luxuriously. "But I'm glad you brought your friends with you. I have friends too."

The door of the shack opened and two gigantic humanoid forms lumbered forth. They were shaped like men, but their skin was like rock and they stood as tall as streetlights. They were so big, in fact, that Makayla didn't think there would have been room for them in the tiny shack and she wasn't sure how they managed to fit through the door. Their eyes were afire and their hands breathed raw power. When they roared, Makayla could feel the heat from their breath across her face.

"Gwyllion," said Brynn's mother.

The two creatures of rock pounded the ground with their fists and roared again, the ground trembling beneath their blows.

"They aren't acting very much like the gwyllion I know," Brynn's father said as the others backed slowly away.

"I can see that."

With the sound of rolling thunder, the two rock-men began a slow lumbering run, each footfall more deafening than the last.

"Get behind us, girls!" Brynn's mother shouted.

Brynn's parents shimmered and changed into their other forms. Her father's limbs lengthened, his ears elongated, his eyes went small and bright, and his skin, from head to toe, turned moss green. Her mother's skin turned as dark as the night sky, replete with comets and galaxies within, and her hair floated around her like waves of starlight. Brynn's father snarled, showing a mouthful of teeth far pointier than Makayla had noticed before. His knees bent into a crouch and his long fingers curled, arms tense, ready to strike. The radiance from her mother's hair was now so bright that it lifted her into the air. Her skin disappeared against the night sky and her hair was a massive bright halo around her body.

The two girls took up positions behind the adults. Makayla did the only thing she could think of and pulled the laser pointer from her pocket. Brynn drew the sword from her back.

"Oh, I don't think so," Seren cried. "I've seen that sword in action."

With a gesture from the tiny woman, the sword was ripped from Brynn's hands and it flew away into the darkness. Brynn grimaced but, without hesitating, her body shimmered and shifted into her goblin form, similar to her father's but with skin of lighter green.

The rock-men were nearly upon them now. One lunged forward, his fists outstretched. Brynn and her father dove to one side to avoid being pummeled. Makayla and Brynn's mother dove to the other. Then Seren was upon them, wings buzzing furiously, a tiny dark dagger in each hand. She slashed and slashed again, driving them apart, pushing Makayla and Llwynog away, giving the rock creatures space to take on the others.

Makayla aimed the laser pointer at the tiny woman, hoping for a repeat performance of the fireball that had destroyed Cath Palug, but when she pressed the button, nothing happened. Seren shot her a contemptuous look and then ignored her. She clearly found Makayla the least threatening member of the party and focused her efforts instead on Brynn's mother.

She flew directly at the older woman's face, sliced her across the cheek with one of the tiny daggers, then darted away. Llwynog lunged at Seren, but the flying woman was too fast. Seren flew in again and sliced Brynn's mother across the arm, twice in quick succession, and buzzed away. Llwynog cried out in pain as the blood began to flow, liquid moonlight seeping out of the cuts on her midnight skin. Desperately, Makayla dug in her backpack and retrieved a piece of fruit, the only other thing she could think of to use.

Seren twirled the tiny daggers in her hands and dove toward Brynn's mother again, her wings tucked tightly behind her, a battle cry keening in her tiny throat. Makayla wound up and hurled the round fruit at the tiny woman, who dodged it in mid-air and screamed in fury. Her wings extended and she glided upward, then tucked them back and dove again. Makayla quickly grabbed another piece of fruit and threw. This one clipped Seren and she spun in the air, sending her to the ground. Her legs bent and she jumped, propelling herself back into the air, but the delay was long enough for Makayla to grab another piece of fruit and throw again. This time, Brynn's mother smacked the tiny flying woman open-handed, sending her directly into the path of Makayla's succulent missile. The fruit was ripe enough that Seren sank halfway inside it, and she fell to the ground, hopelessly entangled and now covered in sticky juice.

Her tiny body sprawled on the rocky ground, tiny limbs akimbo, her tiny daggers thrown aside in her fall. She was disoriented for only a brief moment, but those few seconds were all it took for Makayla to empty the backpack, throw it over the winged woman, and zip it up. The tiny woman screamed in fury and the backpack stretched and bounced as she flew around inside it, lashing out, trying desperately to escape. Brynn's mother found a large round stone from the rocky hillside and she and Makayla worked together to place it atop the backpack, pinning the tiny woman inside.

"Make sure she stays in there!" Llwynog shouted and Makayla nodded her agreement.

Meanwhile, Brynn and her father had been taking on the two gwyllion, although so far, this had mostly consisted of dodging the rock-men and avoiding their blows. After several minutes of this, which was clearly getting them nowhere, Brynn darted under a roundhouse punch from a massive rocky arm and tried to land a blow of her own. Despite throwing the punch with every ounce of force she had, the gwyll didn't even register the impact, and Brynn only succeeded in bruising her fist. She sprinted away, pain spreading across her face.

"That won't work, Brynn," her father called. "You won't be able to damage them that way. They're basically made out of rock!"

"What do we do then?"

"I don't know! I've never fought gwyllion before. I don't know anyone who has!"

Brynn's father crouched and leapt into the air, directly at the head of one of the creatures, arms outstretched, fingers grasping. The gwyll lifted one rocky arm and, with a move quicker than seemed possible, swatted Gafr out of the air. He landed heavily on the ground, the wind knocked from his lungs. The gwyll lifted one leg, thick as a tree, and prepared to stomp directly on the goblin's head. Brynn's eyes went wide, she gritted her teeth in hurried concentration and shouted, "Bad luck for the rock monster, bad luck for the rock monster, bad luck for the rock monster!" The gwyll's foot missed its mark and he stumbled and fell to his knees. Brynn's father scrambled out of the way and scurried back to his feet.

The second gwyll thundered forward and raised his arms to strike, but then Brynn's mother was in his path. The air sparked around her and held her aloft. Her hair, radiant as the sun at twilight, expanded around her and grew brighter and brighter. The enormous creature of rock swiped at her again and again, but each time, the blows were stopped by an unseen barrier. Each punch caused Brynn's mother to recoil and grit her teeth in pain, but whatever force was protecting her held up, and the gwyll roared in frustration.

The light from her hair grew brighter still until it was nearly blinding. Her face was haggard with exertion and her eyes were glowing. The gwyll swiped with unimaginable strength, the force of his blow rippling the air. She raised one arm. The blow was repelled and the rock creature staggered. He swiped again. She raised her other arm and the creature fell to the ground. His fists plunged deep into the rocky earth.

Brynn's mother strode slowly forward, the strain of her efforts clear upon her face. Sweat glistened upon her brow and the galaxies within her skin whirled frantically. The creature roared as she approached, flashing fire from his eyes and throat, but he could not free himself, could not rise to his feet. She walked through the roar and through the fire and when she stood directly in front of his face, she pressed both hands to the sides of the gwyll's head. The stars that lived within her now shone like comets, blazing blinding trails across her arms and neck. Her hair wrapped forward until it grasped the arms of the creature and she uttered several words that Makayla could not hear over the din. The eyes of the gwyll slammed shut and he fell forward with a crash that reverberated across the hilltop.

After being thrown to the ground and almost having his head stomped in, Brynn's father had regained his footing, although he was clutching his side as if something was broken.

"Brynn!" he cried. "Try to get him to follow you!"

She nodded and ducked under another blow, kicking the gwyll in the thigh and scurrying away again, just out of his reach. The rock creature lumbered forward and swung again, and Brynn repeated, darting in again and out, keeping the gwyll moving toward her. With the rock creature focused elsewhere, Brynn's father ran up behind him and leapt, landing on his back and grabbing him around the neck. The gwyll bared his craggy teeth and snarled, fire erupting from deep within him. A rocky fist grabbed Gafr by the arm and tried to pull him off. Brynn's father cried out in pain as the massive hand squeezed with irresistible force. His body swung around but he did not loosen his grip. He now hung from the gwyll's neck, suspended over the rocky creature's chest. Fire flashed from the gwyll's eyes as he released the arm of his attacker and instead used both hands to squeeze

Brynn's father around the chest. Gafr's mouth opened wide and he screamed in agony. Not knowing what else to do, Brynn reached down and picked up a rock as big as her head.

"Leave my father alone!" she screamed and hurled the stone at the rock monster's leg.

The rock struck its target and cracked in two. The gwyll stumbled, one hand sliding down to feel his damaged leg, which had cracked as well and bled golden fire.

The creature roared in pain. His mouth opened wider than seemed possible as he bellowed, and in that moment, Brynn's father spied something inside the gwyll's mouth, something glowing, humming, almost shrieking.

"Brynn!" he shouted. "Hit it again!"

Brynn did as she was asked, and this time when she threw her stone and the gwyll roared in pain, her father reached his undamaged arm into the creature's throat and pulled out something round, glowing, and red, the size of a small bowling ball. The creature of rock immediately fell to the ground, unconscious.

There was utter silence on the hilltop. Two enormous men made of stone lay motionless upon the ground and one tiny woman was trapped inside a grubby backpack under a rock. Whether by skill or sheer luck, they had defeated their foes, and the four of them stood there for a moment, bloody, wounded, and exhausted. Finally, Brynn's father broke the silence.

"They were enchanted," he said. "This was inside him." He held up the fiery, glowing orb. "Gwyllion are usually very gentle. I don't know who would have done this."

He walked to the other creature and, with the help of his wife, rolled him over onto his back. He pried open the gwyll's mouth, reached his entire arm inside, and retrieved a glowing orb identical to the first. He laid them on the hilltop, side by side.

"Brynn," he said, "bring me that sword of yours."

She found it where it had flown in the battle and handed it to him. He held it in one hand and thrust the point of the sword deep into one orb and then the other. The orbs hissed and shrieked as huge clouds of steam erupted forth and the glow within them faded. With a loud crack, they both dissolved into a mass of dull red pebbles.

Instantly, the two gwyllion woke up, groggy and disoriented. They sat up and stared around them in confusion.

"Are we dreaming?" one said to the other, his whisper clearly overheard by everyone on the hill and probably in any towns that happened to be nearby.

"We must be, yes?" said the second gwyll. "How else could we have traveled here from the compound in an instant?"

They were speaking only to each other, completely ignoring the others on the hilltop who were watching them curiously.

"What happened in your dream?"

"There was a human throwing fruit and then a coblyn reached into my throat and pulled out some fire."

"That happened in my dream too."

"Oh, your leg is hurt!" said one, noticing the wound.

"I don't like this dream!" said the other.

"Don't worry, I'll take care of you," said the first, and laid a surprisingly gentle kiss upon the other's brow.

"Let's go home."

"Yes, let's."

The two gigantic men of stone took hands, gave a slight nod to the others standing on the hillside, then walked away together and, hand in hand, disappeared into the night.

"There's only one left now," Brynn's mother said.

The four of them gathered around the backpack, which was still held down by a large stone and which still contained a tiny furious woman.

"You awake in there?" Brynn's mother asked, gently prodding a corner of the backpack.

"What's it to you?" a nasty voice squeaked in reply.

"We defeated the gwyllion. That wasn't a very nice thing to do, enchanting them like that. Probably broke several ancient treaties. I'd hate to think what the punishment might be for forcing those poor creatures into that kind of servitude."

"Why should I care?" the tiny woman shrieked, her voice muffled by the fabric. "I didn't do it. I'm just following orders and they were just sent along to help me!"

"Orders?" Brynn's father asked. "Whose orders? Who sent you to kill us?"

"Like I'd tell you. And even if I wanted to tell you, I couldn't. And also, I don't want to tell you."

"If you don't tell us," said Makayla, thinking quickly, "we'll eat you."

"Coblyns and xana don't eat ellyllon," Seren said, blowing a raspberry. "Nice try."

"But humans do," Makayla said.

"No, they don't," said Seren, but she sounded less sure of herself this time.

"They didn't use to," Makayla continued. "They do now. It's a new thing back on Earth. Eating tiny winged humanoids is all the rage. You should see my dad. He'll go through like twenty at a sitting."

Seren scoffed but then grew silent for several long moments as she pondered this.

"Okay," she said finally. "I'll tell you." Makayla and the others leaned in to listen. "I don't actually know who gave the order. I never saw him or talked to him directly, but he gave me something. To help me out. It's a ring." Her voice was weak now, plaintive, pleading. "You can probably use it to figure out who he is. Please. That's all I know."

They retreated from the backpack and huddled close.

"I don't know if I trust her," Brynn's father said.

"I definitely don't trust her," Brynn's mother replied.

"She's clearly scared of whoever gave her the order."

"Clearly. But she could be telling the truth. And if she is, that could lead us to Conn."

"You're right. I think we've got to take the chance."

They returned to the backpack and Brynn's father knelt down.

"Okay," he said, "I'm going to open the zipper. Just a little. You hand the ring through. If what you say is true, we'll let you out."

"O...okay," a tiny voice replied.

He unzipped the corner of the backpack, ever so slightly, and put two fingers by the opening.

"Give me the ring."

"You got it, Mr. Coblyn, sir. Here you go."

A tiny arm darted outward, the fingers grabbing at Brynn's father. A spark of energy erupted from the tiny hand and he convulsed in pain and collapsed to the ground, writhing in agony. The zipper was open before anyone else could react and Seren flew out, screeching with joy, and zoomed away into the night.

"Suckers!" she screamed. "There was no ring! I made that up! And I totally know who's trying to kill you! But now you'll never find out!"

Then she was gone and it was over. They were left alone on the hilltop. Disheartened, they tended to their wounds, which were relatively minor, considering what they had just gone through. Brynn's father's arm was broken and also several ribs. They arranged a makeshift sling for him and bandaged his chest. Brynn's mother had been slashed by Seren, but the wounds were not deep. They bandaged her as well. Brynn and Makayla had made it through relatively unscathed.

They made camp and slept on the hilltop under the night sky. The other three remained in their goblin forms ("We heal faster this way," Brynn reminded Makayla) and in the morning, they packed up and made ready to resume their journey, which had been so rudely interrupted the night before.

"Well," Brynn's father said, adjusting his sling, "I think we were just about to open this door, weren't we?"

"I think that's where we were," his wife said, smiling.

"Okay, then. Let's give it another go, shall we?"

Chapter 71

The inside of the shack looked just the same as the one that Brynn and Makayla had left behind weeks ago, when they first arrived unexpectedly in Annwfyn. When they opened the trapdoor, they discovered that it smelled the same as well. Beneath the trapdoor, they found a metal ladder and a long tunnel of stone beyond. The floor was covered with gravel and mud and the walls were roughly hewn.

Once they were beneath the ground, Llwynog's hair was bright enough to light their way and they pressed on into the darkness. The tunnel traveled downward at a gentle slope. It did not branch and it did not curve, just continued on, carrying them down into the bowels of Annwfyn. As they walked, it grew colder and colder, until goosebumps rose on Makayla's skin and she could see her breath before her face.

"That shack was on the very edge of the Outerlands," Brynn's father said, after they'd walked what must have been two or three miles. "We must be beyond the boundaries of Annwfyn by now."

"That shouldn't be possible," her mother said. "There shouldn't be any way for a…a tunnel carved out of rock to cross over the boundary. The boundary marks the end of Annwfyn. It's a finite realm. You can't go past the end. That's what 'end' means."

"It appears that someone or something has figured out a way."

After another couple of miles, the tunnel finally came to a stop at a pair of thick metal doors, dull and blocky, made out of what could have been iron, but inlaid with delicate silver runes, faintly glowing.

"Those look like the ones on the floor in your basement, B," Makayla whispered as the four of them examined the doors.

"They do," Brynn said, reaching out a nervous finger to touch one. She immediately yelped and pulled back. "These ones are hot too."

Brynn's father hesitantly confirmed that the handles of the doors moved easily and, more importantly, that they did not burn him.

"Do you...do you think Conn is in there?" Brynn asked him.

"I don't know," he said and pulled the doors open to reveal a large stone balcony overlooking a massive cavern. Hanging in the air was a filmy mist, which lit the vast area with a faint silvery glow. On the floor of the cavern, only vaguely visible from their perch, were rows and rows of people, lined up neatly, filling the cave from edge to edge. In the dim light, it was difficult to tell, but there must have been thousands of people down there, probably tens of thousands—men, women and children, all standing upright and frozen in place.

They descended a long stone stairway to the cavern floor and walked among the silent rows of people. The faces were clearly human, peaceful faces that did not seem to be in any pain or discomfort. Their eyes were open but unseeing. After only a few minutes, Makayla saw a face she recognized.

"Brynn," she said in confusion, "isn't that our gym teacher?"

Brynn looked and slowly nodded and then all four of them were running down the aisles, scanning the faces around them. They found more and more people they knew: another teacher, a neighbor, a classmate, a bus driver, the two women who worked at the comic shop, the Mayor. Each time they found someone they recognized, they shook them by the shoulders, tried to rouse them, but each time, the figure remained stiff and motionless. After ten minutes of frantic searching, they realized that what they were seeing was the entire city of Jeffersonville, Indiana, somehow transported to a dark cavern far beneath the surface of the Land of Annwfyn.

"Everyone," Brynn's father said. "It's absolutely everyone."

"So, when Jeffersonville got filled up with goblins and shadows," Brynn said as they continued to walk, continued to find faces they recognized, "this is what happened to all the people. They got replaced. They got sent here."

"Wait, wait, wait, if all of Jeff got sent down here..." Makayla said weakly, realization rising within her. "My family! My family is here!"

She ran up and down the rows, screaming their names even though she knew they couldn't hear her. It took far too long, twenty or thirty minutes, and by the end she was nearly frantic with worry, but she found them. They were all standing together in a neat line: her mother, her father, her three brothers. She put her hands on her mother's face and she cried. She didn't know when the last time she had seen them was. The real them, that is. She didn't know when they had been replaced by those...whatever those things were that had taken their places in her home. But here they were, standing in front of her, frozen and still.

Brynn found her there with her family and wrapped a comforting arm around her.

"We'll figure it out, Makayla," she said. "We'll get them out of here. You're going to get your family back."

They stood there together for several minutes as Makayla communed with her silent family, before they heard Brynn's father calling to them.

"Girls! Come here! We've found something!"

Brynn's parents were pacing around a huge cauldron that rested in a spherical depression in the very center of the cavern. The cauldron was perhaps eight feet across and looked as if it might be made of pure silver. The stone beneath it was carved in deep grooves forming grotesque images. Within the cauldron was a bubbling liquid, and the steam that rose from the surface formed the haze that lit the cavern with its dim light.

"What...what is that?" Makayla asked.

"Well, I can't say with one hundred percent certainty," Brynn's father said, "but that is what's keeping everyone here frozen."

"Probably," added her mother.

"If we dump it, they should wake up."

"Maybe."

"Are we sure that's a good idea?" Makayla asked, suddenly nervous. "That happened to me once—when Brynn found me after Finian captured me—and I woke up in a really crazy place and it...it freaked me out. Maybe we could get them all home and, you know, wake them up once they're back in their own beds."

Brynn's parents looked at each other.

"I agree, that would be the best option," Brynn's father said, "if it were possible. But I don't see how it would work. There's fifty thousand people here. And there's only four of us."

"Plus, all the beds in Jeffersonville are either occupied or on fire," Brynn said.

"So, I think we're going to have to take the risk of waking them up here," her father said. "We have to get them home and we can't carry them all."

The others looked at Makayla, who thought about it for a minute and then nodded.

Brynn's father, his arm still bound up in the sling, gestured to his wife and stepped back.

"Brynn, come help me," Llwynog said to her daughter.

Brynn and her mother crouched and slid their fingers under the edge of the cauldron and lifted. They grunted with the effort and the bubbling liquid within sloshed over the edge. They heaved again and the cauldron tipped up on its edge and the contents flowed out in a huge wave that filled the stone depression and slowly drained away or evaporated swiftly into the air, until the entire cauldron was dry.

After the cauldron had emptied, a dark, lumpy, misshapen stone fell out with a light clunk. As Brynn and her mother were setting the cauldron back in place, Makayla picked up the stone and looked curiously at it. It was a reddish-orange color and about the size of her hand.

"Is that a diospyrobezoar?" Brynn's father asked her, examining the object as she held it up to the light.

"A what?"

"A diospyrobezoar. Very rare. If someone ate too many persimmons, they might have one of those growing in their stomach. But with that size...that'd be a big someone...and big persimmons."

He walked away to check on his wife. Makayla looked around to make sure no one was watching, then shoved the stone into her backpack.

With the cauldron now empty and the liquid within bubbled away to nothing, the silver haze above them had begun to dissipate, although enough of it remained that it still lit the cavern. As the haze dispersed, the people around them slowly regained awareness and movement. Murmurs from fifty thousand pairs of lips filled the cavern as the residents of Jeffersonville, Indiana, awoke in this strange place.

There were yawns and there were tears. There were reunions and hugs. There were cries of disbelief and shouts of terror. As more and more of the people took stock of the situation around them, whatever emotion had found them when they regained consciousness was quickly replaced by panic. The three goblins and one human in the center of the vast chamber looked around them as chaos and terror emerged, wondering what they should do next. Brynn's father nodded to his wife. Once again, her hair glowed with the light of a thousand stars, and her body rose into the air until she could be seen by every person in the cavern. Whatever power she was using to hold herself airborne also amplified her voice as she spoke to the panicking crowd.

"People of Jeffersonville," she said, her hair swirling around her like a bright cloud, "I know this place seems strange to you. Please remain calm. We're going to get you out of here as soon as we can. All of you. But first I need you to listen. I need you to remain calm."

Her voice had a soporific effect on the milling people and the crowd settled down, their terror quieting as they listened to the strange glowing woman with midnight skin floating high in the air amidst the silvery haze. A few people in the distant corners of the cavern tried to object, tried to demand what right this woman had to tell them what to do, but they were quickly shushed by their neighbors.

"There are some facts you need to know," Brynn's mother continued. "First and foremost, you are not on Earth." There were loud cries of shock and surprise. "Your city, Jeffersonville, is occupied by a hostile force." The cries were even louder now, but Brynn's mother held up her hands for silence. "We're going to help you. We're going to get you home, but when you arrive, your home will not welcome you. You're going to have to reclaim your town."

The hubbub was almost deafening now. Brynn's mother raised her hands again for silence.

"What about the police?" one voice shouted. "Let's call the police! They can figure out what's going on!"

"I'm the police," another voice responded. "And I have no idea what's going on!"

"Also, how would we call anyone?" a third voice cried. "We're in a cave!"

"What about the government, then?" the first voice said. "Let's talk to the government!"

Brynn's mother raised her hands again and the shouts of the crowd fell silent.

"The government will not believe you," she said to them. "The force occupying Jeffersonville is not human." The cries of shock and surprise returned, now joined by cries of sorrow and terror. "It will be up to us. It will be up to you. Your town can be yours once more. We can do it if we work together. Now please, stay calm and let us work. We'll return you to your homes as soon as we can."

At this, she descended to the ground. The crowd around them dispersed, divided into smaller groups, as the residents of Jeffersonville sought out their families, coworkers, their friends. Many were still sobbing or shouting in anger or quivering in fear and many clearly thought they must be dreaming. Those who could provide comfort gave it to those who needed it and those who needed solace found what they could.

"It's everyone," Brynn's father said as they watched the crowd milling around them. "I can't believe we found everyone."

"Well...wait a second," Brynn said. "Not quite everyone."

"What do you mean?"

"Where's my brother? Where's Conn?"

"He's not here," Brynn's mother said, shaking her head.

"Are you sure?"

"Yes. If he was here, I'd be able to feel him. He's nowhere here, nowhere nearby."

Brynn clenched her jaw and tears welled in her eyes. Her mother wrapped her arms around her and drew her close. Makayla knew there was nothing else she could do here, at least for now.

"Everything seems to be okay for a minute," she said. "I need to...I need to go find my family."

"Of course," Brynn's mother said. "I can't believe we didn't think of it sooner. Makayla, oh my goodness, yes, find them!"

Makayla found her mother and her father and her brothers in a far corner of the cavern. The six of them stood apart from all the rest and they held each other and they talked. But what was said then, Makayla never chose to recount, because some things are too important, too precious, to share with others or even (sometimes) to put into words. Some things Makayla chose to keep deep within her heart and this was one of them.

Chapter 72

A few hours later, Makayla found Brynn and her family gathered around the silver cauldron in the midst of a heavy discussion.

"The first thing we have to take care of is getting them all home," Brynn's father was saying.

"Yeah," Brynn said, "but their homes are filled with goblins and shadows!"

"Well, I guess that will be the second thing we have to take care of."

"But how do we get fifty thousand people out of a cavern in Annwfyn and back into a city on Earth?"

"That's a good question," her father answered with a weary smile. "And I may have an answer. While you were all resting, I spent a couple hours examining the cauldron. It may be exactly what we need."

"What do you mean?" Brynn's mother asked.

"Well, I determined that the cauldron is made of silver, as we thought, but it's been plated with illuminated electrum."

"Really?" Brynn's mother said, moving closer to examine the metal.

"Yes! And it looks as though the rim has been washed with iodized abalone."

"Which would allow thaumamalleability."

"That's right. And the feet have clearly been enunciated in transmodal hexography."

"But what about the cache?"

"That's the million dollar question, isn't it?" He smiled. "Provided the actinic cache hasn't been depleted, this cauldron should be able to achieve transdimensional transparency."

"What does all that mean?" Brynn asked as she and Makayla stared on confusedly.

"It means…I think…that we can use this cauldron to craft a portal back to Jeffersonville."

"Do you think you remember how?" Brynn's mother asked him.

"It's been a…a few years," he answered cagily, glancing quickly at his daughter.

Brynn looked archly at him.

"Okay, it's been a few centuries, but I think I can do it. And this actually wouldn't work if we were in Annwfyn, but since I'm pretty sure we're outside the boundaries now…well, I think it's worth a shot."

"But what if you're wrong?" Brynn asked. "What if we're still in Annwfyn? Will it blow up or something? Will it kill us all?"

"No," he said with a shrug. "It just won't work and we're screwed."

"No sense not trying," Brynn's mother said. "We've got nothing to lose."

"Well, I think we might actually have quite a bit to lose," Brynn said, "but let's give it a shot anyway."

Her father smiled and clapped her on the back.

"Great," he said. "Okay, I'm going to need a few things. Something from Jeffersonville, something made of paper, preferably. Then some things from here in the cavern, they have to be hard, some rocks, ore, anything like that. And I'm going to need a little bit of blood. Human blood."

The other three looked at Makayla.

"Sorry, M," Brynn said.

"It's cool. I can spare a little for the greater good."

It took them only a few minutes to gather the necessary materials: a bus schedule, a handful of gravel, and a few drops of blood that Brynn extracted from Makayla as gently as possible with the dragon-pommeled sword. Brynn's father took the materials and spent ten minutes with them and the cauldron, making gestures and speaking words that Makayla didn't find remotely comprehensible.

At the end of it, with a tremendous blast of cold air, the metal at the bottom of the cauldron rippled and grew cloudy and then disappeared entirely. Instead of solid metal, there was now a wide-open hole, and through it, they could see trees and grass and a dilapidated wooden shack. It was the bluff overlooking Jeffersonville and the shack where Makayla and Brynn spent the night after their flight from the shadows.

"That's crazy," Brynn whispered.

"That's magic," Makayla whispered back. "Your parents can do magic, dude."

"It worked," Brynn's father said triumphantly, hugging his wife. "It really worked!"

"The portal only works one way, though," Brynn's mother said, turning to the girls. "Once we go through, we can't come back, so we have to make sure we get everyone."

"And I think we're going to have to do it quickly," Brynn's father said as a loud ripping noise echoed through the cavern.

All around them, threadlike slashes were appearing in the cavern walls, as if the fabric of the rocks was being shredded apart. Beyond the slashes, there was blackness. The cavern was dissolving into nothingness.

"This is like what happened in the barn," Makayla said.

"I was just thinking the same thing," Brynn answered. "That didn't end well for us. Papa, what's going on?"

"I think that giant was right," he said, staring wide-eyed at the tiny rips in the fabric of their reality. "We're sitting in the middle of a dimensional bubble and it's losing cohesiveness. I suspect that cauldron might have been holding the cavern together."

"And now that we've disrupted the cauldron..." his wife said.

"We've disrupted the dimensional bubble and it's falling apart."

"How long do we have?" Brynn asked.

"I don't know. Hours, maybe."

There was a murmur at the edges of the crowd, a murmur that was growing louder as the residents of Jeffersonville began to notice the cavern's imminent collapse.

"Lou," Brynn's father called to his wife, "try to keep them calm. We need to start the evacuation now!"

Brynn's mother rose into the air again, using whatever abilities she had at her disposal to calm the crowd and encourage their exodus from the rapidly eroding chamber.

"Citizens! We're going to be sending you home now! Step into the cauldron at the center of the chamber and you will arrive near Jeffersonville. Once you arrive, do not try to return to town! It's too dangerous. After everyone is assembled, we will return together."

With Brynn's mother directing from above, Makayla, Brynn, and her father helped the frantic crowd into the cauldron and through the portal within. The cauldron was wide enough that ten people could climb in at a time, but even at this rate, it went slowly.

"Keep them moving," Brynn's father instructed. "Keep their attention on the cauldron and keep them moving. The last thing we want is a stampede. We've got to get them all through before this place collapses." He turned to the massing crowd. "Come on, people, keep it moving! Let's get you home! Then we'll come up with a plan to take back our town!"

Brynn angrily grabbed her father's arm.

"What about Conn?" she shouted over the din. "He's still out there somewhere. We need to keep looking for him!"

"That's just going to have to wait for now," he said as he helped an elderly woman over the edge of the cauldron.

"He's my brother! He's your son!"

"I know," he said, his face anguished, "but there are fifty thousand people here who need our help! If they stay here and this bubble collapses, they'll die. If they go through on their own, they're going to have to fight a townful of goblins with no idea what they're facing. They have to go home and we have to go with them. All of us. This has to be our first priority. We'll find Conn. We will. As soon as we can. We just have to do this first, Brynn, I'm sorry."

Brynn clenched her jaw into a stubborn frown but did as her father asked and continued to help the evacuees into the cauldron. It took them hours to get everyone through, but somehow, whether it was the calming influence of whatever magic Brynn's mother was using on them, or the disconnect from the utterly unreal situation they all found themselves in, the citizens of Jeffersonville never descended into full-blown panic.

At long last, Brynn and her mother and her father helped the last few residents into the cauldron, and then it was just the three of them in the rapidly disintegrating cavern, the holes in its reality now making it more hole and less cavern. Brynn's father, his arm still in a sling, needed his wife and daughter to help him over the edge. He gave a friendly wave, slipped down into the portal and then he was gone, leaving Brynn and her mother alone.

"Ready?" Brynn's mother asked, holding out a hand to help her.

Brynn remained silent, her mouth clenched, tears in her eyes.

"You're not coming, are you?" her mother said.

Brynn shook her head.

"Someone has to keep looking for Conn," she said softly. "Tell Papa I love him, okay?"

She reached out her arms and her mother wrapped her in her own and held her daughter close.

"I couldn't...I couldn't tell him," Brynn said, her face buried against her mother's shoulder. "I don't think he'd understand."

"Your father is just trying to do the right thing, you know. Like he always does."

"I know."

"And your father worries about you."

"I know that too. You'll be safe, right?" Brynn asked.

"I'll do my best. You too, okay?"

Brynn nodded.

"Goodbye, my darling girl." She held her daughter's face between her hands. "You have more strength inside you than you could ever possibly know. Find your brother. Bring him home."

"I will, Mama."

Brynn's mother climbed over the edge of the cauldron and disappeared. The cavern was vibrating now, the cracks of its shattered reality growing wider and wider. Brynn adjusted the sword on her back, then turned and ran toward the stairway that led back to the tunnel, hoping to escape before the dimensional bubble collapsed. But just as she reached the stairs, Makayla stepped from the shadows where she had been hiding.

"Hey," she said. "You okay?"

"Makayla! What are you doing here?" Brynn shouted. "You have to go! There's not much time left!"

"After all this, you think I'm going to leave you to finish it on your own? No chance, dude."

"How did you...how did you convince your parents to let you stay?"

"Um..." Makayla shifted nervously on her feet.

"You didn't tell them, did you?"

"I'll tell them when we get back. There was a lot going on and I guess they sort of lost track of me in all the chaos. Or maybe I made sure they lost track of me."

"They're going to be worried sick!"

"They were already worried sick," Makayla said. "A couple more days won't kill them. Let's just finish this quick so I can go apologize and then be grounded forever, okay?" The cavern shook and the floor split under their feet. "I think we better get out of here."

"Agreed."

And they ran, huge cracks appearing in the floor beneath them that they leapt over as they fled to the stairs and then to the tunnel above.

"I'm glad you're here, Makayla," Brynn said with a small smile. "Thanks."

They took the stairs three at a time, then sprinted through the doorway and back up the long rock tunnel, the dimensional bubble disintegrating around them as they ran. Ahead of them, the rock grew more coherent and just as the remains of the cavern and tunnel collapsed behind them, they leapt onto the solid floor. When they dared to sit up and look back over their shoulders, they saw the tunnel opening onto absolute nothingness, the null space that had once been occupied by the vast cavern and the residents of Jeffersonville, Indiana.

"There's no way back now," Brynn said wistfully. "Our parents will just have to take care of whatever happens back on Earth."

"And we're on our own in this crazy-ass world," Makayla said.

"That appears to be the case."

"So now what?"

"Now we find my brother."

ACT 5: THE BATTLE OF JEFFERSONVILLE

Chapter 73

"Look at it down there," Ysbaddaden said to Fan, who was perched comfortably on his shoulder. They were sitting in front of their tent on a bluff overlooking a smoldering town on the planet of Earth. A cloud of smoke hung over the town like a rotting umbrella. They were just finishing their soup.

"What should I be looking at?" asked his tiny winged companion.

"The fires, the devastation, the massive rubble piles, the entire human city with not a single human in it!"

"It's a crying shame, boss."

"That quarry used to be a school!" Ysbaddaden shouted, spilling the remainder of his soup in the process. "That smelter used to be a department store! That armory used to be…well, I'm not entirely sure what it's called…some kind of place where humans go to be physically mistreated by each other…"

"A gym?" Fan supplied hopefully.

"Maybe. But that's not the point."

"What is the point?"

"The point is that this human city is filled with rampaging coblyns bent on its destruction and is becoming a place less and less suitable for humans by the hour!"

The tiny woman unfurled her wings, fluttered to the ground, and looked at her supervisor with concern.

"Kind of looks the same to me as it did yesterday, boss."

"Well, yes, but—"

"And the day before that."

"I know, but—"

"Aaaaaand the day before that." She stood there, tapping her tiny foot, eyebrows raised, but he only glared at her. "We've just sort of been sitting up here watching this town get destroyed for a while now," she went on. "Our tent's getting smelly. We're running out of soup. Are we ever going to, you know, actually do something?"

"There are wheels within wheels moving here, Fan! I must assess and properly analyze this situation. We see below that an entire town has been relocated, every single human stolen away and replaced by coblyns...and not just coblyns but bwgans too! It runs against every known convention, every protocol put in place to prevent this sort of thing from happening!"

He stood up and threw his soup bowl aside. Fan flew over, picked it up, and placed it atop the towering stack of dirty soup bowls next to the door of their tent.

"Our methodology replaces one human from Earth every few years," he continued, "keeping the Tylwyth Teg spread far and wide across this world. One changeling per year at the absolute maximum! Otherwise, we run the risk of detection. With the appropriate protocols in place, any reports of magical mayhem can be dismissed as localized aberrations, errant phenomena, or isolated phantasmagoria, and the changeling can run amok to their heart's content until they tire of their amusements and return to Annwfyn." He waved his hands feverishly at the chaos below. "But this...this is apocalyptic!"

He collapsed to the ground and his head fell into his hands. His voice grew weak and choked. His assistant flitted onto his shoulder and patted him on the back with her tiny hand, trying to comfort him.

"There, there," she said softly in his ear.

"We had three in quick succession last year, all in Jeffersonville. I should have noticed then! And now thousands, tens of thousands of coblyns, here on Earth, in one town. It's an absolute disaster, Fan! What will happen if they're discovered by the general populace outside this city?"

"When, boss," she said softly. "The coblyns are burning down whole blocks and building massive siege engines and battle automata. I think we've moved past if."

"And if the people of Earth learn that there's a realm dimensionally adjacent to their own...filled with...filled with..."

"Beings only seen previously in their storybooks and nightmares?"

"Yes, Fan. Indeed. If they should make that discovery, what will happen to them? What will happen to us?"

She laid her head against his and spoke as gently as she could.

"It's a conundrum, boss. You think maybe we should do something about it?"

He stared at the burning town below them and gave a deep sigh, perhaps the deepest sigh he'd ever sighed in the long centuries of his life.

"Maybe tomorrow, Fan. Maybe tomorrow."

Ysbaddaden was just contemplating returning to the tent for a fretful nap when he was interrupted by a blast of cold air and a loud humming noise. A hole opened in the sky and out of the hole fell a human, who nearly landed on him before he could scurry out of the way. The human was followed closely by another and then another and another and then it was a veritable fountain of human beings falling out of the nothingness onto the ground beneath. The first ones to arrive worked together to catch the newcomers, prevent them from injury, and then clear them out of the way to make room for the rest, who were now appearing at an alarming rate.

Throngs of confused humans were falling from the sky and all Ysbaddaden and Myfanwy could do was watch. They each whispered a small glamour to keep themselves unnoticed while the humans milled about, filled all the available space, then spilled into the forest and the road leading up to the bluff.

"What is going on?" Fan asked, hovering nervously in the air.

"Humans," Ysbaddaden muttered. "So many humans. It must be thousands of them." He glanced around at the bluff, now packed with human beings standing nearly shoulder to shoulder. "Maybe tens of thousands. What are they doing here?"

"I think they're coming home," Fan said quietly, as the realization dawned on them. "I think these are the humans who belong to this town. I think they've come to take it back."

Finally, after hours and hours, while the crowds on the bluff separated into smaller groups, comforted each other, foraged for food, despaired at the sight of their burning city far below, the fountain of humans slowed to a trickle and then finally stopped. After a few minutes, two final beings dropped from the hole and then the migration appeared to be over.

Ysbaddaden hadn't been able to identify any of the other arrivals, but these two he recognized. These two weren't human. They were Tylwyth Teg. A coblyn and a xana that he'd had significant and profound dealings with in the past. He watched as Gafr and Llwynog, Brynn's parents, found each other again below the portal. Gafr seemed to be waiting for another arrival, but the hole in the sky remained empty. His wife spoke a few words in his ear and then embraced him. When they parted, Gafr's face was wet with tears. They turned away, hand in hand, and with another fiendish blast of cold air, the portal sealed itself up tight and was gone.

Gafr and Llwynog were approached by one of the humans, a woman who seemed to hold some authority over the others.

"Probably the Mayor," Fan informed him. "That's what humans call whoever's in charge of their towns."

"I know that, Fan. Shh! I'm trying to listen."

The Mayor spoke to the coblyn and the xana for several minutes, then ascended to the highest point on the bluff and spoke to the masses. Many nearby could hear her and those who couldn't relayed her message to those farther away.

"I know what has happened to us is difficult to comprehend," she said. "We woke up somewhere we didn't recognize and took a journey by means that I would have assumed impossible only twenty-four hours ago. And now, arriving here and seeing the state of our town—dismantled, devastated, aflame—it's terrifying. It's infuriating. I, like most of you, am having feelings of hopelessness and fear. We can't give in to those feelings, though. We need to stay strong. We need to stay strong for each other and for Jeffersonville. Something has happened to our town. Something I'm not sure any of us understand yet, or perhaps ever will understand. But I promise you: we're going to figure this out together. We're going to work together. We're going to take our town back. But for now, please, try to stay calm. I'll have more for you as soon as I can."

This seemed to satisfy the agitated crowd, at least for the moment, and they settled back into quiet conversations and tears. Gafr and Llwynog, however, were avoided and left alone for the most part, as the humans seemed to be unnerved by their inhuman appearance. Ysbaddaden waited until they moved to the outskirts of the crowd and then approached them. He let his glamour fall just enough that the coblyn and the xana could see him while he remained hidden to the rest. When they recognized him, their jaws clenched and their faces tightened as if they had just tasted something terribly sour.

"Ysbaddaden?" Gafr shouted. "What in the hell is going on here?"

"Introductions first," Ysbaddaden said, "angry inquiries after." He gestured to the tiny woman sitting on his shoulder. "This is my assistant, Myfanwy."

"Come on, call me Fan," she said.

"Very well. Fan, this is Gafr and Llwynog."

"Hello," she said brightly.

"Are you done?" Gafr asked, his tone measured. When Ysbaddaden nodded, he resumed his shouting. "What in the hell is going on here?"

"I've spent many days here on this bluff asking myself the same question," Ysbaddaden said. "And then you and this...cohort arrive...most unexpectedly. It raises many further questions. To begin: What exactly are you doing here?"

"We're trying to take these people back to their homes," Llwynog said. "What are *you* doing here?"

"Wondering what happened to their homes."

Gafr and Llwynog took stock of the wounded city below.

"Look at this," Llwynog said. "Flames and chaos. Rubble and smoke. Coblyns and bwgan. Streets patrolled by clockwork chickens. Siege engines in the schoolyards. It's barely recognizable as a human city any longer."

"Did you have something to do with this?" Gafr asked, snapping his attention back to Ysbaddaden.

"No, I assure you," Ysbaddaden said, guilt creeping uneasily into his voice. "I've been monitoring the changelings, as I've always done. Somehow, though…someone else took control of the changeling protocols."

"That shouldn't be possible," Gafr said.

"Oh, I'm aware, trust me. For someone to disrupt the acquisition of the humans, to redirect the relocation of the Tylwyth Teg, funnel them all into one city on Earth. And then to utterly obscure the logistical machinery and the bureaucracy. And then even beyond that, to do all of this without me or any of the directorate having any awareness of their machinations! Whoever did this, the one thing we can say about them with any certainty is that they are exceptionally powerful."

"So…whoever this is," Gafr said, "has been sending all of the changelings here…to Jeffersonville?"

"Indeed," Ysbaddaden answered. "Every single changeling, intended for relocation throughout the multiverse, has instead been placed here. And not only that, the pace of the relocations has increased tenfold."

"How long has this been going on?"

"One year. Almost exactly."

"So then why are *you* here? Are you overseeing? Assisting?"

"I'm trying to figure out how to reverse it," Ysbaddaden said remorsefully. "How to make up for a mistake that falls squarely on my shoulders."

"Boss," Fan said, with a consoling pinch to his cheek, "there's no way you could have known what was happening."

"No, Fan. I should have known. The signs were there...it was clear something terribly out of the ordinary was going on. I just didn't want to see them."

The four of them stood in silence then for several minutes while the massive crowd behind them did the very human things they'd been doing since they arrived: laughing, crying, consoling each other, trying to make sense out of the incomprehensible situation they'd found themselves in.

"We want to take this town back," Gafr said as the sun began to set over the horizon, turning the cloud of smoke which hung over the city a brilliant shade of purple. "We want to return these humans to their homes. We want the changelings gone."

"I want to help," Ysbaddaden said simply.

"What do we do then?" Fan asked. "What's our next step?"

"The first thing we need to do," Llwynog said, "is take care of all the very scared and very hungry people up here on this bluff who are watching their city burn."

"That's probably the first ten things," Fan said. "Maybe twenty."

"Well, let's take care of those things first and then we can figure out what happens next," Gafr said. "Let's take care of the people and then figure out how the hell to get fifty thousand coblyns out of our town."

Gafr held out his hand. Ysbaddaden took the coblyn's hand and, in that moment, their alliance was struck. He turned to his assistant.

"Fan?"

"Yes, boss?"

"We're going to need some more tents."

Chapter 74

The last of the tents was just about set up when the next unexpected visitor arrived. Myfanwy pulled the thousands of tents they needed from the strategic reserves back on Annwfyn, and if any of the humans noticed that the tents appeared from nowhere, assembled themselves when asked, were (of course) bigger on the inside than the outside, smelled like a spring glade, or had running water, none of them mentioned it.

"How many tents left in the reserves, Fan?" Ysbaddaden asked his assistant.

"None, boss."

"Hope no one important tries to go touring then and figures out what we've done."

Food and medical supplies were similarly obtained and were distributed as quickly and efficiently as possible (which wasn't very) by those who had experience in such things. Up on the bluff, an entire city sprang up, almost from nowhere, in the space of just a few hours. The humans within, confused, scared, hungry, and exhausted, finally had food to eat and places to sleep, and eating and sleeping is exactly what they did.

Once all this had been completed, once things on top of the bluff were just about returning to quiet and calm, or at least as quiet and calm as fifty thousand newly inter-dimensionally displaced humans could be, another hole opened in the sky and a mythical blond-haired hero stepped out of it. She was accompanied by a bwbach carrying a baby.

Ysbaddaden's hackles immediately went up.

"Boss! We're in danger!" Fan screamed, pointing at the new arrivals and then promptly disappearing with a tiny pop.

"Some help you are," Ysbaddaden muttered. He backed warily away. "There are entirely too many beings suddenly appearing here."

"I have not come with ill intent," Gwenllian said softly, raising her empty hands as proof. "Thou and thy companion have no reason to fear."

"I think I'll be the one to decide on my fear level," Ysbaddaden said incredulously. "Are you aware who you are? Do you know how many of our people you have killed? Any remembrance of the havoc you've wreaked upon the Tylwyth Teg?"

"I tell it thee again: I mean no harm. I come here unarmed and of my own free will. I know who I have been, yet I also know who I now am. My encounters with the young coblyn named Branwen I do think have forever changed me and the hatred that did live within my soul."

"She does have an effect on people, doesn't she?" He harrumphed. "Very well. I am going to reserve judgment in case you try to start slaughtering me or something. But for the sake of argument, let's say that's all true. Why are you here?"

"I am seeking two coblyns. The parents of this tiny one," Gwenllian said, gesturing to the baby still held in Winnie's arms.

Ysbaddaden went to go find Gafr and Llwynog, but they were already running toward their daughter.

"Hero?" Llwynog shouted as she ran. "Is that you?"

The baby reached for her and she lifted the baby from Winnie's arms and pulled her to her chest. Gafr embraced them both. There were tears enough to share.

"Hi, I'm Winnie," the gray-skinned woman said as they reunited with their child.

"Hello, Winnie," Gafr said. "Thank you. This is amazing. I can't believe you're here. I can't believe you brought her back to us. Where did...how did you find us?"

"I came with *her*," Winnie said, gesturing over her shoulder with her thumb at Gwenllian.

"Since your other daughter was ripped from my care," Gwenllian said, "I have done my best to care for this one. I have been watching, in all the ways that I can watch, in all the realms that I can see, for even the smallest sign of any member of your family. There was nothing. It was as if you had been wiped from the very memory of the worlds. And then I saw you. Back here where it all began. I came as soon as I was able. I did not want this little one to be separated from you for a moment longer than was necessary."

"Thank you," Gafr said. "I don't know if we'll ever be able to repay you for this, or even thank you enough. You brought us back our daughter."

"You've been away from your parents for far too long," Llwynog said to the baby snuggled close against her chest. "Far too long. Never again, okay? Never ever ever. You're going to stay with us now and we're never going to let you go."

Chapter 75

The next morning, they sat on wooden stools as they gathered in the largest tent: Gafr and Llwynog with their infant daughter, Ysbaddaden and Myfanwy, Gwenllian and Winnie, and the Mayor of Jeffersonville. They knew there were decisions to make, and the longer they waited, the worse things were going to get.

"Can you please just explain what is going on?" the Mayor pleaded desperately. "What are those...those things that have taken over our town?"

"I know this is difficult to accept," Llwynog told her. "There are things happening here that don't seem real, that go against everything you've ever been taught. The majority of the beings that you see down below, the ones setting the fires and tearing down the buildings? Those are goblins."

"Or more accurately, 'coblyns,'" her husband interjected.

"Not helpful right now, Gaf."

"Sorry."

"These goblins have been sent here as changelings," Llwynog continued.

"What does that mean?" the Mayor asked.

"It means that in addition to taking over your town, the goblins have taken over your forms. They've taken over your lives. It means there's a goblin down in Jeffersonville right now who looks like you, sounds like you, dresses like you, smells like you. She could fool your closest friend into thinking she was you."

"That's disconcerting."

"The shadows are called bwgans. Less numerous, but no less dangerous."

"What about...I saw some metal things. Some kind of creatures patrolling the streets?" the Mayor asked.

"Ah, those," Llwynog answered. "Those have been constructed by the goblins to keep the town under their control. They're clockwork chickens."

"You've got to be kidding me."

"They're actually a lot scarier than they sound," Gafr said. "You don't want to get into a scrap with one of those, believe me."

"But why are they here?" the Mayor asked. "Where did they come from?"

"They...and we...come from a place called the Land of Annwfyn," Llwynog said. "It's a realm...a dimension...similar to this one, and very close, relatively speaking."

"And you're...goblins, too?" the Mayor asked.

"I am," said Gafr.

"I'm a xana," said Llwynog, "another of the races who live in Annwfyn."

"Ellyll," said Fan.

"Bwbach," said Winnie.

"Human," said Gwenllian. "Well, at least, I used to be."

Gafr looked at Ysbaddaden but he just shook his head.

"This is...this is a lot to take in," the Mayor said, her head sinking into her hands. "All I want...all *we* want, all of those people out there, those scared, confused people, and yes, I'm one of them, all we want is to go home. We just want our town back."

"Unfortunately, that's not an option right now," Gafr said, as gently as he could. "To put it in a parlance that may be better suited to the situation we find ourselves in: Your town is currently occupied by a hostile force."

"Why isn't anyone coming to help us?" the Mayor said, rising to her feet and pacing furiously around the tent. "Where's the Army? Where's the National Guard?"

"They wouldn't have noticed anything unusual," Ysbaddaden said, making his voice heard in the meeting for the first time.

"What?" the Mayor turned on him incredulously. "Jeffersonville is on fire!"

"Here it is, yes. But not for the rest of the world. From the outside, the town would look just the same as it always has. There's some very powerful magic at work here, magic that I don't fully understand. While those of us in here can see the reality of it, an illusion of normality is being projected to the world at large. Only those inside the magic can see the destruction. The enchantment seems very thorough. And only we have the power to remove it."

"How are we going to do that?" the Mayor asked.

"The goblins must be driven out," Ysbaddaden said. "The people must be returned to their homes."

"But how?" Gafr said. "We brought fifty thousand people with us. Fifty thousand people with no magic, no special abilities at all. Fifty thousand soft, squishy, human people. I know they want to help. I know they want their homes back. Many of them will fight for it. But..."

"But perhaps not on the front line," his wife supplied.

"Yeah. So, if we're going to do this," Gafr said, "we're going to need some assistance."

"I think," Ysbaddaden said, arching his fingers sagely, "I think I should perhaps make some calls."

"There's interdimensional telephones now?" Fan piped in.

"Metaphorically speaking."

There was a silence as the weight of the moment hung in the air.

"This is a serious situation we're talking about here," Gafr said. "We're talking about a battle. We're talking about serious risks for anyone who participates. Madam Mayor? I think we need your agreement here to move ahead."

She nodded.

"I can't...I'm not sure I'm prepared for this," she said. "I'm the Mayor of a mid-sized suburb. I can't lead these people into battle."

"We're not asking you to lead them into battle," Gafr said. "We're asking you to tell them what's happening and bring them along if you can."

"Who will lead them, then?" the Mayor asked. "If we're going into battle, someone has to be in command."

"I will lead them," Gwenllian said.

"You?" the Mayor said. "You look like you're about half my age. What possible experience could you have that would qualify you to lead the citizens of my city into this type of battle?"

"Oh, man," Fan said swiftly. "You probably don't want to question her on her age or her warfare credentials. We'd be here all day."

"Suffice to say," Gafr said, "for this kind of endeavor, she is by far the most qualified of anyone here and by 'here,' I mean this planet. Thank you, Gwenllian. It makes the most sense for you to command."

All eyes returned to the Mayor.

"Fine. Yes, I agree," she said. "Yes, I'll talk to as many as I can. Try to convince as many as I can. They all want their town back. I don't know how many will be willing to engage in lethal combat with imaginary creatures—"

"We're not imaginary," Fan interrupted, but she was promptly shushed by Ysbaddaden.

"But if you need my agreement, then, yes, I agree."

"Only one question left, then," said Gafr. "When? When do we do this?"

"On the morrow," Gwenllian said confidently. "At first light. We can wait no longer. If we do, the town will be utterly consumed."

"So, we attack tomorrow then?" the Mayor said, her hands shaking. "Fifty thousand normal citizens are just going to up and attack some crazy mythical beings who look just like us and have moved into our town?"

"Yeah," said Gafr. "That's what we've decided here."

"We're going to have help, though, right?" the Mayor asked.

They all looked at Ysbaddaden.

"Of course," he said sharply. "Yes. I said I'd make some calls."

"How much help?" Gafr said.

"That's to be decided. I'll figure it out."

"So, what is this, then?" the Mayor asked, clearly shaken by the enormity of the moment. "This is just us sitting around, this little group of us calmly deciding the fates of each and every man, woman, and child out there?"

"No one will be forced to endanger themselves," Gafr said. "But if we want to take our town back, we're going to have to do it ourselves. You're going to have to ask the people out there, the residents of this town, to fight for what's theirs. We're going to get some help...if we can. But the burden is ours. In the morning, we're going to march down that road and drive the goblins and the shadows from this town and not all of us will survive. You asked me what this is? I'll tell you. This is a council of war."

Chapter 76

Long after midnight, long after everyone else had gone to sleep, Ysbaddaden was standing alone atop the bluff, waiting. He'd told everyone else at the council of war that he would make some calls. In actuality, he only made one. If this next conversation went well, he wouldn't need to make any others. If it didn't...well, the battle was likely already lost. And, of course, if she didn't even show up, he might as well tell everyone to pack it up and find refuge in some other dimension.

He didn't have to wait very long. She came walking across the sky in the form of an elderly human woman, although he knew that, in her case, "human" was incorrect, "woman" was relative, and "elderly" had little meaning since she was already ancient when the words to describe time were invented.

"You got my message," Ysbaddaden said to her once she was standing on firm ground.

"I did," said the old woman.

"I appreciate you coming. I know your time is valuable."

"Enough of this," snapped Cyrridwen. "Why am I here, Ysbaddaden?"

He pointed to the town below them, flames lighting up the night sky, smoke so thick the destruction could barely be seen.

"Coblyns have taken over this town. What's more, they brought a host of bwgans with them."

"How would something like this even be possible?" she asked, her eyes crinkling suspiciously.

"Changelings," Ysbaddaden responded. "Unregistered, unrestricted. Over the course of a year, they replaced an entire human town with changelings and they did it under everyone's noses, including mine."

"Who is this 'they?'"

"That's the big question, isn't it?"

"Very well," she said with clearly feigned indifference. "A human town is now a changeling town. What has this to do with me?"

"This goes against the bindings placed upon the Tylwyth Teg," he said carefully. "You know that. It goes against every agreement made between Annwfyn and Hannwfyn. The ancient compacts made between the two eternal realms do not allow for noticeable interference with Earthly matters. And I would say this counts as more than interference. This is invasion."

"I am not of the Tylwyth Teg, Ysbaddaden," the old woman said haughtily. "I do not reside in Annwfyn. I do not reside in Hannwfyn. I wandered among the stars and walked the byways of the ancient kingdoms that stood before the realms were spun from nothingness."

"I am aware of this, Cyrridwen. But I feel your involvement may be necessary. I've had a nagging suspicion tickling at the back of my brain since I first discovered that something unusual was happening with the changeling protocols, and I've only just been able to put my finger on it. To put it simply, I fear your grandchildren may be involved."

This finally got her ire up.

"This is not possible, Ysbaddaden!" she said furiously, drawing herself up to her full height and towering above him.

"It has the earmarks of their involvement."

"One of them has been missing for eons and the other is dead!"

"Are you sure?" he said carefully, attempting to tread a fine line between her fury at him and her fury at her progeny.

"I am quite certain that if either of my grandchildren had returned, I would have noticed!"

Ysbaddaden remained silent. He knew that Cyrridwen rarely interfered in the affairs of mortals, had done so less than a handful of times in her unfathomably long life. He'd played his best hand and knew that saying any more could only serve to weaken his position. She stewed on his words for several minutes before she spoke again.

"For the moment," she said, turning her back to him, "let's consider the theory that I might possibly assist you in this battle of yours...which is happening when, by the way?"

"Four hours from now."

"Oh my." She adjusted her clothing primly. "Let's entertain that theory for a moment, shall we? How could we possibly hope to win? Even with the considerable powers at my disposal, a force of coblyns and bwgans of this size is nothing to sneeze at."

"We would need help. What about your daughters?"

"My daughters," she said with a dismissive wave of her hand, "are even less likely than I to interfere in the affairs of Earth. Besides, they have chosen a life among the stars. I do not even know if I could reach them."

"What about Llyn Llyw?"

"The Salmon? You think the Salmon would deign to actually *do* something? He flops around, waiting for humans to come ask him for help, then dispenses cryptic nonsense. It's his thing. He's been doing it for millennia."

"Who else could we ask?"

"I don't know!" said Cyrridwen. "I don't know why I am even considering this."

Ysbaddaden fell silent again, allowing the old woman her thoughts.

"I can't help but feeling that, in some ways," he said, not making eye contact with her, "this may partially be my fault."

"Ysbaddaden Pencawr!" She pointed a gnarled, angry finger at him. "From what you've told me, this most definitely is your fault. In many, many ways." She sighed. "I will speak to my daughters. I will speak to the Salmon. I can promise nothing. I will return in four hours."

Chapter 77

The sun rose, pure and true, over the occupied town of Jeffersonville, Indiana. On a bluff above the town stood fifty thousand people, ready to march down and take it back. A blond-haired woman garbed in light mail armor was marshalling her forces. She carried a golden spear, which she had retrieved from her demesne in the night and which had been borne into battle only once before. She attempted to form the untrained, unarmed citizens into ranks and tried to impart what wisdom she could before the coming battle.

Ysbaddaden stood apart from the masses, his assistant perched upon his shoulder.

"Only about half of them have said they're willing or able to fight, Fan. So a force of twenty five thousand humans, one coblyn, one bwbach, you and me. I don't like our chances."

"Plus *her*, boss."

"Her?"

"Gwenllian ferch Gruffydd! The Warrior Princess! The one leading us into battle! She could probably take on the whole coblyn army herself!"

Ysbaddaden frowned sadly.

"She is our greatest asset right now, it's true, but she can't do it on her own. And Cyrridwen has still not returned. I will see this through to the end but, come nightfall, I wonder how many of those standing on this bluff will still be among the living."

"We've still got time, boss," Fan said consolingly. "Still time for one of those...you know, those things where everything looks terrible and then all of a sudden everything's fine..."

"A miracle?"

"Yeah, boss. Still time for a miracle."

Ysbaddaden grunted unhappily and finished buttoning up his tweed vest and adjusting his bow tie. Even if he was marching to his death, he'd be damned before he'd let himself be dressed inappropriately for the occasion.

Gwenllian gave an order and her force of twenty-five thousand began their march. The road into town was long and dusty and, once moving, the ranks of ill-equipped fighters stretched over a mile. They walked mostly silently, their eyes on the people in front of them or on the ground.

The Mayor walked at the head of the column, just behind Gwenllian, clearly trying to project a confidence that Ysbaddaden knew she couldn't possibly feel. He walked near the front as well, Fan fluttering along beside him, with Gafr and Winnie close by. Llwynog had chosen to remain behind with the baby.

Thirty minutes into their march, they were passing a dark copse of hemlocks when Ysbaddaden heard a familiar voice.

"Ysbaddaden! As I live and breathe!"

A massive form that consisted primarily of bands of knotted muscle hewn from rock and stone walked out from between two trees, a huge smile plastered across his face.

"Lwmpyn?" Ysbaddaden cried. "Is that you? What are you doing here?"

"I thought maybe you could use some help. I brought some friends along with me. Hope you don't mind!"

The ground began to vibrate and the trees began to shake and, with a booming sound at every footfall, a hundred of the massive rock creatures strode out of the woods, flattening the underbrush and the smaller trees as they walked. They fell in beside the humans and joined them in their march.

Ten minutes later, they were crossing over a bridge when Ysbaddaden heard a faint buzzing noise. It grew louder by the second and then he saw its source. A dark cloud was approaching them across the water. It grew closer and closer and then dissolved into countless chirping, tiny, winged creatures, somersaulting and spiraling as they converged with Gwenllian's Army. Fan joined them in the air and they all began talking excitedly, but their voices as they spoke were so high-pitched and rapid that Ysbaddaden could not understand them.

"Hey, everyone!" Fan called out to the group below. "I'd like you to meet my family!"

"Hi, everyone," her family called in unison, all several hundred of them.

The people below waved uncertainly, clearly not sure how to react to the new arrivals.

"That's your family?" the Mayor asked Fan as she resettled on Ysbaddaden's shoulder.

She nodded proudly.

"That's a big family."

"We're small," said Fan. "Our towns don't take up much space. We can have big families."

Ysbaddaden stared in wonderment as their march continued. Their bedraggled force had seemed doomed to defeat only minutes before. But now? Well, maybe they just stood a fighting chance. A very, very minute chance, to be sure, but with the addition of a hundred gwyllion and a few hundred ellyllon, he thought their odds of victory now definitely stood above zero.

"Fan...how did...how did this happen?"

"I made a couple calls, too, Boss."

She smiled proudly and he did as well, but they had little time to bask in the glow before another sight begged their attention. It was Cyrridwen, once again striding across the sky, but this time she was not alone. She was accompanied by nine ethereal figures with long gowns trailing behind and hair floating around them like sepulchral clouds. They did not walk in the sky, as Cyrridwen did, nor fly, as Fan and her family did, but dissolved into mist and coalesced again and in this way moved swiftly through the air. Each of the nine was perhaps twice as tall as a human or maybe thrice but their amorphous shapes made it difficult to tell. They were the color of fog on a winter morning except for their eyes, which were a brilliant blue.

"I told you I would return, Ysbaddaden!" Cyrridwen cried triumphantly. "And I was wrong! My daughters were happy to speak with me and happy to join you today. They say it has been too long since they have sung in battle!"

And thus, Cyrridwen and her daughters, the cyhyraeth, joined Gwenllian's Army as well.

"How on earth did you get the cyhyraeth on our side?" Gafr asked Ysbaddaden, plucking his sleeve.

"A little sweet talk," he answered. "A couple mildly suggestive compliments. A well-timed wink."

"Really?"

"No, of course not! They would have sliced me up and devoured me whole!"

Their conversation was interrupted by a low rumble which shook the trees and rattled their teeth.

"And somehow," Cyrridwen called, "I managed to convince *him* as well!"

Half a mile away, a huge beast rose from the waters of the Ohio River. Despite the distance, they could see it clearly, a vast silver shape glinting in the sun. Scales like shields stood upon its back. Its mouth was as wide as a house and its teeth as tall as a tree. Its neck was long and serpentine, its body as massive as a mountain, and its eyes were fiery wheels. Its enormous fins pulled it from the river and it loured upon the bank waiting for their arrival.

"Behold, Ysbaddaden," the old woman cried from her vantage in the sky, "the Salmon of Knowledge joins your battle!"

The beast roared and the very ground churned beneath their feet. Had Ysbaddaden not been quick to assure all those around him that this beast would be fighting with them and not against them, he was sure they would have lost ninety percent of their force. The humans looked in awe at the curious beings marching beside them, flying above them, and, in the Salmon's case, waiting beyond, throwing the river aside, gnashing its teeth and basking in its own fury.

There were no more arrivals but Ysbaddaden knew that no more were needed. He could not have asked for a better force to take on the vicious horde of changelings waiting for them at the other end of the road. With just these few newcomers, the odds of their victory had rapidly risen and he supposed that there might now be an even chance that he would still be breathing come nightfall.

Half an hour later, they arrived at the outskirts of Jeffersonville, at the line which seemed to demarcate the end of the goblins' destruction. On their side of the line stood twenty-five thousand humans, a few hundred gwyllion and ellyllon, the cyhyraeth and their mother, and in front, the commander of their army, Gwenllian, her blond braid blowing in the wind, her golden spear held lightly in her hand.

On the other side of the line stood a horde of coblyns hissing, howling, shaking their fists at the sky, and brandishing a wide array of weapons they had foraged from the town: golf clubs, parking meters, crowbars, hockey sticks, broom handles, table legs, umbrellas—all blackened in fire and sharpened into sickening points. The clockwork chickens were no longer patrolling but were now standing at attention on the street corners, their red eyes staring balefully at the newly arrived army. The bwgans clung to the sides of the buildings and flew overhead, so thick they nearly blocked out the sun. Beyond the bwgans, all that could be seen was fire.

The humans had been warned that the coblyns had taken over their forms, but even though they understood it intellectually, once the duplicates were standing in front of them, they were clearly shaken by it. Ysbaddaden saw them whispering and pointing as they recognized neighbors, friends, coworkers, in some cases themselves, standing amidst the destruction, snarling and hooting.

At the head of the coblyn army stood the Mayor's doppelganger, dressed in the same muted pantsuit, gray hair arranged in the same messy bun. Ysbaddaden could see the real Mayor, the human Mayor, standing nearby. Her face went white and she clenched her jaw as her exact copy raised a sharpened flagpole into the air. The horde of coblyns behind her repeated the gesture, shaking their weapons at the sky.

Both sides stood staring at each other, neither willing to make the first move. Cyrridwen walked through the air until she stood next to Ysbaddaden.

"I have brought what power I can to bear," she said. "Perhaps it is time that you do the same."

He glanced upward at her, then pursed his lips and turned away.

"How long has it been since you assumed your original form, Ysbadadden?" she asked.

"Ages," he answered. "It's so...cumbersome. Only useful for frightening the meek and scattering the livestock. And it's murder on my knees."

He glared at her, but he knew that she was right. He'd be of little use in his current form. His army needed all the help it could get, even if he'd pay for it later. Assuming he survived, of course.

"Ever used it against the bwgans?" she asked.

"Only once."

"Did it work?"

"Let's find out."

Ysbaddaden allowed his form to slip aside, the threadbare body he'd worn for the last several centuries, as comfortable as a well-worn sock at this point. The bureaucrat, the office worker, the factotum, the problem solver, the messenger, the negotiator—this form had served him well and would hopefully do so again. But today, he needed to reclaim the shape he had worn in his youth, when he had ravaged kingdoms and parleyed with queens and sent heroes to their dooms.

He found the form within himself and set it loose. His body grew and expanded so rapidly that it could barely be seen. At the end, he stood four stories tall and his arms were as thick as tree trunks. His beard grew to his belt and his eyes could see to the ends of the Earth. His teeth could crush stones and his voice could tear down walls. His feet could stomp a herd of cattle flat or his gullet could devour them and he could do either in three minutes flat. He picked up a car and threw it, just to remember how good it felt. It flew almost a mile.

"That's the giant I remember," Cyrridwen said as she strode back into the air.

"Cewri, my dear," he said, and the words blew several of the opposing coblyns into the remains of a nearby ice cream parlor. "We prefer to be called cewri."

A deathly calm settled over the street. Both sides eyed each other, daring the other to strike first. During their march, the people in Gwenllian's Army had picked up rocks, tree branches, fence posts, gardening tools, shovels in the abandoned houses along the way—anything that could be used as a weapon.

Gwenllian held her spear firmly in her hands, her eyes shining in the light from the fires sweeping through the town. Ysbaddaden clenched and unclenched his massive fists. In the sky above them, the nine cyhyraeth began the first murmurs of their song of battle. The gwyllion set their feet deep in the earth, anchoring themselves to the living rock. The ellyllon darted swiftly through the air, chirping incomprehensible profanities. Far in the distance, the Salmon roared once again, and Gwenllian took this as her cue.

The golden-haired hero raised her spear high in the air and, in a voice that was nothing less than velvet wrapped in steel, called her army to battle.

"Forward! Send these foul changelings screaming into the void! Take back your own! Take back your lives! For Jeffersonville...and for freedom!"

With these words, she hurled her golden spear toward the enemy. It arced high in the air, glinting in the light from the sun and from the fire. And behind the spear came her army: the grocers, the bankers, the teachers, the truckers, the nurses, the students, the gardeners, the accountants, and the Mayor, who insisted on being in the front line, saying she couldn't ask others to do something she wasn't willing to do herself. They roared their approval and charged forward, following the spear's flight.

The spear flew straight and true and found its mark in the changeling at the head of the coblyn army, the Mayor's doppelganger. The coblyn sneered but barely flinched as the point of the spear sank deep into her chest. There was no blood. The replica of the Mayor stood her ground, staring straight ahead at the rampaging army that was nearly upon her. She grabbed the shaft of the spear with both hands and, with an inhuman grunt, pulled it from her body.

A laugh was just beginning to erupt from her throat as she dissolved into a pillar of sawdust that fell to the ground and blew away. Behind her, the first rank of coblyns all reached their hands to their chests, just where the Mayor's changeling had been struck, and then collapsed into sawdust as well. The second rank did the same and then the row behind that and then the row behind that and, within seconds, the entire coblyn army splintered away into nothingness. Their remains were picked up by the wind and the sawdust fell down upon Jeffersonville like snow.

The clockwork chickens fell silent and still. Their lights went dark. Whatever power had been commanding them had dissolved along with the coblyn horde. Gwenllian's Army skidded to a halt in confusion. The bwgans were now the only enemies remaining in Jeffersonville. The shadows that had clung to the buildings and flew above the burning town now gathered together, forming a shapeless black mass in the sky that spun and shrieked and wailed.

"Congratulations," a voice spoke from the direction of the whirling shadows. A burst of static filled the brains of all those within earshot. Many grasped their heads in pain and some sank to their knees. "This smoldering ash-heap you once called home is yours once more. Enjoy it as you will for the rest of your brief lives. Our master's reckoning is at hand. There is now no way to prevent it. The days of this world are numbered and we shall rejoice at its demise. Our services are no longer required. We have fulfilled our duties. Do not attempt to seek us out. It will not end well for you."

With a deafening crack of thunder and a blast of glacial air that streaked the ground with frost, the shadows disappeared. The citizens of Jeffersonville walked wide-eyed through the streets, disbelief etched on every face as they saw up close what had become of their town.

The sawdust was now all that remained of the fifty thousand changelings. It threatened to feed the raging fires, but at a suggestion from Ysbaddaden, Cyrridwen and her daughters drew forth a warm rain which settled upon the town until all the flames had been washed away.

Ysbaddaden put aside his massive form and slipped back on his oh-so-comfortable bureaucratic body, made sure his tweed vest and bow tie were adjusted to his liking, then picked up a handful of sodden sawdust, examining it closely.

"Fetches?" Gafr asked him, joining him in the middle of the street.

"It appears so. There were never any coblyns here at all."

"The whole thing was a ruse?"

"It was real. It was just a different kind of real than we thought it was. No coblyns were involved, which is reassuring. But the bwgans were here. They were real. And they appear to be in league with someone who wanted us to *believe* that coblyns had invaded Earth. The town...the town is still destroyed. There must have been a reason for this. Unfathomable powers were unleashed to fashion this destruction and to obscure its origins."

"But what can we do?" Gafr asked.

"For now, nothing," Ysbaddaden said to him kindly. "Go find your wife and daughter. Bring them home. The humans will need your help if they are to build this town back from the ashes."

Ysbaddaden walked apart from the rest, to think on all that happened, on all that had led them to this point, and on the strange turning point he now found himself in.

The Battle of Jeffersonville was won with a single blow. But Ysbaddaden now knew that this battle was but one part of a larger war, a war that he had no knowledge of, that was hidden from his eyes. And how could he fight a war that he couldn't even find?

Chapter 78

Over the next few hours, the rest of the citizens found their way back to town. The city of tents was recreated below as the rebuilding process began. The destruction was not as complete as it had appeared at first. Many houses were still intact, and stockpiles of food, tools, and building supplies were quickly assembled. With the invading goblins and shadows now gone, the people of Jeffersonville were left to resume their previous lives as best they could.

In the dark of the night, most of the beings who had joined Gwenllian's Army departed. The ellyllon and the gwyllion found gates back to Annwfyn. The cyhyraeth and their mother returned to the stars, and the Salmon of Knowledge resumed his previous, less intimidating form.

Winnie asked Ysbaddaden to say goodbye to Hero for her. She said she couldn't bear to do it in person, and she figured that the parents had more than enough to deal with right now without having to deal with an overly distraught bwbach as well.

In the morning, Ysbaddaden found Gwenllian prowling the streets.

"Has there been any further sign of trouble?" he asked her, as they watched the humans begin the long process of cleaning up their streets and reclaiming their town.

"Nay," she replied. "I have searched the city as best I can. All traces of coblyn, fetch and bwgan appear to be completely gone. The city is free."

"My inquiries agree. The enchantment that was laid over the town appears to be degrading fairly rapidly. They should be visible to the rest of the world within a week. They'll have help soon."

"You and I should make sure to be well clear before that happens. Methinks this town needs more help of the human kind, and a significant decrease in the number of meddling heroes and bureaucratic giants mucking up the works."

Ysbaddaden looked at her quizzically.

"Did you just make a joke, Gwenllian?"

"I give myself an allotment of one per year. Methinks I have exceeded my quota."

At that moment, something like a shooting star fell from the sky and hovered above the street. Cyrridwen stepped from the flames. Her eyes stared wildly at the surroundings and her body flickered in and out of coherence, as if something prevented her from connecting with the plane of existence she found herself in.

"Ysbaddaden," she said, and her voice sounded as if it was traveling across incomprehensible distances to reach their ears. "I told you I felt no sign of my grandchildren's involvement. I was wrong!" Her body arched and convulsed in terrible pain. "He's about to do something dreadful. You must find him." Her voice was now a shriek of static. "His sister is in danger! The coblyn children are in danger! The entire world is in danger!"

"Where are they?" Gwenllian asked, but Cyrridwen's form could now barely be seen, and her voice could not reach their ears at all. Cyrridwen reached one staticky hand out and laid it aside Gwenllian's face. Gwenllian grimaced and shuddered as some unseen current passed between them. Then her eyes went wide.

"No," Gwenllian said. "He wouldn't..."

"You must go," Cyrridwen said, her voice finally finding them again. "You're the only one who can face him."

Then her body flickered for the last time and was gone. Gwenllian clutched her golden spear in one hand and made a gesture with the other, opening a hole in the folds of space and time. She stepped to the edge of the hole and dropped in, disappearing to realms unknown.

Ysbaddaden had only a moment to make a decision.

"I'm coming with you!" he shouted and jumped in feet first.

The streets of Jeffersonville were quiet once more.

ACT 6: SHATTERED

Chapter 79

Brynn and Makayla were sitting on a hill in the Land of Annwfyn, home to goblins and pwca and a host of other strange creatures that had mostly tried to eat them or kill them since they'd arrived. The hill they sat on was covered in rocks and moss. Behind them stood a windowless wooden shack. At the bottom of the hill was a crossroads, where three different roads ran off in different directions. There was a signpost at the crossing, but the language was not one that either of them could read. Brynn was wearing a sword. Makayla was carrying a mostly empty backpack.

"Talk about déjà vu," Makayla said. "Weren't we in this exact same position just a couple weeks ago?"

They looked out over the vastness of Annwfyn. They saw roads and forests, mountains and fields, swamps and villages and fortresses. They could travel in any of a million different directions, each seemingly as likely as the other to lead them to Brynn's brother.

"Well, what the hell do we do now?" Brynn asked testily. "Conn could be anywhere out there!" She waggled her hands furiously at the horizon. "Or somewhere else entirely. He might not even be on this plane of existence! I mean, where do we go? Who do we ask?"

"That wouldn't immediately try to eat us before we even finished the question," said Makayla softly.

"I'm in no mood for jokes," Brynn said, not making eye contact.

"Sorry."

Brynn stewed for several more minutes, tapping her feet angrily on the ground and wiping away the occasional tear.

"I...I can't even believe I'm suggesting this," she said finally, "but what about wishing? Like you keep trying to tell me, what's the use of having these stupid powers if I never use them?" She turned to Makayla, eyes pleading. "Could you wish again? I know it's something that I'm *not* supposed to screw around with and every time it's happened it really messed me up. But it worked once before. That's how we found the glass tower. You made it happen that time, Makayla. Make it happen again."

"I don't think I can, B," Makayla said regretfully. "You said it had to be the thing I wanted more than anything else...and I really want you to find your brother." She took Brynn's hand. "But I'm worried about my family now. I really want them to be okay and I'm worried about what's happening in Jeff and I want our house to be okay and I want our town to be okay and I'm worried about you and me getting home...and I don't think I can convince myself to want to find your brother more than any of those things. I'm really sorry."

"No, I understand."

"It doesn't mean I'm not going to stick with you until the end, though."

"I know," Brynn said with a sad smile. "Then I guess we're back where we started. We have to pick a direction. How do we decide? We spent a couple weeks with my parents going all over this place, it's *huge*. Is it just blind guesswork? Is that all we've got left?"

"Well, I actually have an idea about that," Makayla said, slipping off her backpack. "When we were hanging out in the cavern, you remember there was that weird rock that fell out of the cauldron? I ended up sort of taking it and I was messing around with it and it felt like something was inside."

She unzipped the backpack and pulled out the reddish-orange stone that Brynn's father had found. She handed it to Brynn who shook it. A very faint rattle could be heard inside, a whisper, a hiss.

"I was thinking...I don't know," Makayla said, "maybe it could be a clue or something."

Brynn held the misshapen stone in front of her face.

"What if it was put there by whoever is behind all of this...to distract us?" she said, nearly frantic. "What if this is one of those...those things? A what-do-you-call-it...a red herring? What if this is a wild goose chase so that whoever it is has time to do whatever they're planning to do to my brother? I just want him to be okay, Makayla!"

Makayla didn't say anything, just took the stone, smashed it against the ground, and cracked it open. It was hollow, as she had suspected it would be. Inside, coiled tightly, was a long stiff ribbon, once white, but yellowed with age, covered with indecipherable writing.

"It's...it's Conn's ribbon," said Brynn as her eyes opened wide.

"It's what?"

"My mom, back before me and Conn knew what we were—knew that we were goblins, I mean—every night she'd tie a ribbon around my wrist and she'd say this...this chant. It was supposed to stop the other goblins from finding us and taking us away. She'd do the same thing with Conn. This is his ribbon. I'm sure it is."

Brynn gently extracted the ribbon from the hollow in the stone and uncurled it.

"Look at this," she said, feeding it through her fingers, examining every inch. "There were words on my ribbon, letters or figures or something. I used to stare at them every night, trying to figure out what they were, what they meant. I never could." She held it out for Makayla to examine. "These are the same figures on this ribbon, but they've been crossed out. And something's been written over the top."

"Those look like the runes from your basement," Makayla said.

"I think you're right," Brynn said, "except for this one here…and here…and here…"

She pointed out several small rectangular holes which had been cut in the ribbon, excised with surgical precision. Each tiny hole was marked around the edges with a ragged design in a deep rusty red, so dark it was nearly black.

"I think I need to put it on," Brynn said. Her face was white and her eyes were haunted.

"Do you remember how your mom tied it?"

"I think so."

With Makayla's help, Brynn wrapped the ribbon around her wrist three times and tied it with a delicate looping knot. When they'd finished, they saw that the small rectangular holes now all lined up one inside the other. Beneath the holes, Brynn's pulse throbbed erratically.

"A door," she said, her voice shaking. "I mean, that's clearly a door, right?"

"Doors, Brynn. I think it's a door inside a door inside a door, but I don't know what that means."

"Is that where we're supposed to go?"

"I don't know. But I think our choices right now are either figure out what this means or close our eyes and randomly pick a direction and start walking. And that's kind of what we did the last time we were sitting on a hillside in front of a shack and when we did it that time, we almost got killed and honestly, I don't know how long our luck will hold out on that front."

"You're right. Of course, you're right."

"Okay, so we found the ribbon and we tied it on," Makayla said. "What happens after that?"

"So...once it was tied on, my Mom would...she'd say this chant."

Makayla nodded. Brynn closed her eyes and held the ribbon against her chest.

"Egg and Iron encircle this heart,
Fire and Clay crumble apart,
We need no gold,
We need no luck,
There is no child here, nothing but dust."

There was a long silence. Makayla was just about to ask what was going on when Brynn gasped and staggered and opened her eyes.

"I know where we need to go," she said, breathing hard. "I know where the door is." She pointed toward a fortress on the horizon. "And I know that we need to hurry."

Chapter 80

They set off immediately. Makayla tried to press Brynn for more clues about what she'd seen, but her friend was tight-lipped, saying only that she could clearly see the path ahead of them now. More than that, she either didn't know or wouldn't say.

In fact, neither of them talked much on the journey. They were lost in thoughts and worries of family, parents, siblings, town, all facing uncertain fates, lost in fear of where they were going and what they might find there in this vast unknown land that seemed to hold nothing but dangers and questions. Words would have distracted them from the relentless plodding of their feet toward a destination unknown.

Whenever they came to a fork in their path, Brynn would merely point to the left or to the right: around the village or through, toward the fortress or toward the fields, down the stream or up over the bank. When they encountered other creatures, the girls took hands and Brynn would fade them out of visibility until they had passed safely by.

When they grew too exhausted or too overcome to continue, they would stop, have a drink of water if they could find it, let the tears quietly flow if they needed to, and relieve the pressure on their aching, blistered feet as well as they could.

But eventually, night fell, as it did even on this strange world with no sun. The first night, they camped in the hollow of a fallen tree. Muddy, bloody, exhausted, thirsty and hungry, they laid themselves down on a bed of moss, their sleep thankfully dreamless.

The second day of their journey brought more of the same, except they talked even less. Just after midday, they passed around the fortress they had seen from the hilltop and found a narrow winding path that ascended into the mountains. That night, they slept in a crevice of rock that barely shielded them from the elements.

At the dawning of the third day of their journey, the wind bit at them and their hunger made them faint. Brynn's jaw was set in a constant scowl and her eyes were hollow. She told Makayla that they were close, the first words she'd spoken since dawn the day before.

An hour later, after following a narrow path that descended into a scar between the mountains, a path that crumbled under their feet, Brynn grabbed Makayla by the arm, stopping her short. They had walked for two days and two nights through a land more dangerous and more hostile than they could have ever imagined, and as their journey came to an end, they found themselves in a deep chasm between two jagged cliff faces.

They walked a winding path of tumbled stone. At the end, they saw a towering figure carved into the rock, a figure that looked part human and part savage beast. The figure was kneeling, with water in one hand and stars in the other.

Helping each other, stumbling, almost falling, regaining their footing, ascending again, they climbed the statue's lower leg. They climbed up its arm and onto its shoulder and from there climbed the stone tendrils of its hair onto its face until they stood within its empty eye socket.

They were at least a hundred feet above the ground and the wind was whipping around them. They looked into the vacant staring eye of the massive stone figure and at the end of the rounded hollow, they found what they'd been looking for. A thick wooden frame. An engraved rectangular panel. An iron latch.

At the end of their journey, they found a door. And when they opened the door, there was only darkness beyond.

Chapter 81

As Makayla stood looking into the blackness beyond the door, the memories of the Swallowed Hall came roaring back, the memories that came upon her every time she encountered a mystical doorway. They overwhelmed her. Her legs weakened. She stumbled and nearly fell. The smell was intruding on her, infiltrating her, gagging her.

"Did it happen again?" Brynn asked.

Makayla nodded, swallowing the bile back down that had risen in her throat.

"Yes, but also it's still happening," she said, shuffling over to lean against the stone wall.

"What do you want me to do?" Brynn asked.

"I don't know," Makayla said, tears in her eyes, as the memory swirled in the forefront of her brain and the darkness of the doorway wanted to swallow her whole.

"My brother's in there. Or at least he might be. It's the only lead we've got. I have to go through!"

"I know you do."

"But you don't," Brynn said, clasping Makayla's hands in her own. "You could stay here. Find somewhere safe. Hide. I could come back and find you later—"

"No! I'm coming with you."

"I don't know if that's a great idea."

"I'm coming, Brynn! I told you I was going to stick with you until this was all over. I'm coming."

"Are you sure?"

"Yes."

The feelings were rising even stronger now, threatening to wash away every part of her and leaving only the fear.

"Now, Brynn, we have to go now!"

Makayla closed her eyes as tightly as she could. She felt the familiar, strong, sinewy arms wrap around her and lift her and carry her and then she felt a lurch as Brynn leapt through the doorway. Inside herself, she felt the world tear itself apart and piece itself together again and her body didn't know which way was up or which way was down and it didn't know which parts went on the inside and which parts went on the outside. And then, suddenly, all was still. She could smell green grass and violets or something close enough to those two smells that it didn't make a difference.

"It's done," Brynn said. "We're through."

"Are you sure?" Makayla asked.

"Yeah. You can open your eyes."

Hesitantly, her body still shaking, she opened one eye and then the other. The world around her was so bright that it took several seconds for her eyes to adjust. They were in a sun-dappled field of blue flowers that went on and on as far as she could see. She looked above and saw that this world, wherever it was, must not be Annwfyn, because there was real sunlight pouring down. But she could also tell it wasn't Earth, because the sunlight came from three different suns. A little way off, she spied a grove of trees, and hanging from the branches, low and inviting, appeared to be some type of fruit.

"Oh my god, Brynn. Is that food?"

It had been several days since they'd had a substantial meal, or really anything to eat other than a few berries they had foraged while traveling through Annwfyn. They ran.

"Wait," Makayla said as Brynn was reaching for a piece of fruit. "We're not on Earth. We're not on Annwfyn. What if these are made of...I don't know, tungsten or something and they kill us instantly?"

"There's sunlight," Brynn said. "There's clearly oxygen 'cause we're breathing. This place is at least kind of Earth-like. I'm thinking maybe the fruit is too." She took a tentative bite. "I mean, I'm not dead yet, I guess?"

"I suppose it's either this or dying of starvation, right?" Makayla said and they both dug in.

The fruit looked like pears but tasted like tomatoes. Neither of them cared. They ate until they were full and then they ate a little more. And the sudden influx of nutrients made them a bit giddy and then they were laughing. They rolled around on the ground for a while as the suns beat down upon them, still bloody and torn, but at least they were full and warm.

They were sitting together against the trunk of the largest of the fruit trees passing another pearmato back and forth (even though neither of them were really all that hungry anymore), when Brynn pointed at something across the grove.

"Do you see that, Makayla?"

Makayla followed Brynn to a tree at the farthest edge of the orchard. They saw a door in the trunk, narrower and taller than any door they'd ever seen. It must have been ten feet high, but barely wide enough for a person to squeeze through sideways. They stood there in silence for several moments, then Brynn pressed on the handle and pulled the door open. There was nothing but darkness beyond. Makayla screamed.

Chapter 82

"Now, Brynn! Go now, just do it!"

The stink of the dead bodies and the rotting flesh filled her brain and she slammed her eyes shut. Arms wrapped around her and her body was pushed through the narrow doorway. Her head slammed against the frame and she saw stars. Then the world went sideways and there was nothingness surrounding her and gravity disappeared and suddenly there was ground beneath her feet again. She fell to her knees and retched, her hand massaging her head where it had smacked against the wooden doorframe.

Once her breathing had calmed somewhat, she cautiously opened her eyes. They were in a large round tent that looked as if it had once been part of a circus but was now faded and dilapidated. Dull stripes of gray and brown had likely (decades ago) been bright stripes of purple and yellow. Rows of wooden risers sat near the edges of the circle, mostly collapsed. A high wire still shone high above. They had arrived under a flap of canvas. At the opposite wall of the tent, they lifted another flap and saw nothing but darkness beyond.

"Damn it, Brynn," Makayla said, the memory already rising strong within her. "Another door? How many freaking magic doors do we have to go through?"

"Close your eyes, Makayla," Brynn called, her skin already changing from pale to green, and Makayla did as she was told. She felt the canvas slide over her body as she was carried through the doorway. Her chest tightened and her head went light and everything inside her and around her went topsy-turvy and then there was solid ground beneath her feet again.

They were standing at the edge of a frigid pond, the grasses around its edge silver with frost. The pond sat at the bottom of a deep depression, the stone walls too high and too smooth to climb. Beneath the surface of the pond, they could see a free-standing wooden door.

"I don't care for this door at all, Brynn. I really don't."

"Yeah. Me neither. You ready?"

Makayla nodded and squinted her eyes shut. Even though she couldn't see the blackness behind the door this time, it didn't matter. She held her breath as Brynn picked her up and dove into the water and as soon as the ice-cold water hit her skin, the memories flooded her brain and her head grew so light she could barely think.

When the world stopped turning this time, she had to sit for several minutes before she could open her eyes. They were at the bottom of a well. The rough stone walls dripped with water and moss grew beneath their feet. There was an arched stone doorway directly across from them. Makayla nodded wearily, shut her eyes, and Brynn carried her through.

They spent the entire day walking through doors. One door took them into the middle of an ocean and they climbed up a rope ladder to a doorway anchored in the sky. Another doorway dropped them onto an abandoned boat, floating adrift. They found the exit below the deck, in the ship's hold. Another opened into the middle of the air. They fell screaming for only a few seconds before another doorway swallowed them up. One door opened onto a snowfield. One was high in a tree. One door set them in a dark tunnel underground and they had to crawl on their bellies for several minutes to reach the next. Another took them into a dimly lit cave and they had to creep into the mouth of a sleeping dragon to find the exit. Another door was made entirely of fire.

There were so many doors that Makayla eventually lost track of them all. It started to feel like a dream. They went from door to door to door—out one, in another, then out again—until they were almost running from door to door, fearful that if they stopped, they'd never reach the end.

And at every door, Makayla had to close her eyes as memories of the Swallowed Hall rose unbidden, as the smell of death and rot filled her brain and lived within her for as long as the doorway remained, and Brynn would carry her or push her or pull her through.

Finally, their bodies grew too tired to continue. They weren't sure if it was night where they were, but it was nighttime in their brains, and they knew they needed sleep. They stepped through one final doorway and found themselves on a sandy beach. Ocean waves were lapping at the shore. They saw another door built into the edge of a nearby dune. It was dark on this world and there were stars but no moon. It seemed as good a place as any to sleep and resume their search in the morning.

"You know, at that last doorway," Brynn said, as they made themselves comfortable on the sandy beach, staring at the starlight above, "you pretty much went through that one on your own. I wasn't really carrying you, just kind of pulling you along with me. Does that mean...do you think it's getting better?"

"Huh?"

"I mean, you told me you keep having those memories flashing back up in your brain when we see the doors. Do you think you're getting over it?"

"B," Makayla said slowly, "this isn't really something you get over. Something bad happened to me that really freaked me out and now whenever we see those doorways, they remind my brain of the bad thing. I don't know. It feels kind of like a short circuit and all of a sudden I'm in both places or something." She chewed on her lip. "It's not an infection and you take an antibiotic and it goes away. It's not a tumor you can cut out. It's part of me now. It will always be part of me, I guess. You don't get 'better.' You get 'not as bad.' You get 'I can cope with my brain telling me the world is falling apart even when it's not.'"

"Except sometimes the world actually is falling apart," Brynn said sadly.

"Yeah. But even then, you have to learn what there is to hold onto."

"Like each other."

"Exactly."

They reached their hands out and held onto each other in the dark.

"It just feels so stupid, you know," Makayla said, "because it's...it's fear...that's all it is. It's something that every damn human experiences every damn day of their lives. And whatever happens when I see those doorways is just my brain's way of dealing with the fear of all this freaky crap that's been happening to us. I mean, I know we have to go through those doors...but I'm scared, Brynn. Those doors scare the crap out of me."

"Who the hell wouldn't be scared at the crap we've been through? I'm scared too."

Makayla rolled over and stared at Brynn as best she could in the darkness.

"Dude! You've got superpowers!" she said. "You can go invisible and turn into a bird and turn into a super-strong green girl and grant wishes and...and all these crazy things—"

"Doesn't matter. I'm scared too," Brynn said. "All the time. I was scared when the shadows were chasing us out of Jeff. I was scared when Cath Palug had me tied up. I was scared when that cavern was collapsing all around us. I mean, I'm scared right now."

Makayla rolled back over and turned away from Brynn.

"Yeah, except you can walk through the doors," she said, shaking her head. "Every time. I'm the one holding us back."

"What? Come on—"

"Dude, you are literally carrying my weight. You are picking me up and carrying me through each and every doorway we come to. Ever since we left home."

Brynn sat up and leaned over Makayla.

"I don't know what's happening inside you, Makayla. I can't feel what you're feeling. I have no clue how I would have reacted if what happened to you had happened to me. There's no way I could know. But I don't think it's about ignoring the fear or being better than the fear or shutting the fear out. The fear is going to be there. It's in you. It's in me."

Makayla sat up as well, and the two girls sat on the sand, facing each other.

"But my Mom...she used to say that you can't hide from your emotions but you can choose what to do with them," said Brynn. "She always told me I should take my feelings and turn them into bright fire. She said I should take them, hold them, and make something wonderful."

Makayla thought about this for a long time as they nestled themselves back into the sand.

"I kind of wish your Mom was here now," she said, just as she was falling asleep.

"Yeah. Me too."

Chapter 83

They started hopping worlds again at first light. They foraged a few berries (which turned out to be sour but filling), slipped on sword and backpack, and then Brynn swung the door open, revealing the darkness beyond. Makayla squinted her eyes shut and with Brynn's hand guiding her, they stepped through the door in the dune.

They came out in a graveyard and found the next door in the back of a mausoleum. They were launched into an inky black void and swam through the darkness to a door of blazing white. One door dropped them on a mountaintop, and another set them down in the middle of a desert. They arrived in a kitchen, politely declined a dance with an array of singing knives and exited under a table. They emerged into a huge marble room filled with steaming baths and had to dive into one of them to find the way out. One door dropped them in an abandoned warehouse and the next set them onto a swaying rope bridge high above a distant canyon. Each time they found the exit door, Makayla shut her eyes tight and Brynn pulled or carried her through as the memories filled her with fear.

In a field of daisies that grew twice as tall as they were, Makayla grabbed Brynn's arm and pulled her to a stop.

"How many doors have we been through?" Makayla panted, trying to catch her breath.

"Since we started?"

"Yeah, since we went through that first door yesterday, the one in the statue's eye."

"I don't know. Dozens maybe. Less than a hundred, I'm pretty sure."

"How many more, Brynn? We step out of one door and into another. And then we step out of that one and find the next one and then we do it again and again and again. How long is this going to go on?"

"I don't know, Makayla. I have no answers. I just know we need to keep moving."

The next door dropped them into a forest of mangroves and the one after that into a transparent glass sphere orbiting a small moon. Another door set them down on a vast, sticky, white plain that looked and smelled like marshmallows. Three doors later, they were on a seashore and the exit could only be found after they shooed away a large flock of brown pelicans. The next door opened into a clock tower and they had to ride the second hand up to the exit door, which was behind the twelve. A treehouse, a mansion made of metal, a rice paddy, a laundromat—the doors went on and on.

After several hours of jumping from world to world, they sat and rested in a rundown palace on a windy moor, in front of an ornate gilded door, eating a few more of the precious berries they had saved from the morning's forage.

"Just like you said, Makayla. So many doors," Brynn said with a deep sigh. "They can't just go on forever, right? There has to be an end, doesn't there?"

"Yeah," Makayla answered. "I'm sure there does. There has to be an end. Sometime." She looked at Brynn as they sat there in just one of the myriads of worlds upon worlds they had visited since they began this journey, and in that moment, she realized that she'd made a decision. "And there's something I need to find out before we get there."

She turned her body until she and Brynn were sitting knee to knee.

"I've been thinking about what we talked about," Makayla said. "About fear. About what we can do with our feelings. I want to do something with mine. I want to turn them into something else. I want to make something wonderful."

She bit her lip nervously, then leaned over and haltingly put her face right in front of Brynn's, until their noses were almost touching.

"Is this okay?" she asked.

Brynn nodded.

"I'm going to do something now," Makayla said softly.

"Okay."

"Yeah?" Makayla asked and waited for what seemed like an eternity for the answer.

"Yeah," Brynn said, a shy whisper that could barely be heard.

And Makayla kissed her.

She didn't know how long the kiss lasted or precisely what feelings ran through her while it went on, or if she did, she never spoke of it, for this was another moment that Makayla chose to keep deep within her heart.

But once the moment had passed and they were sitting next to each other, side by side, quiet smiles on quiet faces, she said, "I've wanted to do that for a long time. I don't know what's going to happen next, but if...if things get bad...I thought I should do that before things get, um, you know. Bad."

Brynn gulped.

"Was it okay that I did that?" Makayla asked hesitantly.

Brynn nodded nervously.

"I mean, you like girls, right?"

"Yes," Brynn answered, although her voice wavered.

"Yes?"

"Yes...but..."

"But?"

"But not only girls."

"Okay. So...boys *and* girls."

"Yes. Boys and girls," Brynn said, then paused. "And."

"And?"

"Yeah. And."

"And what?" Makayla asked, brows furrowed.

"I'm not sure. I don't know if some of the goblins and the rest of the Tylwyth Teg really think about themselves as boys or girls."

"Huh?"

"I mean, I'm a goblin," Brynn said with a shrug. "But I still think of myself as a person. So I like people. And I *like* people. But I also see a goblin and go, 'hmm.' And there was that hot horse person, the pwca, and I don't know if...if that horse person...was a boy or a girl or what. So yeah, I like girls. But I don't think that's all I like. Is that okay?"

"Yeah. Of course. You like what you like. I can't change that. No one can."

"I like *you*," Brynn said and Makayla blushed.

"We should keep going, right?"

"Yeah. We probably should."

They stood up, buckled on a sword, slipped on a backpack, then opened the golden door. Makayla shut her eyes tight and, hand in hand, they walked through together.

Chapter 84

They stepped out of the doorway into a wide shadowy glade. A stand of trees with massive trunks formed a circle within. Around the edges, brush grew so thick and so tall that it was impassable—a self-contained sphere inside a giant, otherworldly forest. The glade was brown and dry, as if it was waiting for a spring that was never to come. The place was eerily silent, and they looked around cautiously.

"Brynn," Makayla said, coming to a realization.

"What?"

"I don't see another door. Every other time we've been able to see the door as soon as we entered. There's no other door. I think this is the end. I think this is the place all those other doors were leading us to."

"This is it," Brynn said, her breath shuddering, her eyes fixed on the silent glade.

"Yeah."

"This is the end."

"I think so."

"But why are we here?" Brynn asked, her voice growing desperate. "We left Jeffersonville weeks ago and every step led us closer to this...this place. Why this place? There's nothing here."

"Maybe not nothing," Makayla said. "Look."

She grabbed Brynn's hand and they carefully stepped farther into the silent glade. From within the circle, they could see that the trees all had curving wooden staircases winding around their wide trunks. The stairs extended upward among the limbs and leaves and disappeared in the canopy above. Wherever the stairs led, it couldn't be seen from the ground below.

But more curious than this was what stood in the very center of the clearing. A huge oblong mirror in a smooth wooden frame, ten feet tall, floated above the brown, dead grass. In the mirror was the reflection of a woman, bathed in an ethereal glow. Brynn and Makayla walked around the mirror. There was nothing behind it, nothing holding it up. The glade itself was empty. There was only her reflection and nothing else.

The woman in the mirror, frozen and still, had skin as dark as the night sky. Her hair floated around her in a glowing halo, and her open eyes were so pale that they appeared entirely white at first glance. She was dressed in a long gown of blood red, simply made with simple materials. A brocaded velvet belt sat loosely on her hips. Her face was peaceful but also alert, as if it would take but a word to bring her back to life. The light surrounding her washed over her but all else within the mirror was an inky, empty void.

The reflection was so close, so real, that Makayla felt like she should be able to reach out and touch the woman, but when she put her fingers to the glass, it was cold and hard beneath her hand.

"Who is she?" whispered Brynn.

"I don't know," Makayla responded in kind, not knowing why their voices were hushed, but also knowing that it was appropriate. "But she's beautiful." She paused and looked thoughtfully at the woman in the mirror. "No. 'Beautiful' isn't the right word. Is there a word that means 'so beautiful you can't look away but also so powerful you think you probably should?'"

Brynn shrugged.

"Is she human?"

"I don't know," Makayla said. "She kind of looks it but I'm also really getting the feeling that she's not."

"Like she's human but also more than human."

"Except not that she's more than us. Like we're less than her."

"Yeah."

At that moment, they heard footsteps, hard shoes on soft wood, coming from somewhere above them in the treetops. Brynn grabbed Makayla's hand. They slipped into invisibility and then backed away, as slowly and quietly as they could, to the edge of the glade.

A sinewy goblin came clomping down one of the stairways which wound about the tree trunks. He had gray skin and bright green hair and a long, pointed nose. His eyes were small and bright, and he was dressed in a high-collared shirt and a satin vest, with a jeweled brooch at his throat. It sounded like he was humming to himself.

"Oh my god," whispered Brynn. "I can't believe it."

"Who...who is that?"

"That's my little brother."

Brynn was about to rush to him, but Makayla held her back when they saw another figure following close behind, a swaggering figure with incredibly pale skin, jet black hair, and the darkest eyes imaginable.

"What the hell is going on?" Brynn breathed.

"Is...is that Finian?"

"Yeah. Finian or Efnysien or whatever he's calling himself now, I guess."

"But he's…"

"Yeah, he's the one who kidnapped you last year and held you captive. Who came and destroyed my house. Almost killed my whole family. Who burned me."

"But isn't he, you know, dead?" Makayla asked, brows knit in confusion.

"Reports of his death seem to have been grossly exaggerated."

Efnysien followed Conn as they descended to the floor of the glade. He leaned over and said something to Conn that Brynn and Makayla couldn't hear. Conn nodded, a proud smile on his face. Efnysien smiled and patted Conn on the back tenderly, then drew a thin, ornate knife from his belt. Conn knelt down on the dry barren ground and pulled his hair aside, exposing his neck.

"No!" Brynn shouted, and the sound was barely out of her lips before Efnysien reacted. He made a small gesture and uttered a quiet word and then a huge blast of cold air ripped through the clearing. Brynn and Makayla were left frozen in place, gasping for breath. Brynn's concentration faltered and the invisibility flickered away, leaving the girls exposed. Efnysien turned to them, a smug smile plastered to his face, his dark eyes sparking fire.

"Ah," he said, "my would-be Queen has joined us!"

He walked over to Brynn and laid a smoldering finger on her jaw, then looked contemptuously at Makayla.

"You declined my companionship and chose this instead?" he spat at Brynn. "A human?"

Brynn jutted her jaw out but did not respond.

"I can't imagine how much trouble it must have taken the two of you to find us here," Efnysien continued, his ever-present smirk growing ever so slightly wider. "And for what? Come to change your mind? Throw yourself at my feet and beg my forgiveness and ask me to take you back?"

"I'm not here for you, Finian," Brynn said, a calm voice through gritted teeth. "I'm here for him. My brother."

Efnysien rolled his eyes and strolled back to the middle of the glade.

"It matters not," he said. "Your time is past. Your brother will make a far more fitting companion for me than you ever could."

He wiggled one of his fingers absent-mindedly and dusky brown vines rose from the ground and bound Brynn and Makayla's arms.

"Well, in any case," he said, "I'm glad you've come. After all, what would a wedding be without witnesses?"

Chapter 85

"A wedding?" Brynn shouted. "What the hell are you talking about?"

But Efnysien ignored her.

"Come, Cwningen," he said, "look in the mirror. See yourself."

Conn turned and looked in the mirror floating in the center of the glade. His reflection shone and blended with that of the woman within, gray skin with dark, green hair with white, dark eyes with light. Efnysien stood behind the young goblin and looked over his shoulder at the merged reflection.

"Look at you, my magnificent Goblin Queen. Are you ready?" Efnysien held out his hand. "Are you ready to become my bride?"

Conn reached his hand toward Efnysien's with a nervous smile.

"Conn, no," Brynn shouted, "what are you doing?"

"Don't call me that!" he snarled. "My name is Cwningen! I don't use that other name anymore. It was just the name our parents made me use so I wouldn't scare the humans. And guess what?" he said, staring at Makayla and sticking out his long goblin tongue. "I want to scare the humans now."

"This is insane!" Brynn said to him. "Why are you doing this?"

"I'm a goblin, Brynn," he said, turning to her. "I want to do goblin things. I don't want to resist what's inside me. It's part of me. I want to be true to what I'm feeling even if you or Papa or whoever think it's wrong."

"No, come on. Let's go home. Mama and Papa and I have been so worried about you—"

"You never paid attention to me, Brynn! Never wondered how I was feeling about everything that happened to our family. You just...you just figured out about your goblin powers, and about what our family actually was, and how we're so different from everyone else, and do you know when you came and told me about all of that?"

He pulled himself up to his full height and stared his sister straight in the eyes.

"I...I..." she stammered.

"Never, Brynn! The answer is never! I'm your brother and you never told me about it. You know when Mama and Papa told me about it? Only after our home was invaded and we were almost killed!"

"But why *him*?" Brynn asked, finding her voice again. "Why are you here with him? He kidnapped Makayla! He almost killed us!"

"Because whenever I tried to talk to Mama or Papa or even to you about being a goblin, all anyone ever said was, 'oh no, you have to ignore those feelings inside you, those are bad feelings' or 'look at all the humans around us, look at your classmates, be like them.'"

Conn paced angrily around the glade.

"I'm not like the other kids in my class," he said. "I'm not like you. All the people at school are just people. I'm not! I'm different. I'm more than that. And no one...*no one*...in my family would talk to me about what was happening inside me!" He pointed at Efnysien. "He was the only other one who was like us, the only other being I'd ever met who could possibly help me. So I found him. He listened to me, Brynn! He answered my questions. He told me about what being a goblin really meant, what being one of the Tylwyth Teg really meant, about what being from Annwfyn really meant. He told me the truth! He told me the truth about what was going on inside me."

Conn gave a rueful smile.

"What did you and Papa call it?" he asked. "You and Papa used that stupid, stupid word, 'maleficence.'"

"It's not stupid—" Brynn said.

"It *is* stupid!" her brother said. "Because all it means is that we're goblins! And our impulses are not human ones! It's not maleficence. It's our nature. It's our destiny. It's who we are."

"It's not who we have to be," Brynn said, nearly in tears. "We get to choose. There's a better way."

"I don't want to be better. I want to be myself."

"Conn," Brynn said desperately, "you can't get married. You're only eleven."

"I can do whatever I want!"

Efnysien walked up and put a calm hand on Conn's shoulder. He looked Brynn in the eye as her brother glared at her.

"So you see," Efnysien said, "your brother wasn't captured. He wasn't coerced. He's exactly where he wants to be."

Brynn and Makayla stared in silence, their arms still bound tightly to the ground below, as Efnysien walked to the mirror and, with a great effort, pushed his hands into the glass and through it. Using his knife, he cut off a long lock of the frozen woman's hair, and then withdrew his hands from the mirror.

Conn knelt before him again. Efnysien cut off a lock of Conn's green hair and then reached behind his head and cut off a lock of his own. He held the three locks in his hand, the white, the green, the black. He whispered to them and while he spoke, the three locks of hair wove themselves together into a braided ribbon, several feet long.

He held out his hand and raised Conn to his feet. Then, as his whispers continued, the plait wrapped itself around both their hands several times and tied itself into a knot.

"Do you remember the words I taught you?" he asked Conn, who nodded in response.

"*Hearts speak in silence,*" chanted Efnysien.

"*Never more beat alone,*" answered Conn in kind.

"*Eyes for each other.*"

"*Thy visage now my wine.*"

"*Hands bound fast as one.*"

"*Soul and spirit, flesh and bone.*"

"*Blood joined to blood.*"

"*My blood is now thine.*"

After Conn spoke the final line, there was an unnatural silence in the glade—a silence that was quickly subsumed by a thrum of power, a thrum that dried Brynn and Makayla's eyes, parched their throats, and made the hairs on their arms stand on end.

Efnysien raised the knife in the air and plunged it downward, straight through the back of his own hand and into Conn's beneath. Their blood fell and blackened the withered ground. A wave of energy pulsed through the glade.

Conn screamed.

Brynn screamed.

Efnysien smiled.

Chapter 86

"And now our bloods are joined," Efnysien said, the triumphant smile playing on his lips, "the blood of your parents joined with the blood of mine."

Conn stared in shock and horror at the blade piercing their hands. He was shaking his head, eyes wide. His lips moved and a guttural sound came from his throat, but he couldn't seem to form any words.

"You are bound to me now by the oldest compacts, the most ancient of covenants," Efnysien continued. "We bound our hands. We bound our bloods."

"No!" Conn shouted, finding his voice at last. "I don't want this. I changed my mind! Please, let me go!"

Efnysien waved his hand insouciantly, and the same brown, desiccated vines that bound Brynn and Makayla's arms now climbed up Conn's body and wrapped themselves around his mouth, silencing him.

"But I need more than just your blood, my Cwningen, my Goblin Queen," Efnysien said. "I need all that you are. It is only through you that I can fulfill a destiny begun so many eons ago. My sister, my twin, she has been denied to me. But you are the vessel, the door, that will open her essence and join it with mine own."

He closed his eyes and made a grasping gesture with his unbound hand. The glass of the mirror rippled as the woman's body was pulled forward. Her outline was traced upon the surface of the mirror, and then her body slowly pushed through, the shining surface clutching at her, unwilling to let her go. Efnysien increased his efforts, his fingers straining against the force that held her within, and with one final pull, she was free of the mirror, her body fully in the glade, floating a few inches off the barren ground.

She was still frozen, still bathed in the ethereal glow that Makayla and Brynn had first found her in. Her eyes remained open. Her face was calm. Her body remained completely still. Once Efnysien and his twin were standing next to each other, it became clear that they were nearly complete opposites, at least in appearance. The one had pale skin and the darkest eyes imaginable, while the other had the darkest skin imaginable and eyes so pale that they were almost white.

"I brought you here, sister," Efnysien spoke softly, "so long ago, to this realm within a realm. To this tiny portion of Annwfyn that I walled off from the rest. And once I have taken what I need from you, *all of it* will be mine."

"So, what?" Brynn said scornfully. "All of this is just so you can take over Annwfyn? So you can be in charge of it all?"

"I don't want to rule it," Efnysien spat, his eyes sparking with haughty fire. "How petty. How tiresome. Ruling over this world, with all of its squabbling factions, with all of their eccentricities and foibles and bureaucratic machineries would be, to say the least, exhausting."

He turned on Brynn and Makayla, and his eyes were so full of ravenous longing that they feared they would be swallowed up by his gaze alone.

"No," he said. "I will devour this world. I will slake my hunger with it. When I was a boy, I devoured my siblings while we lay in Hafgan's Cauldron and with each bite I could feel my power grow. As I gnawed on their bones, I could feel arcane knowledge and cosmic awareness birthing within me. When the cauldron cracked, I stepped forth, and since that moment, all I have known is hunger. Wine, beasts, blood, loves, lives, souls—I have taken all I can and more, but still it was not enough."

Efnysien licked his lips and fire dripped upon the ground.

"Nothing can satisfy this ache, this void within me," he said. "Nothing could...except everything. I will devour the Land of Annwfyn. All of it. Every seedling, every scrap, every field, every mountain, every den, every family, every clan will feed me, and when I am sated, my fire will course through the very veins of existence. I will be one with this universe. I will flow through her veins, and I will be her, and she will be me."

"And what then?" Brynn asked. "After you've eaten this universe. Time to move on to the next?"

"Perhaps," Efnysien said, almost coquettishly. "My hunger may be fulfilled. It may not. We'll just have to cross that bridge when we come to it. And I say 'we' because you'll be part of it too. You are part of this realm now. And when I consume it, you will be a speck of insubordinate seasoning for my meal. Your essence will be forever a part of me." He held up his free hand with the palm away from them. "Right here, see? I'm going to put you right here on the back of my left hand so every time I itch my nose, I'll remember you." He rolled his eyes, then smirked and squinted at Brynn. "I mean, not really. I've known you for, what? A year? I've had bouts of indigestion that lasted longer."

He turned to his twin sister and gave a deep sigh of longing.

"She's utterly beautiful, isn't she?" he asked. "She was the only one of us to escape imprisonment in the cauldron. After the cauldron cracked, I searched for her, for eons, but she had hidden herself from me, set cryptic barriers between us and let loose glamours that obscured her from my eyes, from my prying charms. I had the essences of seven siblings within me, but without her, my power was incomplete. My hunger grew but my ability to sate it was stunted. I needed her to fulfill my desires."

"But when at last I came to her, I found that consuming her was beyond my abilities. I lacked the strength, the fortitude, the knowledge. As I had grown in power, so had she." He gave a surprisingly human shrug. "Or perhaps it was simply that she was my twin and something within me held me back from devouring the second half of myself. I could not consume her, but I needed her power. So I found another way forward. Ancient magic that lingered from before the creation of the realms was revealed to me."

He tapped a long, pale finger against his lips, his eyes glinting mischievously at Makayla and Brynn.

"The nine peoples of Annwfyn sprang from the nine siblings, did you know this? My twin and I, the bastard children of Penarddun, and her seven acknowledged children with Llŷr. The progenitors of the nine races. And the lowliest of these, the coblyns and the xana, hold bygone magic within their blood, magic held over from a time before time."

"I found one of each, a coblyn and a xana, divided by space and time, one in Earth and one in Annwfyn. And once I had bound them together, once their souls were joined, I used their blood to forge my sister's bindings and here she's remained, bound by lowly goblin blood, for centuries."

"Wait a second," Brynn said hoarsely, her face gone white with horror, "a goblin and a xana, one from Earth and one from Annwfyn. My parents...you're talking about my parents?"

Efnysien gave a look of mock surprise, his hand flying to his cheek.

"They...they were helping you?" Brynn said incredulously. "You're lying. That can't be true!"

"Your parents were part of my life for many, many years," Efnysien said with a cruel, mocking smile, enjoying Brynn's agony. "My spies, my emissaries, my enforcers, my factotums. My loyal servants. Sometimes even more than that. Sometimes less. Their blood bound my sister, but to consume her essence, I needed more. I needed to bind their blood to mine."

He gave a disdainful sniff.

"But they fled before I had the chance. Perhaps they suspected what I was to become. Perhaps they feared my wrath. Perhaps their hearts ached from the love I showered upon them and they could no longer bear my presence. I know not. They fled from me, denying me their blood, denying me the power which flowed from it. They fled from me and escaped my sight. This should have been beyond them. My sister, my equal, hidden from my eyes? Perhaps. For a while. But a lowly coblyn and his wretched xana wife? Utter nonsense. But somehow they managed it."

"I snipped apart this little bubble of Annwfyn and secreted my sister here, while my senses and servants searched for your parents for many long years. There was nothing... nothing... nothing... and then suddenly, two years ago, pop! They showed back up again, nothing masking them, no concealing magics. My two faithful servants were found, only now with two children of their own. And they were found in that most unlikely of places: Jeffersonville, Indiana. On Earth."

"Then it struck me. Your parents had provided the perfect solution to my dilemma. I needed to join both their bloods with mine. But they had already joined their bloods together. In their children. Certainly, it would be much easier to take control of an immature goblin than to wheedle it from two of the Tylwyth Teg at the height of their powers, whose command of their gifts had been growing for centuries. One of their children. That was all I needed."

The smile faded from his face and the fire faded from his eyes until they became pools of utter blackness.

"I went to unimaginable lengths to obtain you, Brynn, so that you could fulfill your destiny and become my Goblin Queen, but you denied me. I tried to take your baby sister, but you and that foul hero killed me. A goblin and a human managed to slay me!"

His head twitched, shaking away an unpleasant memory.

"I mean, it's not like it hasn't happened to me before, but it's still a pain in the ass, to be quite frank. For quite some time, I thought my plan had failed, but as I wandered in darkness, nursing myself back to existence from the infinitesimal speck of my essence that remained, I heard a voice calling to me. Your brother. And I realized that perhaps all was not lost after all."

"Your brother needed answers. Someone to listen to him, to guide him. And I needed *him*. His blood and all the rest of him. Here in this place with me for an hour. Maybe less. And I also needed the rest of his family and all of the heroes and all those who watch over Annwfyn, I needed all of them to be looking somewhere else, anywhere but here. Because what is about to happen will shake this realm to its core. At least for the last few minutes of its existence before I devour it."

"I figured a tornado of goblins and shadows in that insipid little town you seem to love so much ought to do the trick. And it nearly worked, didn't it? The rest of your family and friends stayed there dealing with the lovely little army I assembled. But not you. You just had to find your brother, didn't you? And you did it! Here he is! Ta-da!"

He gestured grandly at Conn, who was shaking, wide-eyed with horror as he realized the extent of Efnysien's plans and clutching at his bleeding, pierced hand.

"Good for you, I suppose," Efnysien drawled. "But guess what? In the grand scheme of things, it doesn't matter a tiddlywink. You'll be consumed along with the rest of this realm. And so will your brother. And so will your little friend here."

"But why?" Brynn pleaded. "You don't need us! You don't need Annwfyn! Why do you need this place? There must be another way to...to satisfy your hunger."

"Why?" Efnysien snarled, drawing himself up to his full height, eyes sparking with baleful fire. "You want to know why? I'll tell you exactly why!"

He held one finger up and drew a deep breath before pausing for only a moment.

"Actually," he said, "you know what...explaining my own motivations is boring even me and I have an unnaturally high tolerance for such things. I'm done talking."

He turned to Brynn's brother.

"Now, Cwningen. My hand is bound to yours. My blood mingles with yours and falls upon the ground. Reach out your other hand. Touch my sister and the binding will be fulfilled. Her essence will come to me through you. My only remaining sibling will be consumed. I will at last be complete."

Conn shook his head furiously in denial, tears streaming down his face, the vines wrapped across his mouth and between his teeth still preventing him from speaking.

"Now, Cwningen! You are mine. I command you."

Conn shook his head again and Efnysien scowled.

"I said now!" he roared.

With a gesture and a word from Efnysien, more brown vines wrapped around Conn's arm and moved it toward Efnysien's sister. Conn struggled against them, but it was no use. Efnysien was too powerful. Conn's hand stopped a fraction of an inch from the frozen woman's arm. The corners of Efnysien's mouth curled upward, he gave the barest flick of his finger, and Conn's hand made connection.

The reaction was instantaneous. The woman's mouth fell open in a soundless shriek, though her eyes remained open and the rest of her body remained frozen and still. A huge flash burst forth from her and visible energy flowed from her body into Efnysien with Conn as the conduit between the two. Wracked in pain, Conn's body arched and convulsed, one hand tethered to Efnysien by the knife, the other locked to the sister. Flashes of energy sparked off him and surrounded him until his whole body was glowing, nearly white-hot.

Efnysien's eyes closed and his body lifted from the ground, though the knife plunged through his hand still bound him to Conn. Brynn and Makayla stared at the two demigods floating above the ground, one as pale as ice, the other as dark as night, with Brynn's brother trapped in between, forced to consume the spirit of one and pass it to the other.

"What is going on, Brynn?" Makayla shouted over the crackling din.

"Nothing good," Brynn answered grimly. "Come on, we've got to do something."

"What the hell are we supposed to do? I can't even move!"

But Brynn didn't respond, her form already shifting fluidly, first into a white raven who slipped out from beneath the vines that bound her, then into a lithe green-skinned goblin who shredded the vines that bound Makayla.

"Come on," Brynn said, "we've got to save my brother. Conn!" she screamed, running to him.

She reached for the knife that bound Conn's hand to Efnysien's, but the energy crackling around Efnysien's form prevented her from touching it. She lunged at the frozen woman, trying to push her body away from Conn's, trying to break the connection, but the energy pouring forth from the woman's body threatened to devour her.

She reached for her brother, the frightened eleven-year-old goblin, his eyes pleading with her, his face contorted in pain. She put her hands to his face and found that somehow, she could touch him. The fire in the air that prevented her from touching Efnysien and his sister did not keep her from her brother, trapped in between the two, binding them together. She pulled the vines from his mouth and he sucked in a deep lungful of air.

"Conn," she said, "I'm going to get you out of here."

"I don't know if you can, Brynn. I made a mistake. I'm so sorry. I made a really bad mistake."

"I know. Just...just try to hold on."

Brynn pulled at his arms, first one and then the other, but his body was bound fast to the two beings on either side of him. She pulled the sword from her back, Gwenllian's dragon-pommeled sword, the most powerful weapon that Brynn or Makayla had ever seen, the sword that had slain shadows and goblins and once, even Efnysien himself, although he had somehow managed to come back from that.

Brynn held the sword in her hands, raised it above her head, and swung it against Efnysien with all the force that she could muster. The sword was repelled by the energy coursing into Efnysien's body, throwing Brynn off balance. She regained her footing, raised the sword and struck again. She hacked and hacked at him with the blade, but each time, the sword was turned aside by the energy field and bounced away harmlessly.

Distraught, she turned to the frozen woman, Efnysien's sister, and tried her luck there, but the results were the same. She swung the sword, with all of her significant goblin strength, against the woman's body, but the blade could not penetrate the field.

"That won't work," Conn said haltingly, the power coursing across him, arcing between his tongue and his eyes. "The binding is too powerful. I can feel them. I can feel what they are. While they're connected together like this, they're practically gods. There's no way to hurt them. Not even with that sword."

"But how...what can I do then?" Brynn asked desperately.

"Me, Brynn," Conn said, suddenly calm. "I'm not a god. I'm just a piece of string tying them together. Just a tiny link in a chain. A chain that wants to destroy the world."

"But what should I do?" Brynn asked him, her hand to his face.

"You have to break the chain, Brynn. You know you have to. He told you what will happen if you don't. Every living thing in Annwfyn will die. And he won't stop there. You know he won't. He'll come for Earth next. For everyone we know...for Mama and Papa..."

He broke down, unable to continue.

"What? No," Brynn said. "Conn, no, I can't! There has to be another way."

Conn found his voice again, found some well of strength deep within himself. His face was resolute and he looked his sister straight in the eye when he spoke.

"You know what you have to do, Brynn. You have to break the chain."

"You can't ask me to do this, Conn!"

"There's only one way out of this, Brynn. You know I'm right."

Brynn just shook her head, almost violently, as Conn's eyes pleaded with her. His body convulsed again as another surge of energy passed through it. He screamed.

"Please, Brynn...it hurts! It hurts so much."

Brynn stared at the sword in her hand and then at her brother, tears streaming down her face. Makayla put a hand on Brynn's arm and gave her a questioning look, offering silently with her eyes. But Brynn shook her head.

"No," she said. "It has to be me."

"Tell Mama..." Conn said, his voice barely a whisper now, his body wasting away as the energy coursed through him, "tell Papa...I...tell them..."

"I know," Brynn said, her eyes holding his. "I will."

"I'm so sorry, Brynn. I didn't know what would happen. I'm so sorry."

"I know," Brynn said, and she plunged the sword into her brother's heart.

Chapter 87

Conn's body fell to the ground, finally released from the binding that held him. His limp hand ripped free from Efnysien's blade and his blood pooled on the barren soil beneath. The conduit now gone, the energy that flowed through him was set free, unconstrained, a nova of light and fire that overtook the glade until it overflowed. The maelstrom grew so bright that nothing could be seen. It passed through the meadow and through all those who remained within it. Brynn and Makayla staggered backward, bathed in blood and power and grief.

Efnysien collapsed next to Conn's dead body, his skin scorched by the explosion. He pulled the knife from his hand and steaming blood flowed freely, blackening and scorching the ground below. His eyes were gaunt and a bedraggled sneer sat upon his lips.

"What have you done, you stupid, stupid girl?" he screamed at Brynn. "Do you know how long I have worked for this day? Do you know what sacrifices I made? All to have it spoiled by some selfish goblin brat!"

He spat a gob of blood and fire onto the ground, where it hissed and sizzled among the dead underbrush. Brynn stared at him in fury, still holding the sword wet with Conn's blood.

"My brother is dead!" she shouted, so angry that her voice was nearly expressionless. "I had to kill him. And it's all because of you."

"Oh, don't be so dramatic," Efnysien said as he staggered to his feet. "He would have died anyway. No mortal could survive that binding."

Acting on pure impulse, her anger now in control, Brynn raised the sword and rushed at him. Efnysien raised a hand and tried to swat Brynn away with his power but could not. His eyes went wide and his nostrils flared. He raised his hand again just as Brynn swung the sword directly at his neck. The blade froze in mid-air. Brynn screamed as she struggled to force the sword into his body. Efnysien's hand shook with effort. A vein in his temple throbbed. He gritted his teeth as he kept the blade away from his skin.

They held this position for what seemed like hours, neither making headway. Brynn couldn't thrust the sword into Efnysien, but neither could he push the blade away. Teeth were bared. Sweat glistened on both brows. Their eyes were locked as they struggled against each other, anger against fear, youthful vigor against ancient power, Brynn's goblin strength against the will of a demigod. And slowly, ever so slowly, it became clear that the goblin was winning.

Efnysien retreated, inch by inch, as she pushed the sword against his power until his back was against one of the massive tree trunks that ringed the meadow.

"Perhaps I misjudged you," he said. He attempted to grin, but bound in concentration as he was, it came off as a sickly grimace. "I wonder if maybe we could come to an…agreement. In exchange for my freedom, for my life, I can offer power, knowledge, riches." He grunted as he struggled to keep the sword from his neck. "I could teach you magical arts unknown to any goblin since the dawning of time. Give you wealth beyond imagining. Power to control the minds of humans and goblins alike. Immortality. I can offer all these to you. And more. Much more."

"Interesting proposal," Brynn said, her teeth gritted with effort. "Here's *my* offer: I'm going to stick my sword in your neck and then you stop talking."

"What about a kingdom to call your own," Efnysien purred, "to rule over with your...whatever you want to call her over there."

"The lady said no!" Makayla shouted. "Now shut up and let her kill you!"

At that moment, a faint hum settled over the glade. It seemed to come from nowhere and everywhere all at once. It was the sound of a flower blooming in a forgotten dream, and Brynn shuddered as she heard it and squinted her eyes shut, trying to hold on to her anger. Her slight distraction was all it took for Efnysien to free himself. He slipped out from under the sword's point and skittered away to the edge of the meadow.

Makayla watched as Brynn held the sword out and slowly advanced on Efnysien, but another movement caught her eye. The woman from the mirror, Efnysien's twin, frozen in place, didn't seem to be quite so frozen anymore. Her hands flexed. Her toes curled. Her eyes fluttered. Light dripped from her fingertips.

"My sister stirs," Efnysien said as he and Brynn circled each other. "I gave too much of myself. Too much of my power was set free when the binding was broken. This is not over," he snarled at Brynn. "Not even close."

Efnysien and Brynn moved slowly within the ring of trees, eyes locked, his hands weaving magic, her hands holding the sword trained on him, but neither willing to strike first.

"Someday," he said, "when you least expect it, I will come for you. For your family, for your humans, for your world." A slow, savage smile spread across his face. "But for now, a safe haven awaits me, a realm of my own making." Their large slow circle had brought him in front of the mirror. "Somewhere not even my sister could follow."

He stepped backward and the glass absorbed him and transformed him until his crystalline form rested just on the surface of the mirror. The crystalline Efnysien waggled his fingers at Brynn and Makayla and then, with great effort, pushed himself back from the glass and into the space beyond the mirror where his sister had once stood. The glass released him and his crystalline form dissolved into the now-familiar pale skin, jet black hair and eyes of unimaginable black. Efnysien put his hands on the inside of the glass and leered at them for just a moment. Then he turned and, without looking back, walked away into the darkness beyond.

Brynn and Makayla rushed to the mirror. They tried to look through the glass, but there was no sign of Efnysien. All they saw were the reflections of two girls, two torn, bloody, bedraggled girls, and the reflection of Conn's body, crumpled and limp, covered in blood, his life drained away. Brynn pounded on the glass and screamed at the mirror in rage and frustration and exhaustion and sorrow.

"It's just a mirror now," Makayla said, trying to pull Brynn away. "Whatever he did, however he got in there, it's over. We can't reach him."

"It's not over, Makayla," Brynn said through clenched jaw. "It can't be. We have to stop him." She wrenched her arm from Makayla's grasp. "My brother is dead. Our city is infested. He sent an army. A freaking army, Makayla! Our families, our classmates, our teachers, they all went to reclaim Jeffersonville and we don't even know how many of them are still alive! We have to stop him. Otherwise, he'll do it again. Or worse. You know he will. Again and again and again and again. He's going to come after my family. Probably yours. Maybe the whole damn planet. We have to stop him. We can't let this happen again."

"But you heard him," Makayla insisted, "he said...he said he lost all his power. He ran away!"

"He'll get his power back," Brynn said, her voice anguished. "He did it before. He came back from the dead. And we didn't even kill him this time."

"But how? How do we stop him?"

"We have to follow him."

"Follow him?" Makayla asked, perplexed.

"In there. We have to follow him into the mirror."

"But how? How?"

"He told us. It's his world. His door that no one else can use. Not even someone as powerful as his sister."

"So it's impossible."

"Exactly," Brynn responded. "Which means there's only one way for us to do it. You ever see anyone do something impossible, Makayla?"

Brynn gave a wistful smile. It took Makayla several seconds to realize what she was talking about.

"But you said...you said we should never use that. You said it was the deepest secret inside you. You said it could only be used for...for the thing someone wants most in the world." Her voice grew faint. "For a fondest desire." Makayla blinked back tears. "I don't know, Brynn, we don't...we don't even totally understand how your powers work—"

"You know exactly how it works, Makayla," Brynn said softly, looking up at the sunless sky. "If a human does a great boon for a goblin, then the goblin is bound by the oldest laws, by compacts drawn up before this world was even a spark, to grant the human's fondest desire."

Brynn looked Makayla straight in the eye.

"Have you done me a boon?"

"Yeah," Makayla said unsurely. "Yeah, I guess I have." Brynn cocked her head. "I...I found your brother for you...but, Brynn, I don't know if that counts, I mean...it didn't end up working out so well."

Brynn put both hands on Makayla's face. She looked over every inch of it before she spoke again.

"You were the one who drove that truck out of Jeffersonville. You were the one who rescued me from Cath Palug. You were the one who found the way into the tower. You were the one who discovered the ribbon that led us to my brother. It was all you, Makayla. It was always you. You have done more for me than I could ever possibly repay."

Makayla nodded nervously.

"And what is your fondest desire?"

"To be with you," Makayla answered, and in that moment, she realized that it was true and more than true. "To follow you wherever you go. In and out of worlds and falling off buildings and stuck in swamps and almost getting eaten and climbing up towers and sleeping in shacks and running from shadows and even if it means chasing the scariest dude I've ever seen through that mirror and into the dark...I want to follow you. Here. There. Everywhere. That's what I want. That's all that I want."

Brynn smiled and all the pain and weariness seemed to fall from her when she did.

"Then make the wish."

"I wish that we could follow Efnysien through the mirror," Makayla said. "Together."

Instantly, Brynn's body filled with the purest, whitest light that Makayla could possibly have imagined. The light lifted Brynn up and suspended her within its power. Waves of light poured through her and out of her, from her eyes, her mouth, her fingertips. The light filled the glade until Makayla couldn't tell where the light ended and where Brynn began. And the light was also a song. Waves of illumination and melody passed through Makayla and surrounded her, until they faded away, leaving Brynn, eyes skyward, floating in the air.

Her body settled gently on the ground, but her skin, her eyes, her hair, her clothes, all of her were now as clear and as sharp as a diamond.

"What happened?" Brynn asked groggily.

"I think...I think you're made of glass."

"I think you might be right," Brynn said, holding her hand up in front of her face "I think I might be part of the mirror now. Which means I should be able to do *this*."

She put her hands together, palms facing each other, and pressed her fingertips against the surface of the mirror. Her fingers slid in easily, as if there was nothing there but water. She pushed her hands apart, and the mirror opened as if it was a curtain. Where there had been a mirror, there was now an open doorway, and there was only darkness beyond. Brynn stepped through the curtain, into the darkness, and held out her hand.

Makayla stood in front of the doorway, and just like every other time she'd looked into the darkness, her chest tightened, her head grew light, the memory of the Swallowed Hall rose unbidden in her brain, and the smell of death and rot threatened to overtake her.

Only this time, she recognized the fear for what it was. She grabbed onto it. She saw the fear, she held it close, and she turned it into bright fire.

The fear wasn't gone. It never would be. It would always be a part of her. It was what you did with the fear, that was what mattered. That's what it meant to be human. And it took a goblin to show her that.

It wasn't easy having a goblin for a best friend.

But the best things were never easy.

She put one foot in front of the other and, eyes wide open, she followed Brynn into the darkness.

Chapter 88

Ysbaddaden fell through Gwenllian's portal and landed roughly, sprawled out on the ground in the middle of a brown, dusty meadow with massive trees in a ring and thick brambled underbrush all around. Gwenllian, on the other hand, landed sprightly and was instantly in motion, running toward the enormous mirror at the center of the glade, spear in hand. However, it was clear that they were too late.

The giant and the hero stared into the mirror's surface. At first, they saw only their own reflections, but then two figures appeared slowly from the silvery darkness within. One carried a sword and looked as if she was made of glass. The other carried a backpack and wore a muddy, ripped hoodie.

Brynn's form shimmered and changed, flesh and blood returning as she drew the sword. Makayla pulled the laser pointer from her pocket and pressed a button on the side. A bright spray of red light shone into the darkness and revealed Efnysien cowering in a corner, torn, withered, burnt. The two girls advanced on him. He staggered to his feet, bleeding freely, hands raised. Ysbaddaden couldn't hear what was said, but it appeared that Efnysien was begging for mercy. He was stumbling, crying, nearly incoherent. He fell to the ground and tried to scramble away, but his hands slipped in his own blood.

Brynn raised the sword over her head and thrust it downward, straight toward Efnysien's heart. But the sword cut nothing but air. The image of Efnysien cowering before the two girls evaporated into smoke, and another Efnysien appeared within the mirror, stepping from behind the frame. This one was hale and healthy, whole, strong, unburnt, untorn.

The real Efnysien wiggled his fingers at Gwenllian and Ysbaddaden. The corners of his mouth curled into a mischievous smile, and his dark eyes sparked fire. He pushed his face into the surface of the mirror, where it merged with the glass just long enough for him to say:

"It's always disappointing when you've found out you've lost, isn't it?"

Then he pulled his head back from the glass and stood within the mirror's darkness. He reared one leg up and kicked, the sole of his boot connecting with the glass with such force that Ysbaddaden felt it in his teeth.

The mirror shattered in front of them and the pieces fell slowly to the ground, a million slivers of silvered glass falling from the wooden frame onto the forest floor, mixing with the blood and dust beneath. A massive wave of cold erupted from the empty hole where the mirror had stood. The glade turned to ice. The frozen frame of the mirror cracked and splintered and rained onto the earth.

The fragments of the mirror were scattered far and wide, and within the countless slices of silvered glass could be seen splintered images. The two girls stared into darkness. They backed slowly away. They heard a sound. Their eyes went wide. They prepared to defend themselves. They ran. And then, Efnysien was in every fragment. He screamed. Flames, sparks, and power erupted from his body. He gave chase.

A biting white light shone from every sliver of glass, so bright it hurt to look at. Ysbaddaden squinted his eyes shut in alarm, and when he opened them again, the fragments of glass showed nothing but red. The color slowly faded away, and then nothing more could be seen within the mirror's remains.

"We were too late," Ysbaddaden said, and Gwenllian nodded, her eyes bathed in sorrow.

The glade was silent for several long minutes, a silence only broken by a faint cracking sound behind them. They turned and saw a woman, ice falling from her form. Her skin was so dark it glowed like burnished midnight, and her eyes were so pale they could barely be seen.

She drew a deep shuddering breath and took in everything around her, as if she was awakening from a long sleep. As she awoke, the glade awoke as well. The ice turned to dew and everything around her returned to life: the trees, the brush, the grass beneath her feet. The wooden fragments of the mirror frame rooted into the ground and began to grow. Within moments, everything within the glade was green, flowering, and alive.

"My lady Nysien," Ysbaddaden said in disbelief, "can it really be you?"

He bowed low before her and the woman gave a simple nod of her head in reply.

"I do not know you," she said, giving him a curious look. "Nor you," she said, turning to Gwenllian.

"We met once before, my lady," Ysbaddaden said. "Although I did not wear this form at the time."

"Was that my brother that was here before?" Nysien asked, her brow furrowed as if she was trying to recover a memory long unused.

"It was. Can you tell us what happened here?"

"I cannot," she said, shaking her head. "It all feels like a dream."

She walked through the meadow, seeing the massive trees with staircases spiraling around their trunks, the blood fallen on the ground, the shattered mirror.

"What a strange place," she said, seemingly to herself. "How long have I been gone?"

"So long," Gwenllian said, "that many now think you nothing more than a myth."

"I am no myth," the woman said with a kind smile, "I assure you. But I do sense that my absence, and my brother's presence, do not bode well for the health of Annwfyn." A sudden thought struck her. "Has the Queen been found?"

"No. Annwfyn still has no one to rule her." Nysien began to speak again but Ysbaddaden held up a polite hand. "I am sure you have many questions, and I would answer them all. But not here, I think. This glade is a place of your brother's."

Ysbaddaden nodded to Gwenllian, who opened a portal for them with a gesture. As they made ready to depart, Nysien noticed Conn's body lying in the newly growing grass. She knelt over him and put a gentle hand to his chest.

"I know not who this is," she said, "but I do not believe he deserved this fate."

The woman with midnight skin rose and stepped into the portal, followed by Ysbaddaden. Gwenllian was about to follow when a flash of light caught her eye. She knelt and picked up a piece of the shattered mirror, larger than the rest.

She gazed into it but saw nothing but her own reflection. She wrapped the fragment in a piece of thick cloth and tucked it away, then stepped into the portal herself.

In the silent glade, life was returning. Buds flowered on the trees. Faint birdsong could be heard. The grass was now so high that it was going to seed, and in the canopy above, green leaves stretched for the sky. In the very center of the glade, flowers sprouted and grew across Conn's body, and he was taken back into the earth, the young goblin reclaimed by the Land of Annwfyn.

Epilogue
Two Weeks Later

It was a time of rebirth in Jeffersonville. Working together, they were rebuilding their town: the schools, the offices, the stores, the restaurants, the homes. Fires were put out. Rubble was cleared. Holes were filled, siege engines were dismantled, and clockwork chickens were melted down. It would be a long, arduous process, but for the people of the ravaged town, the healing had begun.

At least for most of them.

In front of one unassuming house, in the middle of a perfectly normal block, at the far end of a run-of-the-mill neighborhood, a moving van sat in the driveway again, bound for California. A man was loading boxes into the van, while a woman assisted as well as she could with a child in her arms.

An outside observer might have thought that this was a regular human family: a father, a mother, and a baby, their faces holding the usual exhaustion one feels when preparing for a move.

But those who knew the truth could see them for what they were: a coblyn, a xana, and their baby, faces gaunt with incalculable sorrow, the only goblins left in Jeffersonville, Indiana.

"We're sorry to see you go," the Mayor said to the mother and the father. She had stopped by to thank them once again for their efforts in saving her town.

"There's nothing here for us anymore," Gafr said. "Plus, I'm not sure how welcome we'll really be now that everyone knows what we are."

"No one will hold that against you," the Mayor said.

"Everyone in this city has just been through a huge ordeal," Llwynog said. "Not only did they find out that goblins exist, but their homes were invaded by them. Without us around, hopefully that knowledge and those memories will fade and everyone can get back to their normal lives. We'd just be an impediment to that."

"We've had to do a lot of thinking," Gafr said. "Had to ponder some very difficult questions." He blew out his cheeks. "Here's what we know. Or what we think we know." He paused and looked to the sky, trying to find the right words. "This is hard to say. What happened here was the end result of actions put in motion ages ago. Actions that we bear a significant amount of responsibility for...and that is probably putting it mildly. We did something...something terrible...centuries ago and the end result is what you see around you. In our house. In Makayla's house. In every burnt storefront, in every family whose home was destroyed."

"The creature who sent the army here," Llwynog said, "he came here for us. He came here for our family. He seems to be gone, but it's seemed that way before. He may come back, and if he does...and we're still here..." She shook her head, a sad smile on her face. "This town would pay the price for us again.

We couldn't ask the people here to go through this a second time. We put you in danger simply by being here."

Llwynog held Hero tight against her chest and closed her eyes. Gafr came and put a protective arm around both.

"He took two of our children from us. We have to do whatever we can to protect her," Gafr said, stroking the baby's hair. "And I know this doesn't make much sense, but it will be much easier for us to do that in California."

"I can't pretend to comprehend your lives," the Mayor said, "or where you've come from or what you might face in the future. But I do hope you find what you're looking for. I hope you can find safety and peace wherever you end up."

The two goblins bid goodbye to the Mayor and returned to packing the moving van. On a nearby corner, a blond-haired woman stepped into view from where she had been watching surreptitiously. She lifted her sunglasses, unwrapped a heavy piece of silvered glass, and stared into it for several moments before putting it away again.

"You've spent a fair amount of time staring into that bit of mirror lately," Cyrridwen said as she strode out of the night sky.

"I keep hoping," said Gwenllian simply.

"Hoping what?"

"To see something within. Anything."

"If you ever do, let me know."

Gwenllian nodded.

"Have you seen your granddaughter?" she asked.

"Yes. The giant Ysbaddaden brought her to me. She had many questions for me and I had many questions for her."

"Any answers?"

"Far too few."

The two women, both far older than they appeared, surveyed the land around them, a city in transition, half-rebuilt, half-undone. A city nearly destroyed by forces far beyond their comprehension, for a reason that none from this dimension had any inkling of.

"I suppose this may be the last we see of this little town for a while," Cyrridwen said.

"I suspect the town may thank us for that."

"I think you may be right."

"Tell me if you find any answers," Gwenllian said.

"You as well."

The two women left the city behind. One slipped into a fold between the pages of time and space and the other strode away across the sky.

Across the street, the last moving box was loaded. The doors of the van were closed. The lights of the house were turned out. The front door was locked and the key was put under the mat. The baby was strapped into her car seat. The station wagon pulled away, followed by the moving van. And the only goblins left in Jeffersonville, Indiana, drove away into the night.

Acknowledgments

First and foremost, I want to thank my grandmother, Helen Elizabeth (Shetler) Reeder, who passed away while I was writing this book. She grew up on a Mennonite farm in Kansas during the Depression and had to spend much of her youth working to help support her single mother and her ten siblings. But she never let that stop her from learning everything she wanted to. She used to sneak into the living room, late at night, and use her older sister's lesson books to teach herself piano. She taught herself pottery and painting and she wrote letters and stories and plays and she took swimming lessons in her 50's and bought a kiln in her 60's and learned to use email in her 80's and Facebook in her 90's to keep in touch with her two dozen grandchildren. From her, I learned that sometimes you just have to take a quiet leap of faith and try something new.

A few years ago, I thought on the lesson I'd learned from her. I took a quiet leap of faith of my own and, without telling anyone, I wrote a book. Somehow, I managed to get it published. And then I took an even bigger leap of faith and wrote another, which is this one right here. I hope you enjoyed it.

I want to thank Reagan and everyone at Black Rose Writing for giving me the chance to continue Brynn and Makayla's story.

I want to thank my friends Jamie Rothfuss, Jenn Drake, Cynthia Bachhuber, Marni Penning Coleman, and Magi Loucks for invaluable support, assistance, and encouragement.

I want to thank Nancy Mae, beta reader, proofreader, maker of astonishingly useful suggestions, who was willing to read my second draft, when it was still a bit of a higgledy-piggledy mess, and show me all the places where there were far too many words and, especially, far too many, you know, commas. This book is far better for her involvement.

I want to thank my daughter, Lenore Elizabeth, for providing inspiration and joy and exuberance, for those three things live within her, in abundance, and so much more. She makes me appreciate every moment and every day.

I want to thank my son, August Wesley, for constantly amazing me with his kindness and his creativity and his astonishing, unwavering curiosity. Without him, I would have never had the courage to even think of trying to write a book. He makes me brave.

And I especially want to thank my wife, Lisa, who read this book, and then read it again, and then again, and maybe even another time (I lost count), and each time, offered invaluable suggestions and support, and who has also given me the greatest gift, even greater than being an amazing mother to our two children, even greater than going to work every day so I can stay at home and take care of them, even greater than not questioning my sanity when I told her I wanted to finish a book in the middle of a pandemic. She gave me the gift of believing in me, even when I didn't believe in myself, and that is a gift that I can never repay, not even by thanking her in the closing paragraph of the acknowledgments section of an actual, published book.

About the Author

R. Chris Reeder grew up in a tiny town you've never heard of and attended college in Walla Walla, Washington. He founded a theatre company, worked across the country as a professional Shakespearean actor, traveled the globe as an international courier, took a year and a half detour to be a singing activist, and then settled down into the comfortable life of a stay-at-home father and part-time author.
This is his second novel.

www.rchrisreeder.com
www.facebook.com/rchrisreederauthor

Thank you so much for reading
Book Two of *The Coblyn Chronicles*
If you enjoyed our book, please check out our recommended
title for your next great read!

The Changeling's Daughter by R. Chris Reeder

"A timeless, entertaining adventure where nothing is quite
as it seems once curious magic unfolds in an average town."
–Leanna Renee Hieber, award-winning author of
Darker Still* and *Strangely Beautiful

CPSIA information can be obtained
at www.ICGtesting.com
Printed in the USA
LVHW011612080121
675730LV00001B/1

9 781684 336777